BEAUTIFUL SINNERS

GENEVA LEE

IVY ESTATE PUBLISHING + ENTERTAINMENT

Copyright © 2016 by Geneva Lee.

All rights reserved. No part of this publication may be reproduced, distributed or transmitted in any form or by any means, including photocopying, recording, or other electronic or mechanical methods, without the prior written permission of the publisher, except in the case of brief quotations embodied in critical reviews and certain other noncommercial uses permitted by copyright law.

Geneva Lee/Ivy Estate Books www.genevalee.com

Publisher's Note: This is a work of fiction. Names, characters, places, and incidents are a product of the author's imagination. Locales and public names are sometimes used for atmospheric purposes. Any resemblance to actual people, living or dead, or to businesses, companies, events, institutions, or locales is completely coincidental.

Cover Design © Date Book Designs, 2016.

Cover Photo © Adobe Stock.

Previously published as By Invitation Only/Sin Never Sleeps/All Fall Down © Geneva Lee.

What happens in Vegas...

BEAUTIFUL CRIMINAL

Later

I'VE never put much stock in mistakes. Despite the last year of my life, I didn't want my past choices to define me. Now I know I'm doomed to pay for every decision I've made. This is the realization that crashes into me as I fight to stay awake.

Red coats the back of my eyelids as I drift between the real world and the dark. Lights flash, blinding me momentarily as I blink into the rain. It takes a moment for her to come into focus, but when she does everything about her is wrong. Her arms and legs are twisted in unnatural directions like a broken doll. Glass digs into my hands as I claw across the wet pavement toward her. My palm slips as it hits a warm and slippery substance pooling around her head. Her lips are turning blue, but there's a smile fixed on her face as her eyes stare into the starless midnight sky. She looks happy as if she's about to greet a friend. I say her name, I shake her, and then, I scream. And scream. And scream.

Chapter 1

"EMMA, YOU LOOK LIKE HELL," my best friend Josie announces to me as I slide into the passenger seat of her beater Civic. I toss my bag onto the floorboard, ignoring the helpful commentary. Instead I pull my wet hair into a messy bun on top of my head. When I don't respond she sighs and reaches into the pile of random junk that she stores in the center console. She tosses a container of concealer at me before she backs out of my driveway.

"This isn't your color," I point out, eyeing the fair shade suspiciously.

"No." She keeps her eyes on the road, but I spot the grin tugging up the corners of her mouth. "It's yours. You're usually the one who needs it."

I raise an eyebrow, which is seriously risky, given that she'll probably deem them in need of intervention. "Are you sure? Because it seems like you've got a little bitch showing."

"Not my color," she reminds me.

Despite being stuck in standard prep uniform, she looks amazing. Between her corkscrew curls and fuchsia lips, there's an effortless coolness to Josie's style. I guess that's what you get when your mom is a former show girl pretty enough to get knocked up by a high-roller who didn't stick around to place a second bet. Either way he scored big— if only he knew it. Josie has her mom's long legs, ready smile, and way with the men. I say men because she doesn't bother with the guys at school. She prefers to work out her daddy issues with any number of willing tourists.

My dad stands on the porch holding a mug of what I hope is coffee. Josie waves to him cheerfully, narrowly avoiding our mailbox, as I begin to pat the liquid magic on the dark circles rimming my eyes.

"Nightmares? The one about Becca?" She taps the steering wheel, showcasing her fluorescent pink nail polish that looks all that much brighter against her cappuccino skin.

"Test. I had to cram." I lie because I don't want to discuss my seriously screwed up head at seven a.m.

Josie doesn't press it even though she sees through me. She knows the truth because she knows me. That means she also gets that I'm not one to gush about my feelings. What's the point? Talking can't change the shit that's happened.

"Last day," she says instead, "and tonight we party."

"You party," I correct her. "Dad needs me to take over morning shift at the shop first thing on Monday."

"Which gives you a whole weekend, and don't try telling me that you have a hot date."

I flush at the thought. Yeah, hot dates are for girls who haven't been forced into an involuntary vow of celibacy. "I do actually. With laundry and Netflix."

Josie's nose wrinkles and she shakes her head. "You need a life."

"I had one." I stare out the window instantly wishing I hadn't spoken, especially something that made me sound stupid and broken and girly. I'm getting used to the hollow pit my sister's death has left at my core, but today's a day I can't ignore it.

We pull into the school parking lot with my admission hanging like a nasty stink in the air. We both can smell it but we're too polite to talk about it. Josie whips the car so quickly into a space that a nearby frosh jumps out of the way. She shrugs sweetly at him. No one can resist Josie, even if she's just put their life in danger. One of the many reasons that we're an odd couple. I don't smile or chit chat. Hell, I don't make eye contact if I can help it.

"Emma, she wouldn't want you to give up on living," she says in a quiet voice.

"Yeah, well, I wanted to see her graduate this weekend," I snap. She doesn't deserve my reaction, but a year later and I'm still working through the second stage of grief. I prefer when we pretend we're still in denial though.

So much for polite oblivion. I throw my bag over my shoulder, and disappear into the crowd of students scrambling through the front door as the first bell slices the air. This is where I feel safe, lost in a swarm of people who aren't asking if I'm okay or if they can do anything to help. Or worse yet the people who turn those sad eyes on me. I don't want their practiced pity or sympathetic attention. Because there is such a thing as a stupid question and 'are you okay' is one of them. Then there's the jerks that have made it their mission to hold me accountable for what happened that night, because I'm the only one left to blame. The whole lot of them make Belle Mère Prep feel more like the nine circles of hell than high school.

Only a few more hours. But the mental cheerleading does nothing for my apathy, especially when I spot Hugo Roth, my least favorite mistake, loitering near my English class.

"Hey pawn star, ready for summer vacation?" I don't have

to turn to attach the sneer in the voice with his stupid face, but he darts in front of the doorway so I still have to look at him. He's taller than most of the boys in class, which is a blessing given that he has to hold up his gigantic ego all day. I hate to say he cleans up well. Still there's no denying his movie star jawline or his silky blond hair that's just long enough to grab onto when he makes his move. I'd made that mistake once. Never again. "I was thinking of coming into the shop. I have something I know you'll want."

"Sorry. We're all stocked up on junk." My family's Las Vegas pawn shop is considered a tourist landmark, but to me it's just another embarrassment.

I push past him, but his arm flies out to stop me. With his other hand, he grabs his crotch. "What will your daddy give me for this? Or maybe you and I can discuss its value."

"Or maybe I can show it the barrel of one of our many in-stock shotguns." I plaster a smile on my face as I wiggle my pinkie for emphasis. "If I recall, it should slide right in."

Hugo's face darkens as he moves away from the door. "Bitch."

"Good to catch up!" I call after him sweetly from the doorway.

Mr. Hunter doesn't look at me as I rush into the room to the sound of the final bell. "Nice of you to join us, Miss Southerly."

I slide Great Expectations out of my bag and hold it up. "I couldn't stop reading. I didn't get any sleep."

Mr. Hunter has apparently read Dickens because he presses his lips together in disbelief. He probably watched the movie, too, but he doesn't push my tardiness. I slump in my seat as he starts a discussion on whether or not Pip's benefactor did him a favor. Apparently, he didn't get the memo that it's the last day of school. Since I thought the story was stupid—a poor kid trying to impress a rich girl—I stare at the wood-paneling some board member sprung for during the academy's renovation. The result is all Vegas. Oak paneling, bookcases full of dusty leather-bound volumes—a show meant to trick over-qualified teachers and elite college recruiters into thinking that the students here are as competitive as east coast prep students.

Growing up in Belle Mère, I know the truth: all that glitters isn't gold.

"Miss West?" Mr. Hunter calls across the room to a blonde with her back turned to him, catching my attention.

Monroe West glances over her shoulder and stares at him like she's waiting for him to answer. Her Jimmy Choo's probably cost a week of his pay and she knows it. Who said our priorities aren't in place at Belle Mère Prep? But when you're a West, doors open for you. Just not Southerly doors. After Monroe put a pink streak in her hair, Clark County ran out of dye for two months. Girls drove to Los Angeles to get theirs done, and by the time, they had their appointments, she'd moved on. Her latest look is more Miami than pop star, bright citrus hues. She's a step ahead of the game. With her daddy's money and her latest stint on reality TV, wannabe designers are falling all over themselves to send her clothes. It's more proof that life isn't fair. The girl could buy anything she wants and she doesn't even have to. But it's not class warfare that has her on my blacklist. No, she's earned her spot and then some.

"Do you have thoughts on the question?" he prompts her when she doesn't respond.

"Of course, he did him a favor. Everyone wants money. I'd rather be dead than poor." She flicks her bleached locks over her shoulder and returns to her previous conversation.

A snort escapes me and they both turn to stare. Acknowledging Monroe said something is akin to drawing a line in the sand. Generally I stick to cold war tactics like pretending she doesn't exist. It's better for my sanity, but maybe the fact that I won't have to see her for three months is encouraging a little confrontation.

Mr Hunter crosses his arms over his tweed jacket like a nerdy referee. "It seems Emma has some thoughts on the subject."

"Yes." Actual thoughts. "There are so many worse things than being poor like being sick or smug or conceited. I think he knows that. Money doesn't equal happiness." At least, Ethan Hawke didn't seem very happy in the movie, I add silently.

Monroe flips her tan, middle finger at me behind Hunter's back.

"Or class," I add dryly.

She smirks, showcasing how well her coral lipstick matches her manicure. But all evidence of her addition to our debate disappears as soon as Mr. Hunter looks to her. I don't bother to listen as he tries to engage more students in the discussion. It might be Belle Mère policy to educate us until the last possible moment, but we took finals last week. Reading Dickens was the English Department's idea of an end of the year treat. Old Charles would be disappointed to know that we've all checked out, counting the hours until today's final bell heralds the start of summer vacation. Or in my case, summer servitude haggling with gambling addicts over baseball cards and old records. Despite that, this is our version of New Year's Eve as we watch the clock and wait for liberation from one more year.

"If anyone hasn't finished reading, please take your copy with you this summer. The school can afford the loss," Mr. Hunter informs us as the bell rings.

Everyone abandons their unwanted Dickens' novels on their desks as they stampede out of the classroom.

"Emma," Hunter calls before I get to the door. "You're signed up for AP Lit next year, right?"

I nod, chewing on my lip as the hallway fills with students.

Contrary to today's tardiness, I hate being late. There's not much I can control in my life but my punctuality.

"I'll send you the reading list over email. I look forward to having you in class again next fall. Take the book with you."

Translation: he's thrilled that the whole class won't be filled with Housers. Kids who are set to inherit casinos and clubs don't have much interest in literature. "Me too."

I dash into the hallway before he can continue the conversation. Hunter is fine but I'll tackle the reading when I visit Mom in Palm Springs next month. Right now, I want to get to class and finish out this day, so I can leave the worst year of my life behind.

THE TEXTS START JUST after lunch. I sneak a few replies but there's nothing I can do while I'm in class. Dad didn't show to the shop, which is a surprise to no one, except his manager Jerry, who is possibly more sheep than man. He needs someone to follow, so without Dad he's lost. By three, Dad is still MIA. I guess it wasn't coffee in his cup this morning. If I'm lucky our next month's mortgage isn't currently riding on number fourteen.

Jerry: Can you come in?

Me: Nope. Plans.

With a half dozen unfinished television seasons.

Jerry: At least, you'll be here on Monday.

And for the rest of my life. Families stick together in Vegas no matter what cards are dealt to them. I'm not stupid enough to believe I'll get out. Here the House always wins and puts you right back in your place.

Another text arrives, this one from mom, apparently I'm expected at brunch in the morning. My one weekend off before the drudgery of a summer job is quickly being taken over by everyone else. I stuff my phone into my bag and allow myself to enjoy exiting Belle Mère Prep. It's a short-lived pleasure, but then again most are. Outside, the parking lot is a sea of convertibles with their tops down. Apparently it was drive mommy's mid-life crisis to school day. Funny, I don't remember that being on the school announcements.

"We are seniors!" Josie shrieks, lunging toward me as soon as I'm down the front steps. I accept the hug because Josie is a hugger and if after seventeen years she hasn't figured out that I'm not, it's a lost cause.

Over her wild mop of hair, a familiar set of brown eyes flickers my way. I pull back in time to spot Jonas take Monroe's hand. Between his lanky form and dark hair and her platinum locks and petite, swimsuit model body, they're a perfect contrast to one another.

Belle Mère's power couple.

Everyone who is anyone wants to be them. Me? I'll admit it. I just want to be her. Maybe since I used to be the one holding his hand.

Josie follows my gaze and her dark eyes narrow when she sees the pair. "Ignore them."

"I am." If only it were as simple as following her command, but Jonas is the one who broke my heart. He kissed me. He made me fall in love. Then he walked away for her, so I jumped into bed with the school's resident narcissist to get back at him.

It would have been nice to know Hugo had placed a bet on how fast he could get me into bed. I'd known I was a sure thing. At least I could have made some money. I didn't get much else out of it.

"I want to go out tonight." I say it before the thought fully processes.

Josie bounces, looking a bit too much like the ex-cheerleader she is, as she rubs her hands together.

"Nothing crazy," I warn her.

"Don't worry. It will be fun, because I know exactly where we're going." The mischievous glint in her eyes sends a wave of apprehension surging through me.

What have I gotten myself into?

Chapter 2

THE SHADES ARE DRAWN when I reach home. Possibly the only thing more depressing than miles of blazing desert as far as you can see is a dark house smack in the middle of it. The only thing worse than that? The unwelcome scent of stale beer that meets me at the door. I pause for a moment, surveying the scene and wondering why I hadn't signed up for summer classes. I could have graduated early next year, enrolled part time in Las Vegas Community College and used the meager money I made at the shop to get my own place. I allow myself to consider this for all of five seconds before I begin collecting beer cans and cigarettes.

"Hey, pumpkin," Dad greets me, rubbing his eyes. He hasn't passed out yet, which is the only bright spot in this scene. "How was school? Do you have homework?"

My father has been asking those two questions every day of my life since mom left. It's a lack-luster attempt at parenting but I appreciate the effort.

"Last day of school," I remind him, cradling cans in my arms.

"That's right. I got my days mixed up." He scratches his head, smiling sheepishly. "We should celebrate."

Dad tries, which is more than I can say for most parents around here. Most of my classmates were raised by the staff while their parents focused on the casino floor and keeping the whales happy. I wish I could say I was better off than the rest of them, but I'd spent the last five years holding our dysfunctional family together and keeping the business afloat.

He'd never gotten over losing mom, but she'd followed the money away from signed records and sports memorabilia and all the other junk we gave a home to at Pawnography. Apparently a seedy pawn shop blocks from the strip wasn't the kind of wealth she'd envisioned. Mom wanted more and she got it in the form of a new husband and a tasteful compound in Palm Springs where she spent her day sipping white wine spritzers. On her wedding day, she told my sister and I that all her dreams had finally come true. Becca gave her a pass, saying she was simply in love. My sister could see the big picture, including the doors his money would open for us. She'd jumped at the chance to ditch Las Palmas High School when he offered, but I'd wanted no part of her new life. I finally agreed to attend Belle Mére Prep on her dime only after Josie had gotten a scholarship there. I couldn't stand the idea of starting high school with both my sister and best friend there without me.

I drop the cans in the recycling bin, ignoring the fact that he dumped his ash tray in it. As I open the blinds, the sun hits me and I wonder what mom is doing now. Probably sitting by the pool while someone else cooks her dinner. Or maybe she's already on the private jet heading here to grace me with her presence.

"Where do you want to go? I know a guy over at the Rio who can hook us up at the buffet." Dad rubs his hands over his hair to tame it. He looks like a lot of other men in Vegas at the moment: unshaven and unwashed in yesterday's clothes. Unlike those other men, though, he's handsome with a strong jaw and salt and pepper hair. I've had the displeasure of watching women fall all over him since I was a kid. It's how he landed mom—looks and potential. It turns out looks can't make up for failure.

"Actually, Josie is dragging me out, so you are off the hook." I cringe at the thought of graduation parties. They might be as dangerous as the all-you can eat seafood buffet that he's offering me, but she'd made me swear I wouldn't back out.

"Maybe tomorrow," he suggests.

"Sure." I say noncommittally. That way when he forgets tomorrow I won't be disappointed. It's a survival mechanism I'd adopted since the first time he forgot my birthday.

Grabbing a few things from the fridge I start dinner. There's always food in the house because I take care of that. I shop and I plan. Dad doesn't bother to eat unless I put a meal in front of him, so there's no danger of coming home to an empty fridge. I dump sauce into a pan and start boiling water for pasta. I can't claim it's gourmet given the cheap ingredients, but I can produce spaghetti in under fifteen minutes. Take that Spago.

"This is really good, honey." Dad twists his fork, collecting another bite, and shoves it into his mouth.

"I'll put some in the fridge and you can heat it up for lunch." It's a lost cause. His entire diet consists of coffee, beer, and dinner if I'm around to cook.

He nods. We talk about summer plans and the shop. I have to remind him that I'm going to graduate next year. After I clean up the dishes, I peek into the living room where he's turned on a sporting event. I know this because there is a ball and men trying to beat each other up to get it. My father's obsession with sports did not transfer to me. On the upside that probably means his sports gambling problem won't either.

"I'm going to grab a shower. Let Josie in?"

He raises his beer in acknowledgment of my request.

I stay under the hot water so long that my skin is tight by the time I abandon it. I can't wash away my problems, but I can go out tonight and forget them. Wrapping a towel around my head, I wipe off the mirror with my palm. My cheeks are flushed which is the closest I get to having color. Unlike my peers I don't spend all afternoon worshipping the god of skin cancer. Of course that means I have bluish circles under my eyes and every single blemish sticks out like a sore thumb.

By the time I towel dry my hair and head to my room, Josie is waiting. A few shimmery scraps of cloth are scattered over my bed. I narrow my eyes as I pick one up. No matter how I hold it up, I can't decide what it is.

"Is this a scarf?" I ask finally.

Josie snatches it away. "That's mine thank you very much."

As long as she isn't going to make me wear it, I have no further comment on the issue. She strips down and pulls it on over her thong. It's a skimpy, black romper that dips to her naval.

"I have no boobs," she complains as she tugs at it.

"Look on the bright side," I say as I snag a pair of panties from my drawer, "if you did, you wouldn't be able to wear that."

"I guess you're right." She twists around observing herself in my vanity mirror. "How do I look?"

"Older than you are," I say dryly. It's the answer she wants to hear. Josie's hair is a wild, mop of curls that mesh nicely with her high cheekbones and wide, espresso eyes. Her looks combined with that outfit will get her into any club in town. I'll be riding her coattails or rather g-string to get myself inside. "Where did you find this?"

"Frederick took mom to the desert for the weekend. I borrowed a few things." She pushes a dress into my hands. Josie and her mom are as close as I have to female role models in my life. I'm not exactly preening myself to become a trophy wife like my own mother. So Josie and Marion Deckard are the closest I have to a girl squad. That's definitely how it works between the two of them. Considering Marion is only thirty-five, the two of them act and look more like sisters than mother and daughter.

"This dress is missing the dress." I whip around to check the back of Josie's pre-approved party apparel absolutely certain that my ass is hanging out.

Josie shakes her head, pressing a finger to her mouth like she's deep in thought regarding my ensemble. "Emma, you look hot."

"Perhaps," I say slowly, because part of me digs the glittery, slip of fabric she's talked me into, "but I'm going to have to walk with my thighs smashed together all night." I demonstrate what it looks like to walk with my knees clamped together.

"Stop it!" She tosses a throw pillow from the mound of decorative accents I keeps on my bed. "Make sure you have on cute underwear. Have you waxed lately?"

I scrunch my nose up. "The state of my lady bits aren't up for discussion."

"Your lady bits could use a little discussion," she corrects me.

"They have nothing to gossip about. California isn't the only one with a drought."

A smirk curls Josie's lips. "If you really want to end the dry spell, don't wear anything underneath."

"The old no-panties trick? So 1990s. I thought I'd fake a fainting spell instead." There were easier ways to advertise a vacancy than putting it on display. Besides in Vegas what's one more vagina crying out for attention? "So what trouble are you getting us into?"

"Nope." She shakes her head as she holds out a tube of lipstick. "It's a surprise."

I groan and press my hands together. "Please. I beg you."

She only smiles. Whatever she has planned can't be good if she has to drag me there. "Do I get a blindfold?"

"The party isn't that kinky," she says with a snort.

"So it's a party!"

"No shit, Sherlock." She rolls her eyes as she fluffs my hair. It's a lost cause. We are the yin and yang of hair— her unruly, sexy curls and my stick-straight honey blonde locks.

"Why won't you tell me?" I ask her as she continues to make me up.

"That's why you're going easy on me," she says. "Allowing me to put mascara on you isn't going to get me to spill. I'm not that easy."

I stick my tongue out and immediately regret the move when she smacks it with a make-up brush. "That's not what I heard."

"That all you got, Southerly?" She plants one hand on her hip and instantly looks just like her mother. I don't mention this lest I get smacked with another make-up brush. "Because you need to bring it tonight."

That's exactly what I was afraid she would say.

Chapter 3

IT'S a bad sign when Josie wants to Uber. That means two things: she's getting drunk and we're headed to the Strip. It's weird being a duo when we used to be a trio. Becca and Josie used to outnumber me all the time. Now that Becca's gone, we're more evenly matched. Josie still wins most times. I guess she's luckier than I am.

I once tried to see the heart of Las Vegas through the eyes of a stranger—the lights, the people, a million glittering attempts to grab your attention. But I couldn't. Now all I can see is the reality. Behind the crowds of tourists and the Bellagio fountains, under the designer shopping and a-list shows, everyone is broken. It's the ultimate twist of the American dream: pull a lever and you might have it all. Ride out another roll of the dice and you'll become someone. Vegas was built on destroying people. It still is. I wish knowing that could save me, but you don't get out of a town like this. Maybe my luck will change, but I'm not holding my breath.

Our driver flies in and out of traffic so quickly that the neon becomes streaks of color outside the window.

"So what's tonight? Japanese businessmen or the no limits room?" I ask still looking out the glass. We don't gamble, but I know exactly where she prefers to drift when she heads out.

"Neither. Tonight we are young," she announces. "Besides I can always call Richard later."

"The oil guy?"

"No, he's in finance."

"You need a therapist." I abandon the view and turn to her. I've only told her this about a million times.

"Only if he's hot."

I groan. "And old. Where are we going?"

Josie bites her lip and my whole body tenses. A surprise is one thing, but she can't hide the guilt on her face.

"Are you shanghaiing me?" I demand, grabbing for her phone. She holds it away and I resort to tickling her, nervous peels of laughter squeaking from her. But before I can elicit a confession, the car slows down. I stare at the doors to the resort.

"Are you fucking kidding me?" I ask as a bell boy opens the door. I don't wait for her to respond, instead I walk the opposite direction back toward the street. There's no way I'm going into the West.

Josie catches me by the arm before I make it past the entrance, but I don't stop. We're both in impractically tall heels, which means one of us is going down. Spoiler: it won't be me.

"Em," she pleads, "just hear me out."

But there's no point to listening. "I thought you understood the social food chain, but let me make it easy. We're on bottom. If my dad finds out I'm here he'll disown me."

"It's the end of the year party. Everyone will be there!"

"Everyone who was invited," I correct her. My name will never be on a West guest list and I'm one hundred percent okay with that, considering that the price of admission is your soul.

Josie produces a small card from her purse and flourishes it inches from my face. "We're invited."

"Where did you get that?" My anger ebbs into annoyance. That invite is probably enough to get us past security but that's only the first test. The rest of the gauntlet is composed of Monroe and her bitchy minions.

"It doesn't matter. This party is going to be packed."

In Josie speak that means everyone is going to be there, including all the people she'd like to impress.

"You do realize that even with that"—I point to the invitation—"we're not welcome up there."

That finally extinguishes the hopeful glimmer in her eyes. I can't call it a victory because now she just looks pissed. Josie crosses her arms, still clutching the invite, and glares at me. "Since when do you care what people think?"

"I don't."

"Then why not crash, drink their booze, and ruin their nights."

"Well-played." Josie has a point. I can't help but picture Monroe West's face when she discovers the breach in her castle walls. It will be even better to see her horror in person. "Fine, but we stick together and we don't stay long. I have to make a cameo at brunch tomorrow to appease the maternal monster."

I can think of about a million things I'd rather do than spend the evening with a bunch of Housers, including washing my hair, getting a pap smear, and tearing off my own fingernails. Girls just wanna have fun, right?

Meanwhile Josie is positively vibrating with excitement. I let her take my hand and lead me to the entrance of the casino where we're greeted by another uniformed lackey. If only he knew he was letting a Southerly walk inside the West empire. Yeah, we might have just cost him his job, but it's not my responsibility to provide a PSA to the newbie.

Emma Southerly, daughter of Jake Southerly, the mortal enemy of Nathaniel West, owner of the West Resort and Casino.

It sounds melodramatic but it's true. The feud between my dad and Monroe's father goes back from before I was born. They'd been high school buddies. In college they scrounged up every penny they had between the two of them to invest in a start-up. When the start-up took-off, my dad assumed they'd both made it big until he found out Nathaniel had invested it in his name only. Nathaniel West became a venture capitalist super-star and left my dad to take over the family pawn shop. My father had instilled hatred of the type usually reserved for rival sports teams in me my whole life. Since I've never met Nathaniel, I do my part by loathing his daughter. Every one has a role to play after all. Plus Monroe is easy to hate.

Inside the revolving door, the cacophony of the casino floor greets me immediately. Cigarette smoke, dealers calling for bets, hundreds of melodic slot machines. It's enough to make me want to turn tail and abandon Josie but she marches us through the crowds toward the bank of sleek elevators on the other side before I can process any of it. But let's face it, there is no processing it. It's a world of distraction meant to keep you so overwhelmed that you don't notice your savings account is slipping away. The lights, the noise—it's guerrilla warfare at its finest.

Josie walks directly to the elevator at the end and the bag of muscles stationed in front of it. "I'm a guest of Monroe West."

I refrain from gagging at that proclamation.

The private elevator only goes to one floor: the top. Despite that being the seventy-fifth floor, the car travels like lightning, giving me no time to steel myself before the doors slide open to deposit us in a massive entry hall. Because the gold elevator wasn't extravagant enough the entirety of the foyer—floor to ceilings is polished, black marble.

"It's not too late to leave," I point out as the sounds of the party begin to seep toward us.

"Take the chicken exit?" Josie arches her eyebrow.

"Fine, lead the way." My gaze travels up the wall and I catch sight of myself. It doesn't look like me thanks to Josie's wardrobe choices. The girl trapped in the marble is older, put together, sexy. Maybe it's what I hope to be someday. Most days I'm lucky to have all the pieces to my prep uniform clean.

"You cool?" Josie prompts and I realize I've stopped in my tracks.

I tug at the hem of my dress and shrug. "I was just wondering if Nathaniel West read The Great Gatsby too many times, because truly he's compensating for something."

"Not for his money," Josie giggles.

The elevator door dings and I realize that in the time it's taken me to get a hold of myself it's traveled back to the lobby and up again.

"Let's go," I urge her. There's no telling who will be inside. We stand a much better chance of not getting kicked out if we don't come face to face with one of Monroe's minions. I was a Girl Scout. I know there's safety in numbers.

But before we can reach the hallway, footsteps fall behind us. Instinctively, I look over my shoulder and catch sight of Nathaniel West. He's the same age as my dad but he's obviously spent some money on looking younger. That or maybe stress and bitterness are prematurely aging my father. He studies us, a slight sneer creeping onto his lips. There's no denying he's good-looking, exactly the kind of guy Josie throws herself at. Square jawed and broad-shouldered with salt and pepper hair and an expensive suit. But the look he gives me chills my blood, freezing me to the spot. He's a predator and he has me in his sights. One move and I'll be at his mercy. I want to run or hide. Instead I can only shrink back still locked in place and hope his interest in me fades.

Because more than the casual interest he's showing me, there's something in his blue eyes that flickers darkly. It's what holds me in place: this terrifying magnetizing force. Does he know who I am? Would he even care? If Monroe West walked into the pawn shop I doubt my father would blink. He'd probably get a sick thrill out of buying whatever she offered, because it meant a West was in his territory. No doubt that Nathaniel would feel the same way knowing the Jacob Southerly's daughter had found herself in his home.

The men say nothing to us as they pass. Josie tugs at my elbow, urging me forward but before we can follow Nathaniel into the house, one of his bodyguards steps in front of us. He extends his finger, pointing to the opposite hallway.

"The party is that way. This wing is closed to Miss West's guests."

He's firm but not unkind as he speaks. I bite my lip and nod. It takes more than a fair amount of authority to shut me up. This guy has it in spades.

As soon as we're out of earshot, I fall against a wall. "If Dad knew I was that close to Nathaniel West, he'd kill one of us."

Josie nods, still struck dumb by the chance encounter.

I have to admit that after that a swarm of Housers is a welcome sight. The party is already in full swing and in typical Vegas fashion, there's a train wreck everywhere we turn. It's obvious we're not the only ones who crashed or maybe Hugo invited all his favorite escorts. Judging from the scantily clad girls lounging around him, that might be the case. I guide Josie to the outskirts of the room wanting to avoid him.

"Let's get a drink!" I suggest. Maybe it will help wash the taste of self-loathing from my mouth.

Josie only nods.

"Hey, you okay?" I call over the crowd.

She nods again. That's a no. Josie has always craved the attention of the Housers, something I can't exactly fault her for. She's had a lot less time getting kicked around by them. I, on the other hand, floated between the worlds. My dad's business wasn't exactly brag-worthy, but since all commerce in sin city operated in various shades of vice, that might have been a moot point. His rivalry with Nathaniel was what had destroyed any chance I had at belonging. My mother's remarriage to a successful movie producer had nearly wiped that slate clean. When I started Belle Mère, I'd been given a shot at being part of the elite. Monroe, herself, wanted to French braid my hair. Until I started dating Jonas. When she stole him away, I lost my boyfriend and the few friends I thought I had outside of Josie and Becca. The accident just put the final nail in my reputation with the Housers and reduced my inner circle by one.

Josie's never had a cent to her name, though. Knowing me was as close as she came to the in-crowd. She's never had any way to draw attention.

However, she snagged that all-access pass, this is her chance to make a name for herself. I want to warn her against it, but how do you tell your best friend that her fantasy is actually a nightmare in the making.

You don't. That's why I came inside. Because if this is what Josie wants, I'll be beside her.

That also means I'll be there to pick up the pieces.

Until then booze is definitely in order. I drag her through the living room to the bar.

"What will you have?" a kid playing bartender calls over the crowd.

"Two shots of whiskey." I hold up my fingers for emphasis. He dribbles on the counter as he pours. He's going to need a replacement soon. Knowing Monroe, she'll call someone up from the casino to perform the honors. I hand one to Josie and we down them swiftly.

"Better?" I ask when she's recovered from the liquid courage.

"Yes!" She wiggles away from the bar, her mood shifting instantly.

We weave through the crowd, a few lightweights are already on the floor. I step over a girl, biting my lip, torn over leaving her there. But when I move closer, I don't see the girl, I see my sister. Stumbling back, the girl's friend pushes past me. She shoots me a disgusted look.

"I can't believe you would just leave her like that."

I mutter an apology before whipping around to look for a way outside. Anxiety is a bitch and she's always crashing the party. By the time I find one I'm sucking desperately for air.

You didn't leave her, I remind myself. You didn't leave her.

I didn't leave her, and it didn't matter.

It takes a second to catch my breath and then I remember where I am. The rooftop patio contains a collection of cabanas and, even in the dark, it's obvious they're occupied. I look away, feeling like a perv only to discover a pool full of my naked classmates. The pool itself extends to the edge of the building. It probably offers a pretty amazing view but right now, the number of boobs on display has temporarily blinded me. This clearly isn't the sanctuary I'm seeking.

Josie didn't follow me outside, which means I've lost her to the crowd. I wait a few minutes, hoping she'll find her way out to me. Despite the HBO level of nudity in progress, it's still safer here than in there. I count to one hundred before I give up and head into the fray.

"My favorite conquest!"

I force a smile as Hugo greets me at the door with his harem. He's wearing a shirt that proudly proclaims 'STD free.'

"That's false advertising," I inform him, planting my hands on my hips.

"You're welcome to check." He grins widely, tossing his arms around the girls closest to him.

"You really should pay them more. They can't even afford clothes," I say dryly.

The blonde on his left's mouth falls open but the redhead on his right just looks bored.

"Jealousy isn't becoming, Emma." He emphasizes each syllable, the sound of my name on his lips plucks at me.

I've been ID'ed by Hugo, which means it's time to find Josie and get home. I only get a few steps from him before Monroe lunges at me. Her fingers dig into my arm, and I have to resist the urge to slap her. She studies me with disgust. Apparently the scrap of cloth I'm wearing isn't as designer as the scrap of cloth she's wearing. This close I realize she has the same blue eyes as her father. But whereas his blazed, hers are as cold as ice.

"You're going to break a nail," I warn her.

"Who let you up here?"

"Nice guy down stairs. Little head, big muscles. Wait, I'm not sure that narrows it down. How many cavemen do you employ here anyway?" I yank away from her.

Her closest friends flank her, each girl dressed in a slightly different shade of pink. Leighton is blush, and Sabine is bashful. Apparently they've not been given the thumbs up to adopt Monroe's grapefruit hue. Monroe, Leighton and Sabine —the three of them are a veritable spectrum of evil. Leighton is a state-dependent bitch. Get her alone and she's actually not a terrible human being, but either Monroe flips a switch in her or she's far too eager to impress the Housers. Monroe is Monroe.

Sabine, on the other hand? Click on crazy bitch in Urban Dictionary and you'll find her picture. Most of the rumors aren't true. Like the one about her pushing some freshman off the roof of the gym? I sincerely doubt even her parents could cover that up. The rub is that she is totally capable of pushing someone off a roof.

I guess there's a little bit of truth in everything.

"Leighton. Sabine." I nod in greeting. "I had no idea they were filming a Pepto Bismal ad tonight. Congrats on the gig."

"You need to leave." It's amazing Monroe actually produces sound given how tightly she's gritting her teeth.

"Is that anyway to treat a guest?" Riling her up is a calculated risk but I need to buy time before security escorts me off the premises. But even as I scan the crowd around her, I can't find Josie. Over half of Belle Mère but no best friend. I check my phone again, but there's no response to my S.O.S.

Monroe whispers furiously to Leighton. No doubt placing a takeout order. It would be so like her to not even kick me out herself. In the periphery, Jonas moves into view, his gaze flicking from me to Monroe and back again. It's been a long time since I felt those eyes on me, and I hate how it twists my stomach into knots.

Coming here was a mistake.

"Don't bother," I interrupt. "I'm going."

I don't bother trying to look graceful as I push my way through the crowd, but I keep my head up. Jonas and I have had a good thing going, each of us pretending the other doesn't exist. If that unspoken treaty is no longer in effect than I plan to stay as far away from him and Monroe and here as possible. I guess it's a good sign that seeing him no longer makes me want to cry. I think that's what they call progress.

Before I can make it back to the elevators, Jonas intercepts me at the door. His eyes are warm like melted chocolate as he stops. I used to love staring into those eyes. Now I can barely stand to eat a Hershey's bar. That's love for you: the destroyer of life's simple joys.

"Look Monroe is all bark and no bite," he promises, shoving his hands into his pockets. It's a classic Jonas move. He can't stand to have anyone feel left out. If Monroe is the poster child for bitchy behavior, he's the peacemaker. Yet another reason I've deemed their union unholy. Now he's standing here, talking to me, as if I'm just one of the other kids' she's always bullying.

I cross my arms over my chest. He might be able to justify her attitude but there's no way I'm willing to play along. "Then put her on a leash."

"She's just very particular about her guest list. I'm sure if you—"

"We both know why she doesn't want me here," I interrupt him, "but don't worry whatever fit of insanity I suffered earlier is over. I'm leaving."

"You don't have to go." I hate how his voice softens around those words. We stare at each other, and I wonder if this is just him doing his good samaritan act or if he actually wants me to stay. Butterflies stir in my stomach and I squash the fragile hope before I do or say something stupid. I push past him. "I need to find Josie."

He forces a wounded smile, but let's me leave. When I reach the foyer, I still haven't found Josie. She isn't responding to texts. The security guard who pointed us in the direction of the party is gone. It occurs to me then that I'm as lost to her as she is to me.

"You were going to get kicked out anyway," I say to the empty hall before I take a deep breath and follow in the footsteps of Nathaniel. If I'm lucky I'll find her first, but let's face it, lady luck is a bitch.

Chapter 4

THE WEST RESIDENCE goes on forever. There's wealth and then there's extravagance but this rises to the highest levels of selfishness. The other half of the home has been crowded with warm bodies making it too difficult to see my posh surroundings. The marble floor continues down the hallway, satiny gold papers the wall. I trail my hand along it. The slight texture of the wallpaper vibrates across my fingertips. Overhead a series of miniature chandeliers lights my way, dripping like luxury icicles. Who said Vegas was gauche? Sometimes I wonder if this is where interior design flunkies get sent.

I don't mean to count the rooms as I pass them but after the fifth bathroom I'm shaking my head. They can't possibly use them all. Maybe they have a rotation going or they use one for each day of the week. Monday's bathroom. Tuesday's bathroom. Wednesday's bathroom. The maid service should be given the Medal of Honor.

Light creeps through the crack of the slightly ajar door. I pause outside and consider my options. I can keep creeping around counting bathrooms or I can gamble. Pressing my palm to the door, I realize I have a little Vegas in me after all. It swings open to reveal an empty room. A large glass desk perched on chrome legs sits in front of the floor-to-ceiling windows that overlook the neon lights of the strip. A pair of high-back leather chairs in glossy black wait in front of it. It's an office but other than a crystal decanter filled with amber liquid and two rocks glasses, it's devoid of personality. No books. No papers. No art hanging on the walls. Then again what could compete with the glittering backdrop of sin city?

"I don't think you're supposed to be in here."

I startle at the sound of the disembodied voice, my hand flying to my chest like a bad actress.

"S-s-sorry," I stammer as I begin to back out of the room. I've been caught sneaking around by Nathaniel West. I guess I'll finally find out if casino owners really have the power to break someone's legs or if that's just an urban legend.

The desk chair spins around slowly revealing the owner of the voice. As he comes into the light I know he's wearing jeans instead of a suit and that the thin T-shirt hugs his biceps. He clutches the arms of the chair with broad strong hands that bear no signs of age. By the time the light hits his face I know I haven't stumbled upon Nathaniel.

"I don't think you are either, but I won't..." My words die on my lips as his brutally beautiful face is revealed. I've never been the girl who hung pictures of rock stars or actors on my walls. I don't gush over how hot Hottie McHottie is, and I don't turn into a blubbery puddle when I meet a cute guy.

But this guy isn't cute. He isn't hot. He exists on some other plane of attractiveness altogether. His jawline is sharp, chiseled and sculpted by genetics far superior to the rest of humanity. There's a slight crook to his nose that is somehow so perfectly imperfect. A slight smirk plays at his lips. My gaze lingers there wondering what it would be like to kiss him. So much for being above all that boy crazy shit. I'd hang his poster over my bed shamelessly. His tousled brown hair is long enough that I can imagine grabbing it. It's his eyes, though, that arrest me. In the dim light of the room they're deep gray, flashing with dangerous interest. The other half of his face remains in shadow as if I'm only seeing as much of him as he'll allow me to see.

"You're correct." He leans forward pressing his hands flatly against the glass desktop. He's completely in the light now, showcasing the wide curve of his mouth. His eyes are bluer now, the color of the sea after a storm. I could drown in those eyes.

Warning bells ring in my head but my subconscious hits the snooze button. "I won't tell if you won't tell."

"That sounds like a proposition." His eyes trail over my face and my cheeks begin to heat under his watchful gaze.

Two minutes alone with this guy and I've shut down all my defenses. That's the last thing I can allow to happen. "It's not. It's merely playing it smart."

I fold my arms over my chest and tear my eyes from his. He can't be oblivious to his effect on girls, which is why I won't give him the satisfaction of toying with me.

"I didn't mean to offend, Duchess." He shifts in the chair crossing his arms behind his head and no longer bothering to hide his cocky grin.

"You didn't." I study the top of the replica Eiffel tower a few blocks away.

"Then I didn't mean to annoy." He sounds amused but I refuse to check to see if his smile has widened.

"Do I look annoyed?" I shrug and pivot on my heels toward the door. It's well past time for me to take my exit. If Josie is in trouble she'll call. She always does, but not before making me worry a bit. This time though, I'm out. Getting caught trespassing twice in one night is my quota.

He stays silent as I walk toward the door but before I reach the hall, he calls out, "You do look ruffled."

"Ruffled?" I repeat, twirling around to glare at him. "Ruffles are for dresses and potato chips. I don't ruffle."

"Oh, you are definitely ruffled." He brushes a hand over his hair, somehow managing to make it even messier—and sexier. Natural, coppery highlights glint from it as he laughs.

I plant my hands on my hips. When I find Josie, I'm going to kill her. For now, I'd settle for strangling him. "I'm just not interested in playing games."

"Most girls love games," he says.

"I'm not most girls."

"Of course," he continues without acknowledging that I've spoken, "most girls aren't very good at playing."

"Is that so?" I ask. The flush I feel now has nothing to do with embarrassment.

"They never seem to win." He stands and circles the desk, walking toward me with a swagger that sets off my bad boy alarm.

"Try me."

His eyebrow arches up. I've got his attention now. "How did you get in here?"

"I walked," I answer with a shrug. "This is a terrible game."

"I'm just setting the stage, Duchess."

I groan, dropping my arms to my sides as my hands ball into fists. "That's the second time you've called me that. Why?"

"I'm the one asking questions." He takes a step closer and now I can smell his cologne–leather and spice and sex.

"You asked your question. I asked mine. Quid pro quo."

"Fancy words. I'm going to guess you don't go to Las Palmas." A smile twitches at his lips, making him look both kissable and smackable at the same time.

I bat my eyelashes a bit too fast as I answer. "Who says I go to school?"

Hottie McHottie is turning me into a giggling school girl faster than a cheerleader drops her panties on prom night. I step backward instinctively and bump against the door. So much for a graceful exit. My blunder gives him the opportunity to lean over me. He grips the wood frame, hovering dangerously close. I can't help but get the sense that I'm being stalked. Any moment now he might lunge and devour me.

"The uneducated generally don't drop Latin idioms, even common ones." His words dance over my face, leaving a breathy trail of whiskey. "But I'm impressed, so I'll answer your question on the condition that you answer my early one."

I open my mouth to protest but instead I find myself nodding, hypnotized by the magnetic hold of his gaze. Whoever he is, he has more than a few tricks up his sleeve. I know because I'm already under his spell.

His head slants to whisper in my ear. "You look like a Duchess. Regal. Haughty. Untouchable."

I tuck that description away. Later I'll dissect it, fulfilling the biological imperative of femininity. I suspect I'll be annoyed. Maybe even pissed. For now, though, all I can think is that I don't want to be untouchable, not with his lips so close to my skin.

"Your turn," he prompts, pulling away.

I swallow hard, immediately relieved to have a little more space between us. "I was looking for a friend. I guess I got lost."

"The party is in the other room." He backs away, completely liberating me from the cage of his arms.

"No shit." I stand up straighter. If the predator is going to give his prey a chance to escape, I need to be alert. "It's not really my scene. I wanted to find her to say goodbye."

"I was told this is the party of the year," he says, "but you're here against your will."

"Not against my will. More like against my moral code. Hanging out with Monroe West and her minions has to be a violation of the Geneva Convention."

"Minions?" he says with a laugh. "Is that what you call them?"

"Them? Don't you mean us?" I repeat, tilting my head to size him up. He definitely looks like he belongs in her world. He's too pretty for the eyes of mere mortals and his clothes scream upper one percent.

"So I'm classified as a minion? For what do I owe the honor?"

I reach out and run a finger along the neckline of his thin t-shirt. "Gucci," I guess. "And why not? Who doesn't want to drop a couple Benjamins to look like he's not trying? There's no cheap alcohol lingering in your cologne or on your breath."

"So my taste earns me the coveted title?"

"Minion isn't a compliment," I say flatly. He might want to be playful but I'm not in the mood. "Of course, I don't think you go to Belle Mère and Las Palmas kids don't shop Caesar's." I don't bother to add that I don't either. If the forum shops weren't filled with miles of the most expensive retailers in the world, I'd probably still want to avoid the cheesy Americanization of the ancient world. Although it's debatable if Caesar would be with me on that. No, it was a milestone for nouveau riche tourists, but merely a mall to most of my classmates where Spago is the foodcourt.

"Maybe I stole this. You did catch me where I wasn't supposed to be, remember?" His tongue flicks across his full, lower lip. "What would you say then?"

"Did you?" I breathe. "Grand larceny isn't really a turn-on."

He winks before nodding toward the door. "Well, I'm not a student at Belle Mère or Las Palmas."

Does the help here have sticky fingers? That seems doubtful, especially given the confidence that oozes from him. He was probably a boyfriend from out of town who slipped away from arm candy duty. It would definitely explain his entitled attitude. I watch as he slips out the door, heading back to the party or seeking more treasure to loot. It's hard to decide which way I hope he's heading—back to the Housers or to play Robin Hood.

Away from his presence, I remember where I am. Hanging out in Nathaniel West's study is a surefire way to get an up-close and personal look at the West's security. Still someone should appreciate this view. I linger for a few minutes and drink it in. My impression of the man my father hates so vehemently feels justified standing here. Does he look out over the valley below and see the rest of us bustling about like worker ants building his kingdom? No computer. No pictures. There doesn't seem to be much else to do here but play god. That was the difference between a man like West and my dad. One bled and the other doesn't.

Pivoting on my heels, I stride out of the office. But before I can act on my instinct to get out of here, with or without Josie, a shadowy figure on the stairs catches my eye. I freeze in place, realizing with dread that it's no longer moving either.

Busted.

Chapter 5

THIS ISN'T one of those moments when your life flashes before your eyes. Nope, a vision of the next twenty-four hours in a jail cell, waiting for my dad to wake up from a bender, does instead. With any luck Monroe or Hugo will get a couple of great shots of the security hauling me off. By morning, news of my poor judgment will have spread like a pandemic through most of Belle Mère. Oh well. My Instagram feed could use the boost. But when I get the courage to peel my eyes off the floor, I discover the shadow is attached to my new best friend.

"Are you following me?" he asks.

"N-n-no," I stumble over my denial. What is it about this guy that has me tongue-tied? Whatever it is I can't say that I like it. I plant a hand on my hip in challenge. "Are you following me?"

This earns me a smile. The kind that drops defenses and charms parents. I thought I'd built an immunity to guys like him, but here I am coming down with a bad case of wet panties.

He extends his hand and looks at me expectantly. I shake my head. My judgment isn't completely shot.

"I don't bite."

That's disappointing.

"You suck at introductions. I don't even know your name," I point out.

"Is that all that's stopping you?"

That and a few shreds of common sense that he hasn't obliterated yet. What if he tells me his name? Will I take his hand? What if he doesn't? I'm just as likely to follow him, which means I'm in big trouble. Damn Josie for disappearing on me. Usually I'm the one bailing her out of jams. Tonight I wish she'd return the favor. When I find her, I'm revoking her BFF card.

"It must be something terrible," I tease. "Maybe Howard? Or Bert?"

"Bert?" he repeats with a deep laugh. "Two can play this game you know."

I barely process that we've begun walking deeper into the penthouse. Score one for my self preservation skills.

"Ingrid?" he guesses. "Helga?"

"What am I? An old German woman?"

He pauses unexpectedly and I run directly into him. His hands grip my upper arms, steadying me before I can stumble. His touch does strange things to my body – stuff usually reserved for romance novels.

"Definitely not." His answers scrapes up his throat. Maybe I'm not the only one affected by skin to skin contact. "Jameson. My family calls me Jamie.."

Jamie. That feels far too normal a name for him. Familiar. Comfortable. It doesn't fit how he makes me feel. But Jameson does.

"Your turn," he prompts.

"Oh, is that how this works, Jameson? I thought we were

playing coy." At least I can pretend like I have some dignity left.

"We can keep playing, Duchess, but I'm beginning to feel like my opponent deserves formal recognition." The arrogance that's marked his tone since we met softens a bit as he speaks.

"I like the name you've given me. You're right. It's fitting."

His mouth twists into a smirk that's at odds with his strong jaw line, making him look devilish. Why are the wicked boys so much more beddable?

"Duchess it is."

I've won this round and we both know it. It's an unforeseen victory, but I'll take it anyway. I take the opportunity to be the one that leads. A few steps deeper into the penthouse and we find ourselves in a kitchen. Being here has me out of sorts. Scattered mail and magazines clutter the black granite countertops. Judging from the oversized Viking range and large steam hood this is a gourmet kitchen, but the only evidence of food consumption is the dry bits of toast on the plates piled in the sink and an empty yogurt cup.

"I guess the maid has the day off," I note, instinctively picking up the trash and looking for the wastebasket.

"Are you applying for the job?" Jameson asks, nodding toward the offending yogurt cup.

"Maybe for chef." I stare longingly at the stove. I can only imagine the ingredients in the subzero fridge. I bet it's not full of chicken breasts and a half dozen cheap marinades—unlike my house. These people can have whatever they want and they settle for toast and yogurt. Swallowing hard I turn away from the gourmet appliances and spot a neatly disguised recycling bin. It's fitting really: trim out your trash with whitewashed paneling so no one knows that you have any. Who would want the ugliness of the used and discarded blemishing their perfect reality? Not the Wests.

"Chef?" He sounds impressed. It's completely gross that his approval sends a tingle running from my scalp to my toes. I ignore how that ripple hesitates a little too long between my legs.

I shrug, doing my best to look nonchalant. I'm pretty certain that's what Cosmo recommends in these situations, pretend like you're too chill to notice the guy is flirting with you. Except I don't know if Jameson is flirting with me. My boy skills need a tuneup. "I like to cook. It's sad the wicked bitch of the West wastes her caloric intake on nonfat Greek yogurt."

"It's a good source of protein," Jameson advises me as he grabs a stool and makes himself at home in the West's kitchen. "Wicked bitch of the West?"

I cringe inwardly. For all I know Jameson is Monroe's childhood buddy. Or more likely, judging from the pythons of biceps peeking from his T-shirt, her bodyguard. "That's what everyone calls Monroe West. I have no idea who came up with it. I can't believe I said that."

Two truths and a lie.

Wicked bitch of the West. I coined that particular term of endearment for Monroe in ninth grade not long after our introduction when she was released from captivity, or boarding school as the Housers call it.

"I take it you're not a fan."

"I wouldn't say that," I hedge. "I mean I watched her on Pop Princess like the rest of school." Monroe's brief foray into reality television had been the talk of Belle Mère, and it had given me a reason to heckle my screen for a couple weeks. I keep that to myself.

"Then not a friend," he clarifies. Those stormy eyes pierce through me. It's not a question. It's clear he knows the answer, but I can't resist responding.

"We aren't planning any slumber parties. You?"

I'm dying for him to tell me how he wound up here. Maybe that's why I've been answering his questions. Of course, it could just be that he's rattling me. If I'm not careful I'll need to make a cold shower my next stop on this unofficial tour of the West estate.

"I wouldn't call her a friend." It's not much information but judging from the chilly undercurrent in his words he's not the president of her fan club.

Good enough for me.

"Cook something," he says out of nowhere. I shake my head. It's fairly hard to render me speechless but Jameson's just accomplished it.

He snorts at my horrified reaction. "You said it yourself. Someone should appreciate this kitchen. Besides I'm sure one of the—what did you call them? Minions?—will wreck it before the night's over."

He slides off the stool and breaches the subzero fridge, revealing a drawer of artisan cheeses, tins of caviar, and shelves full of perfect organic produce. I have $50 in grocery money to hold me until the end of the month and they have half a Whole Foods in this kitchen.

"Inspired?" He steps aside, holding open the door for me.

"I shouldn't." But now I'm merely feigning a conscience. By this time most of the partygoers will be far too wasted to remember their own names let alone mine. If we get caught I can play drunk. I can't resist the temptation as I pluck a wedge of Gouda from the drawer along with the glass pint of milk. No plastic gallons in this kitchen. Jameson leans against the counter, gripping the edge, as he watches me rummaging through the pantry and fridge for the rest of the ingredients I need. One I've collected the necessities, I fill a Le Creuset stockpot with the special water tap conveniently built into the backsplash over the eight burner gas range. I guess it would have been too much work to use the sink and carry all the way over. "I hope you're hungry."

"I'm starving." His voice is low and gravelly. My eyes flash to his in time to see his tongue flick over his perfectly white teeth.

The better to eat you with.

"Can I help you?" he asks.

"Do you cook?" I don't bother to hide my incredulity at his offer. I can't help but imagine that he subsists on the sandwiches his conquests deliver to him in bed.

"No," he admits slowly and for a moment his cocky exterior slips allowing me a flash of sheepish Jameson. Dammit it makes him even hotter. "But I can set a mean table. Shall we dine poolside?"

He gestures to the private patio just outside a row of sliding glass doors.

"That would be lovely," I practically sing out and he smiles. I can't help my cheerful mood swing now that he's found my soft spot. Not an easy feat. But I've always felt at home in a kitchen. My sister and I used to help our mom cook. She taught me all the basic French sauces. It came in handy when she ditched the three of us for personal chef of her own. I'd split duties with Becca after that. Then everything changed. It had been a long time since I found myself humming over roux.

A few minutes later and I have a slowly thickening cheese sauce and boiling water. Reaching for the bag of penne I found in the cupboard, I dump it in and stir. The pasta momentarily disturbs the waters heat and the surface calms before steam rises to shatter it again. I stare at the bubbles, wondering if I find myself in hot water soon as well.

Jameson returns to the kitchen and I resolve not to look at him. The smell of melted Gouda is drool worthy enough. He passes behind me, opening a drawer, but then his hands are on my hips. My eyes close for a split second, relishing the confident gesture. In that moment I imagine this is my life: cooking without a care in the world for my hot boyfriend. It's so simple that it almost seems attainable.

But it isn't. I gulp against the treacherous ache in my throat. It's a fantasy, that's all. Dreams like that are the lies sold to little kids, and I haven't purchased any for a long time.

He peers over my shoulder, tucking his chin against my neck. It fits there. Maybe a bit too well. "What are you making, Duchess?"

"Grown up mac & cheese," I whisper, not trusting my voice to hide my emotions.

"I might have to see your ID before you can have that." He sweeps his lips swiftly over my throat before he steps away.

I'm in trouble with a capital T. Or maybe I'm just finally having a good dream for once.

"Nice try. But I know what you're really after. Isn't it more fun if you don't know who I am?" I tap the whisk against the rim of the saucier before I take it off the heat. Then I point to the pot of pasta. "Drain that."

"As you wish."

"I love that movie," I say absently.

Jameson pauses at my side, potholders in hand. "It's one of my favorites."

His arm brushes mine as he reaches for the pot. My insides twist as I watch him dump the water. Neither of us speak as he returns the pot to the stove. I add the sauce, not daring to break the silence. We've fallen under a magic spell. Reality will fuck it up soon enough.

. . .

AN HOUR later I'm strewn across a chaise in the pool cabana as Jameson finishes the last of the pasta. I eye him with interest from my carb-induced coma. "Does anyone feed you?"

"Not stuff like this," he says, scooping another bite into his mouth before he pushes the bowl away. "If I could I would hire you as my chef."

That might be dangerous for the chiseled physique I'm lusting after from afar. I keep this to myself. "Let me guess? Mom takes you to the buffets?"

"Mom is more interested in spa fare." He screws up his face. "As far as I can tell, that means no fat, no salt, and no flavor."

"There are more than a few decent restaurants around here," I point out, glancing toward the sparkling lights that glimmer in the night from all angles.

"That is true. I'll add that to my list of reasons why it's good to be back in Vegas."

"Back?" I perk up a little. Mr. Mysterious has slipped and given me a tidbit of information.

He sighs, tilting his head thoughtfully, as if considering how much he's given away. Finally, he nods. "From school."

"Oh, were you exiled? Stole daddy's t-bird? Knocked up the principal's daughter?" I rattle off options in mock horror.

"Do I get bad boy points if I say yes?"

I shake my head. "I've sworn off bad boys for lent."

"It's May."

"What can I say? I'm not Catholic. But the thing about bad boys is true." I'd dabbled in rebels with Hugo. That was enough to make me swear off guys like him for life.

"I'm back from college," he admits.

More information. I push myself up in my seat. Things are starting to get interesting. "Where do you go?"

He hesitates, running his fingers through his hair.

"Nowhere, actually. Not anymore. Tomorrow I get to tell my parents."

Way to go, Emma. How would someone who hadn't embraced the life of cynicism respond to that confession?

"Do you want to talk about it?" I ask slowly.

"Not really." His laugh is hollow. I recognize the bitter edge in it. Apparently Jameson and I are going to keep finding things we have in common.

"I have a knack for disappointing my parents, too," I promise him. "If my dad knew I was here…"

"Why are you here?" he asks bluntly. Maybe the time for games is over.

"My friend dragged me and then promptly left me to fend off Monroe's fury. I'm not supposed to be here." It feels good to admit it.

"Me either," he murmurs. "So neither of us want to be here and neither of us should be here. Tell me, Duchess. Who do you want to be tonight?"

I raise an eyebrow. "I thought I was the Duchess."

"If you like," he promises, "but tonight you can be anyone and anything. What will it be?"

"Carefree," I say without hesitation. "I want to be carefree."

Jameson falls silent as if considering my answer. Studying me for a moment, he finally stands and holds out his hand.

"Another game?" he suggests.

"Twenty questions went so well for us," I say dryly.

"Truth or dare."

Narrowing my eyes, I take his hand and allow him to pull me up. "Truth."

"Why do you hate Monroe?" he asks.

"She stole my boyfriend. Truth or dare?" I don't linger on my answer. There's no way I'll get to carefree if I let thoughts of Jonas sneak into my subconscious.

"Truth."

"Why did you leave school?" I ask.

"I wouldn't call it a voluntary exit," he admits. "I was kicked out. This game sucks."

"Let's liven it up," I suggest. "Dare."

Jameson doesn't miss a beat. "Go swimming with me."

"I don't have a suit." My objection dies on my lips as he tugs his shirt over his head, revealing the hard slab of abs the thin fabric hinted at.

"Carefree, remember? Your turn."

I pause, realizing this might be a good time to gracelessly exit.

"C'mon Duchess. I showed you mine."

"Hardly a fair trade," I hedge, even as my fingers inch toward the hem of my skirt. "I'm only wearing this."

"That's the best news I've heard all day." A grin splits across his handsome face as my cheeks turn red.

"And underwear!"

"That's a shame," he says sadly, unbuckling his belt and sliding it through the loops. The sound of the leather vibrating against denim trembles across me. "Allow me to even things out."

I do my best not to gawk as his jeans hit the ground, but I can't quite help sneaking a peek at his boxer briefs. He taps his foot impatiently. "Do you need me to unzip you?"

I bite my lip before I nod. I barely trust myself to move at this point, let alone attempt the slightest change in position. Jameson circles around behind me, gathering my hair over my shoulder, he draws the zipper down. His hands slip under the straps of my dress as he pushes them down. The flimsy dress flutters into a pool of fabric at my feet as a fingertip trails down my back, between my shoulder blades, to the band of my bra.

I whip around before he can unsnap it. "It's going to take a little more than a dare to get me out of my panties."

He nods in acceptance, but I can see the glimmer in his eyes. I've just made this a challenge. The trouble is I'm not certain which one of us I want to win. He doesn't press it, though. Instead he grabs my hand and tugs me toward the water.

"It's a little bit chilly up here," I call right before he grabs me around the waist and hurls us both into the deep end. Instinct kicks in and I struggle back toward the surface, but Jameson doesn't let go. Instead he smashes his lips to mine, and suddenly I don't need air. I don't need to fight. I go limp in his arms, my body molding naturally to his as the kiss deepens. He pushes us up, not breaking the kiss until we sputter apart for air. We suck in deep breaths, staring at one another. Water drips into his eyes from the strands of wet hair that have fallen across his forehead, but he doesn't blink as if he can't stand to break contact. Then he's kissing me again and I never want him to stop.

Jameson kicks against the water, moving us back until we hit the pool's tile wall. I don't protest as we spin around and I'm pressed against the tile. My arms splay against it as he moves between my legs. The thin fabric separating us rasps against my skin, urging me toward an edge I'm not ready to go over. He begins to explore my neck, his teeth and lips delivering thrills and shivers. When his hand moves up to cup my breast, he pulls back with a sinful smirk. "Any objection, Duchess?"

I meet his eyes, so silver in the moonlit night. He's gained the upper hand, but I have my own cards to play. My hand reaches between us to where our bodies are pinned against the wall, and rubs over the bulge trapped in his boxers.

"None at all," I purr, biting back a moan when his fingers slide under my bra. His thumb circles my nipple and for a second, I nearly lose the last ounce of control I have. Everything with him feels so good—so right. Mostly, because what we're doing and where we're doing it is so wrong.

That's what holds me back though. I'd been down this road before. It's landscape is a bit too familiar. Still, it's hard to turn the car around when we're zooming swiftly toward unknown territory.

"Truth or dare," I whisper through clenched teeth.

Jameson's mouth closes over mine, stealing my words, as if he's through playing games. Then, he pulls away. "Dare, I think."

I can't keep the smile off my face. That's what I was hoping he'd say.

Chapter 6

DAWN CREEPS UP ON ME. I blink against the sunlight before I sit bolt upright and stare at the unfamiliar surroundings. Memories from last night swim to the surface. Jameson's body pressed against mine. His hands gripping my wrists over my head while he kissed me until my lips were swollen. My fingers flutter to my mouth as I recall the vivid details of each hungry kiss. The towel draped over me drops to the ground and I scramble to grab it before someone spots my nearly naked ass waking up in the West's private pool cabana. In the light of day, it looks less glamorous and distinctly less friendly. But more than anything it looks empty.

I'm alone.

I look around for a note even as it sinks in that there won't be one. Two party crashers don't equal a relationship, I remind myself as I scrape up what's left of my pride. No note but my dress is neatly folded and waiting for me on the table next to my phone. It doesn't score Jameson any brownie points, but it keeps him in the neutral zone which is exactly where he belongs. Time to suck it up and do the walk of shame through enemy territory.

My phone vibrates with an incoming text and I grab it, but it isn't from Josie.

Mom: See you at 10!

I check the clock. 9:01. The right curse word hasn't been invented for this scenario, so I blurt all the other ones in existence as I tug my dress on. Gathering my shoes, I tiptoe back inside, praying to every god in history that Monroe isn't a morning person. I pass the dirty pots from last night on my way out, assuaging my guilt by reminding myself that the West's have a full hotel staff at their beck and call. The house is deadly silent, but I can almost imagine the orgy of passed out classmates I would find if I dared to return to the scene of the party. I'm smarter than to press my luck. The door to the study is ajar and I pause only long enough to feel stupid. There's no way Jameson is hanging around here.

"You could have woken me up," I grumble under my breath, but thinking of him recalls flashes of our night together. I'd almost given in to my desire but somehow I had clung to my integrity. The fact doesn't really take the sting out of waking up alone though.

Coming around the corner, two groggy faces greet me.

"Morning, sunshine," Hugo calls. Jonas just looks confused.

Taking a deep breath, I force myself to join them. Unless I want to go to brunch smelling like chlorine with raccoon eyes, I don't have the luxury of waiting around. Also getting the hell out of here seems like a pretty good idea.

"You are looking ravaged this morning," Hugo says. "Who's the lucky man? The bell boy?"

I keep my eyes trained on the glowing, down button. What is the point of having a private elevator if you have to wait?

"Shut up, man," Jonas mutters. "Hey Em, you need a ride home?"

I glance at the sliver of green left on my cell's battery status. I can't call Josie—even if she'd pick up. It will be dead before I can get an Uber. "I can take a cab."

"Don't be ridiculous. I'll drive you," he protests.

"What a gentleman," Hugo says. "First, you sleep on the couch and now you're offering rides to the peasants."

"A cab is not an issue," I say through gritted teeth. The elevator dings and Jonas holds the door until I wander inside.

"I insist. Hugo's headed to the airport anyway. I can drop you before I take him."

I open my mouth to protest, but Hugo butts in.

"Please, I will pay you to stop fighting him on this. I can't handle all the polite tension." He steps between us, folding his arms over his chest and watching the floor numbers descending. "So how was your evening?"

"I fell asleep." I'm not giving him more than that. An inch is more than enough for Hugo Roth to hang me with. "I was waiting for Josie and I got tired."

None of that is technically a lie, which means neither of them question it. The only way to salvage any of last night is if Hugo Roth never finds out that I nearly hooked up with some random guy in Monroe West's cabana.

"Josie was here?" Jonas asks slowly. "I didn't see her."

"That makes two of us." When I finally did find my prodigal friend, I was going to put a tracking device on her.

"Who's Josie?" Hugo asks, looking at both of us.

A sigh in disgust, but Jonas answers him. "She's in our class, man."

He shrugs, satisfied by this answer. That's all he needs to know. If Josie ever did make it onto his radar, he'd be all over her. That's just how guys are around her. The last thing I need is for her to trade in her daddy fetish for a dickhead phase.

"Why'd you even stay last night?" Hugo asks and I realize he's not talking to me. "After Monroe went ballistic like that."

"I wanted to make sure she was okay." Jonas glances at me. "She just gets anxious sometimes."

"I'd call that her permanent state of being," Hugo says flatly.

I barely manage to cover my laughter with a fake cough. For once I agree with Hugo. The elevator delivers us safely to the lobby before I lose my composure. A security guard waiting in front of it steps to the side as we exit, barely acknowledging us. I guess he gets paid enough to look the other way. Then again, everyone knows that Nathaniel West runs this city. No one would dare mess with his daughter's friends.

There are a sad number of people milling around the casino floor as we make our way to the valet stand. I'm not the only girl who didn't go home last night from the looks of it. Desperation mars the faces of those we pass as they hold their breaths as the wheel spins and the dice rolls. I can already tell what's in the cards for them. Being here makes me feel nauseous. I don't understand this world even though I know exactly how and why it works. But after years of finding dad passed out on the couch and the bank account drained, I'm no closer to comprehending what drives the obsession.

Why would anyone want to lose over and over again?

Hugo leans over as we wait for the valet to pull the car around. "Pathetic, isn't it? All that misery for a few minutes of high."

"That's easy for you to say." Contrary to convention, with the amount of money his family has, he can buy happiness. Or at least the equivalent amount of girls, booze, and drugs.

Before we can get into it, Jonas's silver Mercedes arrives.

"I thought Monroe wanted you to get a new car," Hugo says, grabbing the passenger handle. Jonas shoots him a meaningful look. "Oh, I see the chivalry continues. Might as well give her a little thrill."

Hugo opens the door and sweeps his arm out. "Your car."

They say what doesn't kill you makes you stronger, but what about what you don't kill? Because right now I need incentive not to lay him out on the pavement. Considering that I probably have about twenty minutes to get home, shower and throw on clothes, I don't have the time. I take a deep breath and steel myself as I climb into the passenger seat. We pull onto the Strip in silence.

"What's wrong with your car?" I ask conversationally.

"Nothing," Jonas says, flipping on the turn signal. "Monroe likes flashier cars."

Hugo leans forward, poking his head between the seats. "Maybe if she didn't make him sleep on the couch, he'd trade up."

"Put your seat belt on," Jonas barks as a cop car blazes past us, heading in the opposite direction with its sirens blaring. A few more follow.

"Another peaceful morning in Las Vegas," Hugo says dreamily. "This is God's country, I tell you."

For once I'm glad for their noise, anything to drown him out. Turning my attention out the window I stare past the people walking by and past the lights. In the daylight all I see is the trash littering the streets and the homeless man huddled under a collection of blankets.

"What a wonderful world," Hugo pipes up from behind me. I twist around to see him studying the same things I'm seeing, but I don't bother to respond.

The ride home is made all the more excruciating by the fact that Jonas insists on going under the speed limit while Hugo sings loudly to everything that comes over the radio. When I can't stand it anymore I hit the off button.

"I was listening to that," he calls.

"You can turn it on in a minute," I promise as we turn down my street. Dad's car is in the driveway.

"Are you going to be okay?" Jonas asks as he pulls in.

"Yeah, why?" I lie.

"I remember your dad was pretty strict about curfew."

I don't like that he remembers things like that. He has no right to hold onto any memories of us. "That was a long time ago."

"Okay. Have a good summer," he says as Hugo opens my door.

"Have a fun time at the pawn shop." He scoots into my seat, slamming the door in my face.

I wait for them to pull away, waving Jonas on when he hesitates. Was he always such a white knight? Hugo's right. It's a bit off-putting.

"That's the second thing you've agreed with him on today," I say aloud. It might be time to get my head checked.

On the off chance Dad is actually awake the last thing I need is for him to spot two boys bringing me home. When I finally get up the nerve to go inside, he's snoring on the couch with an empty bottle of Jack on the floor.

Saved by the booze.

I don't have time to feel bad for myself or clean up his mess, so I grab a blanket and toss it over him. Heading to my room, I strip down, trying not to think about last night. But undressing brings visions of Jameson flashing through my mind. I push the thoughts aside, plug in my phone and turn on the shower. There's no use, I'm going to be late.

The water feels good but it can't wash away the memory of his hands on me. I turn the faucet off with a groan. My neck is stiff from sleeping awkwardly last night and the last thing I want to do is go to brunch with my mom. But since being dutiful ensures that my tuition gets paid, I rummage through my closet until I find something suitably boring for such an occasion. Stepping into the yellow sundress, my phone begins to vibrate with a series of incoming messages. I grab a few bobby pins from the dresser and twist my wet hair up. It will have to do.

I don't have time to check the texts before Josie's ringtone begins to play. I lunge for it, hitting accept as I flop onto my bed.

"Where the hell were you?" I demand. "I looked for you everywhere."

"Me?" she shrieks. "I heard Monroe kicked you out. I spent half the night wandering through the casino looking for you."

Two ships passing in the night. Sighing, I cradle my phone to my ear and unscrew my mascara wand. "I texted you. I fell asleep out by the pool."

Now's not the time to tell her about Jameson. Not while it's still raw that he left me there like that.

"My phone died," she says quickly, "but that's not what's important. Turn on the news."

"The news?" I repeat.

"Emma!" Her tone is rich with warning, so I flip open my laptop.

"I'm online. What am I looking for?" I ask, still trying to do my make-up. Who says girls can't multi-task?

"Google West Casino," she demands.

A pit opens in my stomach as I key in the words and click on the streaming news link. Neither of us speaks as a reporter's voice comes over my speakers.

We're at the scene of a developing story. Authorities have confirmed the discovery of a body in the penthouse of West

Casino and Resort. The penthouse is the private residence of mogul Nathaniel West and his family. There's been no word yet on the identity of the victim but homicide units are at the scene.

"What the hell is going on?" I whisper.

"Who do you think it is?" Josie asks.

I don't know and that's what scares me.

Chapter 7

ONE OVERPRICED CAB ride later and I'm no closer to processing Josie's bombshell. Today is not a great day to meet with my mom, but I've been summoned and apparently I take my duty as her daughter far more seriously than she takes her maternal obligations to me. Mariano's is packed with the usual late Saturday morning crowd of affluent 40-somethings. Perched atop one of Vegas's stodgier five star hotels, the restaurant offers panoramic views of the city. You don't get to a standing reservation here by playing slots. My guess is Mariano's clientele prefers to retain their view from the top.

Scanning the French twists and bad toupees I search for the pair that belongs to me, and then I spot her: Vivian Von Essen sipping a mimosa.

She used to be Vivian Southerly, but there's very few traces of the woman who used to be my mother. My mom didn't bother doing her hair every morning. She couldn't afford the expensive dress suit she's wearing now. Mom didn't just trade in her husband, she traded in her whole life. Me included. All that's left of our relationship now is our resemblance. Someone once told me I'd be lucky to look like her when I'm older. Our green eyes are identical and we share the same sandy blonde hair. I'm guessing if I want my skin to stay youthful and radiant, I'll need more than good genes. Maybe I should get the name of her aesthetician and plastic surgeon now. I hear it's never too early to start.

I square my shoulders and mutter to myself as I approach her table, "Close your eyes and think of England."

She doesn't bother to look up from her phone. I clear my throat. I don't remember when I began feeling the need to wait for my mother's attention. I'm sure if Sigmund Freud was alive he'd be taking lots of notes. There's probably no one else who could sort out how twisted our relationship has become.

When she doesn't respond I clutch the back of the chair. "Good morning."

"Only for some it seems." Mom glances at me. "I'm just catching up on the news. What a nightmare!"

My smile is tight as I lean in to kiss her cheek. She doesn't know the half of it. As I straighten up I catch a whiff of Chanel No. 5. At least some things don't change. That had been a luxury she always found money for. Becca and I would sit at her feet while she applied it. She would place the precious bottle back on the vanity and tell us, "A girl may not have money but she can always have standards."

A waiter appears, startling me out of the past and into the present.

"I'll have what she's having," I say, nodding to her champagne flute.

She sets her phone down to shoot me a disapproving look. "Emma."

"An orange juice." I feign innocence that neither of us buys. If it comes as a cocktail Vivian Von Essen takes it that way. After last night I could've used a drink, but now I'll settle for shocking my mom into giving me attention. I think Freud had a term for that: desperation. "I didn't expect you to be in town this weekend."

Ice broken. Now to sit and endure the chill for an hour. I unfolded my napkin, which makes a shitty blanket, and wait for her to respond. That's how it is between us now: branches and cheek kisses and awkward small talk.

"You're starting your senior year. I thought that deserved a celebration."

At a place for lifestyle retirees. Gee thanks, Mom.

"There is something we could do if you're interested." Who knew an olive branch could feel so heavy? Extending it is exhausting, but thankfully she grabs for the metaphorical offering.

"Anything. This day is all about you, honey." She presses her lips together, no doubt trying to hold in her excitement.

Here goes nothing. "Could go by Becca's grave this afternoon? The headstone is up—"

"Let's not discuss that right now." She doesn't just cut me off, she dismisses the idea entirely. The interest she'd shown a few moments ago evaporates instantly, replaced by a distant, frosty demeanor.

That's all my sister—her daughter—is to her now: a subject that can be dismissed with one wave of a manicured hand. To my knowledge, Mom hasn't visited Becca's grave since we buried her. Then again given how much Valium she was on at the funeral, she hadn't really been present and accounted for then either. It hurts that I can't share my grief with her. Dad drinks, Mom ignores, and I pretend that I'm not walking around with a gaping hole where my family used to be. No one is going to be asking us to write a book on coping with loss anytime soon.

Meanwhile, she doesn't miss a beat. With a snap of the

fingers a new morning-appropriate cocktail is on the way. "I thought we could discuss your summer plans."

"You know my summer plans already." I force the words past the lump in my throat. "I'm going to help dad at the shop and visit you in a few weeks."

"It's not necessary for you to waste your entire summer babysitting your father."

Actually it is if I want to have a house to return to this fall.

"I don't mind. I like an honest day's work." I can't resist the dig. Since she remarried my mother's occupation can best be described as economic developer. Show her a store and she'll help it stay in business.

But if she catches my none-too-subtle jab, she ignores it. "Filtering through other people's junk is hardly an honest day's work. You need to be focused on yourself right now, Em. With senior year coming up you should be thinking about extracurriculars, not haggling with your father's customers. Have you thought about what colleges you'll be applying to this fall?"

"Maybe Las Vegas Community College. I don't have a lot of options." I shrug, hoping that we can just pretend this subject away. Obviously Hans has been talking to her again. Until he came into the picture a few years ago, my mother's idea of a major was finding a husband. It can't be a coincidence that she's making other plans now. Although if I had to guess those plans still included me finding a husband, just one that would help her indoctrinate me to her lifestyle instead of the one I'd chosen.

"You aren't graduating from one of the premier prep schools in the country to go to community college. This is exactly what Hans and I are worried about." Her voice takes on a blustery tone, the one she uses to dismiss maids and bad foie gras. That means I've landed somewhere between the help and duck liver on her priority list.

I grip my salad fork and butter knife, because I need something to hold onto—something tangible and solid. Between dead bodies and college applications, this weekend is quickly becoming anything but relaxing. This is exactly what happens when you bypass Netflix in favor of living people. The only person who would understand isn't here. Her memory isn't even allowed.

"What are you worried about, Vivian? Having an embarrassment for a daughter? That would be a tragedy. Oh wait. You actually lost a daughter." I don't stop when she sucks in a pained breath, because I hope it hurt her. She needs to prove to me that she can feel something other than disdain and chemical dependency. "Did it even occur to you that Becca should be graduating this weekend?"

"Of course it occurred to me!" she snaps in a low voice. It takes a lot of skill to be pissed and still maintain your face in a crowd. "Do you think a day goes by without thinking of her? But Becca isn't here. You didn't die that night, Emma. I wish I could be discussing her college plans with her right now, but I can't."

So now what? I'm supposed to feel sorry for her. No freaking way. The utensils clatter out of my hands as I stand up in a rush, searching for the next way to needle her. Angry feels good. Vital. It's like a dose of adrenaline straight to my blood, and I can see it's having the same affect on her.

"Sit down," she hisses.

But maybe she's not ready to jump from practiced oblivion to all-consuming rage yet. I consider my options. I can storm out of here and hope it provides even more of a shock to her anti-depressant-riddled system or I can prove that I'm the adult she's afraid I'm becoming.

I sit down. Nothing rattles a parent's cage like fear.

"Accepting that she's gone might sound harsh to you," she

whispers hurriedly, her eyes darting around the room to see if people are watching our little scene, "but it's the truth. I miss her, too. I've already taken two Xanax this morning. Truthfully, she is the reason that I'm here. I never should have left you two with your father."

"Is that why you want me to come to Palm Springs this summer?" I ask. Her guilt is misplaced. She shouldn't feel bad that she left us with our father, she should feel bad that she didn't want to be our mother anymore.

"Partially," she admits. Her new drink arrives and she clutches it like a security blanket. "Honey, you're a teenager. You shouldn't spend all your time taking care of your dad."

"Someone has to." It's supposed to be your job. Apparently my mother had missed the whole for richer or poorer line in her wedding vows. She might have been able to walk away from her marriage with no regrets but I couldn't give up on dad. He'd already lost one daughter.

"Consider it. I want you to have a nice time this summer."

I do, too. Working at Pawnography isn't exactly my dream vacation, but I'd chosen where my loyalties lay a long time ago. "With all the has-beens? Palm Springs isn't exactly a happening place, Mom."

"It's quiet," she corrects me, and she has a point. Vegas isn't exactly known for its calming presence. No, it's energy is exciting at best and frantic at worst.

It's one of the reasons I usually don't mind going to Palm Springs. Yes, the population skews toward senior citizen, but it lacks the stimulus overload of my hometown. Usually, I spend my time there each summer reading by the pool. Hans would stay in L.A., shooting dailies or overseeing edits so Becca and I could hang out with mom. We'd get our nails done and shop for the new school year. We stayed just long enough to pretend that our family wasn't a dysfunctional mess.

"I know your sister won't be there this year," Mom says in a quiet voice. I don't miss the slight tremble she's trying to hide. It's possible she's hurting more than she lets on.

That doesn't mean I can run away from my obligations here, though. "Exactly, I—"

She stops me. "That's why I need you to come."

"I'll be there in June like I promised, but I can't stay longer."

The prodigal waiter arrives with our breakfast entrees in time to soften my proclamation. I've never been so happy to see a stack of pancakes in my life. Across from me, my mother doesn't touch her chicken salad. Instead she stares directly at me, but her eyes remain vacant. Her mind is elsewhere even though she's sitting at the same table.

I cut into my food slowly, wondering if I should clap my hands or shake her. But after a few minutes, she blinks rapidly. Taking one look at my plate, she frowns. "Careful with the carbs, darling."

She's back. I pick up the syrup and pour more onto my plate. So much for the acting like an adult plan. If it means being as checked out as she is, I think I prefer to stay at my current level of maturity.

"Were you at the party at the West's last night?" She picks up her fork but doesn't bother to use it.

But it had the unsettling effect she, no doubt, hoped for. All the questions I'd left at the door when I came in race through my brain. There goes my appetite. "I thought we were avoiding morbid topics at breakfast."

It doesn't make sense to me that she's so desperate to avoid all mention of my sister, but here she is bringing up the latest scandal. The woman really should run for president. She knows exactly how to spin a situation in her favor.

"I cannot imagine what Evelyn is going through right

now." There's an unusual amount of concern in her voice. Given our family history with the Wests, I didn't think she would care. Just like I wouldn't care if I hadn't been there last night.

If I hadn't been in the same house as a dead body and possibly a murderer.

"I didn't know you knew her." I try to sound casual even as my pulse ratchets up.

"Of course, I do." She stops, visibly adjusting as she corrects herself. "Or I did before I got involved with your father. When you take away the tourists this town is smaller than people think. I'd reach out but right now…"

Nerves get the better of me. I'd hoped to avoid the media circus, choosing to foolishly believe that what happened last night in no way will affect me. But most of Belle Mère Prep was at that party. The chances are decent that I know the person. "Did they say who died?"

Her eyes dart to her phone. I know she wants to check for the latest information but she refrains from picking it up. I, on the other hand, wish she would. At least this subject doesn't directly affect us, and it feels a lot safer than continuing to discuss Becca or college or my summer plans.

"Not yet," she says without bothering to check.

"Maybe it was Evelyn." I try to be delicate in my suggestion even if I hadn't known until a few moments ago that my mother knew Mrs. West.

But the suggestion doesn't phase her. "She was out of town. Rumor has it that she prefers to make herself scarce when her children are throwing parties."

"Children?"

"Excuse me," our server interrupts, "can I get you ladies another drink?"

"Yes."

"No," I call over my mother, but she merely repeats herself with a smile.

"I'm the parent, remember?"

Maybe it would be better if both her and my dad had their parental rights revoked. Neither of them seem capable of healthfully dealing with their emotions. It's clearly setting a bad example for me. After all I went to a murder party last night.

"Speaking of, you haven't told me if you were there," Mom points out as if she can read my mind.

"I went, but I didn't stay long." Being put on the spot is making it difficult to come up with a story that doesn't involve skinny-dipping and making out with a stranger for most of the night. Instead I stumble upon a different, but equally true, excuse. "Monroe and I aren't exactly BFFs."

"I can't say I'm sorry to hear that. It's mercenary of me but I'm relieved that you weren't there. God only knows what happened last night." She sighs so deeply that I almost believe she cares.

My clutch vibrates on the table, alerting me to an incoming text, but I ignore it.

"Do you need to get that?" She eyes my bag.

"It can wait." We're nearly through with our meal. Then I can go back to my life and she can go back to hers.

"So Hans and I have been discussing your graduation present." Apparently she hasn't run out of ideas for small talk yet.

I raise one eyebrow. Is she getting me confused with Becca or does she just want to pawn off her present on me? "Getting a little ahead of yourselves. I have a year left."

"Well, we think you could use it now, especially because we both want to see more of you."

"Am I getting a pony?" I ask dryly. It seems fitting for the movie producer step-daddy to buy the affection of his wife's baggage with every little girl's dream present.

The smile creeping across her face is a little frightening. Maybe Hans isn't the only one who wants into my good graces. "Will you settle for a car?"

"I don't think that's a good idea," I say quickly. "It's easier to cab in Vegas. Parking is so tricky and..." I'm blabbering now, because I know what's at the heart of my verbal diarrhea. To my surprise, she does, too.

"You weren't behind the wheel that night," she reminds me gently.

If I had been, we might be sitting here discussing Becca's graduation present. She would have loved a car. I swallow the thought down into the pit of my stomach where I can bury it. "I know."

"Good!" Her concern vanishes, replaced by satisfaction. "It's being delivered later this week. Palm Springs is only a four hour drive. I'm always happy to send the jet for you, but if you ever need to run away..."

"I should run to my mommy?"

Her eyes crinkle at the edges and for a split second I'm little again and she's comforting me. "Yes, honey. You should always run to me."

Chapter 8

IT'S a typical day in the Southwest—bright with a chance of sunburn. I ask my driver to let me off down the street so I can stop at the mailbox and grab the spam and collection notices that tell me I'm home. I've let them pile up for most of the week so I could concentrate on finals. Now ti's time to face the music, which I suspect will come in the form of a funeral march. The house is dark, which means Dad actually went to the shop: a small miracle that provides me a rare opportunity to open the blinds. Then I grab the empty bottle of whiskey he left on the floor and head toward the kitchen. Dropping the mail on the counter, I groan when the doorbell rings. So much for a few blissful moments to myself. It's high season for Jehovah's Witnesses in the city of sin. Truthfully, I think they come for the weather. I trudge to the door, bottle in hand. Might as well have some fun.

But the man at the door isn't in khaki slacks and his badge bears the emblem of the Las Vegas Police Department. He can't be more than a few years older than me, but he's obviously put a lot of a time into building his upper body strength to make up for the slight acne scars that mar his skin. His jaw is smooth, his hair cropped short, and he's sporting a classic pair of aviators.

"Emma Southerly?" The officer at the door nudges his sunglasses down on his nose to study me.

I thrust the bottle behind my back in a sudden fit of self-preservation. "Yes?"

He's either a saint or the sun temporarily blinded him, because he doesn't comment on it. "Would it be possible for you to come down to the station?"

"Why?" Apparently I've been reduced to simple questions. Up next: who, what, when, where. If I don't get myself together there's a breathalyzer in my future.

"We have you on a list of people who attended a party at the West's private residence last night. Is that correct?" His fingers hook into his belt loops as he sways impatiently. He already knows the answer. I doubt the security cameras all over the resort are props.

But since it's a good idea to cooperate with law enforcement, I nod.

"Have you been home all day?" he asks.

"No. I met my mom for brunch," I say slowly.

"Then I assume you heard that a body was found this morning at the West Resort," he continues, helpfully filling in the blanks as I try to comprehend that a policeman is standing on my front stoop.

"Yes, we discussed it over croissant." I refrain from rolling my eyes because I doubt he missed the sarcasm in the statement. "But I don't see what that has to do with me. Most of Belle Mère Prep was at that party last night."

This time he takes his sunglasses off and stares me down. "Most of them left before dawn."

"I bet you've been practicing that move for years. Did it feel good?"

His stare turns into a glare. Do not get on the bad side of Johnny Law.

"Okay, then. Do I need a lawyer?"

"Do you?" he asks.

He's taking this moment way too seriously, but I suppose most cops don't join the force to hand out parking tickets.

"Look if you want to call your parents, I can wait," he offers.

"No!" Calling parents equals my dad finding out that I willingly went to the Wests' house last night. "Sorry, I'm new to this. I think I've been watching too much CSI."

"Do you need a ride?" He puts his aviators back on.

I look past him to the squad car parked in my driveway. Thank God most of the neighbors work weekends. "Do I have to sit in the back?"

"Not this time."

"Okay, give me a minute." I back away from the door and attempt to surreptitiously deposit the bottle on the couch. Briefly I consider changing. Then again, I'm wearing a dress so I could just take off my panties and rock the whole Sharon Stone bit. This isn't how I saw my Saturday afternoon playing out, especially not the part where I fulfill some cop's wet dream.

"Get it over with, Emma," I mutter, grabbing my purse. As I head out the door I check his badge.

Officer Mobie.

"It couldn't have been easy to have that name in school," I say as he opens the passenger door for me.

He doesn't respond as he waits for me to get in. Mental note: bringing up childhood bullying might not be the best way to start conversation with the person putting you into a police cruiser.

I stare out the window, surprised when we pull into a small, residential station only a few blocks from my house. There are no reporters with flashing cameras or hordes of gawkers. Save for a few expensive cars parked awkwardly next to the force's Crown Vics, nothing's going on. Since it was a shorter ride than I expected, it didn't give me much time to prep myself for my first official police questioning. I'm sure that living in Vegas means it won't be my last. Not that there's much to sort through. Mostly all I feel is unfiltered dread and the need to pound my head against a brick wall. Bad things happen when I attempt socializing. When will I learn?

I study the Belle Mère Police Station before I turn and check the officer's badge again. Las Vegas Police Department. Is he lost? "I thought they found the body at the resort."

"They did, but the Belle Mère special crimes unit has been tasked with handling this case. We're assisting." Translation: since the situation involves people with money, it would be dealt with delicately.

"I'm guessing the media is camped out at your station, waiting for a press conference that isn't going to happen."

"I wouldn't know, miss." But this observation earns me the slightest twitch of the lips. I'm right and maybe Officer Mobie is human after all.

He escorts me inside. The waiting area looks more like the lobby of a nice hotel, complete with nondescript art and carefully selected, stain-resistant furniture. A receptionist with flame red hair pulled into a top knot shoots Officer Mobie a warm smile.

"Apparently she heard those school yard rumors about Mobie and his…" The look he gives me shuts me down. "So much for trying to pay a guy a compliment."

"Miss Southerly?" A tall woman approaches us as we near the elevator.

"Emma," I offer. I'm making all sorts of new friends today.

"Thank you, officer. I have her from here," she tells him.

I can't help but notice Mobie strutting over to the receptionist. He leans down and starts to chat her up. I love a happy ending.

"I'm Detective Mackey." She pushes the button on the elevator panel. "I apologize for dragging you down here on a Saturday."

Peeling my eyes from the fledgling romance in the lobby, I give her my attention. Mackey sports the typical blunt bob of a career woman with not much time to care about her hair and make-up. But her black suit is tailored precisely to her trim body, which means she cares enough to shop and exercise.

"It's not a problem. Bodies don't keep, do they?" I wince as soon as it's out of my mouth. Nervous humor strikes again.

To my relief, she ignores my tasteless joke. When the elevator delivers us to the second floor, she waits for me to exit. "Can I get you a coffee or a soda?"

"No thanks." I rub my palms on the skirt of my dress. The interview room looks like they stole it from a police procedural, and it's making my hands sweat. Apparently my body is feeling guilt by proximity.

The chair's metal legs scrape mercilessly against the tile floor as she takes the seat across from mine. "I'll get to the point. We simply need a statement from you about last night. Just what you remember and who you saw."

"Honestly, I didn't see much. I was being anti-social." Why does such an easy request feel so hard? I guess when you have nothing to hide, you have nothing to share either.

"Anti-social," she repeats, scribbling something into a black notebook. "So you were alone in the house?"

"No! I was with someone," I correct her quickly, even if having a partner in trespassing doesn't exactly make it right. "We just weren't at the party. We looked around."

And now I sound like I was casing the joint.

"Can you tell me the name of this person? I'll just need to corroborate his or her story. This is all routine. We need to get a picture of the evening's events and who was where." Her pencil stays poised over the pad of paper.

"His," I answer. If Jameson isn't already dealing with this mess, I'm about to throw him into the mix. I don't feel too bad, considering he didn't leave a note. "I only know his first name. Jameson. We were just hanging out. I made us some food in the kitchen and we went for a swim."

And kissed. A lot. I keep that tidbit to myself. It's fun enough admitting I made myself at home. She doesn't need the details of my sexscapades.

"I see." Detective Mackey pauses and makes another note. I crane my neck trying to read it. "Jameson. Do you know his last name?"

"No." I also don't have his phone number, I add silently. Maybe last night wasn't as electric as I thought it was. Or maybe he'd been more drunk than I'd realized.

"If we showed you some pictures could you possibly identify him?" Detective Mackey's next question interrupts my analysis.

"Are you interested in him?" I ask slowly as realization creeps in.

"We're simply following up." Her face remains passive but her eyes study me. "Could you identify him?"

Jameson couldn't have anything to with this, but, honestly, the most I know about him is how his tongue feels down my throat.

"I got a pretty decent look at him." Understatement of the year. "I should be able to."

"Is there anything else you remember about that night? Anyone you saw?" she presses.

She's serious but I can't help laughing. "Are you kidding? Most of my school. Monroe's dad when we first came in. Some security guys."

"We?" Mackey perks up at this revelation. "Who were you with?"

"I came to the party with my best friend, Josie, but we got separated. She left early."

Which is why I'm here, and she isn't.

"So you didn't come with Jameson?"

"No, we met at the party. I've never seen him before last night." With all the circles we're running around this topic, I hope this counts as my daily cardio.

"Were you drinking?"

I'm surprised it took her this long to ask. Of course, that's what they would think, especially given that the whole party was a scene out of teens gone wild. It might be nice to blame my decision to spend the night making out with a random guy on tequila but I can't, even if she probably won't believe me. "Nope. All my poor choices are the result of my own stupidity."

She doesn't even smile, but there's probably not much room for a sense of humor in her vocation.

"Excuse me. I'll only be a moment and then we can wrap this up."

Rocking my chair onto its back legs, I study the room. There's the two way mirror that fools no one. Who knew that was a real thing? One window, a table, chairs, and four pastel green walls that are likely meant to be calming but just remind me of puke. Life on the inside isn't so bad. No worse than being stuck in a doctor's office. It's more purgatory than hell.

My gaze drifts to the hallway, waiting for her to return. A few people pass by and one stops. Jonas waves timidly at me from the other side of the glass. He's dressed in sweats and t-shirt, and dark hair is plastered to his sweaty forehead. I can imagine Officer Mobie rolling up to greet him at the lacrosse field. The sport is his one true love no matter what Monroe thinks. Jonas left this morning, too, which means they'll want his statement. Thank God Hugo is on a plane.

If Jonas was there, he might remember more than I did. I stand up and walk toward the door. Since he's so close to the family there's a good chance that he'll know more than I've been told, but as I reach for the handle, Monroe appears.

I shrink away. Not because I don't want her to see me, but because of how she looks. Monroe once came to a big lacrosse match with the flu and no one knew until she threw up all over the referee. She doesn't do public appearances without full hair and make-up. Today she's a mess though. Mascara remnants ring her eyes and her golden locks are thrown into an unbrushed ponytail. Jonas wraps his arms around her and she melts against him.

I've never seen her look so small or so vulnerable.

Backing up from the door, I accidentally catch her eye. She shoves Jonas away and points at the window. Detective Mackey rushes toward her, and although I can't hear what's being said, I can guess from the scarlet shade Monroe turns as she continues to yell. After a few minutes of enduring her mute, tonsil gymnastics, Jonas coaxes her away from the window.

Detective Mackey ducks back into the interview room, setting a file folder on the table. strait-laced. It's a state I like to call the Monroe effect.

"You have a fan," she says.

"We just love each other." I can only hope her curiosity doesn't extend to more questions about my relationship with Monroe.

"She seemed confused as to why you're here. According to her, you were asked to leave the party." Mackey waits with her finger poised on the folder's edge.

Maybe I should start sewing my scarlet M now. Uninvited party guest? Check. Don't know the full name of my alibi? Check. Caught sneaking out by doting boyfriend? Check. I might convict myself.

"She did ask me to leave, but I got lost looking for my friend."

"That's how you met Jameson. Did he ask you to stay?"

"He's very persuasive." The truth is that he didn't convince me at all. He didn't ask me to stay with him or raid the Wests' pantry or swim in their pool. Thanks to him I'd left a trail of fingerprints that Hansel and Gretel could follow all over that penthouse.

"Can you tell me who this is?" She flips open the folder to a picture of Jameson. Just not my Jameson.

It's him, but not the boy I met last night. He's smiling in this picture, dressed in a button-down and pressed slacks, as he stands in front of a very expensive looking sports car. He seems happy but as I study the picture, I spot the distance in his eyes. They're vacant as if he's simply going through the motions. But the most puzzling aspect of the photo is that his arm is around Monroe. She's beaming at the camera, hugging him tightly.

"That's Jameson," I answer in a quiet voice, pushing the photo back to her. I don't want it to be the truth.

Mackey purses her lips and looks to the mirror on the other side of the room.

"Is someone behind that? Like on TV?" I wave at it. I've been here for over an hour and I have more questions than answers. I hope whoever is back there has more figured out than I do. "Do I pass the test?"

"Yes, you do as a matter of fact."

I turn back to her. "I was only joking. I tend to eat foot when I'm nervous."

"You're free to go, Emma." She puts the photo back into the folder and stands up.

"Wait. That's it?" I'd expected hours of grilling. Maybe a light or two shined in my face. Now she's saying I can just walk out of here.

She stops at the door and peers over at me. Distrust flashes in her eyes but she quickly hides it. "Unless you have something you want to tell us…"

"I've told you everything." I'm officially out of patience.

"We might need you to come in again. Please let us know if you'll be traveling." She opens the door but I just gawk at her.

"I'm going to see my mother in Palm Springs in a few weeks." I force myself onto my feet. The next question I have for her I don't want answered sitting down. "Am I suspect or something?"

"Everyone who was there last night is a person of interest." It's a stock answer that does nothing to assuage the panic welling in me.

"That's a very long list."

"Yes, it is." She gestures toward the door. Pulling out her phone, she taps the screen not bothering to look at me. She's through with me.

For now.

My head is still spinning when I step into the corridor. Before Detective Mackey can disappear, I call after her. "Detective?"

"Yes?"

"I don't even know what happened. Was someone murdered? Who? If I'm a person of interest, I'd like to know." This doesn't feel like an unreasonable request after answering all her questions.

"Yes, someone was murdered," she confirms as she clips her

phone back on her belt. "At the moment, we're waiting to release that information."

"I guess I'll wait for the press conference." Nothing like being questioned for a crime you know nothing about.

Mackey presses her lips into a thin line. Not a smile or a wave or even a goodbye. When she's gone I slump against the wall. There's absolutely no way I'm asking for a ride home in a police car. I'm guessing that Monroe isn't going to offer. More than transportation, I need someone to help sort through my feelings.

Emma: I need you to pick me up.

Josie: Sure. Where?

Emma: Promise you won't freak out.

Josie: Now I'm definitely going to freak out.

Emma: At the Belle Mère police station.

Chapter 9

IT TAKES her so long to respond that I almost call to make certain she hasn't fainted. I'm going to wind up calling an Uber so I can go peel her off the floor.

Josie: On my way.

She'll have figured out why I'm here. It wouldn't take a genius to do that, but maybe a genius could sort out exactly what I've gotten myself into.

Footsteps shuffle closer and I discover Jonas clutching a Styrofoam cup. He holds it out to me. "I thought you could use this."

"I'm good." I fiddle with my phone for a few seconds, trying to ignore the awkward silence that's so obvious I can almost hear it. "Did you get a mug shot?"

"Um, no."

"Me either." I abandon my phone to my blackhole of a purse. "All those questions and nothing to show the grandkids."

Jonas chuckles and takes the wall next to me. It's odd being so close to him after all this time. It's been nearly two years since we broke up, and I've spent each of those days pretending he meant nothing to me. Today there's no flutter in my stomach or pangs in my chest. He's become someone I used to know.

I'd spent years thinking I loved him, and although I'd never admit it, even if I was being tortured, I wondered what would happen if he broke up with Monroe. But there's no electricity, no unseen force tugging me to him now. I guess I hadn't let myself get close enough to realize my feelings for him were an illusion. Now we're here and there's nothing to say to one another.

"So did you do it?" I ask conversationally. "If we're stuck together we might as well compare rap sheets."

"No!" Jonas stares at me, horror-stricken. "I would never hurt Monroe or her family."

I can't say the same when it comes to Monroe, but I bite my tongue. A police station probably isn't the best place to crack that joke. It might go over worse than saying the word bomb at an airport, and I don't think I can handle a cavity search on top of everything else this day has brought.

"I'm kidding," I reassure him. "I'm not even sure what they think we did."

"Us?" He tilts his head and a few dark strands flop over his forehead. "Nothing. They have a suspect already."

"Who?" I'd been right when I guessed he would know something. Now I just have to get him to fess up. Maybe I could borrow the interrogation room.

"Don't you know—" He struggles to find the words. It makes me want to draw him a map. If he's sitting on the answers to what's gone on in the last twenty-four hours I want to know. But before I can get anything out of him, Monroe rounds the corner and he does his best impression of a clam.

"What are you doing here? Haven't you done enough?" She marches straight up to me and sticks her face inches from my own.

I want to tell her to brush her teeth, but I take the high road. It's not a favor she'll ever return for me. She probably got woken up by a homicide squad this morning. Instead I cross my arms, pointing my elbows out in case she decides to move any closer. "I haven't done anything except crash your stupid party. I don't even know why I'm here."

I can take the high road but being nice to her is another story, even though this close I can see her eyes are bloodshot from crying.

"Don't play dumb. It makes all of us look bad when girls act stupid." Jonas grabs her hand but she shakes him off.

"Not acting, sugar. I really don't know," I inform her. Maybe I need to write clueless on a Post-It note and stick it to my forehead.

"You're not even worth yelling at," she mutters, sounding more tired than annoyed. She pulls away, turning her attention to Jonas, and grabbing my coffee out of his hands. Taking one sip, she scrunches her nose as if she expected it to be Starbucks. "That's terrible. They reached mom, so they said I could go home..."

She trails off as her voice cracks. I'm torn between wanting to melt into the wall and sneaking away. Watching your enemy break down isn't as thrilling as I might have suspected. It's just awkward. Right now I wish I was actually invisible to her, so that I could sneak out without prompting another round. She shakes her head once as if willing away tears. "Mom won't be back until tomorrow."

From now on I'm taking a vow of social celibacy. My only friends will be on my recommended watch list. Yes, I will miss out on nights like that night—and boys who can kiss like Jameson.

Jameson who might be a murderer, I remind myself, before I take a mental vacay down memory lane. Jameson who might be dead. It hurts to even consider it. But the truth is I don't know anything about Jameson, particularly why he was there last night, but Detective Mackey seems very interested in him. If my boy barometer is that off it might be best if I stay at home from now until the only thing that excites me is the local Bingo night.

"You can stay at my place. My parents are in Maui," he says, rubbing her shoulder in a soothing gesture.

Yesterday afternoon it would have made me physically ill to be near this, but today I'm almost glad he's here to take care of her. It's as if I stepped through a funhouse mirror. Suddenly I'm over Jonas and worrying about Monroe. I need to get out of here before I join the pep squad and start wearing cardigans.

"I can't believe he actually did it," she whispers, obviously forgetting I'm still within earshot. "They didn't get along, but this? I have no idea when they're going to release Jameson. If they're going to..."

I take a step closer at the sound of his name, and Monroe's silver eyes narrow. "What are you looking at?"

But I'm not looking at her, I'm listening to her. "Jameson."

I don't know what reaction I expect to get out of her when I say his name. I simply can't help myself.

"Yes, you've helped him get away with murder."

Jameson. Murderer. The words crash into me but I don't feel them. They're as empty as the hollow pit left from where my stomach dropped out. I kissed him. I liked him. Until this moment, I'd mostly been able to dismiss all the strange questions I was asked this afternoon. Now the pieces are starting to fit, and as the whole picture comes into focus, I realize I'm in it. I'm not merely some girl who was in the wrong place at the wrong time.

"You don't know that he did it." That's Jonas—always the

mediator. Would he still believe that if he knew that I'd woken up alone this morning?

Stomach acid bubbles into my throat and I swallow it—and the urge to vomit—down.

"Who else then? You? Her?" She shoves her thumb in my direction.

"They think Jameson did it?" I'm asking a question but I don't want the answers.

"Are you having some type of fit?" Monroe hisses, hurling a disgusted look my direction. "Yes, Jamie killed our father."

My family calls me Jamie. Everything clicks into place, and I reach out to steady myself against the wall. The photo of Jameson with Monroe. Everything Jameson said the night before. Jameson is Monroe's brother. Nathaniel's son.

Nathaniel is dead. Jameson is a West. And somehow I've found myself in the middle of a murder.

"You're here to be his alibi," Monroe continues. "I don't know what's more disgusting, knowing that a slut like you touched my brother or that he'd admit to everyone that he stooped so low."

"Monroe." Jonas says her name sharply, but I step forward and wiggle between them.

"Let her finish. She's been wanting to say this for a long time." I'm tired of being used by the Wests. First my father was a pawn in Nathaniel's schemes and then I endured years of shit from Monroe. I hate them all, especially Jameson for using me to get himself out of trouble. All they do is take, and I'm about to give a little back.

"You never should have been there last night, but I guess I can't be surprised that you threw yourself at him. It's your typical pathetic move." She's practically spitting at me now.

"My typical pathetic move?" I repeat. "Like when you got Jonas drunk at the Freshman Desert Party and had sex with him on a car in front of half of the student body. Classy like that, Monroe? Because one of us is actually pathetic. There's a mirror in there if you want to see what she looks like."

Jonas looks positively constipated as I haul up this unpleasant memory, but hey it takes two to tango.

"Feel free to jump in any time or did she take your backbone along with your virginity?" I tell him.

"You know Hugo will be back tomorrow to give his statement if you need a pity fuck," Monroe steps in before I can unleash three years of anger on her boyfriend. "Sorry I can't be more help but I have to plan my father's funeral."

She drags Jonas toward the elevator, dumping the coffee cup on the floor. I suppose Monroe and her brother are a lot a like: they both expect other people to clean up their messes.

Brother.

The fight had been a welcome distraction from that piece of shrapnel that's now lodged in my chest about dead center. Jameson didn't know who I was last night, because he never would have touched a Southerly. Now conveniently I'm his alibi, which no one can ever know. It might kill my dad to know I was out all night with a guy, but if he found out that it was a West, he might kill him. And me. Belle Mère really doesn't need any more murders at the moment.

"Come on, Josie. Where are you?" Saying her name a loud works like an incantation because a second later the phone buzzes with a message that she's outside. I can't blame her for not wanting to come into the police station. If Detective Mackey is telling the truth and everyone at that party is a suspect, she'll get her fifteen minutes soon enough.

Texting her that I'm on my way out, I hit the elevator button. But as I step inside, the door next to my interview room opens—the one on the other side of the mirror. Jameson steps out followed by a man in a suit. He's dressed in his clothes from last night and a five o'clock shadow darkens his jaw. The hair my hands tangled through last night is a mess of coppery, brown tangles.

Because he slept with it wet. After our time in the pool. After we spent half the night with our bodies entwined. Did he sleep next to me? I push the thought as far back into my gray matter as I can, because if what Monroe told me is true, then he's dangerous. He pauses to talk to the man who must be his lawyer. Meanwhile the elevator doors are taking the length of a Bible to close. Jameson turns as if he can sense me watching him, and our eyes meet. A charge of electricity runs over my skin as he stares at me. The recognition and the hunger in his gaze calls my body to him while I scramble to press buttons on the control panel. His mouth opens as I stumble my salvation and the doors slide shut between us.

Chapter 10

"YOU LOOK PRETTY." Josie eyes the yellow dress I'd worn to appease my mom this morning. "Personally I don't dress up to go to the station, but to each her own."

I shoot her a look that says I'm not currently to be fucked with. Seeing Jameson ratcheted the warning level on my personal stupidity watch. I'd disregarded my instincts yesterday—a mistake I'd be paying for indefinitely.

When I don't offer any information, she presses forward. "Dare I ask?"

"Give me a minute." I close my eyes, squeezing them until spots of light appear. Then I hold out my arm. "Pinch me."

"What?" she asks.

"Pinch me," I request again. "I need to be woken up." A second later a sharp throb bursts across my skin, and I snatch my arm away from her. "I didn't really mean it."

"You asked me to do it twice!" Josie huffs as she puts the car into reverse and backs out of the parking lot.

For all intents and purposes, she did jolt me out of my hazy state, which is why I notice that her hair is frizzy like she just woke up. Today she's the one with the dark circles under her eyes and no make-up. She looks like how I feel. "Hey, you okay?"

"I was really worried about you last night." Her eyes stay glued to the road as if she's waiting for a chance to pull out of the station's parking lot, but the road is free of traffic. She continues, gazing blankly ahead, "I didn't get much sleep and then I've been watching the news all morning."

No. No. No.

"Don't work yourself up," I beg her. Last summer after the accident, Josie consumed every piece of media that focused on Becca's death. She watched the crash scene news video every night. She collected clippings from the paper. I even found a copy of the obituary stuffed inside one of her textbooks. When I confronted her about it, she admitted that none of it felt real. I understood that, and helping her through it had been easier than focusing on my own grief. I didn't want to see a repeat of that level of obsession from her again. "This has nothing to do with us, so you need to let it go."

She flinches at my gentle redirection, and her voice takes on a wild, uneven tone that mimics the screech of her tires as she pulls out hastily. "They aren't even saying anything on the news. And don't tell me it has nothing to do with us when I just picked you up at the police station."

"Turn here," I demand, pointing to the street ahead.

She swerves into the right lane and does as I ask, navigating to our favorite ice cream shop, Coffee & Cream. We pull into a spot and scramble out ahead of a large family in a minivan. For five blessed minutes, I focus on nothing but deciding what ice cream flavor to choose: a scoop of coffee and a scoop of tiramisu. But as soon as we both have cones in our hands, I'm back to reality. The outdoor patio is empty thanks to the afternoon heat. We might melt but we'll have our privacy.

"Spill," she says after a few licks of her mint chocolate chip. "Where were you last night and what were you doing at the police station today?"

I pause from my ice cream coma and give her a guilty look. "I stayed at Monroe's last night."

"Like a slumber party?" Josie asks in confusion, which quickly shifts to disbelief. "Did you two freeze each other's bras and practice kissing?"

Considering that I cost her a night's sleep and called her for a jail pick-up, I probably shouldn't have hit her with any more of the bizarre details of the last twenty-four hours so quickly. "I didn't stay with Monroe."

"Oh this is getting good!" she squeals.

"Eyes on the prize! For all you know I'm a murderer," I remind her.

"I know for a fact that you aren't."

"How?" I ask, barely catching a drip of ice cream before it melts on my skirt.

"Because I know you," she says dismissively, "but you definitely were up to no good last night if you wound up at the police station. Just not murder."

I wish I had as much faith in myself as she has in me. Maybe I didn't kill anyone but I might have kissed someone who did. But the worst part is that after seeing him at the station, I know I would spend the night with him all over again in a heartbeat if I had the chance no matter the outcome. I'm not as innocent as she believes.

"It sounds like they're going to be pulling in everyone that was at the party," I say, not ready to delve into the psychological quagmire that my impromptu rendezvous has left me in.

"What?"

She pales a shade or two, so I hurry on. "I don't know for

sure. It would take them forever, and they already have a suspect."

"Okay, you need to start sharing the details right now." It's a demand but the edges are brittle. Josie's nerves are clearly shot, and I'm not helping.

"I don't know where to begin," I hedge. Maybe going to her with this isn't the best idea. My best friend is as vibrant and carefree as a butterfly, but she's delicate like one, too.

But she's having none of it. Her lips purse before she releases a deep sigh. "How about you start with why you wound up spending the night at the Wests'?"

"I met this guy." I have to force myself to say it.

"How come stories of poor life choices always start that way?"

"More of your stories than mine," I remind her, even though Poor Life Choices should be my new band name.

"True. Continue."

"He was funny and sexy and a little arrogant, but it didn't turn me off." I might as well work through my feelings if I'm going to rehash all the details of last night.

"You can say that again," she says with a smirk. At least talking about a boy is distracting her from all the worrying.

"We didn't do it," I clarify. I'd given myself a nice checklist to meet before I got back in bed with a guy after my disastrous decision to lose my v-card to Hugo. At the very top of it: fall in love first. Cheesy, I know. But my mom is right about a girl having standards. "We just kissed and skinny-dipped and cooked."

Josie snorts at this revelation. "So you didn't do it, but you cooked? You have a weird idea of what is supposed to happen during hook-ups."

"Thanks for the reminder. I'll ask your expert opinion next time—if I can find you!" I know she doesn't get why I keep my knees together but it doesn't really matter what she thinks on that topic.

"So what went wrong?" she asks, a note of impatience coloring her tone.

They accused him of murdering his father. I might need to break that to her a bit more carefully. "Apparently I really have a thing for bad boys."

"You've lost me again."

"Hang on." I pull out my phone and do a search for Jameson West; Google knows just who I'm talking about, I realize with a rush. I can't pinpoint if it's fear or excitement. I tap images and dozens of pictures flow onto my screen. Thanks to his father's high profile in business and his sister's brush with reality show fame, the Wests are Internet fodder. I hold up the phone so that Josie can see the photo. "Meet my latest poor decision."

"He's about twenty years too young for my taste, but I'd hardly call that a poor decision," she says with approval.

"Look at his name," I prompt. "I didn't know who he was."

"Wait, so if he's Jameson West and he was at the party that makes him…Monroe's brother? Did we even know she had a brother?"

"I didn't, but I'm not exactly President of the Monroe Appreciation Club."

She grabs my phone and scans the information. By the time she's done reading it, she'll probably know more about him than I do. "He went to military school and then attended Stanford," she tells me.

"That surprises me." I snatch the phone back and scan the short biography included on his father's Wiki entry.

"Nathaniel's son." She pauses and stares at me, completely neglecting her ice cream cone which drips all over her hand. "Holy shit, Em. Your dad is going to freak out."

"You can say that again." I brace myself for telling her the part I've been leaving out. "Nathaniel is dead. The police called me in to check Jameson's alibi."

"Did he actually do it?" she breathes.

"That's what I don't know," I admit. Part of me wants to say he couldn't have done it, even while the rest of me calls me out on my own BS. Two tiny voices have been whispering their opinions since we left the station, and I can't decide which one to listen to.

"What did your dad say?" she asks.

"He doesn't know, and I hope he doesn't find out." I know she won't say anything to him. I can't say the same for the rest of the world. How long can I really keep this a secret?

"As if this isn't going to be headline news." Josie drops her unfinished cone onto a napkin and rubs her stomach. "I feel sick."

"Imagine how I feel. I made out with the son of my father's worst enemy, who also might be a murderer. I'm winning at life, wouldn't you say?"

"You didn't know." But that line isn't any more comforting coming from her. "So Nathaniel West is dead."

"Yeah. Monroe was at the station. I felt bad for her."

"Of course you did. You have a heart." Josie's head drops to my shoulder.

"Then I told her off for screwing Jonas," I add.

"You also have moxie. This is going to be a really long summer."

"I know. I've been thinking…maybe I should go to stay with my mom in Palm Springs." There's going to be media scrutiny. I could hope that my name wouldn't get dragged into this, but given that Nathaniel West consistently ranked in People magazine's most interesting people articles and he'd once been interviewed by Barbara Walters, it seems like a safe bet that anything and everything that has to do with his murder will get leaked.

"Will they let you?"

"It's not that far away." This morning when my mother suggested it, it was dead last on my list of summer activities right under 'take a pottery class' and 'go vegan,' but my stepfather knows a thing or two about nosey reporters coming from Hollywood. "It's my best bet not to wind up on the cover of every tabloid in America."

"What about Jameson?"

It's strange to hear her calling him that. Even if it is his real name. "What about him? We kissed. We didn't elope."

"That kiss dragged you into a murder investigation," she points out.

"Yes, no first date will ever live up to that one again."

"Did you talk to him?"

I shake my head, remembering how he tried to call out to me at the station. Part of me wants to hear him out, but what good could possibly come out of it. The police had a reason to suspect him. "I was in the right place at the right time. He needed someone to say he was busy during the murder."

"And you were busy," Josie waggles her eyebrows, and I elbow her in the ribs. "Maybe he really was with you when it happened. You should call him."

"I didn't get his number. I woke up alone with no note."

"Ouch!" Josie exclaims and I can already feel her sassy side coming out. "Never mind if he played you like that, let him fry."

"He did fold up my dress," I say in his defense.

"That doesn't make up for stealing the booty," she chastises me.

"He didn't steal the booty." I can't help but laugh at the indignation on her face. Now I remembered why I called her, because now that I've spilled my guts and we've faced the worst possible scenario, the whole situation is a lot less nightmarish. Time to return the favor. "What about you? Meet any prospective sugar daddies last night?"

"Oh look at the time." She holds up her bare wrist. "I have to get you home."

"You are avoiding the question," I accuse.

"You hate hearing about my papa bears."

"Oh that is gross!" I clutch my throat, pretending to gag.

"My point is made. I have to meet mom for dinner soon. Want to join us?"

I shake my head, recalling my vow to never leave the house again. "I think I'm going to stay home tonight. Going out with you gets me in trouble."

"Marion would never allow us to misbehave," Josie reminds me as I dump the remains of my ice cream cone in the trash. "That's why I'm glad she works nights." She winks as she unlocks her car.

"I think I just want to be alone. I know that sounds super pathetic," I add before she can state the obvious. "I need to think about stuff."

Like packing up and heading to Palm Springs. Josie doesn't argue with me. A few minutes later she drops me off at home. Dad's car is still gone and the blinds are only half opened since I got interrupted earlier. It feels like my whole day has been spent coming back to an empty house, and as much as I want to stew, I feel lonely looking at how quiet it is. Maybe being with mom this summer wouldn't be so bad.

The window rolls down behind me. "Call if you need me. I could be convinced to stay in tonight."

"Promise."

Inside, I stare at the fridge for a long time before I slam it shut. Nothing sounds good. The television binge I'd been planning seems a little less thrilling now that I've been pulled into my very own drama.

I spot the bottle I abandoned on the couch. I pick it up and deliver it successfully to the trash. The pile of bills from earlier gloat from the counter. Going to stay with mom might protect me from getting dragged into this any further, but it will also leave dad to his own devices. I pick one up and tear along the envelope seam, drawing out the letter, I nearly fall over. Three months behind on our electric bill. That means any minute the lights could go out. There's only one thing to do. An hour later I've sweet talked the utility company into letting me pay one installment. I hang up the phone and any thoughts I had of leaving Belle Mère along with it. I don't want to be stuck taking care of my dad forever, but I also don't want to lose my house.

Falling into an old routine seems like the most mind-numbing option, so I gather laundry. But even after listening to the whir and rumble of the machines, I can't silence the inner debate bouncing around in my head.

On my way to my room with a basket full of folded clothes, I pass the door that's remained closed since last summer. This was Becca's house, too. With each day that passes, I forget her a little more. Stupid things like how her laugh sounded or the face she made when she was angry. All those tiny bits of a person that add up to a whole. I'm losing her piece by piece. I can't lose this house or her room. I need it if it's going to keep her memory alive. If Becca was here she would know what to do, and that's exactly what I needed to remember. Heading to my room, I strip off the sundress I wore for my mother and find a comfy pair of shorts and a tank top. Then I pull my hair into a ponytail and throw on my running shoes. I need to clear my head. I need to run. Not away from here but to someone. It's easy to forget that there's one other person I can always talk to —as long as I'm okay with her not responding.

Chapter 11

I CHOSE the Belle Mère graveyard because it was close to home. Dad wanted to be able to visit. But he visits as often as mom does. If I hadn't worried about it there wouldn't even be a headstone marking her grave. Maybe it would be easier if I could pretend she was just off at school or if I could drink away her memory, but I'd been cursed and blessed to spend the last few moments with her before she died. The run to the cemetery is boring, but it gives me time to clear my head. I run faster until my muscles burn and I'm drenched in sweat. I know I can't outrun what's happening, but that doesn't stop me from trying. By the time I reach the graveyard, the shade trees and green lawn are a welcome site. It's a bit strange to spend so much time and energy tending to the final resting place of the dead. In the desert, most of us don't get to look at green grass while we're alive. It's not comforting to think I'll be buried under it someday.

I jog along the path, reading names and dates. Nearly everyone here lived a nice, long life. They had decades on Becca. She didn't even get eighteen years. We buried her under a fledgling willow tree. A strange choice for Nevada, but rules don't seem to apply in graveyards. Reputations don't matter. Everyone here is beloved and missed and dear. Drought regulations don't exist or maybe the unnaturally green grass has evolved to soak up the tears of its visitors.

Becca's face greets me when I reach her site. Mom considered having her headstone laser-engraved with her image tacky, but I'd fought her on it. Her grave didn't need to suit anyone's taste but mine. It had been a good call. Over the last year, her photos began to vanish as her Facebook page was deleted and her Instagram stopped updating. Then they disappeared from our house, leaving only faded patches where they had hung for years. But it's even harder to think about all the photos she won't get to take.

Plopping down in front of the headstone, I give her a small grin. Her face beams back at me, locked in a happy moment from earlier that summer. It's one of the last pictures I have of her. My memory fills in the rest of the picture. Becca posing in front of a tall cactus, her red hair billowing behind her. She'll always look like this to me: young, happy. She'll never age, while I've gotten older in the last twenty-four hours. I blink back tears. "Hey sis, have I got a story to tell you."

With Becca I leave nothing out. I tell her about sneaking around Nathaniel's office and meeting Jameson. I tell her that it seems impossible to have fallen in love with him a little bit in one night. I tell her that makes me feel stupid. Then I tell her it was all a lie. I ask her if I should go to Mom's and I tell her about Dad and his drinking. I know it's impossible but I can't help but hope that she'll speak up and offer me some insight. Although it would probably scare me to death.

I sit for a little while, soaking up how good it feels just to get it all off my chest, even though the only response is the wind in the willow branches. "I've never really thought much about what happens after we die, but I like the idea that you're listening somewhere. There's no way you landed the angel gig. It'll take you centuries before you work off all the trouble you made here."

As twilight falls in dusky hues over the cemetery, I stand up.

"I miss you, Becca," I whisper. I should have brought her flowers but I think she'd be okay just knowing that I brought her love. If I hurry I'll be home before dark, but as I turn I nearly jump out of my skin. Jameson's leaning against a tree. He's changed since I saw him last. He hasn't shaved but his hair is combed into neat chaos. In the dusky light, it's darker than I remember. His jeans hug his narrow hips but not as tightly as his shirt clings to his muscular torso. My thoughts flash to what he looks like out of his clothes and I blush. Striding up to him, I fold my arms over my chest and glare.

"How long have you been standing there?" I demand. Then a more important question occurs to me. "Did you follow me?"

"A little full of ourselves, Duchess." He shifts ever so slightly and I find myself doing the same.

Dammit, he is not who you thought he was, I remind myself.

"Don't call me that," I warn him. Did he think we would just pick up where we left off? That ship sailed when I woke up alone.

"Then I guess I'll call you Emma or would you prefer Ms. Southerly?" he asks, a chill runs so deeply in his words that I feel it in my own blood. Last night I thought he might devour me, tonight it feels like he'd settle for a mere mauling.

"I'd prefer you didn't call me anything." I move past him but his hand flies out and catches my wrist, stopping me in my tracks. I tug against his hold but he only tightens his grip. "Let go of me."

"We need to talk first."

"We needed to talk this morning," I tell him. "But I'm a little tired after spending most of the day covering for your ass with the homicide division."

"I appreciate that." But there's no gratitude in his face. He's reciting the obligatory thanks.

"I think getting someone off a murder rap deserves flowers or maybe chocolate," I bite back.

Jameson steps closer, still keeping my wrist pinned. "Did you think you got me off, Duchess?"

"You're using that word again," I warn him.

He ignores me. "Believe me, this is far from over."

"It is for us," I tell him.

His eyes flash, lightning in the stormy gray. I've upset him, which is a pretty stupid thing considering that he may or may not have killed someone in the last twenty-four hours. But as angry as I am at him, I can't find it in myself to be scared of him. Apparently reason, logic, and common sense have all deserted me for the time being. Jameson drops his hold on me.

"Why didn't you tell me who you were?" he asks.

"Oh, okay, Jameson West. Did you enjoy the part where I talked crap on your sister? Or when I basically said horrible things about your whole family? Let's not pretend we were honest with each other. "

"Agreed," he says to my surprise. "I'd suggest we start over. Jameson West."

He holds out his hand, but I don't take it.

"Emma Southerly," I say coldly. "We don't shake hands with Wests."

"That was our fathers' fight. It died with them."

"My dad is still alive," I tell him.

"Then he wins. I have no interest in continuing their petty feud."

"That's an incredibly enlightened sentiment, but not really one I share."

"So what do you have against the Wests, Miss Southerly?"

I hate how formal he sounds when he calls me that, but I can't exactly ask him to call me Duchess. Talk about sending the wrong signal. "My grief with your family goes back a few years."

"Ah yes. My troublemaker of a sister stole your boyfriend," he recalls.

"You were paying attention."

"I liked paying attention to you."

"Really?" I ask, "because I don't recall you leaving a note. Not very attentive, Mr. West."

"Check your phone," he orders.

It's in that moment that I realize it's sitting on the kitchen counter. I've ran all the way here without it. Now I'm talking to a murder suspect without a way to call for help. I might not be afraid of him, but I can't believe I was so stupid as to leave it behind. "I don't have it."

"You came all this way without your phone." Annoyance colors his disbelief.

"There was a time when people walked miles without cell phones," I remind him. Where does he get off treating me this way?

"Don't be cute, Emma. I can't allow you to run home."

"Excuse me?" I repeat, not bothering to hide my shock. "Did we just jump through time and wind up in the 1950s? I'm not helpless."

"It's not safe," he ignores me, which only brings my rage from simmering to full boil. "You shouldn't be running without a way to call home."

"And it's safe to get in the car with you?"

"It's the safest place in the world for you. I need you alive."

A shiver races up my spine, but I channel my energy into convincing him to let me walk away. I have no idea what he's capable of, and I can never forget that. "I'll be fine if I leave now."

"We're not through talking."

"Listen, I don't know who you think you are—"

"I'm Jameson West," he interrupts me.

"That's so impressive," I mock him, "but I've been taking care of myself for a long time."

"You mean like staying out all night with men you don't know?"

"If by men, you mean you, then yes." Does he have some type of personality disorder? Dr. Jameson and Mr. West. "But it's not a habit of mine. I must have been suffering a bout of insanity."

"Then I suppose I was lucky," he says.

"You have no idea," I mutter. "You probably should have thrown a quarter in the slots. Luck was on your side."

"Others might disagree with you."

Oh, right. Dead dad. Whoops.

"I should go."

"Emma you can get in my car or I can follow you in my car. Those are your options."

My eyes narrow into slits so thin that I can barely see him. "Suit yourself."

I take off on a full jog before he can respond. Cutting through the gravestones, I narrowly make it to the street before a sleek, black BMW catches up with me. It slows down to match my pace, which would be comical if it wasn't so infuriating. I speed up my pace but it's no use. One, I'm not really much of a runner, so there's no way I can keep up that speed for long. Two, he's in a freaking car. By the time he's been following me for a mile, I dart right and take a side street. I have no idea if I can actually get to my house from here but I'm willing to chance it. The last streaks of daylight are fading into a milky blue sky as I quicken my pace. The desert is particularly dark at night and I have no desire to get stuck too far from home, especially with an innocent-until-proven-guilty murderer on my trail. But just as I round a corner, the BMW appears again.

"Do you even know how to get home?" he calls from the rolled down window.

"Yes."

"You're lying," he accuses. "Get in the car, Duchess."

"I told you not to call me that!" I yell between panting breaths.

"It seems to really suit your attitude at the moment." He continues to idle alongside me. "If you get in, I'll drop you off a few houses down. If not, I'll be parked in your driveway before you can unlock your front door. Is your father home from work yet?"

I halt in my tracks. His scale of kissability to smackability just tipped heavily in favor of a backhand across his face. But he's hit the mark: I don't want to explain him to my dad. Reluctantly I jog around to the passenger side. The interior is sleek if a little bit utilitarian, but it hardly matters since he's turned the air conditioner on full blast. I want to pretend that I'm overheated from running, but his presence is also a contributing factor. My whole body turns traitor in his midst, remembering how his lips felt as they explored my skin.

But that was before I knew who he was or what he was capable of. If I couldn't bring myself to be scared of him, I could try to maintain some self-control.

"Buckle up," he commands me.

I grimace at him, abandoning the glorious chill coming from the vents and reach for my seatbelt. "I always buckle up."

"I imagined you'd say that, given…"

"Given what?" I press when he leaves his thought hanging between us.

"What happened to your sister," he finishes as he peels out of the neighborhood.

Yesterday he didn't know my name. Now he knows how my sister died? Uneasiness mixes with the Molotov cocktail of emotions I'm trying to suppress.

"How the hell do you know about that?"

"Public record," he answers with a shrug.

"Until today, you had no idea who I was," I remind him.

"I've done a little research. It probably occurred to you today that I might be guilty of my father's murder. I felt I needed to know who I was dealing with."

"And something you found led you to believe I could be pushed around?"

"Quite the opposite. As soon as I found out your last name, I assumed you'd be trouble."

He has no idea. "Look I told the police the truth, and that's all I'm going to tell them. I'm not adding to my story."

"I wouldn't ask you to." He frowns as if the suggestion that I lie is completely unpalatable.

"So you're just going to follow me now?" I ask him, "and look up news stories about my family and invite yourself into my life?"

"I'm inviting myself?" he repeats. He throws the stick shift into the next gear and speeds up until the engine roars. Now I see why he wanted me to put on my seat belt. "According to my sister, you weren't even invited last night."

I should have known this was going to come up, but it

hardly seems like he has the right to be calling me out. "Lucky for you I crashed, I suppose."

"I couldn't agree more." He whips around a corner and I clutch the armrest between us. "You okay, Duchess?"

I shoot daggers at him. "Maybe you should slow down a little."

"Don't you trust me?" he asks.

"Really, this is where you want to go with this conversation?" Relief floods through me as we reach my street.

He switches gears, slowing down and coming to a halt a few houses away from my own. "Safely home, like I promised," he says. "You haven't answered my question. Do you trust me?"

I don't think we're talking about his driving skills anymore. "I don't know you."

"That hurts." The wounded quality in his voice speaks more to actual sincerity than flirtation.

"You let me believe that you were crashing that party, too."

"You believed what you wanted to believe." He has a point, but I'm not about to let him know it. He unbuckles his seat belt and twists to face me from the driver's seat. "I think you can let go now."

I release my death grip on the armrest, but I don't relax. His silvery eyes drift across my mouth. I feel them there as acutely as I felt his lips on my own last night. When his gaze finally reaches mine, I find the same questions there that I've been asking myself all afternoon. "Maybe I did," I admit slowly, "but I still didn't know who you were."

"I told you my name," he interrupts me. "You were the one playing coy."

"And you liked it," I blurt out.

A wolfish smile creeps onto his face, the wickedness reaching all the way up to those perfect gray eyes. "I did."

"Glad we've settled that." I tear myself away from his

magnetic gaze and focus on the street ahead. Night has fallen. Most of the houses are still dark. Only a few lights twinkle from behind curtains, most of them left on to greet their owners when they arrive home from work or pleasure. People don't stay in on Saturday night in Las Vegas. We might be the only ones here right now.

"Looks empty," Jameson says, following my gaze.

I nod. In some aspects our worlds aren't so different. Most of the housers have house maids substituting for their parents who are too busy on business trips or entertaining clients or jetting off to some exotic vacation without them. It's the same here, even if it's on a smaller scale. My neighbors run small restaurants and grocery stores. They manage the casinos off the strip and in their free time, they pour their take-home back in to the Vegas economy.

"They're at work," I say aloud.

"Does it scare you to be with me?" He asks.

"No," I whisper. Admitting this to him feels like opening a door that I might not be able to close. I chance a quick peek at him.

His profile is stunning in the moonlight that streams through the windshield, etching him in blunt lines and hard edges. He claimed that he had been away at school in California. The slight sun-kissed tone of his skin that glows faintly in the dim light suggests he'd been somewhere sunny, but he's not tan. Not like most of the people around here.

"What were you studying?" I ask before I can stop myself.

He turns to me looking a little surprised, but also pleased. "Business. No surprise, right?"

"You look like you didn't get outside much," I note.

"That seems a little hypocritical coming from you, Duchess, not that I mind." I flush at the appreciative tone in his voice, which only proves he's right.

"I buy stock in SPF 200," I tell him. "Even at the pool, I'm one of those girls with a hat and sunglasses that pauses her reading to slather as much sunscreen as possible. Skin cancer is a bitch."

"True enough," he says with a chuckle.

"I know I don't fit in here," I tell him.

"No, you don't," he murmurs. "You stand out."

"Is that why you talked to me?" I ask him.

"I spoke to you because it was rude not to acknowledge the fact that you were trespassing."

"Right." Embarrassment rolls over me in waves and I search for the door handle. That's all the reminder I need that I made a huge mistake wandering into that office, sticking around, getting into his car tonight. How many more huge mistakes would I be allowed before I had to pay the price?

He reaches across and grabs my hand. "I didn't mean it like that."

"Yeah, you probably didn't," I say, "but let's face it. I don't know you. You don't know me."

"I'd like to get to know you." I stopped trying to open the door and turn on him.

"Why?" If I discount the murder investigation focused on him, then I'm staring at the heir to a multi-billion dollar company who has the sense of humor to charm the panties off whomever he wants and the looks that mean he doesn't have to. He's the whole package. Compared to him, I'm nothing.

"Because last night I was more honest with you in the few hours we spent together than I've been with anyone my whole life and since then all I can think about is spending more time with you. I want to know you. Maybe I'm imagining it, but I think I've gotten under your skin, as well. If I'm wrong, tell me to leave, but if you felt even a hint of that last night, don't push me away."

"Would you let me?" I breathe. There's something about him that overwhelms me. I won't be able to let him in to part of my life. He'll simply consume me whole.

The hand gripping my own drops it, but only so he can reach up and cup my jaw. "Think about it."

My body leans forward instinctively, but his hand falls away breaking the spell.

"Okay." It's the most I can promise him. I throw open the door before he can convince me to change my mind.

"Duchess," he calls after me. I duck down to the open window. "Check your phone."

Jogging across my neighbors yards, I can feel him watching me from the car. He turns on the headlights to guide my path, but I don't hear the engine roar back to life until I step inside the house. I pause for a moment, catching my breath against the door, then I remember what he said.

My phone is waiting for me on the kitchen counter. Sliding it on, I search through the messages, but there's nothing there. What is he hoping I'll find? Then it hits me and I open my contact list. Skimming through it, I get to 'J.' He's typed in his full name. I select it and find a note written in the contact information. "Call me, Duchess. Please."

"What have you gotten yourself into?" I say to the empty kitchen for the two-hundredth time today. He's left what happens next up to me, but I'm not stupid enough to believe I have a choice. I should stay away from him. It's the smart thing to do. It's what I've always done, keeping my distance is a safe bet. Too bad I can't.

Chapter 12

MONDAY, it's back to routine. I'm switching gears despite my dad's constant absence from work. Pawn shops thrive on their own in Las Vegas. There's always someone willing to gamble on their own treasures. Ninety percent of people don't come back, which means we have an unusual and original stock of junk for tourists to peruse. Nothing thrills a Midwestern farmer more than taking home a Billy Joel tour jacket. I've never claimed to understand it, but if it keeps the lights on and my stomach full, I can work with it.

Jerry is already waiting by the door when I pull into the lot. When I was a lot younger, Dad kept the place open 24 hours. He did some pretty good business considering he didn't mind taking items off drunk people's hands. He also got robbed a few too many times. Then Mom walked out, and he had to be practical, not that there weren't many nights that Becca and I spent sleeping on cots in the warehouse.

"Hey, Emma," Jerry greets me, holding out a Starbucks cup. "Cappuccino, right?"

"Jerry, if you're trying to get on my good side, it's working."

I take the cup from him, and he starts to unlock the door. It takes longer to roll up the metal security gates than it does to turn on the computer, but there's little else that we have to worry about. The shop has a bookkeeper, a toddler could run a transaction. The rest is all instinct.

"Is your Dad coming in?" Jerry asks as I rearrange a pile of Star Wars memorabilia. I put Princess Leia in the front of the case because she's my favorite. I shrug in response to his question. "Your guess is as good as mine."

"I just thought maybe…" He trails off before he wanders away.

I'm not sure, but I think I make him nervous. I can't exactly blame him for assuming that I might know if Dad was coming in, but as usual I left him snoring off a hangover on the couch. The shop is closed on Sundays, and through some miracle Dad hasn't heard about what happened to Nathaniel West, which means he doesn't know that I was there that night. I guess Mom has been keeping secrets from him long enough that it didn't occur to her to mention it. Not that they're on speaking terms unless major parenting intervention is required.

I'd taken the coward's path and decided to stay in my room all day. We'd passed each other a few times coming in and out of the kitchen, but he'd been asleep before I'd put dinner in the oven. Usually I'd push it and wake him up, but I figured I'd better enjoy the calm before the storm. I have no idea when Jameson is going to show back up, but I have no doubt that he will. Eventually, even that will filter through Dad's alcohol-soaked brain.

By 2:00 pm I've bought a handful of old Beatles records and calmly informed a hysterical woman that her five carat diamond was a knock-off. I'd count it as a successful day except Dad still isn't here. Apparently, I'm going to be doing more than help out in the shop this summer. The melodic tingle of bells alerts me to a new customer, but when I glance up I find Jameson stalking through the entrance. I'm out from behind the counter before Jerry can greet him.

"What are you doing here?" I demand trying to sound more forceful than flustered and failing. I can't have Jameson showing up whenever he feels like it. He might not care about going toe to toe with my dad, but I have to live under the same roof as him. "You should go."

Jameson looks around at the store. Apart from the cluttered collections of pawned treasure, the place is vacant. "Is your dad here?"

"No." I begin to tap my foot on the floor. "He could walk in any minute though."

"Then we'll deal with that, if it happens." His tone is dismissive. What must it be like to never think more than ten minutes in advance? I guess he has the luxury to live that way.

Jerry walks over and eyes us suspiciously. He shoves his hands into his pockets, and puffs his chest out. "Can I help you with something?"

He directs the question at Jameson who merely looks at him like he's a bug that needs to be squashed. "I'm being helped already."

"Jerry, this is a friend," I say quickly trying to defuse the situation before Jerry picks up the phone. "He came by to drop something off. We'll just be a second." I grab Jameson's arm and pull him into the back room.

"This is interesting," he says as he takes in the stock of odds and ends.

Vintage toys sit forlornly next to unlit neon signs. In the corner, a dusty jukebox no longer plays music. He studies an old Monte Carlo half covered by a tarp. If the store is like a closet of junk, the backroom is a graveyard of sorts. This is where we send the items no one wants. "If there was a place on earth comprised of other people's treasures, this is it."

He picks up a Fender guitar. "I always wanted to take lessons."

I take it away from him and place it carefully back on the shelf. I don't even want his fingerprints in my world. "You break it, you buy it."

"Maybe I'll just buy it, Duchess." But he makes no move to pick it back up.

"Let's try this again, why are you here?" I'm rapidly losing patience with his air of mystery. It might have been sexy the other night, but now that the veil has been lifted, I know what's underneath: another spoiled rich boy who has the power to buy himself out of trouble.

"I wanted to see you. Isn't that reason enough?" he asks.

Considering our family history and the events that drew us together, it shouldn't feel like enough, but I have to work hard to keep myself from softening in his presence. He looks good today, as if that's news. Unlike the last time I saw him, he's cleanly shaven, and his hair is styled into that messy, wild chaos that begs to be grabbed onto. His grey shirt accents the silver in his tumultuous eyes, and there's a devious grin playing at the corners of his far too kissable lips. It's totally unfair that someone can look this good and be that rich too.

"You're staring at me," he accuses, but he's not put off. In fact, he seems turned on.

I look away quickly. "I thought you had something on your face."

His hand flies up to brush against his chin. "Did I get it?"

"No," I lie softly, moving closer. I brush my fingers along his smooth jaw. "Now it's gone."

Before I can pull back, his palm covers the back of my hand, holding it against his face. "I wish it wasn't," he says.

It takes far too much willpower to draw away from him. If I could bottle up the amount it requires, I'd make a fortune off people who wanted to quit smoking or to lose fifty pounds. Maybe what they really need is a moment trying to resist him to see how much easier everything else in their life feels after.

"I want to take you out," he says.

"I'm not sure that's a good idea." I hear it coming out of my lips while my body screams yes. My self-preservation goddess is working overtime today. I'll have to give her a bonus.

My answer seems to surprise him. Then again, he probably doesn't hear no very often.

"I found what you left on my phone."

"Would you have called?" he asks me.

"Probably not when I saw your last name."

"And now?" he presses, taking a step towards me until our bodies are hovering mere inches from one another's. He's so close that I can smell the spicy notes of his cologne and feel the heat radiating off his body. My own remembers what it's like to have it pressed against it. An invisible thread seems to tug me in his direction.

I lock my knees and force myself to stay in place. "I'm still not sure it's a good idea."

"How can I convince you?" He steps closer again, unknowingly doing a lot of the work. The nearer he comes to me, the more fuzzy the lines become.

"Maybe you should go," I suggest.

"If your dad isn't here, what's the problem with me being here?" he asks.

"He could show up." I'm on the defensive, and he doesn't even know why.

"Does he often not show up? I thought this was his place."

"Do I want to know how you know that?" I'm beginning to wonder if he's ordered a full dossier on my entire family. I'm not the one that needs a background check. "Dad hasn't had the easiest time," I struggle with what to say. "He has some issues."

There, that covers a whole range of evils, especially given the multifarious smorgasbord of vice that we reside in.

"Since your sister?" Jameson guesses.

I shake my head wondering only momentarily if he's distributed some type of truth serum to me. "Since I can remember," I admit, "some people handle their booze better than others."

"I'm prying," he says, but he doesn't apologize for it. I suppose given the amount I now know about his family, it's only fair.

"I've definitely pried into your personal life."

"Quid pro quo," he says.

"I thought you were a college dropout," I mock.

"I learned it from some girl I hooked up with. She was pretty smart."

"Are you attempting to flirt with me Mr. West?" I meander past him shamelessly shaking my ass a little as I go.

"I've never claimed to be a saint," stopping at the water cooler, I poor myself a Dixie cup full and sip it slowly. "Did you check your phone?"

"You're bypassing my question," I accuse him.

Refilling the cup I hold it out to him, "No Duchess. I just asked you a more important one. The answer to your question is obvious," he takes a drink, careful to place his lips exactly where my lip gloss smudged on the rim. I suspect it's not a coincidence, so does my body judging from how a thrill tingles through me landing with a burst of anticipation between my legs. "Yeah, I checked my phone."

"Then can we stop dicking around? I gave you my number, would you have called it before...?"

"Maybe if I found it. I suppose they might pull tricks like that in California, but where I come from, it's still good manners to leave a girl a note. Especially if she's still in her underwear. It's also considered polite to wake her up."

"You looked peaceful. I didn't want to disturb you." It's a half ass excuse, and one that does nothing to sway my opinion as to his innocence.

"Where did you go when you left me," I asked casually. I have to consider that there's a reason that Jameson is the one the police are focused on. Even if I don't want to.

"Wrong question again Duchess. I think what you really meant to ask is did you kill your father?"

"We've been over that," but my voice peaks up a notch.

"Betraying the truth. It's okay if you don't believe me yet, but I'll give you my word that I didn't kill him, and someday that will mean something to you."

"Someday?" I raise an eyebrow. He's awfully sure of himself. Then again why wouldn't Jameson West be certain of his ability to sway the opinions of a woman. "Maybe you can start proving that to me by telling me where you were that night because you weren't there when I woke up."

"You want all the sordid details?" He asked. Anger contorts his face into a mask of rage, "You want me to tell you how I found my father's body? That I checked his pulse and tried to give him CPR?"

I take a step backward, needing to put distance between us as his voice continues to rise. But even when I do a magnetic force pulls me back toward him. I grab onto a shelf and brace myself, trying to break the power he seems to hold over me.

"That I was covered in his blood, and that, plus his will and testament make me guilty as sin in the eyes of the Belle Mère Police?" He's yelling now and I flinch at the brutal accusation running through his words. I'd brought this response on myself.

"Or maybe you want to know about earlier when he came out onto the patio and found us there, and I pulled him inside before he could wake you up? Or about the argument we had after? If you like I can give you a timeline. It'll be an easier sell to the gossip magazines. Be honest, this is just another one of your little games. I only want you to tell me one thing."

"Is this what you think of me," I break in, choking back my own rage, "because if so, there's the door. Get the fuck out."

"I asked first." He ignores my request completely. Maybe I need to be a little less polite about it.

He leans so close to me that we're nearly kissing. "Are you looking for fame or fortune Duchess?"

I want to scream at him that I want the truth, but it's a little too A Few Good Men for me. Instead, I settle for walking over to the door and throwing it open.

"Out." I don't scream, I say it softly.

He strides past me, casting one hottie glance before he walks back into the store. I follow him out only to spot Jerry scurrying as far away from the two of us as possible.

"You get what you came for?" he asks Jameson as he walks toward the door.

"No," Jameson barks at him, "you have nothing I want here."

Jameson West is as hot and cold as a bad faucet. If I turn him on I don't know what I'll get. I spend the rest of the day replaying the conversation in my head, wondering how it got exactly from lighthearted banter to serious topics to accusations so quickly. But like everything centered around him, I'm left with more questions than answers.

Chapter 13

A FEW HOURS LATER, I'm still fuming. I slam down the baseball card I've been analyzing and glare at it's owner. I'm not sure how he manages to keep his eyes wide and innocent underneath the bushy caterpillars that he calls eyebrows. Usually, I try to kill them with kindness. Even scammers often have a guilty conscious. Nine times out of ten, they'll grab their own junk and take off before I have to call them out. Sometimes they even apologize, but this guy must have brass balls. Too bad I'm about to hold them to the fire. "Wow. A baseball card signed by Babe Ruth."

I play dumb for a minute, simply because I enjoy watching the puppet dance. He leans against the counter and nods his head before he adjusts the collar of his tracksuit, "Yeah. One of my clients was running a little low on cash. He offered me this. I guess he didn't know what he had."

Okay, I didn't expect that. Now I almost feel bad for the guy. "What's your business?"

"Private investigator." He magics a business card out of his back pocket and hands it to me. "Dominic Chamber."

I suck in a breath and prep myself to give him the bad news. "Mr. Chamber," I begin, but he stops me.

"Dominic, please."

"Dominic, maybe you should stick to taking pictures of married men and tracking down lost puppies."

"Oh, man," he scratches the back of his head. "Are you telling me that's fake?"

"Yeah," I slide it across the glass to him. "Babe Ruth probably didn't use a blue Bic to sign autographs."

I could go into details about the Ruth's signature or how rarely he actually autographed something, but there's no need to rub salt in the wound. Hopefully, he stops accepting payment in the form of sentimental memorabilia.

"The card has to be worth something, right?" He scoops it up and studies it for a minute.

"Reproduction," I tell him gently. Why not tackle all the bad news today?

"Well, thanks."

"For what it's worth, I'm sorry. I wish it was real too." Even though I'm surrounded by authentic comic books and baseball cards, vintage guitars and more, ninety percent of what passes through this shop isn't real. It's easy enough to turn away the scammers, but far too many of the people who drag their treasures into us find out that they're clinging to another man's junk.

"Don't worry about it. I sent the guy the pictures he needs in an online gallery." He takes out his phone and swipes the screen a few times. "Poof. It's so easy to make evidence disappear."

Evidence; the word lands heavy on my chest. I do my best to smile, wishing him well. As soon as he's out the door, I notice he's left his card. I throw it in the drawer. You never know when you might need a private dick.

Checking my phone, I find half a dozen missed texts from Josie.

Josie: Have you seen this?

Josie: I'm freaking out right now.

Josie: You're totally hooking up with the world's sexiest killer.

I groan as I click on the link she sent me. Sure enough Jameson has been dubbed The World's Most Eligible Murderer. I guess it's time for him to have this fifteen minutes in this, outside the shadow of his father. The story mentions little about Nathaniel or the case the police are bringing against Jameson. Instead, it's a laundry list of complaints from Jameson's former college roommate. Most of it sounds like sour grapes, but I keep reading anyway until I reach the point where the roommate complains about the parade of women constantly showing up in their apartment.

Even though it's little more than musty laundry, I can only imagine how it feels for Jameson to read about himself in a national paper.

Emma: When did this story come out?

Josie: I saw it a few hours ago. It's trending on Facebook.

I scroll to the story's bi-line and check the publication information. The story was uploaded to the website this morning. Jameson had come to visit me after his former roommate, and I suspect former friend, served up a steamy dish of Jameson's secret sauce.

"You are so stupid," I mutter to myself.

"What's that?" Jerry calls from across the room.

I wave him off, "Nothing."

I choose to continue my chastisement in my head. Jameson had come here earlier to get away from the attention, but also because he seemed desperate to prove to me that he wasn't who they said he was. Maybe part of that desperation stemmed from having all his bad habits and mistakes on the front pages of papers at newsstands all over the country. It also explains the accusations he'd leveled at me, but it doesn't absolve him of what he'd said.

Josie: Need a ride?

I glance at the clock; two more hours. I shoot back a message telling her to pick me up at 6:30 when the night manager will be in. Hitting the back button, my phone takes me to my contacts list. Jameson's name sits two slots above Josie's. I select it and hit the compose button. I can't seem to find the right words to let him know that I'm sorry and not sorry at the same time. Who knew being involved with a murder investigation made flirtation so difficult?

By 6:30, I still haven't come up with the right message. Waving goodbye to Jerry and the night manager, I flee the shop digging my phone out of my purse. I catch the faint purr of an engine idling nearby, but it's not Josie's beat up Honda Civic waiting for me. I don't even have to look up to know that. There's no screeching metal or flapping belts. Nope, this car sounds like it runs on sex.

I straighten up to face him. Jameson's lounging against the side of his car, against the side of his black BMW. He's not smiling, or frowning—or holding a weapon—so it's hard to get a read on his mood. "Waiting for someone?" I call.

"Waiting for you," he admits. His tone is still icy, but I shrug it off reminding myself that he's had a much worst day than me. "Need a ride?"

At the same moment, Josie pulls into Pawnography's parking lot. She slows to a stop when she sees the two of us staring each other down across the pavement. Despite what's happened to him, he doesn't deserve for me to get in his car. He doesn't need another free pass in life, but I can't look away. His gaze has locked onto my own, and the storm raging in those eyes when he left earlier has calmed. There's still so much I don't know and don't understand. He owes me answers. I turn toward Josie and gesture for her to leave. She doesn't need any more instruction thanks to best friend ESP, or maybe she defaulted to one of the unspoken rules of sisterhood and made herself scarce. She blows me a kiss before she circles around and heads back out. Shouldering my bag, I walk directly at him.

"Friend of yours?" he asks.

"Yep, and my ride home." To my surprise, he circles around the car with me and opens the passenger door. "You don't drive?"

I swallow against the raw nerves this question inspires. "I try not to."

Given what he knows about my family, he might be able to guess exactly why that is. He doesn't pressure me for answers. Unlike how you pressured him earlier, I accuse myself.

"Do you need to learn?" he asks. "I can teach you." We're changing gears before he's even released the brakes. Earlier he'd written me off as a gold digger. Now he's offering me private lessons. Maybe I could offer him one on not being a dick.

"I know how," I let my tone do the work for me. It's not really a subject I feel like getting into at the moment. I can't trust him.

Thankfully, Jameson switches subjects as he switches gears. "I apologize for earlier. Things have been complicated and..."

He leaves the unfinished thought hanging in the air.

"You don't know who to trust," I finish for him.

"You're perceptive," he notes.

If I'm going to earn a spot on his trust list and he's going to earn one on mine, now's the time to start being honest. "No. I read the interview with your college roommate today. He sold you out."

"The worst part is, a story like that might have got him some vacation money. I had Thanksgiving at his house last year, and he sold me out for a Mai Tai."

"Probably, an ocean view, too," I tag on. "Personally, I demanded they pay me in diamonds and sign over the Taj Mahal. I guess I have higher standards than him."

"I'm sorry I accused you."

"Look …" I struggle with exactly how to put this, "The night we met, it was fun to play games. We both wanted to pretend to be someone else, but you're using my name to keep yourself out of jail. If whatever this is is going to work, you're going to have to start being honest with me."

"Does that work both ways, Duchess?"

I melt a little at the nickname. We're surviving our first unofficial fight, pet names intact.

"I have nothing to hide," I promise him.

He stops the BMW a few houses down, then he turns his flickering blue eyes on me. He reaches out, his thumb brushing over my lower lip as if considering this—considering me. "We all have something to hide, Duchess."

Chapter 14

HEY PRINCESS, I have a business meeting at the bank. See you later.

I pluck the post-it note off the fridge and shake my head. I hope he's talking about a meeting with an actual employee and not just an ATM on his way to the race track. Crumpling it, I check the clock on the microwave and curse. No time to make coffee this morning. Instead I grab a granola bar from the cupboard and dart out the door, stopping in my tracks when I spot Jameson's BMW in the driveway.

The low rumble of bass rattles his window as I knock on it. He turns down the music and rolls it down.

"Is this loitering or trespassing?" I ask.

"I call it chivalry," he corrects me. "Come on. I'll drive you to the shop."

I hesitate for a minute then I shoulder my purse and turn toward the bus station.

Jameson calls out again. "You're not going to walk all the way there."

Somehow I don't think he'd let me. Glancing down the

street to make sure my dad is nowhere in sight I get into Jameson's car. All I'd need was for Dad to finish up his meeting early. But when we make it to the next block with no sign of him in sight, I finally relax in the leather seat.

"I wasn't going to walk," I tell him. I tap on the glass to point out a sign as we pass. "The bus drops me off down the street from the store."

His eyebrows knit together as if he's considering this. His hand drifts over and for one moment I think he's about to take mine but then he changes gears. "I know a pawn shop isn't a Fortune 500 company," Jameson says slowly, "but I'd think your father would be able to afford a car."

"He has one." I shrug, letting his judgment roll off my shoulders. It's a skill I've developed over the years.

"For you," he states the obvious.

"I don't want one." There, that's not a lie. I don't want a car. For a crazy second, I consider if my mother has arranged for Jameson to sway me into accepting my early graduation gift.

"You really shouldn't be taking the bus alone."

"Why? Because working yourself up over it screams first world problems."

He bypasses the question as he drifts effortlessly across lanes. "Do you take it at night when you don't have a ride?"

"Sometimes. Other times, Josie picks me up or Jerry takes me home."

"Jerry?" Jameson repeats stiffly.

"You met him yesterday," I remind him. Am I actually detecting a hint of jealousy in those broad shoulders? "The store manager."

Jameson relaxes with a laugh. "Oh, that guy."

I don't need to ask to know what he meant by that. Jerry's nice but he's not exactly a catch. The familiar melody of nursery rhymes builds outside the car windows. We stop at a traffic circle to yield to an ice cream truck, I sigh as it passes us.

"Do you want a popsicle?" Jameson asks and I realize I've been staring after it.

"Becca and I used to keep some money in one of those magnetic hide-a-key boxes under the mailbox. We'd run out as soon as we heard him coming."

"What did you get?" he asks.

"A bomb pop." I tell him. "I liked that it turned my tongue funny colors. What'd you get?"

"Me?" He shakes his head as if its a silly question, but I know better. A guy's favorite frozen dessert says a lot about him. "Nothing."

"No, when you were a kid," I press.

"Nothing," he repeats. "It's hard for the ice cream man to visit a gated community."

His answer tells me more than I expected. It doesn't take a talk show host to know that lack of ice cream means he had a sad childhood.

"You should have told me," I squeal, eager to remedy the situation now. "I would have jumped out and gotten you something."

"It's nine in the morning."

"You can read a clock!" I say in mock surprise. "Gorgeous and he can tell time. Where's the chapel?"

Jameson's eyebrow arches up. "Gorgeous huh?"

"I shouldn't have said that," I admit.

"Maybe we can catch the ice cream man another time," he suggests as he pulls up to Pawnography. "You can help me with my first time. Give me tips"

"You still have a first time available? I figured you'd handed all those out."

Relaxed Jameson vanishes, replaced by his rigid, distant

alter ego. "Don't believe everything you read in the papers, Duchess."

"I don't," I rush to assure him. "But boys who kiss like you have had some practice."

The praise boosts his ego and puts the haughty smirk back on his face. "You could say that. I guess I saved one first to share with you though."

"Careful West, that's starting to sound like a date."

"We both know dates are off limits," he says, reminding me of the rule I had set. "Maybe I can sway you with a bomb pop."

I climb out of the car and lean down to look at him through the open window. "You can certainly try."

INVENTORY IS A WRECK. There's supposed to be standard procedure at the shop but with a constantly changing schedule and an absentee boss most of that's gone by the wayside. Items need cataloging and files need updating. I'm about to throw in the towel when a man in a white uniform approaches me by the register.

"Ms. Southerly?" he addresses me.

"Yes?" I'm not exactly fond of giving out my name these days, especially to strangers.

"These are for you." He hands me two cold, colorful packages.

Bomb pops. My pulse takes off like a rocket as I accept the treats.

"What do I owe you?" I ask him bending to grab my purse from the lower shelf, trying to ignore that my fingers are going numb from the ice.

"It's a gift from a friend," he says dismissing my offer. He refuses even to take the tip I hold out to him. "That's not necessary. He's a very good friend."

If only he knew the half of it.

I don't bother to hide my enthusiasm as I unwrap the popsicle and clutch the wooden stick. Holding up my camera I take a selfie licking it then I send it to Jameson.

Jameson: You're giving me ideas, Duchess.

Emma: That was unintentionally pornographic.

Jameson: Unintentional porn is my favorite kind.

My cheeks heat as I consider what he's thinking as he stares at my photo. I know what would be on my mind if he sent me a picture of his tongue, and it wouldn't be ice cream.

Time to change the subject.

Emma: Thank you for the Bomb Pop but what about you? Did you get one for yourself?

Jameson: No. I'm saving my first Bomb Pop to share with someone special.

Emma: Ice cream doesn't wait. It melts.

Jameson: Then maybe you need to reconsider going on that date with me.

I respond with another tawdry selfie with my lips wrapped around the tip of the popsicle. I'd said no more games but I might as well leave him guessing.

MY PRIVATE CHAUFFEUR service continues throughout the week. More than once I have to rush out the door before Dad sees that I'm getting a ride from someone other than Josie. The ten minutes to the shop and the ten minutes home have been the only alone time we've gotten this week since Dad decided to start making appearances at the store. At least it means I won't have to work on the weekend.

This morning, there's a cappuccino waiting in the cup holder for me. As soon as I pick it up I know it's dry with extra foam. Someone's been paying attention. I take a few cautious sips, but he's silent next to me. I almost always wait for him to speak because he's nicer in the mornings than I am, but today he's quiet.

"How was your night?" I ask.

"Uneventful." He doesn't elaborate further, but he dares to glance over at me. Dark circles under his eyes mar his otherwise perfect face.

My fingers twitch, and I realize I want to reach out and rub his back. I want to reassure him that everything's going to be fine, but that's not a promise I can make him. "Is your mom back yet?"

"No." Apparently he's answering in one word sentences today.

"How's Monroe?" This question earns me a genuine reaction.

His gaze flickers to me in surprise, a bemused grin taking resonance on his lips, "Do you really want to know how Monroe is?"

"No," I admit, setting my cup back down in the holder, "but I don't want to ride in silence the whole time either."

"She's begging me to talk to a psychiatrist, probably so she can buy my files and see if I did it. As if I'd walk into some quack and confess all of my sins."

Is there anything to confess? The question is on the tip of my tongue, but I swallow it down. The more time I spend with Jameson, the more convinced I am of his innocence, but that's when he's in a good mood. When he's happy it's as if the sun is shining directly on me—until a dark cloud descends. I can't always see it coming. More often than not, it has nothing to do with me. He arrives in these moods. Sometimes he loosens up, other times he barely cracks a smile. Each time I seem to pinpoint exactly how I feel about him, his mood changes, shifting as abruptly as an unforeseen storm.

"You know, there's one thing you can do to cheer me up."

I tilt my head in interest, "And that is?"

"Agree to go on a real date with me." He's not giving up on that. I should have known that's what he was getting at, but he finds a new way to ask everyday.

"I need time," I tell him. The air between us thickens, pulsating with negative energy. Forecast: hurricane. Category: Jameson.

"Take all the time you need." There's far more annoyance than reassurance in his statement. His knuckles are white from gripping the steering wheel so hard.

I groan as I reach for the door handle and swing it open.

"Wait," he calls. I swivel in my seat. Jameson catches my chin with his cupped hand, "Patience isn't one of my virtues."

"I can see that," I try to remain detached, but it's harder when he's touching me. My body craves that skin on skin contact. I want to melt into him.

"I'm trying," he says in a low voice that raises goosebumps along my arms.

I swallow and nod, at a loss for words. For one second I burrow into his hold, pressing my cheek against his open palm. Then I scramble out of the car before I give in again.

DAD IS A MAN POSSESSED. In the last week he's done more to organize product and file forms than he's done in the last three years. He tears through the store. Jerry and I stay out of his way. If he wants to work, neither of us are going to stop him. Gives me a chance to focus on the customers. It also means I don't have to close every single night and open the next morning.

Peeking into the back room I find him at the computer

sorting through what looks like years of receipts, "You want something for lunch?"

"I'm fine." He doesn't look at me, so I step into the room and lean against the door frame.

"Need something?" he ask, his eyes crinkle at the corners as he beams at me.

"It's been awhile since I've seen you enjoy the shop so much."

"It's been awhile since I got good news," he admits to me.

"News?" I repeat. "You didn't share."

He leans in his chair, crossing his hands behind his head, "I didn't have to honey. It's all over every newspaper in the country."

It takes a second for his words to sink in, but when I realize what he's referring to a hollow pang hits me square in the chest. "You mean what happened to Nathaniel West?"

"I know." He waves a hand at me. "It's morbid, but for a long time I'd stopped believing in karma."

"And now you do again," I finish for him despite my cotton ball of a tongue.

"What Nathaniel West did to this family is unforgivable. Do I have to remind you of that?" His mood slips for a moment, allowing me a glimmer of the hatred he'd wasted on him.

"You were friends once," I say in a soft voice. It had to count for something.

Dad shakes his head, rubbing the scruff on his chin. "You're too young to understand this, but sometimes people aren't who we think they are. Don't let your guard down, honey."

I want to tell him I've been understanding this for a couple of years now, but that I hadn't let hate consume me. I had allowed myself to be bitter, though. If I didn't get that in check would I wind up like him? Practically throwing a party for a dead man?

"You okay?" He studies me momentarily, but the wheels aren't turning behind his eyes. As far as he's concerned, I'll reach the same conclusion he has.

"Low blood sugar," I lie. "I think I'm going to go grab lunch."

"You're working too hard," he says with a sigh. "This is your summer, you should enjoy yourself. Grab lunch and take the afternoon off."

I mumble in agreement to this plan and back out of the room. Nathaniel West was my father's enemy. I'd taken that feud seriously, even when I didn't have a horse in the race. Now that the man was dead, that hatred had evaporated. Now my mixed feelings toward the West family had a lot more to do with the legacy of his children than the bad blood from before I was born. I hate Monroe, but I like Jameson. I can't take sides any more, and now, even my afternoon off feels tainted by the macabre joy my dad is taking in these events.

I dig my phone out and call Josie, but she doesn't answer. I could get an Uber or catch the bus... or I could call my personal driver.

It doesn't take me long to make my decision.

Chapter 15

THERE'S NOT a cloud in the sky. It's bright blue, and Jameson is happy. I tuck the copy of *Wuthering Heights* I filched from the shop in my purse as soon as he parks his BMW. At least from where I stand there's no Heathcliff glower frozen on his face. But just like the wind on the moors, that could change any minute. Before I can shoulder my bag and head toward him, he's out of the car, opening the door.

"I'm starting to get used to this," I tease.

"Good."

"Is there any way we can stop at the store?" I ask him as he pulls out. I guess if he's going to insist on being my driver then he can help me run errands. "I need to grab some lunch stuff."

"Already taken care of, Duchess." He hitches his finger towards the back seat where a wicker basket sits.

"Is that a picnic basket?" I stare at it like it might disappear or transform into an everyday object. Because real life does not include hot guys and picnic baskets.

"I assumed I'd need to feed you," he explains. He assumed

correctly. Somehow Jameson has managed to steadily outnumber his mood swings with surprisingly sweet gestures.

"I didn't know picnic baskets were a real thing." I hope he didn't catch the slight break in my voice, even Yogi Bear didn't cry over picnics. It's been a long time since a guy surprised me with something as sweet as this. Actually, a guy never has.

"They are," he informs me. "It's just one of the many perks of living in a casino. I have a staff that can find picnic baskets."

"And make the picnics."

Jameson clutches his chest, shaking his head. "I'm wounded, Duchess. I made everything in that picnic basket."

"So you made me lunch, and now you're taking me where?" I search the scenery outside my window for a clue.

"That's a secret," he says.

"Secrets don't make friends," I grumble. "A picnic lunch and a surprise location? If I didn't know better, I'd think this was a date, but since I haven't agreed to a date, I can't possibly be right."

He blows off my none-too-subtle accusation with a whistle. "This is just two friends having lunch. Don't read into things, Emma."

I check out his outfit for clues, but that hardly tells me anything. He's in his standard T-shirt and jeans. If Calvin Klein were a god, Jameson would be his muse. The shirt seems to caress his body and his jeans hang low on his hips as though his clothes were making love to him. It's enough to give a girl wicked thoughts. I squirm a little in my seat trying to squash my hunger. I doubt whatever he's packed in that basket will actually satisfy me down there.

Jameson weaves in and and out of traffic until the busy streets of Vegas are behind us, and we're on the open road. The desert slowly evolves into the peaks of mountains. I have no idea how far away from home he's taking me, and I don't care.

As we climb higher, I start to spot scraggly pines and patches of snow. Coming from the desert to this feels like a fairy tale.

"Is this Mount Charleston?" I ask him, gawking at the vacation homes tucked into the mountainside.

He nods, his eyes glued to the winding road. "Have you ever been up here?"

"No. We've never made it." Despite the city's reputation, there actually are plenty of things to do outdoors. My family had just never done any of it. I'd like to say we're indoor types, but really mountains are just outside our comfort zone. Fresh air instead of lingering cigarette smoke. Scenery carved by nature. Not our scene. Despite the fact that the mountains have always been there hanging in the distance like an old film backdrop, they'd never felt real to me until now.

"What do you think?" Jameson asks, calling me from my thoughts and back to the reality of him.

I search for the right words to describe how it makes me feel. "They're magnificent."

"These aren't even great mountains," he confesses to me. "Someday I'll take you to the Appalachians or up to Colorado. We have a house in Aspen."

I press my lips into a thin smile. His family has vacation homes while my family's idea of a vacation has been jumping from one desert location to another for as long back as I can remember. "My vacations rely on the terms of a custody agreement."

"My family's vacations usually center around business. I don't know how you're supposed to break the cycle."

"Kill all the lawyers," I suggest.

"Right now, I'm a pretty big fan of lawyers." The conversation screeches to an awkward halt at the reminder of his legal troubles. It's as if there's a monster lurking in the room with us.

Occasionally we forget it's there, then one of us slips up and reminds the other, and we're stuck watching our backs.

We lapse into silence until he turns down a rocky lane.

"Wow," I gasp. Tall trees flank either side of the drive as he zooms along to an unknown destination. The road deposits us in front of a breathtaking chalet perched cliff side. I get out before he has a chance to come around and perform his gentlemanly duties.

The air is cold in my throat and its crispness makes my lungs hurt, but I drink it in greedily. There's no pollution or fumes tainting it. It tastes like pine needles and sunshine. I walk closer to the edge. Jameson gathers the picnic basket as I gawk at the amazing views. Vegas is a speck in the distance, and for once instead of neon signs and blinking lights, trees and rocks rise around me. When I finally turn away from it, I find Jameson standing a few yards away watching me.

"Is this your house?" I ask.

"Yes." His response is colored with a sadness I don't understand, and before I can reconsider, I cross to him and press my lips to his.

"What was that for?" he asks as we break apart.

"For sharing this with me," I tell him, "and because I don't want you to be sad here. Promise me."

He agrees to nothing. Instead, he gives me a half-smile and tugs me toward the house. It might be hard for a building to compete with the natural beauty of the mountain setting, but this house does. Jameson leads me through a living room that I can fit my whole house in, and out double doors to a back deck that jets precariously over the side of the rocky precipice. I wait patiently as he lays out his feast, trying not to laugh when he produces peanut butter and jelly sandwiches and a bag of chips.

"You're the gourmet cook," he reminds me, but his eyes twinkle like stars, reflecting some of my own amusement.

"No complaints. This is perfect." I unwrap my sandwich and take a large bite.

"It's crunchy peanut butter. I hope that's okay," he tells me as I begin to chew.

I swallow hard, nodding enthusiastically. "Crunchy is the best."

"Duchess, I think you're the peanut butter to my jelly," he says before he takes a bite of his own sandwich. It's a cheesy sentiment, but my stomach flutters.

When we finish, he hands me an apple. "Dessert?"

"There's a lack of frosting on that dessert." I scrunch up my nose. I guess even billionaire guys with model-level good looks can't get it right all the time.

"I'll keep that in mind for next time," he promises.

But I munch away at the apple, still mesmerized by the scenery around me.

"You know, I did come to the mountains once," I say, as I begin to recall a hazy memory from childhood.

"Didn't leave much of an impression," Jameson says.

I can't help but laugh as the memory grows clearer. "Actually, I think I blocked it out because it was traumatic. My parents took us on this road trip into California, and we went through the mountains."

"Road trips are the absolute worse."

Somehow I doubt that someone with a private jet can actually commiserate with me on this topic, but I nod in agreement. Jameson reaches for my hand, entwining his fingers through mine, and I wonder if he can feel my pulse starting to beat frantically in my veins.

"What happened?" he prompts.

I shake my head trying to clear it before I continue,

suddenly overcome by his nearness. "We brought my cousin, Ellie, along. I have no idea why. We had to stop to use the restroom. Mom told us to stay near the car, but we'd been cooped up for hours, so of course we started running around like bats out of hell. Anyway, I was racing Becca to a tree behind the rest stop. I'm sure it wasn't that far, but it felt like it at the time. I beat her there, but when I turned around, she was gone, so I ran back to the parking lot, and my parents were gone."

"What did you do?" he asks, trying to unsuccessfully stifle a laugh at my predicament. His thumb rubs circles on the inside of my wrist, and I have to take a deep breath.

"I sat down and cried," I admit. "I thought they left me because I wasn't listening to my mom. As it turns out, they forgot they had Ellie with them. All they saw was two kids in the backseat. It took twenty minutes of my sister raising hell before they turned around and realized she was trying to tell them I wasn't there."

"Were they angry at you," he asks, "when they got back?"

"No," I shake my head, feeling the slightest prick of tears in the corner of my eyes as the memory turns from amusing to bittersweet. "I just remember my mom hugging me so hard, and then Becca grabbed my hand and promised she'd never leave me again."

I nearly choke on the words. Jameson drops his hold on my hand and wraps his arms around my shoulders, drawing me against his hard chest. How can he feel so sturdy and muscular, and still be such a soft place to land?

"My parents took us on a road trip once," he tells me, and I'm grateful for the distraction. "I don't remember much. Dad packed us all in the car and drove us out to this little city in California. There was a boardwalk and a giant ferris wheel. He gave us twenty bucks and let us play as many carnival games as we could. I'll never forget that city. It was called Heaven."

"Heaven?" I repeat in disbelief.

"Yes. Heaven is a place on earth," he says bemusedly.

"Did you ever go back?" I ask in a soft voice.

"No. I went to boarding school the next fall. Mom was convinced that military school was the right way to go."

"I can't see you at military school," I admit. "It actually seems more suited to Monroe."

"I don't think military school could handle Monroe" he says dryly. "But I tried to go back there once." His voice fades into the past, and even though we're pressed closely together, I can feel the distance of memory between us. "The whole town had been bought out. The boardwalk, the ferris wheel, the games. They were all gone."

"What happened to them?"

"Someone came in, developed everything into condos." He barks a hollow laugh. "I wasn't surprised when I found the project in my dad's portfolio."

Pulling back, I stare at him. "Are you telling me your father took your family on a vacation, then bought the place out, and turned it into senior living?"

"It's also very popular amongst young professionals," he says. "The city isn't even called Heaven any more."

"Did they rename it Purgatory?" I nuzzle into his arms, trying to think of the right thing to say. I'd thought my family was dysfunctional. But the Wests made my parents look like parents of the year. "If I had enough money. I'd buy a little town on the coast and name it Heaven."

"Could we build a boardwalk?" he asks.

"Oh, yes. Heaven has to have a boardwalk," I promise him.

"I like the picture you're painting of the afterlife."

"It's not an afterlife," I say. "It's just a dream."

Jameson presses his lips to my forehead, lingering there. It's a gesture filled with warmth and promises of its own. I want to stay here with him where everything is quiet and simple, and bad memories are only stories from the past. He buries his face in my hair and breathes in. Then, he speaks so softly that I barely catch it. "I hope your dreams come true, Duchess."

THAT NIGHT, I stare at the ceiling, unable to sleep. I replay every touch, every brush of his hand over mine, the few kisses we stole. Maybe tomorrow I can hang up some pictures of boy bands. I don't know what Jameson West is doing to me, but I know I don't want him to stop. I roll over and grab my pillow tightly, clamping my eyes closed, but nothing works. I'm still lying there when a soft tap catches my attention, followed by another. It takes a second to realize it's a rhythm. I go to my window and peek through the blinds. Two eyes stare back at me and I nearly jump out of my skin.

"Smooth," I muttered to myself as I tug on the cord so that I can unlock the window. "Trying to scare me to death?" I hiss at Jameson through the screen.

"I thought of something I wanted to ask you," he says.

"You could have tried using the phone." I crossed my arms and wait for his question.

"Why would I do that when your first floor window is so convenient? Come on, let me in, Duchess." He tosses me a crooked smile.

I glance over my shoulder at my closed bedroom door. "Have you lost your mind? If my dad comes in here and finds you, he'll kill you and he'll claim self-defense, *and* he'll get off."

"I'm not staying." He holds up two fingers. "Scout's promise."

"I doubt you were ever a Boy Scout." I pinch the metal tabs

on the screen, wiggling it out of place, and set it against the wall.

Jameson ducks inside my window. Straightening up, he brushes off the dust from the window sill and looks around. "Not what I imagined," he admits.

"What did you imagine?"

"Something regal. Four poster bed. Hand maidens."

"We're fresh out of hand maidens," I say flatly. "I'm lucky if I have clean sheets on the bed."

The bed. The innocent thought has my eyes darting over to the rumpled sheets and comforter. Jameson's gaze follows mine in that direction. "Were you asleep?"

"No, I couldn't sleep. My head's too full." *Of you.* I keep that part to myself.

He holds out his hands. "Come here."

Now would be a very good time to share my parents' no boys in the bedroom rule, but the words stick on my tongue. It's easier to respect parental edicts when parents are around to enforce them. My dad might be home, but he's not really present. All I really have is my own instinct, and that's split decidedly down the middle on what I should do. The smart move is to show him the window. Instead, I take his hands. He leads me to the bed and I follow without objection. But when Jameson kicks off his shoes, then he reaches for the hem of his shirt, my internal panic button goes off.

"What are you doing?" I whisper furiously. The only thing worse than my dad finding Jameson in my bedroom would be he finding a half dressed Jameson in my bed.

"I feel overdressed." He tips his chin toward me. It's at that moment I remember that I'm in a tank top and boy shorts. I try to tug my shirt down.

"No need to cover up," he reminds me. "I saw more than that on our first date."

"That wasn't a date," I correct him. "And before you get excited about the proximity of the bed, you should know that I have a checklist."

"A *checklist?*" he says like I've piqued his interest.

Why would I bring that up? Probably because I'm half-naked in my bedroom with him. "I, um, have a checklist before I'll have sex with a guy."

He's quiet for a moment before he runs his hand through his hair. "Duchess, are you a virgin?"

"No." Heat burns my cheeks and I pray he doesn't ask any more questions. "But, honestly, I made a huge mistake and I don't want another one on my record."

"Will you tell me what's on the checklist?" He grins widely.

"Absolutely not! You aren't gaming this system."

"I wouldn't dare," he promises. He drops onto my bed, grinning wildly and putting his upper torso on display. Instinct takes over and I crawl in next to him. Slowly he guides me to my side and slides his arm under my waist. My body molds to his, effortlessly. "What did you want to ask?"

But he doesn't answer. Instead, his nose and lips skim along the back of my neck, before he settles his mouth on my shoulder. The heat of his breath on my bare skin sends tingling emissaries of anticipation running through my body. "I wanted to know what you were dreaming about," he murmurs, "but you weren't sleeping."

"I was thinking," I say shyly.

"That's dangerous when you're trying to fall asleep." Anguish coats his words and I struggle in his grasp until I flip over to face him.

"Why aren't you asleep in your own bed?" I ask.

"Yours is more comfortable. I like this body pillow." He presses closer to me until I can feel *every* rock hard inch of him.

Jameson wants me—his body betrays that much. I can feel the proof of it pressing into my hip.

I imagine what it would be like to let him slip between my legs. I'm not sure if it would help me sleep or keep me wide awake. Although something tells me that getting Jameson naked would make the night pass far too quickly.

But wanting him doesn't explain why he's here now. If it's company he's looking for, there's no end of women willing to help him out. He had come to me.

"And?" I press him. I refuse to be distracted by him.

"Nightmares." He leaves it at that.

I don't need him to tell me about nightmares. I know all too well how often the worst moments of your life revisit you in your dreams. "Sometimes I have nightmares about Becca," I confess to him instead. "It's like it's happening all over again and I can't wake up."

"You were there that night." It's a statement, not a question as if this is only now dawning on him. Wherever he'd gotten his information, it didn't include that little detail. "I'm sorry you had to see that."

"There's no use apologizing for life or tragedy. Both are inevitable."

Our foreheads press together and my breath falls into sync with his. "Maybe we're doing this wrong," he suggests.

"What?" I say in a sleepy voice.

"Strength in numbers, Duchess. I don't think I could have a nightmare with you in my arms."

"Then stay," I offer in a small voice before giving him my lips to convince him.

Chapter 16

"I CAN'T BELIEVE you're Jameson West's girlfriend," Josie says, as she sifts through the pile of clothes strewn across my bed. "I've been doing some research on him, and you're totally going to wind up on the cover of *People* Magazine."

"Or *US Weekly*, and I'm not his girlfriend," I grumble. "Is my navy dress over there?" The police department should consider hiring Josie to be an interrogator. Despite making Jameson promise to keep the status of our relationship a secret, I had spilled to her in less than two minutes. "No one's supposed to know, remember?"

"It's my secret." She pretends to draw a zipper over her lips. "Why is it a secret again?"

"Because my dad will have an aneurism if he finds out we're hanging out."

"Hanging out? Dating? Which is it, sister?" Josie demands.

"I don't know," I finally admit. Plopping onto my bed, I consider the question. It feels like my answer should be obvious. "I don't think I'm ready to be his girlfriend."

Josie groans as if she's half as frustrated as I am. "But you want to kiss him and practice making babies?"

"Maybe I should cancel." We both know that this thing between Jameson and I is a ticking time bomb. I pause at the mirror and mess with my hair for a moment, wondering if I should wear it up or down.

"You are not canceling," she insists. A moment later, she triumphantly holds up my navy dress.

It's one of my favorites since it never wrinkles. Plus its a simple A-line, but the second I see it, I realize it's all wrong. The simplicity I loved feels boring and uninspired now. I'll have to rip out my own tongue before I say it a loud but I want to impress Jameson.

"I think I'll wear jeans." Opening my drawer, I pull out a pair and shimmy into them.

"You're going on a date with a billionaire in denim?"

My eyes narrow in response to her disapproving tone. "I *can't* tell what you think of that. Jameson wears jeans all the time." And he looks good in them "Look, I know this is hard for you to believe, but for some girls, finding a guy they can hang out with in blue jeans and flip-flops is kind of a dream."

"Okay," she agrees, reluctantly. Her eyes flicker to the bag she brought with her. I haven't had the courage to ask what's inside. "As long as you realize there's a time and place for Louboutins."

"Between you and my mother, how could I ever forget?" I tease. I choose a soft black tank that flows to my hips, managing to achieve the pinnacle of lazy girl fashion: successfully mixing style and comfort.

"Just please wear these?" Josie begs, pulling a pair of strappy, gold Louboutins out of her bag. "It will dress it up just enough."

"No promises," I warn, but I hold out my hand. Slipping

one on, I fasten it around my ankle and observe. It kills me to admit it, but it's actually kind of sexy.

"Oh, those are perfect," she squeals, clapping her hands like she got her birthday present.

"Where did you get them, anyway? You just started waiting tables." These shoes cost at least seven hundred dollars. I can't bring myself to consider dropping a Benjamin on new shoes. But even though Josie has a penchant for extravagance, she doesn't have the means to indulge her tastes.

She tips her chin up and rolls her eyes at me as if it's the most obvious thing in the world. "Do you really want to know?"

"A gift from one of your admirers," I guess. I try to block the vision of a drooling, forty-something business man blessing her with a shoe shopping spree, but even in my head, it can't be unseen. "Do you think I should spray these with Lysol?"

"I haven't even worn them yet." She pretends to pout as she flops backward onto my bed.

"That's why they're so tight." I wiggle my foot around before I take a few tentative steps. I wobble a bit but it's mostly successful. Maybe by the time Jameson arrives, I won't look like a newborn colt in high heels.

"I figured you could break them in for me," she says with a wink.

Josie oversees my hair, opting to gather it in a high ponytail and loosening just the right amount of hair to wisp around my neck. She digs out a pair of simple gold hoop earrings. I grimace as she hands them to me. "It's not too much," she reprimands.

"Okay, okay." I put them in and turn to check myself out in the mirror. I have to admit that I look good even if Josie's glam touches feel a bit unnatural.

"Fit for the arm of the world's most eligible …" I shoot Josie a warning look before she can finish that statement, "…bachelor. You landed the whale, baby. Enjoy it."

. . .

JAMESON PICKS me up at home after my dad leaves. My heartbeat stutters like a scratched record when I glance out the front window and spot the black BMW idling in my driveway. When his face appears over the roof of the car, my stomach starts doing flips. This is why people write love songs. Maybe even why they listen to them. I'd never understood that before, but meeting him has opened my eyes to a world I'd turned my nose up to. Perhaps that's how he managed to sneak in under my radar.

I lock the front door and grip the handrail of our stoop as I brave the two steps. His eyes drift from my head to the expensive shoes on my feet. I blush a little as I brush past him.

"You can't argue with the name 'Duchess' now," he says to me before he shuts my door. I wait until he's in the driver's seat to ask why. "Because you look like a million dollars."

It's the oldest line in the book. Probably because it still works. I can't keep the goofy grin off my face.

"So," Jameson pauses as if he's struggling to get something out. "Do you trust me yet?"

I only have to consider for a moment. "Yes."

"Thank God because I wouldn't take you where we're headed if you didn't." I gulp at the underlying threat in his words. "I'm really sorry about this," he continues. "If there were any other way …"

"Maybe I should stay home," I say slowly.

"You probably should, but I want to spend the day with you." If he feels sorry there's no regret in his voice. Instead he casts a devious grin at me. I shiver under his wolfish gaze. I'm not used to how he makes me feel yet, and I don't think I ever want to be.

But the thought that I might not get to spend the day with

him makes me want to pout, but I reign in that impulse. "Look, if you have something better to do ..."

"No," he says, quickly. "But it is unfortunately something I can't get out of."

"Fine," I say before he can overthink our plans. "I'm in."

He doesn't wait for me to ask any more questions before he throws the car in reverse and speeds out of my neighborhood. "So where are we going?"

"To the airport."

"Are you supposed to leave the state?" I ask, before I consider an even more dangerous problem, "And I need to be back by curfew."

"We're not going anywhere," he says, tacking on, "this time." He takes the exit for the Las Vegas private airfield. We're cleared through security, and Jameson zooms toward this small outcrop of buildings that oversee the private runways high rollers use when they come to visit.

"My mom sends her jet here to pick me up for my summer trip." I tell him.

"What summer trip?" he asks in a strangled voice.

"I stay with her in Palm Springs over summer vacation." I don't miss how his knuckles tighten on the steering wheel as he processes this information. "I only go for a week."

The rigid tension in his shoulders doesn't dissipate. "Good to know. My mom's finally getting in. I don't trust a car service not to spill the details on her arrival. The last thing she needs to deal with is the press hounding her, so I need to pick her up and take her to our house on Mt. Charleston."

"I'm meeting your mom?"

"Is that a problem?"

It shouldn't be, but given the fragility of our connection, I hadn't expected to meet parents yet. Plus, we've known each other for a whole week. It's not like I'm buying bridal magazines, but I keep this to myself. If he wants me to meet his mom, it shouldn't be a big deal. "We just haven't had a real date yet."

"By my count, we've had several, Duchess." His mood lightens as he teases me, "But you say the word and I'll get us tickets to Blue Man Group."

I groan and bat him on the arm. "Don't you dare."

"Britney Spears?" he suggests.

"Getting colder."

"I hear Elton John might be coming to town." This time he's serious. He glances at me for approval, and I tap my nose and nod enthusiastically. "I'll look into tickets, but if we're not officially dating, then maybe I shouldn't be knocking on your bedroom window."

"That was a matter of survival. Neither of us were going to be able to fall asleep." At least that's how I sold that poor decision to myself. I bite my lip, remembering the dreamless peace I'd found thanks to his presence and the note waiting on my pillow in the morning.

"Sorry I had to sneak out like that," he says, as if he's reading my mind. "But I didn't want your dad to catch me."

"Probably smart," I agree. The shop has more than a few shotguns in its inventory.

"So are we officially dating or not?"

"Can I get back to you on that one?" I hedge. He doesn't say a word, but I see the muscle in his jaw twitch. A shadow descends over us as moody Jameson returns.

When the car is parked, he circles around to my side. As soon as I'm out, he grabs my hand tightly and leads me toward the edge of a runway. He doesn't speak as a small speck of a plane comes into view, barreling faster as it descends toward the strip in front of us. My hand is starting to hurt from his grip, but I don't dare remove it. As soon as the jet is on the ground, he yanks me forward.

Attendants rush over and open the door hovering nearby as a woman in a black wrap dress takes the steps. Her face is obscured by the brim of a large, black hat and a pair of oversized sunglasses. When she reaches the bottom, she takes off the glasses. Even from a few feet away, it's easy to see the red rimming her eyes. She's been crying, but when her gaze lands on Jameson, she lights up. Her arms stretch out and he drags us toward her. "Jamie!"

"Mom," he greets her in a thick voice.

"Oh, darling." She crushes him into a hug, but he doesn't release my hand. I clear my throat awkwardly after a few minutes not wanting to feel like a third wheel.

"Maybe I should give you two a moment," I begin, but Jameson cuts me off.

"That's not necessary."

"I'm so sorry." Mrs. West opens her purse and pulls out a handkerchief, dabbing at her nose. She forces a smile onto her face. "We haven't been introduced. I'm Evelyn West."

I open my mouth to give her my name, but Jameson jumps in. "This is my girlfriend, Mom. Emma Southerly."

I can almost swear I feel the tarmac vibrate as the bombshells hit. It takes a concerted effort to stay on my feet. Girlfriend?

"*Southerly?*" His mother repeats in surprise, but she instantly regains her composure. "It's lovely to meet you. I'm so glad you've been able to be here with my Jameson. I just couldn't leave my father in his condition."

"It's okay, Mom," Jameson promises her. He loops his free arm through hers and guides us both back toward the BMW. "I have everything under control here."

She tenses when he says this. But if she has an opinion on the situation, she keeps it to herself. Jameson opens the front passenger door and drops my hand to help me in, but I shake my head. "I'm fine back here." I get into the back seat before he can protest.

"That's very sweet of you," Mrs. West says.

On the way to Mt. Charleston, she peppers us with questions. How did we meet? How long have we known each other? Jameson manages to skillfully answer them all without giving anything away. Now doesn't seem like the best time to mention exactly what party it was we met at or that our relationship was founded on an alibi. When we arrive at the mountain chalet, he carries her bag inside and she takes my arm as we head into the house.

"I'll admit I was a bit surprised when I heard your last name." She chooses her words carefully, but I can hear the edge to them. "Does your father know you're seeing my son?"

I consider lying, but then I shake my head. "No."

"Word to the wise, tell him sooner rather than later. Parents hate finding out they're being lied to." Her tone is gentle and I see now where Jameson gets his softer side as well as his looks.

Her eyes are the same silvery blue as her son's and her aristocratic features are the feminine equivalent of his brutal beauty. She removes her hat and I see that her hair is light like her daughter's, nearly white at the temples.

"I believe you know my mother," I say, looking for a subject of conversation while we wait for Jameson to return.

"How is Vivian?" she asks.

"Remarried living in Palm Springs."

Evelyn frowns at this revelation. "Do you see her often?"

"I stay with her during the summer. We split holidays. It's all very scheduled."

"A daughter's time with her mother should never be scheduled." She perks up as Jameson enters the room. "Speaking of, where is my daughter?"

"Probably with her boyfriend," Jameson informs her. "She's been shacking up with him all week."

"Are you two fighting?" she guesses, not at all perturbed by his implications.

"Considering Monroe thinks I did it, you could say that." A chill creeps into his words and I feel the urge to go to him and reassure him, but I force myself to stay still.

"Your sister is confused. This was traumatic for her and she doesn't know what to believe."

"She seems pretty eager to believe the Belle Mère Police Department." His broad shoulders go rigid with pent up tension and shadows seem to fall over his face, making it impossible to read how he's feeling.

"I'll speak with her."

"Let me know how that goes," he says coldly.

"I'm afraid my daughter and I have a typical relationship. I remind myself she's a teenager," Evelyn says to me conversationally, before redirecting her words to her son. "And we're all under a lot of stress, so we need to remember to be kind to one another."

He inclines his head. "Of course." His Adam's Apple bobs as he swallows. "I had the staff stock the kitchen. The maid should arrive tomorrow, so until then—"

"I do not need a maid," she interrupts him. "I'm perfectly capable of picking up my own laundry and cooking my own meals."

"I simply want to reduce your stress level," he suggests gently.

She looks to me with an eyebrow raised. "I think my son just mothered me."

"He can be a little controlling," I sympathize with her.

"I hope you fight him on that."

"Oh, I do," I promise her.

Jameson stoops down to kiss his mother's cheek. "Before you two conspire against me further, I should get her home."

"Do you have to go?" Evelyn asks. "I could whip us up a little dinner."

Jameson locks eyes with me and I can see his desperation to leave. I don't understand it, but I can sense it.

"I need to cook for my dad," I explain to her. "But some other time."

"I'm holding you to that." Before I realize it's happening, she's hugging me. This is way outside of my comfort zone, but I accept it because she's grieving and because she's my boyfriend's mother and because holy crap, Jameson is my boyfriend.

Chapter 17

I'VE BYPASSED trust and gone straight to infatuation. My hand stays tightly knitted with Jameson's as he pulls into my driveway an hour later. Somehow he managed to steer and shift gears with the other as if he couldn't bare to relinquish his hold on me. Meanwhile, I'm still trying to wrap my head around the events of this afternoon. Apparently Jameson has made the decision about our relationship for me.

"I'm sorry that you had to spend the day stuck in the car."

But I shake my head at his apology. "It was nice to meet your mom."

"Said no girl ever."

"No, really," I say defensively. Meeting Evelyn West shines a light on the shadowy reputation of her family. After all the years hearing about the evil Nathaniel West I'm beginning to question which party was actually wrong.

"What was your dad like?" I ask Jameson. He flinches at the mention of his father, and I immediately regret bringing it up.

"This is taking a turn for the worse if you're asking about my dad. Is it too late to take you to a movie?"

"I'm used to much more exciting dates," I tease him.

"Then you admit this is a date." There's a note of triumph in his voice and the feeling is contagious. Even though I'm the loser it makes me feel like the winner.

"I'm told I'm your girlfriend. What's with the label, West?"

"If it was up to me I'd actually plaster it on your forehead, but I'll settle for getting to tell people you're mine." He lifts my hand to his mouth and brushes a kiss.

How am I supposed to fight that? Sighing, I tug my hand free from him and put on my serious face. No matter what's happening between us, there are things I need to understand. "The only things I know about your dad is what my dad has told me."

"I imagine that's not good," Jameson says. "Dad was complicated."

Do they make father's day cards for complicated dads? I could imagine them sitting in the slots next to the empty spot for absentee fathers. *Here's to another year of never knowing how or if I'll meet your approval. Happy Father's Day.*

"He had this tremendous vision," Jameson's voice takes on a wistful tone that I understand. My voice sounds the same when I talk about Becca—half wishful, half regret. "He could see things other people couldn't but he was blind to what was right in front of him."

"Which was?" I prompt in a soft voice.

"A wife who was way too forgiving and two kids who just wanted his attention." Anger streaks through his words.

Empathy forms a lump in my throat. It aches there while I blink back tears. I'm used to my own disappointment when it comes to my genetic donors but they're both still alive. There's a chance I'll be able to fix my relationship with my parents.

Jameson is going to have to live the rest of his life wondering what his dad really thought of him.

"Emma," he turns his silver eyes on me "Do you think I did it?"

"No." I reject the idea firmly. My lips form the shape of the word but no sound comes out. It's a truth that I feel deep within me. I don't need to speak it or claim it. I know he's innocent, because I've come to know his heart.

He clenches his eyes shut momentarily and when they open again they're flaming with a need that takes my breath away. Jameson reaches up and plucks the tie from my hair allowing my blonde locks to ripple down to my shoulders. His fingers rake through it gripping tightly as he smashes his lips against mine. There's a hunger in the kiss that I haven't completely felt since the night we met. It's been hiding in the background the whole time, but now we've unleashed it.

We fight closer. The kiss deepening as our tongues tangle greedily together searching for more. I want all of him no matter the consequences. My hand flattens on his hard chest. My heart jumps when I feel the speed with which his is racing.

He is my shouldn't.

My impossibility.

My can't.

And I'm not about to give him up.

When we break apart we pant for air pressing sweaty foreheads against one another. "I need to go," I say finally. "Dad will be home any minute."

"Maybe I should stay," he suggests.

"I think that kiss went to your head," I tell him.

"Emma, we can't avoid him forever."

"We can try." I trace an index finger along the curved lines of his abdomen. "We need a plan. Throwing this at him is the worst possible scenario."

He kisses my forehead and the sensation of his lips lingers there, making my head swim. "We'll discuss it tomorrow."

"You have a lot more things to worry about," I remind him. "Your mom is back now and—"

"I don't want to sneak around with you anymore," he stops me. His eyes sear into mine and the weight of what he's implying settles heavy on my chest.

How can I want to be with him and still be so afraid of the consequences? I lick my lips before I nod in agreement. "We can figure it out tomorrow."

I can still put the brakes on this before we make any stupid decisions like announcing our relationship to my dad. What's the rush to tell the world about?

"Do you have breakfast plans?" he asks pushing a strand of hair behind my ear. His fingertip grazes down my neck and it's all I can do to concentrate on what he's asking.

"Sleeping in. I'll probably get up for lunch."

"I like the idea of sleeping in."

I shake my head. "Sorry, my bed's invitation only tonight. The store is closed tomorrow. My Dad will be home all day."

Jameson leans forward slanting his head so that his lips hover over mine. "I really need to get a lock on your door, Duchess."

My core tightens at the thought of being alone with him in bed again. I haven't had time to go through my mental checklist but I'm pretty sure there are very few boxes left to mark. The pulse beating a war drum between my legs seems to agree with that assessment.

"Now get out of this car before I devour you," he threatens. His breath whispers over my lips before he pulls back and turns the engine on.

I practically stumble up the front walk and into the house. It's worse than drugs the effect he has on me but before I can turn my key in the lock, the door flies open. My dad glowers at me from the doorframe. His eyes flashing to the black BMW still idling in his driveway.

"Where the hell have you been?" he demands. The vodka on his breath nearly knocks me over and I move to shut the door but despite his condition he's too fast for me. He's on the front stoop before I can stop him.

"You get the hell out of here and stay away from my daughter," he screams. "I know who you are!"

"Dad!" I clutch his arm and try to drag him inside but he shakes me off so forcefully that I fall backwards. Jameson is out of the car in an instant. I shake it off and scramble into my feet to put a stop to this before it starts, but Dad reaches back and grabs a hold of my shoulder.

"What are you thinking?" he demands. "You can pack your bags. I've already spoken to your mother."

"I'm not going to Palm Springs," I shriek. I struggle to pull away from him but his grasp only tightens sinking into the soft flesh of my upper arm until tears smart my eyes. Jameson arrives and steps between us forcing him to release me. "You won't lay a finger on her."

"I am her father. I say who touches her and who gets the hell out of my house." He lists a bit as he directs his attention back to me. "Emma pack your bags. Your mother is sending the jet."

I step out from behind Jameson and regard him directly.

"No," I tell him hoping he can't see how hard my lower lip is trembling.

"I will not have another slut in this house. If you want to be your mom, you can live with her." He hurls the insult at me and it hits me square in the chest. After everything I've done for him, it takes so little to shatter my relationship with him forever.

"You won't speak about your daughter that way," Jameson sounds too calm as he continues to instruct my father regarding his unacceptable behavior.

"She's nothing to you." My dad turns his fury on Jameson pressing so close to him that their chests bump. "Don't let him fool you, Emma. The Wests should be studied by scientists. It's amazing how they can walk around without hearts."

"She is everything to me," Jameson interrupts him in a low voice. A thrill of fear ricochets through me as he reveals this.

I spot my dad's fist before Jameson does, and I jump in front of him in time to catch it in the stomach. The impact flattens me and I curl into a ball at their feet. Jameson drops to my side instantaneously.

"I need you to breathe, baby. I know it's hard," he says when I shake my head gasping for air that won't come. "Look at me. In and out." He demonstrates a slow breathing pattern and I suck at the air around me until I'm able to imitate it.

"Emma I'm so sorry." My dad tries to kneel down next to me. I see the tears on his cheeks but they mean nothing to me. Jameson shoves him away from me, knocking him onto his ass against the door.

"You don't deserve to look at her," he spits before he scoops me into his arms and carries me out the front door.

I tuck my body against his, willing myself to believe the reassuring words he whispers as he places me back in the passenger seat and buckles me up. I can't tear my eyes away from my childhood home. Dad stands in the doorway gripping it to stay upright. He looks defeated and small— and for the first time in my life I'm not sure I'll ever be able to forgive him.

Chapter 18

JAMESON DOESN'T PRESSURE me to talk as we head toward the lights of the city. I stare out the window, not processing the blur of life that we pass. Keeping my knees tucked against my chest, I try to ignore the tender ache in my belly. It's not really what's hurting me anyway. Dad didn't mean to hit me, but I can't erase the look of hatred on his face as his fist made impact. It was aimed at Jameson, but I felt his vehemence as acutely as I felt the punch. Without realizing what was happening, I'd started to see Jameson's problems as my own. If Dad hates him he might as well hate me as well.

I don't ask where we're going. I keep my mouth shut to hold back the sobs threatening to spill over. When we finally pull into the far valet circle in front of West Resort, I still can't bring myself to move.

He unbuckles my seat belt and patiently coaxes me into his lap. I curl into a ball that he doesn't try to loosen. Instead he strokes my hair and kisses my forehead. He doesn't offer me meaningless words of reassurance or excuses for what happened. He's simply there, and that's all I need.

When my eyes are finally dry he tips my chin up with one finger, gazes down at me. I understand the look I see shining behind his blue eyes even though I've never experienced the feeling before this moment. The sensation wraps around me and I sense it doing the same to him, binding us together. Our lives become inextricable in that moment. We're inseparable and unbreakable. I'll carry his pain as he carries mine, and in these strong arms bracketing my body, I'll find protection.

"Do you want to talk about it?" he prompts.

"No," I croak, my voice still raw with the tears. He doesn't push it. We both know it was an accident, but accidents aren't always easily forgiven.

Out the window it begins to rain, which is as rare a thing in Las Vegas as finding true love. Both have been known to happen, just not often. The raindrops beat an irregular pattern on the roof of the car and slide down the windows like tears.

"I think we're stuck here," I say, finding my voice once more.

"If I'm with you I could be stuck anywhere." He guides my mouth to his and kisses me softly, then he sighs. "I know you don't want to talk about it, but I do need to know if you're okay physically. Do I need to take you to a doctor?"

"I'm not made of glass," I huff, but he won't let me pull away. "Believe me, I know that Duchess. You're far more precious than that. Gold, maybe? But even gold can be broken."

"He didn't mean to do it." I have to face this sooner or later. I had known there would be consequences when my dad found out about Jameson. I hadn't anticipated they'd be physical. Or that he'd throw me out. "He's sending me to Palm Springs."

"Yeah, I caught that." Jameson buries his mouth in my hair and silence descends over us once more.

"Do you have a house in Palm Springs?"

"I could," he says, but the playful tone in his voice remains flat. We both know he can't leave. Not while there's an active investigation into his father's murder, and he's the primary suspect.

"Who else would want to kill your father?"

"What?" He blinks in surprise at our rapidly changing conversation. I don't have time to explain that we need to figure this out. "The people here are toxic. Our lives are toxic. We need to get out."

"But we can't," he reminds me. "Not while they're investigating me."

"Did they tell you to stay in the city?"

He nods. "You?"

I shake my head. "They only asked if I was planning to leave this summer."

"I knew they didn't suspect you." There's a finality to his tone that leaves me confused. His eyes drop down, and when he looks up they're full of regret. "Have you ever needed to tell someone something even though it might ruin everything?"

I suck in a breath. "That doesn't sound like a hypothetical question."

"It's not."

"Should I get back in my own seat for this?" I ask him.

"I'd rather keep my hands on you for as long as possible." Uh-oh. Whatever is about to come out of his mouth has the potential to change everything. "I was in the other room when they questioned you the day we found his body."

I nod. I'd seen him coming out as I got into the elevator. It didn't take a membership in MENSA to know why he'd been next door. "When they wanted me to corroborate your alibi?"

"Yes." He pauses before adding on, "and no. You have to understand, you were this mysterious girl who showed up and was lurking around the house. I liked you. I really did, but it would have been stupid of me not to mention you to the police."

"Wait. What are you saying?" I pry myself from his grasp, and even though there's very little wiggle room I pull away until the steering wheel digs into my shoulder blades.

"I told him just that. That I'd found a girl in my dad's study who wouldn't tell me her name, and that she'd stayed the whole night."

"How did you know I stayed?" I asked angrily. "Because you weren't with me."

"After I left you on the patio, I went to speak to my dad. We had words. He handled me leaving Stanford as well as you might expect. After that I found a bottle of whiskey and made a new friend for a couple of hours. Sometimes darkness overcomes me, Emma. It's not something I like about myself, but I can't deny it. I left you out there because I couldn't bear for you to see me like this. Then I saw you leaving with Jonas and Hugo, and I knew Monroe would be able to tell me who you were."

"You wanted to know who I was?" I ask, softening too much.

"I wanted to run after you but I stopped myself."

"Why?" I demand. The question covers so many unanswered things from that night.

"I'd been drinking for hours. I passed out with my head on the bar. It wasn't a proud moment for me."

"And then you found your dad." My stomach begins to churn as I relive the night with him. I don't like experiencing it through his eyes.

"Yes, and I didn't think. I tried to stop the bleeding and checked his pulse. Then I realized it was too late. Monroe found me like that: covered in his blood and drunk off my ass. She called the cops. All I can remember is her screaming 'what did you do?' over and over again. She couldn't hear a word I was saying. She still can't.

"So, when the police brought you in, I told them about the girl," he repeats himself. "I let them draw their own conclusions. You were my alibi."

"But I was also your primary suspect," I guess. Betrayal rips my heart in half, and my hand flies to my mouth to hold back a sob, but Jameson won't let me scramble away from him. He grabs me by the hips and holds me on his lap. "The day in the cemetery when I found you, you didn't trust me. You suspected I might have killed him. Am I right?"

I force myself to nod.

"But you didn't want that to be the case," he continues.

I nod again.

"That's exactly how I felt the whole time," he says. "I needed to find out if I could trust you. I needed to find out who you were. As soon as Monroe told me you were a Southerly, it was a strike against you."

"The feeling's mutual," I spit at him.

"Calm down, Duchess," he urges me, but I dodge his hand when he tries to stroke my cheek. "I stood there and listened to you talking to your sister in the graveyard, and I knew then that you could never hurt anyone."

"But you had to be sure, I guess."

"It sounds like you're familiar with the stakes."

"I am," I admit slowly. I want to be angry at him for suspecting me. This whole time he had been putting me to the test, but hadn't I been doing the same to him? It was a classic case of two wrongs don't make a right. Now we'd found ourselves at a crossroads.

"I had to know for sure, so I sought you out."

"You stalked me," I correct him.

"Fine, I stalked you, Duchess. You're incredibly stalk-able."

I choose to take that as a compliment.

"Then at some point it stopped being about looking for answers and it just became about spending time with you," he confesses.

As hard as I try to hold on to my anger I feel it slipping slowly away from me. It leaks from my blood until I feel nothing but exhaustion. Jameson waits, his eyebrows furrowed, as I stay silent.

"I get it," I say finally.

"Because you were doing the same to me?" he asks.

"Maybe," I hedge. What's the fun in showing all my cards at once? Except I know he's already seen them. He's seen right through me. I won't be getting any tricks past him. The good news is, he won't be getting any past me either.

"So where do we go from here?"

"I don't care," he murmurs. This time I let him take my hand. "As long as we go there together."

"I don't think they make co-ed prison cells," I say flatly.

"Touché, Duchess."

"Please tell me you have a really, really good lawyer." We can't keep avoiding this, or avoiding the practical discussions that need to happen. "Speaking of which, do I need a really, really good lawyer?"

"Believe me, Detective Mackey is not interested in you," he says. "She had a few words with me for dragging you into this. I think she's convinced I paid you to say we were together that night."

Despite the conflicting emotions swirling inside of me I take offense at this. Maneuvering myself in the seat, I straddle him and wrap my arms behind his neck. "Did she honestly suggest my boyfriend needs to pay someone off to spend the night with him?"

He smirks, allowing a glimpse of the arrogant boy I'd met

that night in his father's study. His hands circle my waist and press flat against the small of my back, drawing me closer to him.

My heart begins to pound along with a few other parts of me as our bodies press together, and without thinking I begin to rock against his groin seeking relief. "Maybe we should go inside, Duchess," he suggests, sweeping his lips lightly over my own.

"Too far," I whimper as I push the ache at my center against the rock hard bulge between my legs. His hands slide under my tank top to trail down my bare back.

"Tell me what you want," he groans, as I continue to rub myself against him.

"You."

"What about your checklist?"

"Fuck my checklist," I whisper into his ear, nipping it with my teeth.

"You're making it very hard to think clearly, Duchess."

"Then don't think," I urge him. "I just want to be someone else tonight," I say, recalling the words I spoke to him when we met.

"Carefree?" he offers, and I nod. "Believe me," he mutters with a frustrated groan, "I want nothing more than to strip you down and give you exactly what you're asking for, but I think that plan benefits from adding a bed to it."

"But the bed is so far," I moan, "and it's raining."

"And we're parked outside one of the busiest resorts in Las Vegas," he reminds me. But even as he speaks his hands tangle in my hair, drawing my lips to his once more. His body begins to move in unison with mine, meeting each push and grind of my hips with a thrust of his own. The denim of my jeans rasps against the sensitive spot begging for attention, and I begin to whimper.

"That's it, Duchess," he coaxes, his hands guiding my hips to move faster. "This is only a taste."

My muscles tense and I dig my fingernails into the back of his neck just as a rap at the window startles us apart.

"Um, Mister West?" The valet looks politely away as he calls through the window. "Can we park your car for you?"

I look around and I'm embarrassed to see a number of hotel guests clustered around the entrance, phones in hand.

"Yes," Jameson calls back. The valet opens the driver door and offers me a hand to help me extricate myself from my precarious situation. As soon as I'm around the car I take a bow, careful to make sure my middle finger is hidden in plain sight. Enjoy the photos.

"That's enough, Duchess." Jameson puts a hand on the small of my back. He keeps it there as we make a dash for the entrance, and under its comforting warmth, I don't even notice the rain.

Chapter 19

NO ONE'S prepared for rain in the desert. We're half-drowned by the time we're inside the lobby. Jameson catches me around the waist, and spins me behind a column.

"Let's finish the game we started the night we met," he suggests, nuzzling along my jawline. He trails upward, until his lips find my earlobe, but he doesn't kiss me. Instead, he catches the tender shell between his teeth. The nip is playful, but the ache that elicits inside me is very serious.

"Truth or dare," I moan, not caring that half of Vegas could be Snapchatting us right now.

"Truth," he murmurs. The heat of his breath whispers unspoken promises, but it can't distract me from the question I need answered.

"Why did you come looking for me that day in the graveyard?" I ask.

"That's what you want to know?" He seems surprised, but he doesn't pull away from me. Instead, he moves his mouth back up to my ear. "There are three reasons, Duchess. Two I will share, but the other, I'm keeping in my pocket."

Does he feel the need to keep me guessing, too? It's a twisted game we're caught in, neither of us sure what the other's intentions are, and it's made all the more dangerous, because we've put our hearts at stake. "I'll settle for two," I breathe.

"Because I wanted to see you," he admits. It's not the answer I expect. That day, of all days, he should have had more important things on his mind, but as his hands grip my hips, I push the troubling thought down where it can't distract me.

"You want a better explanation," he guesses. He pulls away, only far enough so that our eyes can meet. "I didn't plan to leave you there that night. I didn't plan any of this, and I suppose I wanted you to know that."

"And the other reason?"

"I wanted to convince myself you did it, but instead I think I fell for you."

"How did you know I was there? Did you follow me?"

"I went to your house," he says, "And then I saw you running. So yes, Emma, I did follow you. Does that upset you?"

I swallow and nod. I can't admit that his explanation is reasonable, because if whatever's happening between us is going to work, there has to be some boundaries. "I need to know I'm still my own person and that you respect that."

Given how it hurts when he steps away from me, I need to remind myself of that, too.

"I'm sorry." Sincerity shines in his silver-blue eyes. "I suppose now isn't the time to bring up the security detail I'd like to place on you."

I raise one eyebrow, sliding my palms up his chest, and then I push him away. "I'm starting to think everyone's right, and you are crazy."

"Does that make you insane by association?" he asks.

"Maybe." I close my eyes and let out an annoyed huff of air.

"You have a terrible habit of ruining perfectly good dates."

"So this is finally a date." His mouth twists into a haughty grin that screams I told you so.

"Don't look so self-congratulatory," I warn him, "Not when I just told you that you're a first-class date wrecker."

He reaches out and fiddles with the hem of my tank. "But you have to understand, I was told those weren't dates."

"So you weren't trying?"

"Oh, I've been trying since the minute I met you, Duchess. It's just nice to know that I might be succeeding." His knuckles graze against my stomach as he continues to play with my shirt. Even the hint of his touch blazes a trail of fire in its wake. I know two things, then. Jameson West can take me when he wants me, and two, I'm totally screwed.

"Come on." He urges me away from the pillar. It's strange to think about going back upstairs. The place where our relationship began is almost where it ended. There's no security guard waiting at the private elevator, and I flash a concerned look at him.

"So you want to put a security detail on me, but no one's watching the gates to the kingdom?"

"Don't worry, Duchess," he says as he presses the elevator button. "I've had four times as many security cameras installed in the last week. You can't blink here without security knowing about it."

"But why not have the extra muscle?"

He laughs at this. "For someone who looked very resistant to the idea of having a body guard, you seem awfully concerned about my safety."

"I can't stand the idea of someone doing you bodily harm." I run my fingers across the flat plane of his abdomen. Of the two of us, he's in much more danger than I am. At least that's what I want to tell myself, even as I ignore the real danger I face. How I feel about Jameson is morphing and evolving so rapidly that it's hard to wrap my head around, but the very fact that I've never felt this way about anyone before tells me all I need to know. Yes, I am in danger of losing my heart to him.

"Then you understand how I feel," he says huskily.

At least if I do lose my heart to him, I'll be getting one in return.

"Your turn," he prompts, as the elevator light signals its imminent arrival.

I look him squarely in the eyes as the doors slide open behind us. "Dare."

"God, I was hoping you'd say that, Duchess." His hand fists in my shirt, dragging me inside the compartment. "This elevator only goes up," he reminds me. "So the only button I need to worry about pushing is yours. But," he backs me into the mirrored wall, his hips pressing roughly against mine. "If I hit this button, we'll have two minutes alone in here before security responds."

I follow his gaze to the panel, where a stop button is located next to one marked panic. "So what's your dare, then?" I ask him.

"If I hit that button, you have to accept it." He shifts his groin harder against mine, so that I can feel the long, hard outline of his dick.

I want more than two minutes with that, but I'll take what I can get. "I said dare, didn't I? Wait, are there cameras in here?"

The wicked grin that splits his face is answer enough. "But doesn't that make it better?"

"Dare," I repeat.

He presses the button. The elevator screeches to a halt as his lips cover mine.

"I dare you to hold out" he breathes against them. I lose that dare on the spot.

"You only have two minutes," I taunt.

"With two minutes, I could get you there twice, but I think I'll take my time." I get the sense that isn't a boast, but my heart sinks a little at the thought of having to wait. I have absolutely no intention of holding out on this one. Our mouths crush together as he slants his head, deepening the kiss, allowing his tongue to capture my own. When we break apart a few seconds later, we're breathless, but I shake my head.

"You're a good kisser, but you're not that good, West."

"I think you want to lose, Duchess. Now I'm going to make you wait even longer." He bends his head, denying me his kiss, but only so that he can start the slow progress from my collarbone to the valley between my breasts. My eyes clamp shut, as my head falls back, knocking against the mirror. When I feel the heat of his mouth settling over the peaks, I open one eye, and watch as he slowly begins to suck it through the fabric of my tank and bra.

Seeing it is almost as amazing as actually feeling it. It might not be enough to get me there, but I'm not going to complain. After a few seconds, he switches to the other side, repeating the move until I've begun to whimper. Then he releases me, and it takes all my willpower not to grab his hair and shove him back where he belongs.

Jameson straightens up, and traces a finger along the bow of my upper lip. "I could get you off that way," he promises, "but I'm feeling very selfish tonight." His finger runs along my lower lip, down my chin, and neck, forging a line down, down, down, until his hand reaches the waistband of my jeans. With one practiced move, he unbuttons them.

"Pink panties," he says with approval. "God, you're going to kill me, Duchess."

In fact, I am going to kill him, if he doesn't finish what he started soon. I buck against the hand still gripping my jeans. He takes the hint, and his hand flattens against my lower belly. He slides it past the thin satin of my panties, stopping just before he reaches the promised land.

"Look at me," he commands. "Show me your green eyes, Duchess."

I bite my lip as I open my eyes, trying to stay still.

"Still determined to win?" His finger slips to the precise point of my desire and begins to rub slow circles around it.

I nod, but my breath hitches in my throat.

"Don't pass out," he warns me quickening the pace. He crushes his body against mine, trapping his hand in place. His hips begin to imitate the rhythm, adding an insurmountable amount of pressure. "Show me how pretty you look when I'm giving you what you need, Duchess."

The breath I've been holding releases in a throaty cry as I crack apart at the seams. My muscles spasm and I crumble into him. His mouth finds mine and he sucks his own pleasure from my lips. I have to press my thighs tightly together when he doesn't stop. Jameson takes the hint and withdraws his hand. He grabs my hip and kneads it as I come down from the amazing high of his touch.

"What happens when you lose a dare?" he asks.

I stare dreamily at him and smile. "I think you win the game."

Chapter 20

MY LEGS SHAKE as Jameson hits the button to restart the elevator. Best two minutes of my life. Judging from the pleased smirk on his face, he's happy about it, too. But when the elevator deposits us onto his private floor, we're greeted by the loud beat of bass. Jameson grabs my hand and drags me out, cursing under his breath. Given the shattering experience I just had, it takes more than a little effort to keep up with him, especially in heels.

"I cannot fucking believe this," he mutters as he leads me into the entertainment suite. It looks like a scene from last weekend: classmates passed out on the furniture, girls doing body shots on the bar, even Hugo waves from the couch.

Jameson turns to me. "I'm so sorry about this. Can you give me a minute?"

I nod but he's already abandoned me. I stand awkwardly in the midst of my drunk schoolmates. So much for the romantic evening of bliss I've been promised. This is like a bad Vietnam flashback.

"Pawn star!" Hugo calls to me. "Did you miss me?"

"Like I missed the stomach flu," I respond with a grimace.

Hugo ditches the girl hanging off of him and wanders closer. "I see you traded up but I suppose damaged goods can be bought at a reduced price."

"I'd advise you to shut the fuck up before Jameson hears you." I'm through with his insults.

His mocking attitude evaporates and he takes a menacing step closer. "You have to do more than screw yourself into this crowd. I thought you figured that out when I left you there after that night, but since you didn't let me make it clear. You don't get to speak to us like that."

"Why, because the Housers always win?" I ask.

"Because you're trash."

"Sticks and stones Hugo," I say with a sigh. "If you'll excuse me I feel the need to throw up now." I turn on my heel and walk away my hands balling into fists at my side. If today has taught me anything is that's violence isn't the answer, even if it would be very satisfying.

"He's going to see through you," Hugo calls after me. "Just like Jonas. Just like the rest of us."

I refuse to turn around and acknowledge the last comment even as it sticks in my back. Knowing something isn't true on a rational level doesn't always make it hurt less. I escort myself back to the entrance. The last time I walked around here unchaperoned bad things happened, but I'm not about to stand there and let Hugo hurl abuse at me. Crossing my arms over my chest I lean against the marble wall and wait for Jameson to return. After a few minutes I send him a text but I get no response.

I'm just about to head back into the chaos when the elevator slides open. Detective Mackey strides out, zeroing in on me. "Ms. Southerly."

I force a smile that's not fooling anyone.

"Are you here with Jameson West?" she asks.

I'm not sure how to answer that but it's not like I can hide the truth. "Yes."

"It sounds like there are quite a few people here with Jameson West." She cocks her head as if she's listening to the music. "We just got here," I rush to explain. It can't look good to be having a party on the one week anniversary of murder but I can tell from the calculated look on her face that she's not interested in my excuses.

"Where can we find him?" she asks me.

"What do you want with him?" I make a mental note to get the name of Jameson's lawyer and put it on my speed dial.

She pulls an envelope from her bag. "It's private business."

"I think he's with his sister," I say finally, "or at least he's looking for her."

"So then this is Monroe's idea of grieving?" Mackey guesses.

For no explicable reason I find myself growing defensive. "She's had a bit of a rough week."

"Emma." Mackey leans forward and lowers her voice to a conspiratorial whisper. "Don't try to excuse their behavior. Stay above it."

Is that what she thinks of me, that I'm above all of this? Jameson must have been right when he said she didn't suspect me but the fact does nothing to soothe me. The only way I can stay above this is with Jameson by my side doing the same, but he's not here.

"Excuse us," she waves on the officer waiting behind her. "We need to find your boyfriend."

I guess news travels fast. Then again with any luck the beginnings of our first sex tape have already made it onto YouTube. I slam my fist against the wall, remembering too late that it's marble. Clutching it, I groan. Then I hurry after her.

Whatever Jameson has to face tonight, he won't do it alone. I catch up with her just as she finds him arguing with Monroe.

"Excuse me, Mr. West. Perhaps we can speak somewhere privately," Detective Mackey interrupts. Both Wests fall silent immediately and stare at her.

Jameson's eyes dart to mine over her shoulder. "Take care of her?" he asks me, glancing toward Monroe.

"You did not just ask her to do that!" Monroe stomps into the other room either oblivious to the fact that her brother is probably going to be arrested or indifferent to it. Despite his request I follow behind them as he leads them into a hall away from the crowd.

"Jameson West, I'm here to arrest you for assault."

"Is that what we're calling it?" he asks in confusion. "That's a majorly reduced charge."

"We received report of the assault," she continues ignoring his interjection, "this evening."

"Wait," he stops her, "who's claiming I assaulted them?"

"Jake Southerly."

I gasp and heads swivel in my direction but Jameson's eyes warn me to stay silent.

"Did you miss me that much, Detective? We both know these charges won't stick."

"Be that as it may we have a nice jail cell waiting for you." She turns to the officer behind her and nods. He walks forward cuffs in hand and begins to read Jameson his Miranda rights.

"Please find Monroe," Jameson calls ignoring him completely. "Check on her, then take her phone and call my mom."

I want to defend him and tell Detective Mackey that Jameson was protecting me but from the look in his eyes I know he doesn't want me to do that. It takes everything I can muster to keep my mouth shut.

"Some date," he says to me as they haul him toward the elevator.

"Maybe next time we could just grab some dinner," I suggest. Before they can stop me I run over and kiss him full on the lips. The officer leading him out breaks us apart.

"That's quite enough!" Detective Mackey warns us. She studies me curiously as we all stand there and wait for the elevator to arrive. When it does, she lets the officer take Jameson inside.

"Just a moment," she tells him. Then she turns to me. "What does he have on you?"

"Nothing." I hate her for even suggesting that I can be bought.

"I thought you were a smarter girl than that." She leaves the proclamation hanging in the air before she disappears into the elevator.

The doors shut and I stand there listening to the throb of music coming from the other room.

"You couldn't have broken up the party while you were at it," I say to the elevator doors. Then I steel myself and head back inside.

Monroe is nowhere to be found. I navigate through the crowd, careful to avoid Hugo. Coming around the corner to the kitchen where I cooked for Jameson, I halt as two voices rise angrily. Tiptoeing to the wall I get as close as possible, trying to listen in without being seen.

"You have no idea what you saw!"

I peek around the corner and find Monroe and Leighton in a face off. Given Leighton's knock-off of the Wicked Bitch's wardrobe, right down to the mournful black from head to toe. Is imitation still the sincerest form of flattery?

"I would never say anything," Leighton starts.

"No, it's about how you're mistaken because you couldn't possibly have seen that."

"But I did," Leighton says.

God does the girl have any sense of self-preservation about her? Even from here I can see the anger practically vibrating off of Monroe. "I saw him that night with him. I saw what he did to him, and I just want you to know ..."

"No," Monroe cuts her off. "You saw nothing and if you can't remember that, then remember this: without me you're nothing. I can destroy you just as fast as I made you."

I flatten against the wall as Monroe turns and stalks back to the party. Leighton stands there for a moment before she does the same.

What the hell was that about? What had Leighton seen? Why was Monroe so intent on keeping her quiet?

The fragile strands of trust binding my heart to Jameson's begin to fray. There's only one thing that Leighton could have seen that would scare Monroe this badly, but if she did why hasn't she said anything? But I already know the answer. Because she's scared of what will happen to her. Earlier I decided that I trusted Jameson. Now I have to face the possibility that despite that, he still might not be innocent. He told me himself he was drinking. If he lost his temper, could I blame him for what had happened? Would it change how I felt about him?

I want to believe it couldn't but as the pit in my stomach grows, I force myself to face the fact that it might. Rushing back into the other room, I search for Leighton. I finally find her near the bar doing tequila shots. I suppose blacking out might be preferable to remembering tonight. She spots me and shakes her head dropping the lime she's sucking on to the counter.

"You should go," she suggests. "If Monroe sees you here she is going to lose her mind."

"Believe me she already knows I'm here." Grabbing Leighton by her thin wrist, I tuck her away from the cluster of people at the bar and over near the windows overlooking the patio. People brush past us and the noise offers us cover. "I overhead you talking to Monroe."

She pales and glances nervously around us. Meanwhile, I keep my back to the crowd. Hopefully if Monroe is circling, she won't spot us. "I don't really care what anyone here thinks of me but I do care what they're saying about my boyfriend."

"Your boyfriend?" she says in confusion. "Look, obviously I didn't see what I thought I saw."

I want to yank her bleached blonde locks at the root and shake her until she breaks like a piñata. "I heard you," I repeat. "I just need to know what you saw."

"Monroe was right," she says in a hurry. "It probably wasn't what I thought. I mean why would Jonas ..."

"Jonas?" I cut her off. "I thought we were talking about Jameson."

She blinks rapidly before she giggles. "Jameson? Why would I be talking about him?"

"Maybe because he just got arrested," I say.

"The Wests have more money than God." She rolls her eyes and flips her hair over her shoulder like she's auditioning for a Barbie commercial. "He'll be playing golf faster than O.J."

"O.J. sat in prison for nearly two years," I tell her. "So try again. What were you talking to Monroe about?"

"It has nothing to do with Jameson," she repeats. "I know he didn't kill his father, because..."

She breaks off smiling widely at someone over my shoulder. It's the last thing I see before I'm thrown forward. My mind tries to put together the pieces as I slam into her. A hand. My back. Glass shattering as we crash through it. I don't have time to think as we fall the few feet onto the concrete.

I've never put much stock in mistakes. Despite the last year of my life, I didn't want my past choices to define me. Now I know I'm doomed to pay for every decision I've made. This is the realization that crashes into me as I fight to stay awake.

Red coats the back of my eyelids as I drift between the real world and the dark. Lights flash, blinding me momentarily as I blink into the rain. It takes a moment for her to come into focus, but when she does everything about her is wrong. Her arms and legs are twisted in unnatural directions like a broken doll. Glass digs into my hands as I claw across the wet pavement toward her. My palm slips as it hits a warm and slippery substance pooling around her head. Her lips are turning blue, but there's a smile fixed on her face as her eyes stare into the starless midnight sky. She looks happy as if she's about to greet a friend.

I say her name, I shake her, and then, I scream. And scream. And scream.

Ready for another sinful installment?
1-click BEAUTIFUL SINNER, book 2 in the Sinners Saga trilogy now! Turn the page for a sneak peek.

Want to know when the next Sinners book releases? Text Geneva to 31996 or click her to be added to the list: https://slkt.io/63E4

If you loved this, you have to read my newsletter-first story sent twice a month only to subscribers! Become a VIP: http://www.genevalee.com/vip

Need another free read? If you loved Beautiful Sinner, you'll love the dark, sensual, and dangerous *New York Times* Bestselling Royals Saga, book one COMMAND ME is free for a limited time! *A glance, a kiss, and nothing would be the same...*

Join my Facebook reader group, Geneva Lee's Loves, for exclusive giveaways, sneak peeks, live videos and more.

Keep reading for a sneak peek of **BEAUTIFUL SINNER**!

———

A NOTE on the fridge stops me.

Getting a blow out. Back by 1!

I have the house to myself and I've wasted that time stalking some perv's idea of a good time. Sighing, I reach for the fridge door and freeze when I catch a figure reflected in the stainless steel. I spin around and blink a few times as if he might disappear. But he's still there leaning against the doorway. In my defense, he looks too good to be real, but then again, he always has. His wild coppery brown hair is longer than the last time I saw him, falling just over his ears. He rakes it back with one smooth, self-assured motion, but despite the smile playing at his lips, he doesn't greet me. Instead, we stand and stare at each other. Can he sense the line in the sand between us? We'd parted on good terms, at least as good of terms as one can when their boyfriend is being hauled off in handcuffs, but things got a little more complicated since then.

"I'm sorry," I blurt out. "I should have come to visit you."

Lightning flashes in his silver-blue eyes. Without a word, he straightens and strides towards me. Reaching out his hand, he cups the side of my face with his palm, and my eyes close involuntarily. Time didn't dull the electric connection of his touch. Jameson West caught me the first time we met. While we were apart, I questioned that, but now I know I'm gone hook, line, and sinker.

"Don't," he warns me. My eyes flicker open, and I see my questions reflected in his eyes. "Never apologize to me."

I start to pull away, but his hand shifts to grab my chin.

"I should have—" I begin.

"I don't care about any of that," he stops me. "When I heard what happened, I lost it. Are you okay?" He pulls back and grabs my hands, studying the fresh, pink scars marring my skin. "Not being able to come to you nearly drove me crazy."

Is that what happened to me? I wonder. Had being apart from him driven me to insane thoughts? It must have, because here in his presence, all my fears seems ridiculous. His touch erases my doubt, leaving only certainty behind. Whatever happened the night his father was murdered, Jameson isn't guilty of what they think he did. Looking into the depths of his blue eyes, I know he still has secrets, but who doesn't? I have to trust he'll share them with me when the time is right. There are a million things we need to discuss, but being so close to him that I can feel the heat roll off his body, none of them seem to matter.

"This is your home away from home, huh?" he asks, looking past me into the gourmet kitchen that's barely used. There's probably still plastic wrap on the appliances.

"My mother's, mostly. She never really took to Hollywood. It reminded her too much of Vegas." I can't help but wonder what he thinks of the place. My stepfather's sprawling, private estate stretches across the patchy desert, nestling into the foot of the mountains. Someone else might be impressed, but Jameson owns a casino and a mountain home and God knows what else. I really should take the time to Google his real estate holdings.

"Is she home now?"

"She had an appointment in town," I tell him.

He releases a heavy sigh I didn't know he was holding onto. "Thank God."

In one swift movement, his hands slide along my torso, lingering on my hips before they slide further down. Jameson lifts me off my feet and I instinctively wrap my legs around his waist. His face slants towards mine, but he hesitates a fraction of an inch before our lips meet. I can already taste the sweetness of his breath.

"Where's your room?" he murmurs.

It's hard to find words, given the promising situation I've found myself in. My tongue darts out to wet my lower lip, then I jerk my head backward. "Down that hall."

He doesn't need further information. Our mouths crash together as he carries me with the confidence of a man who's walked this corridor his whole life. I barely process him kicking open the door before he deposits me onto my bed.

"I hope I got the right one, Duchess," he says, "Because my patience just ran out."

My fingers clutch my familiar, yellow bedspread, and I nod.

"This is my room," I say softly. "There's a—"

He winks at me. "Give me the tour later."

I gawk as he reaches behind his neck and pulls his t-shirt over his head. Scientists could study the anatomical miracle that are his abs. Perfectly stacked and carved deeply, they narrow to showcase the top of a deep v that I assume continues past the jeans that hang temptingly off his hips. Thousands of tiny butterflies dance in my stomach as he lowers himself with torturous slowness over me.

"Is this okay?" he asks. I bob my head, not trusting my voice. "That is excellent news, because I spent a considerable amount of time imagining what I was going to do to this body."

"What if I'd said no?" I tease, finally finding my voice.

"Then I would have had to persuade you otherwise." His index finger traces across my lower lip, then trails down my chin, along my neck, and further until he pauses in the valley between my breasts.

"Think it would be that easy to convince me?" I breathe, despite the biological urge I have to pant and beg for more.

"I think I could have made you see my side, but I'd be happy to show you exactly how I would have done that."

"I already said yes," I murmur. This time, the smile that's been threatening to appear curves over his face. A strand of hair falls over his eyes and I reach up to push it back.

"That feels good, Duchess," he moans, and I rake my fingernails through his locks. "You've been in my head so long. Feeling you touch me is like waking up from a bad dream."

"I'm right here," I whisper, my voice thick with promise.

He drops lower, nestling his trim waist between my splayed legs. I can feel the rough denim of his jeans through my thin bikini bottom. I wiggle lower, trying to see what else I can discover, but his hands shoot out to keep me in place and I find myself pinned under a very, sexy push-up.

"I promised myself that when I got you in this position, I'd take my time," he says. He bends forward, pressing his lips to the curve of my jaw. "I've waited a long time for this, Duchess."

Ready to binge-read? **1-click BEAUTIFUL SINNER**

All that glitters...

BEAUTIFUL SINNER

Later

Lies are so easy to tell, and sins are so hard to forgive. It's odd how even something as simple as a coat of paint can be deceptive until viewed in the right light. I never knew what I preferred—a pretty lie or a sorry sinner—until now.

The room has been redone to have a sleek, modern appeal. Everything is white and minimal with clean lines and the most abstract of abstract art, but the stale scent of cigarette smoke still hangs in the room. It's proof that Vegas is a city out of time, or maybe just one unhinged from reality. If it weren't for the acrid smell assaulting my nostrils, the space might actually seem luxurious. No doubt the renovation had been a ploy to try to convince visitors the hotel is worth the hefty price tag.

Next month, I will have some serious explaining to do when my mom and Hans get my emergency credit card bill. But if this situation doesn't count as a crisis, nothing ever will.

I sit on the edge of the bed and wait with my hands folded in my lap. Being nervous is strange. Of course, I've never called a service before. Until a few days ago, my only contact with call girls had been my shoes on the fliers littering the streets.

Somehow it still feels inevitable. I'm in too deep not to follow the clues.

But *this* room, in *this* hotel, in *this* city could never hope to be more than a mirage. Because the one thing tourists never see is the truth. The bones of Las Vegas are rotten, weakened by greed and excess. Even in a fancy hotel room I can't see past that fact.

A knock on the door startles me, and I stand, smoothing my dress as if I need to impress her. When I open the door, I'm met by familiar, if surprised eyes. The shock mirrored in them quickly shifts to anger.

Stepping to the side, I hold out my arm. "Won't you come in?"

Chapter 1

"DON'T FORGET YOUR SUNSCREEN," Mom calls to me from across the patio. She eyes me watchfully from under the black brim of an oversized sun hat.

If only this were about sunscreen. I sigh and pick up the bottle of SPF 50 she sets out for me every morning. Slathering it on my legs, I'm careful to avoid the cuts that are still healing from *the incident*, as she calls it.

It's only 10 a.m., but I've already reapplied twice. That's Palm Springs for you. If you don't melt in the sun, your sunscreen will. In some ways, the desert city is a lot like Vegas, particularly when it comes to their heat indexes. But what had once been the exclusive playground to Hollywood is now more of a retirement community.

There isn't much to do here, which is why I like to visit. It's a break from the frenetic hustle of Las Vegas. But given the circumstances of my early exodus to my mother's house, she's been constantly hovering. It's like having a bodyguard without the perks of being a rock star. No sex, drugs, or rock-n-roll under her watch.

Lying back on the chaise, I shut my eyes tightly to the sun, which is creeping steadily toward the center of the sky. I can still feel its heat as its blazing light burns through my eyelids.

Palm Springs is my place to relax—at least it usually is. But Zen is in short supply these days. On the glass table next to me, my phone buzzes. I don't have to look at the message to know who it's from. There are only two people in the world who would bother to text me, and one of them used his one phone call weeks ago to reach someone else. I can't exactly blame him. After he was arrested for assaulting my father, the police had held him while they continued to investigate his father's murder. Without a law degree, I'm useless to Jameson West. It's been even harder to be supportive since my mother whisked me from the hospital straight to California. Between my absence and my paranoia that he might be a murderer, I'm a shoo-in for girlfriend of the year.

My dad didn't object to the rearrangement of custody, but he'd been avoiding me since our last father-daughter brawl. So I know the text is from neither of them, which only leaves Josie. Pushing myself up, I catch the strings of my bikini top and tie it tightly around my neck. I grab my sunglasses and my phone, but as soon as my feet hit the searing heat of the cement, Mom's face appears from under her hat.

"Drink some water," she advises.

"I will," I promise, forcing myself not to sound too sarcastic. If she doesn't ease up, I'll make good on that promise by drowning myself. The weight of the water would be a lot less oppressive than her nagging.

She's scared, a small voice in my head reminds me.

That makes two of us, another retorts.

Great. Now my inner monologues are fighting, too.

I pause near the sliding glass doors and for a second, the sound of shattering glass and the sharp sting of shards piercing through skin overtakes me. The memory overrides the present until I shake it off.

"Everything okay, Emma?" Mom asks.

I swallow before I nod. "Everything is fine, but I wanted to talk to you about something."

She abandons Oprah's latest book club pick and turns to face me. "Yes?"

"It's just...I promised Dad that I would be around this summer..." I begin, leaving out that I no longer feel obliged to keep that promise—not after I'd been the unintended recipient of his fist. I self-consciously stroke the yellow remnants of the bruise he'd given me. He might have been aiming for Jameson, but he got me. Conveniently for him, no one questioned where the injury on my stomach came from after the accident that night. "So I think I need to head back to Belle Mère."

Her lips purse as if my words taste funny, and she shakes her head slowly. "I don't think that's a good idea. With everything going on there—"

"That's exactly why I need to go back," I interrupt. She had to know this was coming. I've never stayed at her resort in Palm Springs longer than two weeks. As of today, I've been here almost a month. "I've been here a lot longer than usual."

"And you spent the first week on narcotics," she reminds me.

"I'm fine now." I cross my tan arms over my chest, my golden skin serving as further proof that I've spent enough time lounging poolside.

"And you haven't outstayed your welcome," she says as if that's the reason I'd feel obliged to go.

"Look, Josie needs me. The shop needs me—" I stop myself before I add Jameson to that list. Mom doesn't need to know that he is also pulling me home, not after what happened at his house. Honestly, I'm not even certain he wants me to return to Belle Mère.

And my Mom may not want to admit it, but the strange events plaguing my small community concern her. It doesn't take a degree in psychology to know she's choosing to avoid the reality of the situation.

She pulls off her hat and wipes sweat from her damp forehead, then turns the full intensity of her gaze on me. Meeting her cold, emerald eyes is like staring into a mirror. "Hans and I have been talking. We think it would be best if you transfer here for your senior year."

"Here?" I ask in disbelief. "What happened to 'I need to worry about college'? Does Palm Springs even have—"

"Here as in California. There are plenty of options in Los Angeles," she stops me.

"Los Angeles?" I explode. "No way. You might not like it, but I have a life back in Belle Mère."

"A life you almost lost," she says flatly.

"It was an accident," I remind her, even as a shiver ripples up my spine. I'd been too freaked out to tell her the truth, so I'd gone along with the story that Monroe West had concocted about that night. Leighton had been drunk, and when she stumbled, she took me with her, falling through a plate-glass window a few feet to the patio below. I'm certain it was easier to buy off the cops to overlook the underage drinking and partying than it would've been to undermine an investigation into something more sinister. No one has questioned the story, even though Leighton is still in a coma.

But I can't deny the truth to myself: we'd been pushed. Mom didn't know that. Theoretically, Monroe didn't either, even though she'd conveniently fed a story to the paramedics.

"Accidents aren't always innocent," Mom says. The shiver running through me turns into a full chill that settles deeply in my bones. She isn't talking about me and what happened at the West penthouse. She's talking about Becca.

"I'm going to be fine," I promise her softly. I only hope I can make good on that claim.

"We'll talk about this later." She picks her book back up and returns her attention to the dog-eared page. I've been dismissed, but I'm not free to go.

"WHEN ARE YOU COMING HOME?" Josie asks as soon as FaceTime connects. Half of her head is covered in Bantu knots while the rest of her hair is recklessly curly. Josie, like her hair, is a study in contrasts. Both prim and responsible with a wild streak that carves a bigger path through her personality with each passing year. I plop onto my bed with my computer.

"Hello to you, too." The glare of afternoon sun makes it hard to see the screen, so I shimmy toward the headboard.

"It's a serious question, Em. I need you to come home. I need your help."

Her panic raises my eyebrows. Josie Deckard doesn't *need* anything—at least not from me. She could use a little validation or maybe a call from her absentee father, but she certainly isn't the type to ask for help.

"What's going on?" If she isn't having a melodramatic moment, I might be forced to make good on the threat I made to my mom to leave Palm Springs sooner rather than later.

"There's just a lot of stuff going on," she says. "Leighton is still in the coma, and they've hauled in half of Belle Mère for questioning in the West murder."

"At least they're still looking for suspects," I interject. It doesn't take an advanced degree in forensics and criminology to see that the FBI has already pinned Nathaniel West's murder on his son. It isn't something I want to consider, because I need to believe that Jameson West is innocent. I told him I believed he was, and I did believe it at the time. Also, because he's my boyfriend. Or was my boyfriend. I'm not entirely sure about that now. I rub absently at the still healing cuts covering my forearm. Jameson couldn't have been the one to push Leighton and me through that window, which helps his case with me. If someone wanted to shut us up that badly, they were probably hiding something. However, I'd never gotten the full story from Leighton about who she was protecting. I'd overheard her telling Monroe that she wouldn't tell anyone about *him*. I assumed she was talking about Jameson, but the only thing she managed to tell me was that she was protecting Jonas. Then someone shoved both of us through a plate-glass window. No one can claim the Wests don't throw killer parties.

"It's more than that," Josie interrupts my thoughts. "Do you have your phone?"

I hold it up, and she breathes a heavy sigh that is definitely not one of relief.

"I sent you a message on Instagram," she says.

"Snap a pic of your lunch to share with me? Did you pin some bikini-ready, summer workouts, too?" I ask dryly as I slide past the lock screen on my phone.

In my Instagram messages, I find her note. Clinking on the link she sent, I'm taken to an account I've never seen before. But even though I don't recognize the username—TheDealer—the photos are full of people I know.

"Check out the fifth one down," Josie says in a quiet voice. My eyes flicker back to the computer screen, only to find her own eyes clenched shut. When I reach the photo, it takes a moment for me to see past the blurriness of the picture. It had clearly been taken from some distance. Someone else might not recognize the girl with the wild mop of curls and the petite figure, but I know my best friend when I see her. I don't know the man she's with, though.

"What is this?" I ask in confusion.

"That's Tom," she says. "Or maybe Aaron, I don't remember. It's not important."

"It's important enough that you called me freaking out in the middle of the afternoon to beg me to come home. Who is this guy, Josie?"

"Who do you think?" she asks in measured syllables.

"Oh." Realization dawns on me. Despite how often she ditches me to hook up with random men, I haven't seen her in action until now. "Did you and he ..."

I suddenly wish that I was playing *Madlibs*, so I could finish that sentence with something innocent or benign. *Did you and he save a kitten? Did you and he play miniature golf?* Instead, my mind fills in the blank with visions of rendezvouses that would make E. L. James blush.

"Yes," she answers pointedly, putting me out of my misery.

"How did someone take a picture?" I ask. While Josie might be working through a daddy complex, she's not stupid. A stream of selfies will destroy her life as much as it will this man's. She doesn't take pics of her hook-ups, and she doesn't allow them to either.

"Look closer," she whispers. I scroll through the feed and realize it isn't your typical narcissistic teen feed. No selfies. No documenting every minute detail of a single day. All the pictures on this account are of *other* people—other people we know. Each one is an odd mix of photojournalism and surveillance camera.

"Do you know who took these?" I ask her.

I can't stop looking. It's almost addictive, and I catch myself wondering if I'll make an appearance. The photos are captioned with initials and a location, but nothing else.

"My mom is going to kill me," Josie moans, ignoring my question.

"How is she even going to see these? Your mom's not really social media savvy."

I don't admit that I understand what has her so freaked out. Just the existence of that photo reveals a side of Josie that she keeps under wraps. If this whole feed is full of photos of our Belle Mère cohorts, more than a few people might have already seen it.

"Where did you even find out about this?" I try a different tactic to get the information out of her.

"The account followed me," she says. She pauses as if struggling with whether or not to tell me the next bit. "They're following Monroe, Hugo, and Jameson, too."

"Jameson," I repeat. My heart sinks into my stomach. What photos of him might be on display?

"Are you talking to him yet?" Josie asks.

I shake my head, relieved that there's something more pressing to focus on. "So they're following all of you, but that doesn't mean—"

"Emma," Josie interrupts me. "They're following your account, too."

I put my phone on the desk uncertain I want to unearth my own incriminating moments captured with someone else's camera. "Why would someone do this?"

"To ruin my life," Josie informs me immediately. She's put some thought into this, obviously.

"It's only a photo—" I begin, but she cuts me off.

"That's easy for you to say," Josie shrieks. "If my mom sees these pictures, I'll be enrolled in the Bellevue Girls Academy for the summer session with no parole in sight."

"This isn't *Hamlet*," I stop her, wishing I had a few hundred Xanax on hand. Josie is clearly on the verge of a nervous breakdown while I've been avoiding reality in Palm Springs. "Your mom's not going to send you to a nunnery."

Josie falls backward, disappearing from sight momentarily. The screen goes black, and I squash the panic that rises in my chest. Then she blurs back into focus. I spot her familiar polka dot comforter, and a pillow clutched to her chest. When she finally speaks, her voice is small. "You only see the nice side of my mother."

"At least your mother has a nice side," I grumble. "My mom went nuclear when I told her I was thinking about leaving Palm Springs. It's going to take some serious ego massaging to calm her down if I go." I leave out that she wants me to stay in California permanently. Right now isn't the time to deliver more bad news.

"Look," Josie continues, drawing my attention back to her problem. "My mom is cool, but she obsesses over making sure I have a better life than she had."

"I'm pretty sure that's all parents," I point out. Even though my own have a warped sense of what that actually means, I know their hearts are generally in the right place.

"Let me translate that a little bit better. She's obsessed with me not getting pregnant."

"Can you blame her?" I ask.

She shakes her head and for a moment the screen is filled with her wild, uncontrollable curls. "No, I can't, and that's the problem. I mean, she was only nineteen when I was born, and it seriously set back her dancing career."

"Does she know that you're..." I trail away, glancing out the window to the placid surface of the pool outside. There's no easy way to ask this, because, in truth, even I don't know the answer. When Josie started targeting older guys, I tried to let it roll off my back until she slept with one of our teachers. After that, I asked her to keep the pornographic details to herself. It's easier to take a calculus test if you don't have your best friend's impression of Mr. Barrett's O-face stuck in your head.

"Does she what?" Josie prompts.

"Does she know you've had sex?" The question rushes out of my mouth.

"The list of topics that are off-limits between my mother and I is long and exhaustive, but sex is at the very top of it." Josie presses her fuchsia lips into a thin line, grimacing at the thought. "I'd already be in a *nunnery*, as you put it, if she knew. I mean, I hide my pills in an Altoids tin."

"I guess that answers that question." A million questions tumble through my head. How many men has she had sex with? Why? Is she using condoms? Getting tested? Somehow I manage to swallow them all.

"Does your mom know about you?" Josie asks even though she knows that my sexual rap sheet only has one entry. I was completely honest with her about my first—and only—time. Not that there was much to tell.

"I didn't feel the need to clue her in on my lackluster first time, especially since I pretty much pretend it never happened," I remind her. Sleeping with Hugo Roth had been a knee-jerk reaction to a terrible situation. I mean, what better way to get back at your cheating boyfriend for having sex in front of half your freshman class than to screw his best friend? I won't be putting that proud achievement on any college applications.

"I don't think my mom would welcome any of the men I've been with in this house."

"Probably not, since they're as old as her boyfriend," I remind her.

Josie smacks her forehead. "Oh, I forgot to tell you. They broke up last week. Men suck."

"How's your mom?" I ask, genuinely concerned.

"She cried for a day. Then she put on some lipstick and met someone new." Josie shrugs but her words are tinged with cynicism. Like mother, like daughter. The Deckards employ a nonchalant attitude toward the "love 'em and leave 'em" philosophy followed by most men in Vegas. The ones who live there full time generally aren't prime cuts of male. Not the single ones, anyway. And the rest of them are tourists whose presence is as fleeting as their luck.

I pick up my phone and stare at the Instagram feed again. It's definitely her, and while whoever's blessed us with this account only identified her by her initials, it hardly feels anonymous. I scroll through the handful of other photos that have been posted. Hugo Roth practically dragging an unconscious girl down the hall. Monroe West, peeking guiltily over a pair of black sunglasses like she knew she was being watched. There's nothing outright incriminating in any of the photos. It's simply the suggestion contained in each one. It wouldn't take a nut job to weave conspiracies in all these pictures. It's clear that's what The Dealer wants his audience to consider. Or her audience, I guess. There's no sexism in stalking.

"Who do you think took these?" I ask.

"If I knew, I'd already have strangled them and stolen their phone," Josie admits.

I study the picture of her for a few more seconds, this time zeroing in on Josie's dress.

"Wait." My mouth goes dry, and I lick my lips. "This is the dress you were wearing the night of…"

But it seems she's already realized that because she gulps and nods. Thumbing back through I find the picture of Hugo with the blonde draped over his shoulder. I can only make out part of his shirt. A *D* and two *E*'s.

"STD Free," I mutter to myself as I picture the shirt Hugo wore that night. I'd called it false advertising. Staring at this picture, I stand by that claim. *Conscience-free* would have been a lot more fitting.

"What?" Josie asks in confusion.

"Nothing. It's not important." There's no need to fill her in on the details. "This picture is from that night, too. Why would someone be posting pictures from the night Nathaniel West was murdered?"

I glance up from the phone just as Josie's eyes zero in on me through the screen.

"I have a better question for you," she says. "How many more pictures did they take?"

Chapter 2

AN HOUR LATER, I finally pry myself away from the feed and head into the kitchen. All the paranoia is making me hungry. But a note on the fridge stops me.

Getting a blow out. Back by 1!

I have the house to myself and I've wasted that time stalking some perv's idea of a good time. Sighing, I reach for the fridge door and freeze when I catch a figure reflected in the stainless steel. I spin around and blink a few times as if he might disappear. But he's still there leaning against the doorway. In my defense, he looks too good to be real, but then again, he always has. His wild coppery brown hair is longer than the last time I saw him, falling just over his ears. He rakes it back with one smooth, self-assured motion, but despite the smile playing at his lips, he doesn't greet me. Instead, we stand and stare at each other. Can he sense the line in the sand between us? We'd parted on good terms, at least as good of terms as one can when their boyfriend is being hauled off in handcuffs, but things got a little more complicated since then.

"I'm sorry," I blurt out. "I should have come to visit you."

Lightning flashes in his silver-blue eyes. Without a word, he straightens and strides towards me. Reaching out his hand, he cups the side of my face with his palm, and my eyes close involuntarily. Time didn't dull the electric connection of his touch. Jameson West caught me the first time we met. While we were apart, I questioned that, but now I know I'm gone hook, line, and sinker.

"Don't," he warns me. My eyes flicker open, and I see my questions reflected in his eyes. "Never apologize to me."

I start to pull away, but his hand shifts to grab my chin.

"I should have—" I begin.

"I don't care about any of that," he stops me. "When I heard what happened, I lost it. Are you okay?" He pulls back and grabs my hands, studying the fresh, pink scars marring my skin. "Not being able to come to you nearly drove me crazy."

Is that what happened to me? I wonder. Had being apart from him driven me to insane thoughts? It must have, because here in his presence, all my fears seems ridiculous. His touch erases my doubt, leaving only certainty behind. Whatever happened the night his father was murdered, Jameson isn't guilty of what they think he did. Looking into the depths of his blue eyes, I know he still has secrets, but who doesn't? I have to trust he'll share them with me when the time is right. There are a million things we need to discuss, but being so close to him that I can feel the heat roll off his body, none of them seem to matter.

"This is your home away from home, huh?" he asks, looking past me into the gourmet kitchen that's barely used. There's probably still plastic wrap on the appliances.

"My mother's, mostly. She never really took to Hollywood. It reminded her too much of Vegas." I can't help but wonder what he thinks of the place. My stepfather's sprawling, private estate stretches across the patchy desert, nestling into the foot of the mountains. Someone else might be impressed, but Jameson owns a casino and a mountain home and God knows what else. I really should take the time to Google his real estate holdings.

"Is she home now?"

"She had an appointment in town," I tell him.

He releases a heavy sigh I didn't know he was holding onto. "Thank God."

In one swift movement, his hands slide along my torso, lingering on my hips before they slide further down. Jameson lifts me off my feet and I instinctively wrap my legs around his waist. His face slants towards mine, but he hesitates a fraction of an inch before our lips meet. I can already taste the sweetness of his breath.

"Where's your room?" he murmurs.

It's hard to find words, given the promising situation I've found myself in. My tongue darts out to wet my lower lip, then I jerk my head backward. "Down that hall."

He doesn't need further information. Our mouths crash together as he carries me with the confidence of a man who's walked this corridor his whole life. I barely process him kicking open the door before he deposits me onto my bed.

"I hope I got the right one, Duchess," he says, "Because my patience just ran out."

My fingers clutch my familiar, yellow bedspread, and I nod.

"This is my room," I say softly. "There's a—"

He winks at me. "Give me the tour later."

I gawk as he reaches behind his neck and pulls his t-shirt over his head. Scientists could study the anatomical miracle that are his abs. Perfectly stacked and carved deeply, they narrow to showcase the top of a deep v that I assume continues past the jeans that hang temptingly off his hips. Thousands of tiny butterflies dance in my stomach as he lowers himself with torturous slowness over me.

"Is this okay?" he asks. I bob my head, not trusting my voice. "That is excellent news, because I spent a considerable amount of time imagining what I was going to do to this body."

"What if I'd said no?" I tease, finally finding my voice.

"Then I would have had to persuade you otherwise." His index finger traces across my lower lip, then trails down my chin, along my neck, and further until he pauses in the valley between my breasts.

"Think it would be that easy to convince me?" I breathe, despite the biological urge I have to pant and beg for more.

"I think I could have made you see my side, but I'd be happy to show you exactly how I would have done that."

"I already said yes," I murmur. This time, the smile that's been threatening to appear curves over his face. A strand of hair falls over his eyes and I reach up to push it back.

"That feels good, Duchess," he moans, and I rake my fingernails through his locks. "You've been in my head so long. Feeling you touch me is like waking up from a bad dream."

"I'm right here," I whisper, my voice thick with promise.

He drops lower, nestling his trim waist between my splayed legs. I can feel the rough denim of his jeans through my thin bikini bottom. I wiggle lower, trying to see what else I can discover, but his hands shoot out to keep me in place and I find myself pinned under a very, sexy push-up.

"I promised myself that when I got you in this position, I'd take my time," he says. He bends forward, pressing his lips to the curve of my jaw. "I've waited a long time for this, Duchess."

"Then why are you stopping now?" An impatient hunger blooms within me, and I struggle against the hold he has on my wrists. He laughs softly before he releases them.

"I'm waiting, because I'm not in a hurry. I'm going to make

you feel things you've never felt before. I'm going to strip away all the distance time has placed between us, and when I'm done, there will be no doubt that you belong to me," he raises his head and gazes down at me, "if that's okay."

"I guess." I roll my eyes a little at the ridiculousness of that question. My body's been screaming *yes* this whole time. He hardly needs to ask now.

"Where should I start? Your lips?" he muses. He brushes his own over mine, drawing the attention of my nerves upward, if only momentarily.

I moan my approval.

"Or maybe here." He runs his mouth slowly down my neck, settling in the hollow of my collarbone. A slight gasp escapes me, and I grip the comforter tighter. "See? We're just getting started."

It takes all my self-control not to throw my arms around his neck and pull him against me. I'm not entirely sure what stops me, except maybe the fact that I still feel guilty that he's been sitting in a jail cell, or maybe curiosity. I want to see what he can do to me as much as he wants to show me, but before that can happen, I hear the front door slam.

"Shit!" I yelp, pushing him off me. He lands with a thump on the floor. "Put your shirt on."

He reappears not bothering to hide his amusement as he plucks the t-shirt from the floor and tugs it overhead.

"Emma?" Mom's voice echoes through the large open foyer. I glance towards Jameson and brace myself.

"I'm in my room," I call. Standing, I smooth out the bedspread and point to a desk chair. I grab a pair of jeans and a tank top to throw over my bikini.

"You: there," I command in a low voice. He salutes me with his index finger and promptly takes his assigned seat, assuming a saintly position.

"Emma, I was thinking that we should..." The words die on her lips when she steps inside my bedroom. "Um, hello."

Jameson nods in greeting. "It's nice to meet you, Mrs. Von Essen."

She stares at him for a moment longer, frozen in place, then she shakes her head as if to clear it. She smiles warmly. "Vivian."

"Vivian," he repeats, but whatever spell Jameson has cast over her doesn't extend to protect me. Turning in my direction, she shoots me a questioning look.

"Mom," I brace myself for what I'm about to tell her, "This is Jameson West."

"Ah. The famous Mr. West." Her voice piques on his name. She doesn't hold the same animosity toward the Wests that her ex-husband, my father, does, but she's not welcoming him into the family either.

"I'm afraid my reputation does precede me." He stands and extends his hand.

"I've heard a lot about you," she says as she shakes it. I flinch, because if that's true, she hasn't been hearing it from me.

"Mom," I say in warning.

"I have," she says with a shrug.

"Yes." Jameson's eyes dart to mine. "I believe your husband is currently in negotiations with Paramount to do a film based on my father."

"I don't know much about that." It's an obvious lie, but one that most would willingly swallow. If she knows about it, she's kept it from me. Probably to keep the peace this summer.

"Perhaps I'll discuss it with him, then. I'd like to know more." The tension in the room has a greenish tinge that threatens to suffocate each of us, but my mother is oblivious.

"I'm sure he would enjoy that. He has quite a few questions about what happened."

"Don't we all?" Jameson tilts his head. "Maybe he can tell me how the story ends."

Now that our bodies are separated, I can think a little more clearly, which means questions are racing through my head. Apparently, I'm not the only one still trying to figure out what happened. If Jameson doesn't know, the FBI doesn't either. So how did he get out of police custody?

"I didn't know you would be visiting us." Mom walks to the side of the bed and picks up a pillow that's fallen to the floor, no doubt cataloging every wrinkle in my bedspread to use when she interrogates me about him later.

"I wanted to surprise Emma."

"And you did," I jump in. "Maybe we should check out downtown. There's…"

"Will you be staying long?" Mom interjects. Somehow, I've found myself in the middle of a socialite standoff. The weapon of choice? Who can be more polite to the other while slowing bleeding them dry.

"Only as long as it takes to convince Emma to come home."

"And why would she want to do that?" This time she doesn't bother to sugar coat her words.

"Because that's where she belongs."

"In Belle Mère?" Mom asks.

"With me," Jameson corrects.

I step forward, wedging myself between them. "I'm going to take Jameson downtown."

"You'll have to bring him back for dinner," she says, not bothering to tear her eyes away from him.

"Sure," I agree. Grabbing Jameson's hand, I drag him out of the room and toward the front door.

"Your mother is…"

"A piece of work?" I offer. I come to a stop when I spot the white Porsche Carrera with its top down, parked in the circle drive. "Is that yours?"

He grins at me, and this time he's the one leading me away from the house and toward the car.

"If your mom saw my car, she knew she had company," he says. There's an undercurrent of annoyance in his voice.

I wave my hand. "She probably thought it was a spare Porsche that Hans keeps around. I mean, who would notice this?"

"Get in, Duchess," he says, swinging open the door. As I climb into the seat, he bends over and kisses me full on the lips. He circles around the back, and I realize there's so much I have to tell him about what happened that night, about what I heard, and more than anything, he needs to know about the Instagram account before his picture pops up on it.

"Jameson, there are things you need to know," I begin.

He hits the ignition switch. "We'll get to that. First, there's something I need to tell you."

Before I can protest his trumping of my news, he twists in his seat to face me. "They haven't dropped the charges against me."

"Then why are you here?" I ask. "This is a different state." I look around as if police helicopters and a SWAT team might appear over the mountains.

"Don't worry about that."

"Don't worry about that?" I shriek. "Are you out on bail?"

"I am," he confirms coolly.

"Then why did you come here? They just released you."

"To bring you home," he says.

"I want to come back," I tell him, "but maybe my mom is right. Maybe distance is the best thing right now."

"You won't have distance for very long." A cloud passes over the sun as he speaks, momentarily casting us in shadow.

"What does that mean?" I demand.

"They're questioning your alibi."

"My alibi? Don't you mean *your* alibi?"

"*Our* alibi. Emma, they're building a case against both of us."

"Case?" I repeat in confusion. The reality of what he's telling me refuses to sink in or maybe I'm not allowing it to.

"They want to charge us both with my father's murder," he clarifies. Reaching out, he takes my hand. "But I'm not going to let that happen."

"What are we going to do?" I breathe.

Dropping my hand, he takes a pair of silver aviators from the console and slides them on. Then he leans over, bringing his lips to my neck. He drops a soft kiss and a moment later I feel the seat belt snake over my shoulder. "Buckle up, Duchess."

Chapter 3

I SHOULD BE surprised when Jameson pulls into the driveway of a mid-century, mini-mansion—the kind Palm Springs is famous for. I stare him down expectantly, as he waits for the privacy gate to open.

"It's not mine," he assures me.

"Good, because you don't have to buy real estate in every city you visit."

"Believe me, if I was going to buy a house here, Duchess, it'd be next door to you." He pushes his sunglasses down the bridge of his nose and winks at me. "Easier to sneak through your window that way."

And into my panties. "If you can get past Hans' security, go for it, otherwise I suggest walking in through the front door."

He laughs as he hits the gas and speeds into the driveway. Apparently, the Porsche doesn't do slow. The grounds of the house are as immaculate as the lines characteristic of the time period—sharp and neatly edged. Large, orange blooms cascade over the retaining wall that surrounds the house. It's smaller than my stepfather's place but it gives off a retro-hip vibe that I can't help but admire.

"So whose place is this anyway?" I ask as I climb out of the car. Jameson is at my side instantly, shutting the door behind me.

"A friend's," he says like this is an answer before he throws his arm around my shoulders and leads me toward the front entrance.

Judging from the severe lack of furniture inside, his friend is either really into minimalism or a dude. Inventorying the living room, my suspicions are confirmed. "I'm going to guess your friend is a guy."

"How did you know?"

"Psychic," I say dryly. "One couch, two chairs, every gaming system. A TV that takes up half the wall, and no pictures."

"You're a regular Nancy Drew."

I spin toward him, and trail my index finger along the hard planes of his chest. "Is your friend home?"

He catches my waist and pulls my body against his, dropping his lips to my ear, he whispers, "Does it matter?"

I'm guessing that, according to bro code, friends don't cock-block friends in their bachelor pads. But as if to undermine my theory, an amused voice interrupts us. "Don't mind me, I like to watch."

I'm so wrapped up in Jameson that it takes a second for the familiarity of the voice to seep into my giddy brain, but when it does, I turn and gawk at the equally familiar face.

"Never fails," Jameson grumbles. "Levi, you have terrible timing."

"I have excellent timing," Levi calls, grabbing an apple from a bowl on the kitchen counter. He takes a bite, and continues to talk as he chews. "That is, according to Michael Bay."

"I wouldn't brag about that, man."

Neither of them seem to remember I'm here. I elbow Jameson in the ribs. There's no point in trying to play it cool now, not when I've been staring like a catatonic fan girl for over a minute.

"Sorry, Duchess." Jameson shifts, and puts one hand possessively on the small of my back. "Emma Southerly meet Levi Rowe."

"I know who he is," I hiss. "What I don't know is what we're doing here."

"Nice to meet you, Em," Levi says, before his movie star white teeth crunch into the apple again. He swallows hard and I follow the slide of his throat. How on earth does he make that look sexy? "I figured Jameson had to have a girl up here if he was coming back to California."

I raise a questioning eyebrow at my boyfriend. "This is the part of the scene where you tell me how you two know each other."

Between the Wests' money, and his sister's brief bid for fame, it shouldn't shock me that he knows Levi Rowe, former teenie bopper heartthrob turned up-and-coming action film star. I'd been safely passed my tween years when he'd been doing his Disney Channel stint, but even though movies about transforming robots aren't my cup of tea, I drooled over his abs like every hot blooded female I know.

As if on cue, Levi steps away from the counter, his unbuttoned linen shirt fluttering open as he strides towards us. *Those abs.* "Jameson brings all his girls here to impress them."

Levi extends his hand, and the two grip each other's forearm as they lean into a masculine hug. Two seconds and a chest bump, I'm beginning to wonder if I stumbled into a frat house by mistake.

"Levi was at Stanford with me," Jameson says. "For what,

like two weeks? Turns out his serious college plans were a publicity stunt designed by a movie studio."

"I plan on finishing someday." Levi's lips twitch into the grin that casting directors are willing to pay millions for.

"He plans on getting an honorary diploma," Jameson clarifies.

"Jodie Foster got a doctorate," Levi tells us.

"You're going to have to find a script with less running, and more lines to snag one of those, professor," Jameson advises him.

"I'll have you know my agent sent over a serious part this morning." He glances from Jameson to me, and back again. "And you know, I think I need to go read that now."

"Sounds like a good idea," Jameson agrees.

"Yep," Levi says as he backs down the hall. "I'll be in my room with my headphones on, deep in thought, completely oblivious to the outside world. If you scream for help, or"—he fakes a cough—"any other reason, I won't hear you."

"You're overselling it," Jameson calls after him, but he doesn't miss the opportunity to haul me in the opposite direction. "Come on, Duchess."

I steal a glance over my shoulder as Levi disappears into another room. "We're at Levi Rowe's house."

"Yes," Jameson says.

"You know Levi Rowe."

"Yes."

"Do you introduce all your girlfriends to him?" I ask.

"Not if I can help it."

"Ooh, want to make some wine with those sour grapes? Are you threatened by your friend's brutish masculinity?"

Jameson groans before he laughs. "Are you attracted to my friend's brutish masculinity?"

"Not particularly. Why settle for a movie star when you can have a billionaire?"

"That's my little gold digger," Jameson pauses before a closed door. "I don't introduce my girlfriends to Levi."

"Somebody like to play with your toys?" I ask, but when he turns to stare at me, the light mood vanishes. In the darkness of the corridor, his eyes are shadowy gray and my stomach clenches as they bore into me.

"I don't do girlfriends."

"I thought I was your girlfriend," I breathe.

"You are," he says pointedly.

"Wait." I struggle through the hormones muddling my brain to piece together what he's telling me. "Am I your first girlfriend?"

"I think there was one in fifth grade, Kyla or Kaylee."

"You haven't had a girlfriend since fifth grade?"

"I find girls usually want me for one thing."

"And you're happy to give it to them."

"Money, Duchess," he corrects my assumption. "They want me for money. I want them for sex."

"Let me guess which one of you gets what you want."

He backs me against the door. "Do you know what kind of depraved things people are willing to do if they think there's a pot of gold at the end of the…"

"Blowjob?" I offer dryly. My guess is that Jameson could get most girls in any number of compromising positions even if he were dirt poor. He grins wolfishly, and I wonder if I'm leading myself to the slaughter. "So your friend went to Stanford as a publicity stunt, and you went for…"

"An *education*," he says.

There's a double meaning to that.

"I haven't even taken AP Biology," I whisper. Jameson leans forward, bracing his hands on the door and effectively caging me. I don't want to be just one more sacrificial lamb, but I don't want him to stop either.

"You should know what you're getting into," he says gruffly.

"I'm not as innocent as I look," I protest, but a flutter of panic surges in my chest. Now I'm the one overselling it. Being willing is different than being experienced.

"Don't lie, Duchess." He bends forward and presses his lips to the hollow of my throat.

"I'm not wearing white to my wedding," I remind him.

His laughter tickles across my bare skin. "What? Because some kid sweated on you for thirty seconds?"

"It was more like a minute."

"I stand corrected." His mouth glides along my collarbone. Despite the heady cocktail of frustration and desire swirling inside me, I push against his chest in annoyance.

"If we're going to have a pissing contest, we should do it in the bathroom."

Jameson straightens and meets my eyes. "You have the wrong idea. I like that you're innocent. I like knowing that my hands, my fingers, my lips, my tongue, this"—he presses his hard-on into my soft lower belly and I feel it through the layers of clothing separating us. "get to educate you."

"You sound awfully sure of yourself," I murmur. The kiss he brushes over my lips proves he has a right to be, and a moan escapes me. He wraps an arm around my waist, and I know two things: he's caught me and I don't want to escape. But before the kiss can deepen, he throws open the door behind us. Despite his firm grasp, fear thrills through me in a jolting split second of weightlessness.

"I won't let you fall," he promises.

Something tells me I already have.

We stumble back toward the bed, fumbling with our clothes, leaving a trail of discarded clothes in our wake until I'm stripped to my bikini and he's down to his boxer briefs. A rare bout of shyness overcomes me, and I'm torn between how much I want to rip off his underwear and my inexperience. When I finally get up the nerve to slip my fingers past the elastic waistband, he catches my hands and draws them over my head.

"Not so fast," he advises me. "I want you to know exactly what you're getting into."

"I have a pretty good idea," I pant, not bothering to hide my annoyance as my shyness shifts into shamelessness instantly. But Jameson keeps my wrists pinned over my head.

"I got you off in the elevator," he recalls in a lowered voice. "Has any other guy?"

I shake my head, feeling my cheeks flame.

"Then I'm guessing no one has had his mouth on you."

It takes a second for me to realize what he's suggesting. I bite my lower lip, and shake my head again, the flush on my cheeks probably turning to a lovely shade of candy apple red. "Don't be embarrassed, Duchess. I'm going to let go of you now, but I want you to keep your hands up here. Can you do that for me? At least until..."

I nod. I'm not entirely sure what the end of that sentence is, but I have a few ideas what comes after *until*. He kisses downward between my breasts past my navel, sliding his hands along the path until they stop on my hips.

I resist the urge to bury my face in a pillow when he plucks the ties of my bikini bottom. He waits for a moment, as if letting me get used to the idea of what's about to happen, then he draws it slowly down. Suddenly I can't remember if I shaved this morning. Or if I shaved enough. I've seen a Playboy, and I know he has, too. I open my mouth to apologize, but before I can speak, I feel the warm wet plunge of his tongue, nudging its way to the throbbing pulse between my thighs. I arch up, lost for words except for a strangled cry that vibrates from a part of me I didn't know existed. Now I understand what he meant by *until* because my hands fly to his head, grab hold of his hair and push him against me as his tongue works magic. He reaches up and pries my fingers loose. Gripping my wrists, he pins my arms to the bed. He's in charge now. I give in to that reality, allowing my hips to move in unison with his mouth. Dozens of half-formed thoughts flit through my head, prematurely dismissed by a flick or suck, each growing shorter as the pressure builds inside me. Before long, I can't stop myself from bucking against him, and his pleased groan vibrates against my sensitive swollen flesh.

It's enough to send me crashing over the edge. I'm not sure if the screams are in my head, or if I'm bellowing them out loud. All I know is I can find no other word except his name. When I can't take any more, my legs clamp instinctively against his head. Trembles wrack my body and I grip the comforter. I need something to hold on to, because I'm not entirely convinced that I'm not dreaming. He frees himself, then he slides his arms under my torso and gently moves me farther onto the bed. I curl into a fetal position—an instinct they don't tell you about in *Cosmo*—and blink languidly as he climbs in beside me. I reach a trembling hand toward his waist, but he stops me.

"Not right now. That's all I needed." He cradles me to him and presses a kiss to my forehead.

"I...I..." Thoughts are still slow to form.

"Speechless," he notes with satisfaction. "Rest up, Duchess. There's more where that came from."

. . .

I BLINK INTO THE SUNLIGHT, then sit straight up, clutching the sheet thrown casually over my lower half. "Oh my god. What time is it?"

Jameson glances up from his phone and smirks. His hair is a tangled mess, and I wonder for a second if it got that way from me trying to pull it out. "Relax. It's just after four."

"Oh my God."

"No, just Jameson."

I flop back down on the bed, sneaking another quick peek at him as I pull the sheet higher. He flips onto his side, and traces the edge of it.

"I have to say that I find your sudden modesty a bit too enticing."

I pull it to my chin. "Mr. West, what big eyes you have."

"Skip to the part where I say, 'The better to eat you with,'" he encourages me, and I slap his shoulder. He falls back beside me, laughing.

"That was ..." I hesitate, before landing on, "Incredible."

"Feel free to write songs and sonnets singing my praises."

"I would, but I don't think it's safe for your head to get any bigger." I turn onto my side, already thinking about round two, until my eyes land on his phone. I stop breathing when I spy the Instagram feed on his screen. "The Dealer should be called The Mood Killer."

"Don't worry about him," Jameson says.

"So it's a him?" Maybe while I slept off the orgasmic coma he put me in, he's found some clues.

"Or her," he adds.

Or maybe not. I scoot up in the bed, shaking my head. "How am I not supposed to worry? That's seriously creepy shit."

"Agreed, but I don't really see the point. Whoever it is needs to be charged with stalking. We should go to the police."

He hasn't been looking closely at all. I reach for his phone, and scroll through the feed. "These two are from the night your father was murdered," I inform him. "I don't know about the rest."

I return to the top of the feed to find I've made my first photo appearance. The photo that posted seconds ago is definitely from that night. I stare at the picture of me sleeping in the cabana. It's dark enough that I can't make out much, except for one important fact.

I'm alone.

"That's new," Jameson says in a quiet voice. I want to reassure him, but we both know that if anyone finds this picture, it could undermine the alibi he's established for that night. He had been honest with me about what happened after I fell asleep, but I'd kept those facts to myself. I might believe that he did nothing but fight with his father and then drown his sorrows in a few drinks, but whoever posted this knows that a picture is worth a thousand words. In this case, all thousand of them are *guilty*.

"We need to find out who this is before anyone else sees these photos."

"Too late," Jameson takes his phone from me, and tosses it to the foot of the bed. "The Dealer already has a few followers."

"What is he advertising for fans?" I lunge forward to retrieve it, but he holds me back.

"None of his followers are going to tattle."

"How can you possibly know that?" I ask.

"Because so far, his entire following consists of Monroe, Josie, *you*, and now me."

"Should we send an engraved invitation to Hugo? I doubt he'd want to miss this party," I snap. Hugo's cameo in The Dealer's stream is more incriminating than most.

"For now, I think we're safe," he continues.

"But for how long?"

"I have a guy who can check into this. Whoever this is can't hide behind a username forever."

I don't ask him what we'll do when we find out who's been collecting a scrapbook of our intimate moments, because once we know who they are, they'll have nothing left to hide.

Especially our secrets.

Chapter 4

IF THE DEALER hadn't already put the fear of God in me, facing my mother at the dinner table will. She meets us at the door, offering a simpering smile to Jameson as she directs us to the dining room.

"I hope you like shrimp," she says, but before I can remind her of my aversion to the creepy, ocean spiders, she grabs my elbow and hauls me to the side.

"You're glowing," she accuses.

I half expect her to haul me to the ER to check to see if my virtue is intact. I pull away before she can lose control and make a scene. "Summer love," I say casually before dashing into the dining room.

Hans glances up from his tablet and grunts a greeting. I'm not certain if that's just hello in his native tongue or if we're not worthy of full syllables.

"We have a guest," Mom trills as she enters behind us. Hans still doesn't bother to look up until she adds, "Jameson West."

That gets his attention and confirms my fears that my stepfather is actually a big enough dick to do a biopic accusing my boyfriend of murder. I guess that really puts the fun in dysfunctional family.

"The infamous Mr. West." Hans's accent is muted by years of being in the US, but it still curls around his words. Between that, his broad shoulders, and what is left of his wispy, blond hair, it's obvious he is an import.

"It's nice to meet you, son." He stands and holds out his hand. The two shake once. I'm not an expert on male greetings but I'd give theirs an eight for formality and a ten for tension. "Hans Von Essen."

"I know who you are, Mr. Von Essen." Jameson doesn't hide the insinuation in his words.

We take our seats as Hans begins to scoff, ignoring Jameson's coldness. Meanwhile, I wish I had a blanket to cope with the chill. "Please, call me Hans."

"I suppose that's fitting." Jameson unfolds his napkin and places it in his lap without bothering to look up from his place setting.

Hans smiles tightly and beckons for the maid to take his tablet. "I'm sorry?"

"To call you Hans. After all, I'm dating your stepdaughter," Jameson offers the alternative explanation, dangling it like a carrot overhead. If Hans goes for it maybe we can spend the evening in awkward silence, making small talk, and escape unscathed.

"I had no idea you two were so close."

Or maybe not.

Hans studies me with interest and I can almost feel the future interrogation now. My love life has never really come up with my stepfather before now. Probably since he had little real interest in me, other than to offer parenting advice to my absentee mother and back up all her paranoid plans for my future. But now I have something he wants, and he's never going to get it out of me. I turn my full attention to the flatware to avoid meeting Hans's gaze while wondering if a butter knife is sharp enough to commit harakiri.

"We're very close," Jameson tells him and I distinctly hear another nail being driven into the coffin that now holds what's left of my stepdad's disinterest. I'm going to miss it. Two parents is bad enough. Now I'll have three at me all the time.

"Oh yes, I have no doubt of that," Hans waves him off dismissively. "I'm afraid I haven't been around as much as I would like. I just wrapped a major film for Paramount and I'm in pre-production on two more."

"They don't want to hear about the business darling," Mom interjects. "People only want to go see the movie, remember?"

"Not at all. What are you working on?" Jameson asks and the question hangs in the air.

The arrival of our salads grants a brief reprieve, but any hope I had of Hans choking on a cucumber slice is dashed when he ignores it entirely. "I'm afraid the projects haven't been announced yet, so I'm not at liberty to share."

"I understand the need for discretion." Jameson tips his head in acknowledgement. But if the butter knife wouldn't be enough for ritualistic suicide, it could definitely cut through the tension in the air.

"I was telling Emma about our thoughts about Los Angeles," Mom pipes up, as if somehow this topic will be less uncomfortable than the first. Jameson's eyes flash from her to me for confirmation.

"And I told her hell to the no," I add.

"Oh, Emma," Hans begins, "there are some very good schools in Los Angeles."

"I'm happy where I'm at," I protest, dropping my salad fork on the table. "Where I *was*."

"I had to beg you to attend Belle Mère Prep," Mom reminds me, "And now suddenly you love it there." I don't miss the none-too-subtle glare she casts at Jameson. "I think you would be more concerned about getting into a good college, then."

"I told you I would take a few classes at UNLV," I say without hope that it will stop her from digging into this topic.

I never intended to make good on that promise. As far as I'm concerned, I don't need more than a high school diploma to take over the family business. Of course, that was before what happened with my father. Given that the police had used his false claim of assault to hold Jameson for nearly a month, I probably need to reconsider that life plan. "I'm not about to be bullied into becoming a valley girl."

"You don't have to go," Jameson says with an air of authority that makes me cringe. At any other time, I'd find it seriously hot, but considering that we're in the presence of my mother, it only makes me queasy.

"It would be selfish to ask her to miss this opportunity." Hans spears a leaf of lettuce onto his fork, but instead of eating it, he spins it in the light.

"What about the East Coast?" Mom suggests as if we've been discussing my matriculation to Harvard and Yale for years.

"What about it?"

"There are some good schools there," Jameson tosses his opinion into the ring.

I narrow my eyes at him and mouth, *Traitor*.

"Why would I want to go someplace I've never been?" I point out with a shrug.

"You've never been to the East Coast?" Jameson asks. He stares at me like I just announced I'm from a different planet.

"Emma doesn't like to travel," my mother says offhandedly.

"I haven't really gotten the opportunity to." Mom's revisionist history of my travel preferences kills my appetite entirely. I push my plate away. Ilsa appears and whisks it off to the kitchen. I'm like that plate of salad. Suitably filling until Mom grows tired of me. Then it's back to the kitchen for me. She loves to travel, but I haven't been invited on those trips. Over the years, she'd made a few noncommittal statements about taking me here or there, but she's never followed through on any of them. It shouldn't sting as much as it does. But how do you explain to someone that your mother has access to a private jet and you've only seen two states?

"We should go to New York," Jameson suggests, and for a moment it's just the two of us. We gaze at each other across the table as I imagine us frolicking through Central Park. The whole scene is very reminiscent of the opening credits of *Friends*. But the longer he and I stare at each other, the more those scenes start to shift to ones that remind me of *Sex and The City*.

Mom clears her throat and the spell is broken. "Emma is seventeen."

"Thanks for the fact check, Mom," I mutter.

"I don't allow my seventeen-year-old to go halfway across the country without my permission," she continues.

"It's a good thing I'll be eighteen in two weeks then," I jump in.

"Two weeks?" Jameson asks in surprise. "Maybe it will be a birthday trip."

She glowers at him. I want to warn her that her face will freeze like that, but considering the amount of Botox comprising her body, it probably already has.

"I would've thought your people would be a little more thorough."

"Come again?" he asks.

"Someone with your level of wealth has certainly run a background check on my daughter." She folds her manicured hands on the table in challenge.

"Obviously," he admits, "but I didn't memorize it."

"Not something as important as your girlfriend's birthday?"

I don't miss how she makes girlfriend sound like a lot nastier of a word. "Gee, mom. Do you mean slut? Or maybe whore?"

I push my chair from the table, but before I can continue my dramatic exit solo, Jameson stands. "Not everything in this world has to be subject to contracts and legalese and security procedures. I want my relationship with Emma to be real."

"Do you even know what that word means?" she asks him. But despite the coldness of her tone, she shrinks against her seat. Meanwhile Hans watches the entire scene unfolding with interest. I half expect him to yell cut or offer director's notes.

"I'm not hungry," I announce loudly. "Let's go for a drive."

Jameson sucks in a deep breath and squares his shoulders before he gestures towards the door. "After you."

Apologies crowd my lips as we make our way through the hall, but none of them feel adequate.

"Don't even think about apologizing, Duchess," he says as if he can read my mind.

"But they're my parents."

"Only one of them is," he corrects me, "but I can see why you wouldn't want to claim either."

His keys are out of his pocket before we hit the front door, but mom chases after us. "A word, Emma."

It's more than she deserves, but I pause. "Go ahead. I'll be out in a second."

He looks torn as if he's leaving me to fend off a rabid dog on my own while he saves himself. Nothing could be closer to the truth.

"I can handle myself," I assure him. He doesn't need further prodding.

Mom doesn't beat around the bush about why she stopped me. "I don't think it's a good idea for you to see him."

"Really? And I thought you were planning our wedding." I cross my arms and begin counting down the minute I've given her in my head.

"You have no idea who he is."

"I have a better idea than you do. You didn't even give him a chance."

"I don't have to," she explodes. "I know his family. I know what they're capable of."

"Excuse me," I interrupt her, "but you're the one who was ready to call his Mom a few weeks ago."

"There's a difference between being a West by marriage and being a West by birth," she says.

"Could you be more self-righteous?" I ask her.

"Blood will out, Emma." She speaks as if she's giving me the code key to decipher her cryptic insights.

"If we're done with the riddling portion of the evening, I need to go." I don't wait for her to respond before I turn on my heels and leave my mother—and her opinions—behind.

Chapter 5

"YOUR MOTHER and my father would have gotten along," Jameson informs me as soon as I'm inside the Porsche.

"But who would be the other two Horsemen of the Apocalypse?" I slump into my seat, feeling more than a little sorry for myself.

"Seat belt," he commands. Groaning, I tuck it over my shoulder. It's not like me to forget, not after what happened to my sister, but if my mother can accomplish anything on a daily basis, it's to suck my will to live.

"Where are we going?" I ask him.

"What's the farthest point on the planet from here?"

"I don't know. New Zealand?" Sadly, I don't think this car floats. He revs the engine and peels out of the driveway. Considering how fast he's going, it might just be able to make it across water, but as we reach the main drag of downtown Palm Springs road closure signs greet us. For a brief second, I wonder if my mom now controls the Department of Transportation, too. I wouldn't put it past her to do something that dramatic to stop me from seeing Jameson. But just beyond the white and orange obstacles, a number of tents are set up in the street. People wander, many hand-in-hand with loved ones or children, and music floats through the air toward the car.

Swiveling in my seat, I touch the hand he's using to grip the drive shaft. "Let's do something normal."

"You're going to have to give me some ideas, Duchess. I'm fresh out of normal these days, considering most of our dates end in murder, interrogations, or arrest."

I understand exactly where he's coming from. I tip my head toward the street carnival.

"Really?" he asks incredulously.

"Street food and music and hideous arts and crafts. It's perfect." I unfasten my seat belt and open the car door. "I need normal."

Before he can stop me, I'm halfway to the fair. The tents host various artists and crafters hocking everything from paintings to handmade soaps to any of the hippie paraphernalia necessary for a Californian lifestyle. I peruse them until a familiar pair of hands grabs my hips.

"Come on," he murmurs. "I'm hungry, if that's okay with you."

"Eating is normal," I assure him. But when he heads for a restaurant, I grab his hand and yank him towards the food trucks. "This will be faster."

"What is it?" He stares at the truck as if it is a spaceship.

"What can I get you two?" The man calls from the window.

"How hungry are you?" I ask Jameson. He holds his hands out wide and grins. At least he's going to be a good sport about it, even if dinner doesn't come on bone china. "Four carne asada and four al pastor."

Jameson leans so close to me that I can smell his cologne.

My mouth begins to water and I'm not sure if it's from the promise of food or him.

"You forgot to order the side of salmonella," he whispers

"I think they throw that in for free," I mutter.

A few minutes later, and he's devouring his own words with a side of garlic-lime salsa. "Okay, you were right," he grants me, when we toss our empty taco trays in the trash. "I'm converted. Now I'll only order food from trucks."

"I hear there are a lot of food trucks in New York." I throw it out like bait to see if he'll bite.

Instead he spins me around and pulls me close to him. "So you are interested in going?"

"Of course I am." The Empire State Building. Broadway. Fifth Avenue. Why wouldn't I be dying to go?

"Why have you never been to the East Coast?"

"It's complicated and I don't feel like telling sad stories tonight. You know the saying: 'and baby makes three'? Well, according to my parental units, three's a crowd."

"No need to say more, Duchess. I'm going to take you to New York, then London, and maybe Tokyo after that."

"Paris?" I suggest nonchalantly.

"Definitely Paris." Neither of us mention the fact that if he's already in violation of the terms of his bail by being a state away, Europe is out of the question. "I guess it's your birthday, so which one do you want to go to?"

"We don't have to go anywhere," I reassure him. We can dream, but we can't actually revise reality.

"We do." He brushes a sticky strand of hair from my forehead. "They can't cage us."

"They already have," I say softly.

"Then we'll break free."

"Do you really think we can?" I ask. We stand for a moment, clinging to each other despite the oppressive Californian heat. Above us, strings of light twinkle in the twilight like dozens of wishing stars but they can't grant our desires any more than we can.

"What do you want, Duchess?" he asks, reading the silence in my eyes. "The moon, the stars? Say the word, and I'll give them to you."

"You," I whisper. "I only want you."

WHEN WE'VE EXHAUSTED the carnival's delights, we drive to the base of the San Jacinto Mountains. But the farther we get from the lively downtown scene, the quieter we each become until we've left normal behind entirely. Jameson's eyes stare into the distance as he parks the convertible. "Your stepfather's right. It's selfish for me to want you back in Vegas."

"But inevitable," I remind him. If he's right and the police suspect me too, then my return can't be avoided.

"Maybe not," he admits slowly. "Between my lawyers and Hans's lawyers we can probably keep them tied up for a while."

But not forever.

"You shouldn't have to face this alone. If they have questions about what happened that night, *we* need to answer them."

"Emma, we both know we weren't together the entire evening. I left you by the pool. I want you to rescind my alibi."

"But you were with me." Panic boils in my chest bubbling over in a rush of unfamiliar emotions. "You were with me most of the night. Besides, there were dozens of people there. Anyone could have done it."

"But my fingerprints are all over the scene."

"Yes, because you found the body, and what about my alibi?" I ask. "They found him in his office and that's where we met, so…"

He nods grimly. He might want to believe the investigators are going after me to rattle him, but we both know I had just as much opportunity that evening. Plus, given my family's history with the Wests, nearly as much motive as well.

"You weren't with me the whole night," I repeat, latching on to that fact. If he thinks I'm going to let him play the martyr, he can climb right back off that cross. "Which means *I* was alone, too. If they're going to make you a suspect, they might as well make me one as well. Besides that, you're not going to be able to find who did this by yourself. Not if you're constantly being dragged in for questioning."

"You think they're going to give you an extra recess while I stay in the principal's office?" he points out dryly.

I don't admit that he's right. Not when I need to sound confident about what's at stake. Instead I fall back on classic diversionary tactics. "Why are they so focused on you anyway? You weren't the only one there with motive. I think they're just being lazy."

Judging from how his fingers tighten on the steering wheel, I've hit a nerve. "It's more than that. Mackey has a vendetta. My lawyers say she wants to see me burn for this."

"Why?"

"I don't have an answer for you, but I'm going to find out the reason she has it in for me."

"Sounds like step one of a plan." Mission accomplished. If he's going after the real murderer, he'll need my help—especially since the cops already think he's guilty. We can't rely on justice being done.

"You should stay," Jameson says as though he can read my mind. There's a firmness in his words that dares me to question him.

"Too bad I'm not the type to take orders," I inform him. "I'm coming back."

"Emma, I thought I needed you to come back with me and even though I miss you, I'll never forgive myself if something happens to you again. We don't know who murdered my father, but we also don't know who pushed you through the glass that night."

"Considering you live in a casino, there's a distinct lack of surveillance cameras in your house."

He blows out a hollow laugh before reaching over to clutch my hand. "Dad called that penthouse his oasis. He said nowhere was safer than at the very top of what he had built. I guess he never considered how far he had to fall.

"Whoever did this came into my home invited because there's no other way they could've gotten past the security team. One of us opened the door to his murderer and let them walk right in."

"It's not your fault," I say in a soft voice. He won't believe it, but he needs to hear it.

"Maybe not," he admits. "My relationship with my dad was complicated, but I owe him justice."

The sun fading swiftly behind the mountains casts a purple haze across the horizon. As the blazing orb disappears from view and the moon takes up its watch, I get out of the car and go to the driver's side. Before he can protest, I climb in and straddle him. Wrapping my arms around his neck, I gaze into his eyes.

"I want to come back with you." I cut him off before he can respond. "I'm pretty damn good at taking care of myself in case you failed to notice."

"I didn't," he says, a wry smile playing at his lips. "Sometimes I think that scares me more than anything."

I raise an eyebrow at this revelation. "Strong women scare you?"

"No," he assures me in a gruff voice as his hands dig into

my hips, urging me closer. "I like strong women; I just don't want you to do anything stupid to protect me. Whoever did this, Duchess, isn't going to confess if we find them."

"I don't want them to confess," I say in measured tones. "I want them to pay."

"My father wasn't a good man, but he was my father. I can't help but think that whoever did this probably had a good reason." His words send a chill rippling up my spine. It settles in the roots of my hair until I feel the coldness of it all over.

If the murderer had a reason, what would stop him from piling up more collateral damage? Because in order to get past the lies, we'd have to get closer to the truth—and the person who killed Nathaniel West.

Chapter 6

THE HOUSE IS dark when I tiptoe through the foyer. I refused Jameson's request for me to stay with him at Levi's house. I wouldn't put it past my mother to file a missing person's report. After all, as she recently reminded me, I'm only seventeen. The last thing I need is to get Jameson any more police face time. Given the traumatic dinner earlier, my guess is that mom popped a few Xanax and drifted into the Valley of the Dolls.

But light catches my attention as I make my way to my bedroom. It seeps through a crack in Hans's office door. I hesitate while considering my options. I can go on having a detached relationship with my stepfather or I can call him out on his plans to make a movie based on my boyfriend's life. Neither seem like very appealing options, but I can't go on living under this roof if he plans to use me as a source of information about Jameson.

I creep toward the open door, then knock softly. When there's no answer, I push it open to discover the room is empty. A few scripts are strewn across the desk and curiosity gets the better of me. Wandering over, I sift through the pages and head shots left out until a photo of a familiar face slips out of a file folder marked "Jameson." My heart sinks when I see the notes scribbled on the bottom of the photo of Levi Row. I wonder how much they offered him to sell out his old college buddy. He mentioned that he was about to take on a serious role, and the Academy loves biopics. I stuff him and his traitorous smile back into the folder and sit down not certain what will be worse: if I tell Jameson or if he hears it from *Entertainment Weekly*.

After shuffling through a few more piles, I find a script titled *Wild West*.

Cringe.

I can only hope that's a working title. Flipping through the pages, I discover how thoroughly Hans has researched the situation. He might have played dumb about Jameson being my boyfriend at dinner. But unless he hasn't read his own script, he had no problem agreeing to direct a sex scene that hadn't happened between our characters. With my luck, they'll get some blonde bombshell like Blake Lively for me and I'd get to spend the rest of my life feeling inferior to my fictional counterpart and her fictional sex life. I know better, but I keep reading. It turns out that fictional me is a bit of a slut. My stomach turns over and I rip the page in half, crumple the pieces into balls and throw them into the trash can. If I had matches, the script would already be on fire. Picking up the rest, I dump it on top of the torn pieces. I'm not wasting my time ripping up one-hundred pages sensationalized lies about myself and my boyfriend. Opening the desk drawer, I search for matches. Instead under a pile of office supplies, I find a file marked *Becca*. My hands tremble as I flip it open to find a police report detailing the accident that killed her. I can't bring myself to read about the crash. I lived through it. No amount of clinical objectivity and police lingo could erase those memories. For just a moment, the smell of burnt rubber wafts around me and the rolling sensation in my stomach gets worst. I shake my head until the memories fade. The file doesn't contain much else: an insurance policy, obituary, and the death certificate. I suppose someone had to care enough to keep these things, but it surprises me that it's Hans. I trace her name. That's all she is now, words on paper. Becca is a collection of memories and facts-date of birth, time of death, mother, father. The tip of my index finger stops on the word typed under name of father.

Unknown.

Why would Becca's death certificate list her father as unknown? Mom and Dad had been divorced before the accident but that didn't mean he wasn't her father. It didn't make any sense unless...

I continue to stare at it as if it will start to make sense or forge a new meaning, but I'm no closer to making sense out of it when Hans clears his throat from the doorway. I slam the folder shut hurriedly.

"Can I help you, Emma?" His large body fills the door frame and I shake my head. "I see you've been reading my script."

"You've got a few details wrong," I inform him in a cold voice. I shove Becca's file underneath the ones containing head shots before I lounge back in his office chair and grip the arms until my hands hurt.

"I'd be more than happy to consult with you and Jameson on the project."

"I doubt he's interested in helping make a movie that claims he's guilty of murdering his father."

"Don't you know that fame is the new jury of your peers?"

"Jameson isn't on trial for his father's murder." My protest sounds weak, even to me.

"He will be," Hans assures me. "Let me help him."

"And you making a movie saying he did it is going to get him off. Pardon me, but I call bullshit." Hans doesn't balk like my mother at my use of curse words. Instead, he walks inside the office and takes the seat across from me.

"He's young, good looking. He had to have a reason to do it. If the audience likes him it won't matter if he's guilty."

"He didn't do it," I repeat myself, but Hans either doesn't hear me or doesn't care.

"Perhaps there's a tragic story. His father hit him or molested him."

"Oh my God. Do you hear yourself?" I stand up knocking a few pieces of paper to the floor. "You can't just make things up."

"Of course I can. I work in Hollywood," Hans chuckles derisively.

"Does mom know that you put a sex scene featuring her daughter in this movie?"

"She already knows that you're his alibi," he says meaningfully.

"That doesn't mean we have sex."

"You're really so winningly innocent." He pauses and looks me up and down. "It's going to be hard to cast you. I need an actress that can play naive but fuckable."

"I need to go throw up now." My hand flies to cover my mouth as I try to keep the churning at bay. But as I round the corner of the desk, he stands and steps in front of me.

"Aren't you going to ask me about the other thing?"

I swallow and try to channel some of that winning innocence. "I don't know what you're talking about."

"It's part of the charm," he says, "how terrible of a liar you are."

I try to push past him but he holds me in place. "Ask me."

There's a threat running through he's words now.

"Why do you have that file on Becca?" My voice is small, because I don't want to know the answer. Not while I'm still trying to wrap my head around that one word: unknown. I knew my sister. She'd been there every day of my life. I'd been born into a world that was already hers and nothing has felt right since she left it. The idea that her existence—and my life—are comprised of lies is too much to bear.

"Becca was very special to me," Hans says. His grip on my arm loosens but he doesn't let me go.

"I know." As much as I don't want to fill in that unknown with his name, it can't be helped.

"You do?" he asks in surprise.

"I saw..." What exactly did I see? The certificate itself proves nothing, which means I'm about to take a big leap without a safety net.

"Saw what, Emma?" he demands. He presses his palms flat on the desk and leans in to catch my eye. "How long have you known?"

"A few minutes," I answer in confusion.

He bristles as if my lack of long-term study of the subject affronts him. "You never suspected?"

"Why would I suspect that?"

"She didn't tell you?"

"She knew?" If Becca had known that we had different fathers, she'd taken that secret to the grave. If that's true, she'd been my best friend and I hadn't known her at all.

"You gathered the truth from that stack of papers. You're very intuitive." His fingers slide up my bare arm. It takes a second to process the meaning behind his touch but my body backs away before my mind catches up.

"What the hell do you think you're doing?"

"I miss your sister," he says. "You look like her, you know?"

My mouth goes dry. "We were sisters."

"You remind me of your sister. You're as beautiful as she was, maybe even prettier." He moves toward me and I scramble to think of a way out. "I used to screw her on that desk."

"You were her father." The accusation spills out of me and stops him in his tracks.

"What?"

"That's the secret. The one that you were hiding." Even as I say it, the truth forms with startling clarity, but now I want it to be something that's as benign as my mother lying about an old fling and then marrying him later. Because the new picture in my head can't be erased.

"I'm afraid only he and your mother know who her father is. Although I suspect your dad knows as well. Your sister was ambitious," he continues, and I want to scream at him to stop talking about her because I don't want his memories of her. I want mine. I want to believe I was her best friend. I want to believe that the furthest she ever got was with a Topher Drake at his Halloween party her junior year. "I loved your sister."

"No, you didn't," I correct him.

"That's not fair. I love you both."

"I didn't ask for your love." I rush toward the other end of the desk but my foot catches on the rug and I tumble down into the chair.

"Becca had dreams," Hans tells me, "and dreams take money."

"Do you even know the difference between the truth and lies anymore?" I start to push myself up but he leans over me.

"That pretty little mouth of yours will get you into trouble." His hot breath, still stinking of tonight's shrimp entree, makes me gag. "I'm a reasonable man. For instance, take this sex scene that's bothering you. Maybe you didn't sleep with him." He stands up and his fingers find his belt buckle.

NO. NO. NO.

It's the only word I can process but I can't get it out of my mouth. My heart pounds against my rib cage like a trapped animal trying to break free. I want to run, but I'm frozen in place, afraid that the slightest movement will encourage my predator to lunge.

"Maybe you gave him head," he suggests. "I can see you doing that."

I struggle to find my voice and when I do questions flood from me. "Is this how it was with you two? You forced her into doing what you wanted?"

"Becca liked to please me. Maybe you should be a little more like your sister." He unbuttons his trousers. "Why don't you show me what happened that night? Show me how I need to rewrite the scene."

Sensing my opportunity, I find the courage to stand up. I'm careful to push the chair back to give myself more room. Hans mistakes that for acquiescence.

"That's good," he coaxes. His hands reach to rest on my shoulders so that he can gently urge me to my knees.

"I think the whole scene needs a rewrite," I tell him before I swiftly introduce his groin to my kneecap. He's down long enough for me to get out of the room and into the hall. I pull my cell phone out of my pocket and dial 911. When he stumbles to the doorway and starts to lunge, I hold up the screen. "One more step and all they hear is me yelling for help."

"You're nothing like your sister." He spits at my feet.

"No, I guess I'm not."

IN MY ROOM, I lock the door and shove a few things in a bag, makeup, a couple T-shirts, my swimsuit, and grab my laptop. There's a 10% chance I can convince my mom to mail me the rest, but I can't tell her what happened, so she'll probably hold it hostage until I'm brave enough to show up at her door again.

You remind me of your sister. Hans words swim in my head until I'm dizzy trying to forget them. It's not like the first time I've been compared to Becca, but this was different. I resist the urge to walk into the shower, fully clothed, and turn the water to the melt-your-skin off setting. Nothing can wash this away.

I send two text messages, the first to Jameson. I didn't bother to type more than SOS. Not while my fingers are still shaking. To Josie, I managed to get out two words: *Coming home.*

Now I just have to wait and not go crazy, which feels impossible. I want to get away from here and pretend this never happened.

Instead, I stare in the mirror for a moment trying to find Becca hiding in my green eyes. I'm having a hard time picturing her. I can recall all the facts: strawberry blonde hair instead of my sandy blonde, more freckles, particularly on her nose. She never tanned if she could help it. I have all the pieces of the puzzle but it's getting harder to figure out how to put them together. That's the real cost of grief. People you lose slowly slip away until they're nothing more than a list of memories you can't recall.

"Get yourself together," I command the girl in the mirror, but she looks scared and small. I don't want to hug her, though, I want to slap her. Instead I wander back into my bedroom. I could pack another suitcase, but somehow I don't want any of these things anymore, not if they were bought with Hans's money. My eyes fall on a framed picture from last summer. Becca and I are laughing as mom and Hans try to look serious in the background. We need a family picture, mom had said. This was as close as we'd gotten. Now it's all we have. I grab it off the desk and fling it to the ground.

You break it, you buy it, right?

I'd been bought with private school tuition, a new car, and my mother's happiness. What had he bought her with?

Bending down, I pick up the frame, shaking the rest of the broken glass free so that I can pluck the photo out. It should be comforting to see my sister staring back at me given literally only moments ago I couldn't conjure up her face, but it's the exact opposite. I've looked at this picture every day this summer, but today Becca seems different. Is her smile forced? Is she really laughing? Did he assault her and she covered up for him, thinking no one would believe her, not even me? Hans wants me to believe the worst, but what if he's telling the truth? What happened between Hans and Becca?

"It's really inconvenient that you're dead," I say to the photo. A rush of hot tears aches in my throat, but I swallow against the pain.

Digging through my desk drawers, I find another photo of the two of us, shot at closer range. We're hugging on a beach in La Jolla. Becca's blue eyes stare back at me.

The only blue eyes in the family. Mom's voice floats to my mind. I'd need a biology text book to be positive but, if memory serves, it's pretty rare for my father's brown eyes and my mother's green eyes to produce a blue-eyed child. Recessive genes, my ass. The shrill ring of my phone startles me, and I toss the picture back on my dresser.

"I can't get through the gate," Jameson says, and I detect a note of panic in his voice.

"I'll open it but meet me at the front door as soon as you can."

"What the hell is going on, Duchess?"

"Just meet me."

Shouldering my duffle bag, I brace myself as I unlock my door but Hans isn't waiting for me. Running down the hall, I'm a few steps from the front entrance when Jameson's headlights glare through the window. A sob of relief bursts out of me.

"Where on earth are you going?" my mother calls from the top of the stairs.

"Home," I tell her.

"I did not give you permission."

I ignore her and open the door. "I'm not staying in this house a minute longer."

"You seem to be under the mistaken impression that you make the rules around here—" my mother begins.

"You're under the mistaken impression that it's safe for me here." I'm not even sure she can hear me past the sobs that choke my words. I can't hold any of it back. Not anymore.

Even in the dark house, I see her face pale. She takes a few stairs down but stops again. "What does that mean?"

"Ask your husband."

Chapter 7

I DON'T HAVE to tell Jameson to drive fast. He's off the Von Essen property in record time. I don't ask questions when he heads away from the city. Jameson could take me anywhere as long as it was far away from that twisted dollhouse.

Moonlight casts stark shadows over Palm Springs. Tonight it looks black and white and every shade of gray in between. It's a city of ghosts. No place for me.

Jameson pulls into the private airfield just beyond the public airport.

"What about the car?" I ask as he collects our bags from the back seat.

"What about it?"

A one-time use Porsche? Jameson West is so out of my league.

"You have a pilot available to pick you up at midnight?" I stare at the crew refueling the small private jet.

"That surprises you?"

"No." I shrug trying to look nonchalant and failing miserably. "I mean, the rest of us are stuck search Travelocity and taking red-eyes."

"I think this qualifies as a red-eye Duchess."

A man in a pressed uniform approaches us and Jameson hands off our bags. "Are you jealous of my private jet?"

"My mom has one." Which isn't exactly true. Hans's studio does, and there isn't a shot in hell that I'll be going aboard Hans's flight deck anytime soon.

"Then we're two peas in a private jet pod."

"Been waiting your whole life for another girl with a private jet?"

He knits his fingers through mine. "Private jets, questionable childhoods, we were made for each other."

I rest my head on his shoulder thankful that he's not pressing me for more information about why we're waiting at a private airstrip in the middle of the night. I might have used up my allotment of normal for the day, but I'm grateful that he's here cracking jokes. It's strange that the circumstances surrounding our relationship are so dramatic, given how easy it is to be with him.

"They're ready for us," he announces. I follow him on board and immediately remember that there's West money and what's left for everyone else on the planet. Apparently private jets can be divided by class—and Jameson's is clearly platinum. The seats are upholstered in buttery leather and champagne-gold subtly accents each surface.

"Do you want to get some rest?" he asks hitching a finger toward an open door. I peek inside and find a small but adequate bedroom that might have come in handy if I felt like facing the inevitable onslaught of nightmares about tonight's events. Instead, I shake my head. I figure there's two ways to deal with my trauma: self-inflicted insomnia, or dreams Freddy Krueger wouldn't dare enter.

"I don't feel like sleeping." I don't have to say anything else. Jameson takes the hint and we settle into two leather seats facing one another. A stewardess, who must have trained to be a ninja in another life, appears instantly beside us.

"May I bring you something to drink Mr. West?"

"A whiskey and soda. Laura, allow me to introduce Ms. Emma Southerly."

She turns her warm bubble gum pink smile on me. "What can I bring you Ms. Southerly?"

I refrain from ordering all the booze in the world because that certainly isn't going to help me stay awake. "Can I have some coffee?"

Caffeine is not only a safe bet, but a necessity at this hour.

"Absolutely, I just put a fresh pot on," she chirps. She scurries out of the private compartment and I wonder how many pots of coffee she's had. No one should be this alert at this time of night.

Looking back to Jameson, I find him studying me, but he doesn't speak. The silence stretches through the delivery of our drinks and take-off. When Laura excuses herself after we've been in the air for a while, he unbuckles and comes to my side. Kneeling next to me, he takes my hand. "I need you to tell me what happened."

"Nothing," I lie because I don't want to tell him. Repeating what happened between Hans and I means facing the information he gave me, not just what he tried to do. I know how to protect myself against pervs, what self-respecting Vegas girl doesn't, but nothing can change what he told me.

"Emma," Jameson prompts when I'm quiet for a few more minutes. "Did Hans hurt you?"

"Yes," I stammer. "No! Not like you're thinking."

But then again, hadn't he?

"What did he do to you?" His voice is dangerously low,

quiet with a rage that anything I tell him will only fan into uncontrollable fury.

"Nothing happened," I say in a rush, choosing to cling to obliviousness.

"Jesus Christ, Emma." His grip on my hand tightens. "You're scaring the shit out of me."

"He tried." I leave it at that.

"Did he...touch you?" Jameson asks in a strangled voice.

"He tried," I repeat, "but I kneed him in the balls."

"That piece of shit. Why didn't you tell me?"

"Because I knew you'd react this way, and the last thing I need is another member of my family charging you with assault."

"That man isn't your family."

He doesn't have to tell me that twice.

"Do you want to talk about what happened?"

I shake my head quickly. Maybe when I've had a chance to process the things Hans claimed happened between him and Becca, I'll need to talk about it. For now, I'm more than happy to pretend that it's all lies. I need to pretend, because missing my sister is hard enough without worrying about whether or not I knew her at all. My thoughts flash to Hans unbuckling his belt and I swallow against a bit of bile that rises in my throat.

I got away, but I almost hadn't. The idea that he might have forced me to do that to him when I never have before only makes it worse.

Without thinking, I jump to my feet. Jameson drops back to his heels and stares at me.

"Stand up," I order him.

"Duchess?" But he complies, and I kiss him hard on the lips resting my palms against the ridges of his abdomen. The contact gives me the courage I need to slide one of my hands lower, past the loose waistline of his jeans to the warm, rock-hard bulge that seems as eager for this as I am. But as soon as my fingers sweep over it he pulls back, circling my wrist with his hand.

"Duchess, I don't think it's a good idea."

My eyes narrow in annoyance. "I've already had one guy try to tell me what to do with my body tonight. How about you let me make my own decisions?"

It's logic he can't argue with, but before he tries, I drop down on one knee and then the other, sliding both my hands to the button of his jeans. I unfasten it, then I slide the zipper down until I can draw them off his narrow hips. I might be the one on my knees, but I feel powerful. My newfound courage surges through me, and I tug his boxer briefs down to his ankles.

It's not the first time I've touched a dick, but it's the most face time I've ever had with one. Until this moment, the whole process seemed pretty simple: take off pants, put in mouth, suck. Now that I'm getting a chance to study Jameson West's most impressive asset—and that's saying something—I wonder if I'm in over my head.

It's different than I remember. Strained, veins bluish with trapped blood, and long—so long that I am wondering how it will fit in my mouth.

And, for that matter, anywhere else.

"Duchess," he whispers in a hoarse voice. "You don't have to." He rakes his hand through my hair gently, reminding me exactly why I want to do this. I wet my lips with my tongue then I lean forward and lick. In the back of my head something Josie told me once comes to mind and I giggle.

Treat it like an ice cream cone.

"You're going to give me a complex," he warns. "Is it funny?"

I bite my lower lip and peer up at him. "No," I breathe. "It's delicious."

"Then feel free to have another taste," he says with a smirk. I take him up on the offer, running my tongue up and down and swirling it over the broad tip until I'm brave enough to lower my mouth over him.

The hand on top of my hair fists as a low growl of pleasure rumbles from his chest. "That's it, Duchess," he encourages me. "Oh fuck, just like that."

I bob my mouth up and down, my confidence boosted by the dirty words spilling from his mouth. "Your hand," he grunts. "Use your hand."

I grip it firmly, and he reaches down guiding my fingers along his length in unison with the rhythm of my mouth.

"Fuck, I'm going to come," he warns me in a strained voice, but when he nudges my head to push me away I hollow my cheeks and suck harder until a strange heat floods the back of my throat. It takes a little effort to gulp it down, but I manage with a couple gags. Apparently, I won't be going pro at blow jobs anytime soon.

He hauls me up by the elbow, his eyes half masked with pleasure and kisses me deeply. When we break apart he takes a deep breath. "Oh my God, that was ..."

"Not God," I stop him, "Just Emma Southerly."

Chapter 8

IT'S JUST past two in the morning when we land in Vegas. We're far enough away from the neon signs of the Strip, that the only light is from the blanket of stars overhead. I spot Josie leaning against her beat-up junker. Judging from the shorts, tank top, and vacant expression, she's still half asleep. Jameson raises an eyebrow when he spots her. "I could give you a ride home."

I force a tight smile. "I'm not going home."

Realization flashes in Jameson's eyes. With everything else that has been going on, it's easy to forget that home is not my happy place currently. "You could stay with me, and we wouldn't get into trouble at all."

I shake my head, and this time the grin on my face is real. The thought at staying at Jameson's house turns me into a puddle of melted jelly, and that's exactly why it's a bad idea. The thought of waking up next to Jameson is tempting. But I doubt we'd ever go to bed, or at least to sleep.

"My parents are already really pissed at me," I remind him, and given the events of tonight, I doubt that's about to change.

"Screw your parents. You'll be eighteen soon."

"Yes, I will," I confirm with a peck on his lips. "Call me crazy, but that's a little young to be living with my boyfriend."

"Okay, you're crazy," he teases, hooking his fingers in the loops of my jeans. "I think we're old souls."

"That might be true, but according to our driver's licenses, I'm a minor and you're already in enough trouble."

"I've never seen either of those facts on my license." He tilts his head in acknowledgement of that fact, but I can tell he's still not buying what I'm selling. That's okay, he doesn't have to. I'm the only one who has to live with my decision. "You sure I can't convince you otherwise?"

"I'll visit," I promise him. "You're going to be sick of me, Jameson West."

"I could never be sick of you."

"Wanna bet?" Part of me hopes that's true, but even with my questionable background in relationships, I don't think that's how it works.

"We won't know until we try."

"Spoken like a guy trying to get into my pants."

He leans forward, each of his breaths tickling my ear as he whispers, "I've already been there, Duchess. I just miss my happy place."

"Are you saying my vagina is your happy place?"

"Baby, it's my personal Disney World."

Josie coughs loudly behind us, and we startle apart. "Now that you two have ruined my childhood"—she pauses to yawn—"can we get going? Some of us need our beauty sleep."

I throw my arms around her and squeeze. Some people go home. But for me, some people are home. But before I can join her in the car, Jameson catches me around the waist. "Are you sure I can't convince you otherwise?"

"Well, no," I say a bit too forcefully. He drops his hold on me. "I mean, no. It's not a good idea."

He glances from me to Josie, then he kisses my cheek. "I'll call you tomorrow, Duchess."

"When?" I asked, as he starts to back away. It's a little sad that I want to plan my entire day around him. Sometimes a girl has to give in to her cravings. He shrugs, looking like a definition of the word cocky, as he stuffs his hands into his jeans pockets. "Depends on when I get up and around. I have a hard time getting up out of bed."

"Do you?" I ask.

"Sure you don't want to come over and see what I mean?" he offers.

I roll my eyes. Then I turn and loop my arm with my best friend's.

"Why are you passing up that invitation?" she hisses under her breath.

"Trust me, the invitation is open."

I MAY HAVE WOKEN Josie up, but her mom is just getting off her shift at the MGM Grand. She throws open the door to the tiny matchbox the Deckards call home as soon as we reach the front stoop. Her face is freshly washed, her dark skin glistening with moisturizer, and her hair is pulled into a tight knot at the top of her head. She's also doing her best impression of a pissed-off lioness.

"What the hell do you ..." she stops as soon as she sees me. "Oh my God, darling."

Marion throws her arms around my shoulders and gives me into the perfect hug. When you see moms and daughters in movies and on TV, this is what it looks like. At least that's the closest approximation to maternal affection I've ever known. Vivian Von Essen isn't known for warm hugs.

"I didn't know you were back."

"I just got in," I told her. "Josie gave me a ride."

"Emma's just going to crash with us, if that's okay."

"Your daddy knows?" Marion asks. But even as she begins her interrogation, she hauls me inside. A few minutes later, and she's got omelettes cooking on the stovetop. "Okay, now that I don't have a knife in hand, spill. Why are you staying at our house?"

"If it's not okay," I begin, but she holds up a hand, showcasing long, teal nails that undoubtedly match her costume for the latest show she's dancing in.

"You're always welcome in this house. But I saw how you hesitated when I asked about your daddy."

"We had a fight before the accident," I admit to her, "and things got ugly. Then Mom wanted me in Palm Springs… "

As much as I love Marion Deckard, I don't want to go in to more details about the shit sandwich life's been feeding me of late.

"He's probably worried about you."

"Yeah, well…" I press my fingertips into the tines of the fork she sat out on the bar. "Trust me, he doesn't expect me to come home."

"Do you want to talk about it?" she asks.

I shake my head. I'm just about all talked out. The talking never seems to cease. First everyone wanted me to talk about my parents' divorce. How was I feeling? Who did I want to live with? Then mom got remarried and I had to talk about her new husband. Was I excited? Did I like him? Where did I want to live *again*? At the time, I didn't have anything to say about him. That's certainly changed. But nothing was worse than when they started pleading with me to talk about Becca. *Share what happened that night. Share your favorite memories of her. Share how you're feeling.* No one wants to know when all you feel is numb.

At least when the police came around and started asking me to talk about Nathaniel West's murder they wanted facts, not emotions. They didn't need to know if I was sad or happy or scared. They just wanted a play by play. After tonight and the accident last month, there are going to be a lot more things for people to ask me about. I need to gather strength for the oncoming inquisition.

Marion shoves the carton of eggs into the overly crowded refrigerator and closes the door. Leaning against it, she stares me down. "Do you feel safe there?" One bad choice couldn't change a lifetime of feeling at home, right? But when I open my mouth, all that comes out is a small "no."

"You stay here as long as you need." She doesn't press me for further information. There's no threatening to call the police. No after-school special drill about talking with adults you trust. She's known too many men in this town not to read between the lines.

Josie reappears from the bathroom and takes the barstool next to mine. "That smells good." She peeks past her mother to the omelette pan.

"You better make one yourself if you want one."

"Oh, I see, Emma gets spoiled," she teases as she heads to the fridge. Pretty soon she's standing next to her mom, tending her own pan. Marion begins to hum, and Josie jumps in, singing the lyrics of what sounds suspiciously like a Taylor Swift song.

Marion whirls around and drops the omelette on my plate with the skilled ease of someone who lives primarily on eggs. I've never said no to her signature dish. Then again, I've never been offered anything else.

Turning around, she bumps her hip against her daughter's, and the two continue their duet while I take small bites. Between the buttery smell permeating the kitchen and the easy atmosphere, my appetite returns.

I try to help with dishes, but she shoos me away. Josie excuses herself to bed, but I linger in the small living room, staring at an old photo of me with Josie and Becca. Marion had taken it at some little carnival that had popped up in a grocery store parking lot. We had just come off the spinning cups, and we were still giggling and falling all over each other out of dizziness. One simple snap of the lens and she'd managed to capture pure happiness.

"I miss her every day," Marion says quietly.

I nod, my mouth too dry to agree with her. Somehow given Hans' revelation, I miss her even more. She feels farther from me than ever. Time is supposed to heal grief, and instead, it seems to keep finding new ways to open up the wound.

"Did she ever talk to you about a boy?" Boy is definitely the wrong word, but saying anything else might give away the situation. I don't give a crap what happens to Hans, long may he burn in hell, but I do care about how people remember my sister, especially about how I remember her.

"I wish." Marion moves beside me and shakes her head sadly. She wraps an arm around my shoulders and pulls me in closely. "But getting a Southerly girl to talk is a bit of a challenge."

She might be right, but no one wants to hear what I have to tell.

"I met her boyfriend." My stomach clenches on the white lie. "Or at least some guy who claims he'd…you know."

Marion pulls a few inches back and bites her lip guiltily. "I did take her to the doctor to get on birth control."

"Oh." I want something to hold on to. I need something to

hold on to. I should be used to grasping at straws and holding on to whatever shred of happiness reality tosses my way. I don't know how to find my footing with this. Becca definitely wasn't with any guys here. It doesn't prove Hans' story, but it supports it.

"Was the boy nice?" Marion asks.

For a moment, I forget the lie I fed her, but even when I process what she's asking me, I can't stop myself from telling her the truth.

"No."

Chapter 9

I SEE Becca in my dreams. It's her face. When she laughs, it's her voice. She glances towards me with a stranger's blue eyes, but she doesn't see me. She walks past me and through an unmarked door. When I follow behind her the room is dark and empty. I sit down and cry. There are a million questions I want to ask her, but even in the dream I know she's gone and that I'll never receive the answers I want.

Before, not knowing bugged me; now it hurts. Each second in the dark room seems longer than the last and the sadness takes over until the sobs roll powerfully through my body. Then there's a hand on my shoulder. I blink against the tears, trying to see in the darkness, certain Becca has come back for me, but as my vision returns, it's Josie's face that greets me.

"Are you okay?" she whispers, her voice groggy with her own dreams. "You were crying in your sleep."

I swipe a few tears lingering on my eyelids. "I'm fine."

"Do you want to talk about it?" Josie scoots lower in the bed until we're face to face. I'm not sure what to tell her. I still don't know how what I've learned about Becca will affect my memory of her, but I want to keep the information to myself. Josie shouldn't have to shoulder the burden of looking at one of her best friends differently. After all, the living can make amends, but the dead can never change.

"I was dreaming about Becca," I admit to her. "I don't remember much else."

"Was it hard to be in Palm Springs without her?" Josie asks. It's an obvious question and one she's nearly asked me a dozen times. I've known her long enough that I can tell when she's chickening out on addressing a topic.

I gulp against the sharp stab of ache her question produces. If she only knew how much Palm Springs had changed everything. "Yeah. It was weird."

"Is that why you left?"

Whatever has been holding her back from drilling me this summer is obviously no longer an issue. I can't expect to avoid questions when I up and run away in the middle of the night and land on my best friend's doorstep. It's a tad bit comforting to know that she's still here and willing to force the uncomfortable topics. But I don't want to talk about what happened in Palm Springs.

"I think I missed home," I say instead.

"Does home have an adorable dimple when he smirks?" Josie guesses and just like that the mood lightens, shifting subtly like the sky outside her window that's slowly changing from inky black to the purplish hues of dawn.

"Yes." It's one truth I don't have to hide. It's not as if I can camouflage my feelings for him. "Jameson isn't the only thing I missed about Vegas, but he's definitely top three."

She clucks her tongue in reproach. "I'd put him higher than that."

"Are you checking out my boyfriend?" I smack her shoulder playfully.

"Girl, you can't miss that ass."

"No, you cannot."

Josie can brag on my boyfriend all day long. The thought of being jealous where she's concerned is so ridiculous, I nearly laugh. Not only do I know he's not her type, but I also trust her with my life. That means I definitely trust her with my boyfriend.

"Does he look that good naked?" she asks in a hushed voice like her mom might be standing with her ear pressed to her bedroom door eavesdropping.

I bite my lip suddenly feeling a little self-aware even as my mind flashes to memories of his chest and arms, of his legs and *everywhere* else. "I haven't exactly seen him naked."

"I cannot believe you aren't tapping that," she squeals. "'There's picky and then there's prude."

"And nothing in between," I note dryly. Trust Josie to stick to the black and white ends of the sex spectrum. "We've screwed around and I'm pretty sure I've seen most of him."

"Details?" She insists, clutching her pillow like she's settling in for a bed time story.

I give her the laundry list of what we have done together, which might be short but I still think it's impressive. When I finish, she feigns wiping drool from her mouth. "So you're going to have sex with him, right?"

"I guess," I hedge.

"Oh my god, what is stopping you? Is it that stupid checklist of yours?"

What is stopping me? Jameson has proven to be nothing short of perfect. Well, he might be a little controlling, but it's not like I'll put up with that shit so it hardly matters. "No," I shake my head. "I'm pretty sure he's hit all the requirements."

She grabs my hand and squeezes it so tightly that she nearly breaks a finger. "Even love?"

Fuck a duck, that's a big one. Even though I've never written down all the requirements I had for my second time, love has always been at the very top.

"It's a simple question," she prompts me.

Am I in love with Jameson West? I haven't felt like I've been falling for him so much as hurtling with him for the last few weeks. But doesn't the fact that I didn't hesitate when she asked if he met *all* of the requirements mean something? The problem is neither of us have actually said it. We've tossed the term around, trying it on to see how it sounds, but we haven't gotten to those three little words.

"You're in love with him," Josie says it for me.

"I don't know, I mean..." I stammer as I try to think of a way out of this subject. But as the first sliver of sunlight appears on the horizon, everything becomes illuminated. "Yeah, I am."

Josie, for her part, is practically seizing in the bed with excitement. The realization just makes me feel nauseated.

"What if he doesn't love me?" I ask her in a quiet voice.

She abandons her mattress jig and props herself up on an elbow, wagging her finger at me. "I've seen how that boy looks at you. He's been waiting at the love party for you to show up for a long time."

"He hasn't said it," I tell her.

"Who cares if he says he loves you? He shows he loves you. It's a lot easier for a guy to say *I love you* than to prove he means it. Trust me."

And I have to because of the two of us, she's the one who knows.

Neither of us can fall back asleep so we get dressed quietly. I borrow a light cotton t-shirt and a pair of cut-offs from her when I realize my bags are full of unmatched outfits. At least I grabbed underwear.

"Maybe we should swing by your house?" she suggests. "You

could grab some stuff."

I bite the inside of my cheek and look for an excuse but she's right. Josie and I aren't exactly built the same way, which means our sartorial overlap is limited. Going home means I might run into my dad, though. The last time I saw my father was a bit of jumble. I have a faint memory of him visiting me in the hospital after the accident, but I was too drugged out at the time for it to count. Going back home, even to retrieve my belongings, might send the wrong message. After what Hans did, Dad looks better in comparison. But it doesn't undo what he did.

"Okay, spill," she demands when I remain silent. "What happened between you and your dad?"

I thought my fight with him was the low point of that evening until things got much worse. I'd been in no shape to tell Josie about it and from the time I wasn't on a perpetual dose of opioids, I'd wanted to forget that it had ever happened.

But you can't crash in your friend's bed indefinitely without giving up the goods. "He found out about Jameson and me."

"Oh, shit." Josie freezes and gives me her full attention leaving one eyebrow unlined. "I'm guessing he didn't take that well. Did he kick you out?"

I shake my head. That would have been far less complicated. "No, he tried to start a fight with Jameson and I got in the way."

"What are you saying?" Josie asks slowly. She's starting to put the pieces together, but she's still going to make me say it.

"He hit me—punched me to be precise." The nonchalant attitude I'm going for is completely undermined by the way my voice cracks when I say it aloud.

"Oh my god, I'm going to kill him." Her tone rises to an octave somewhere between shrill and ear splitting.

I wave my hands frantically before she gets too loud and

wakes up her mom. "He was aiming for Jameson. I jumped in front of it."

"That doesn't make it right, Em."

"Agreed." She doesn't have to tell me that twice. "But it's also not abuse, so don't even think about calling him in."

"You mean like he did to your boyfriend? Did Jameson pummel him before or after he hit you?"

"After." Admitting it is cringe worthy.

"I'm sorry but I have to say this; what a piece of crap."

"I think he was trying to protect me," I say, dredging up one of the many theories I'd overanalyzed for the better part of the last month.

"By hitting you? Don't play that game, Emma."

"No, by turning Jameson in. He honestly thinks the Wests are dangerous."

"Someone did kill the patriarch," Josie points out.

"You make it sound Shakespearean." I take my phone off the charger and toss it into my bag.

"Shakespeare knew a thing or two about fucked up families," she reminds me.

"Mr. Hunter would be so proud of you right now," I tell her, thinking about the overeager English teacher at Belle Mère Prep.

Josie leans into the mirror to finish her other eyebrow. "Speaking of Hunter, what do you think of him?"

"As an educator?" I say with meaning.

"In general," she says bypassing awkward and going straight for uncomfortable. At least, she's abandoning the topic of my dad.

"I think you already do well enough in that subject."

She flashes me a wide grin in the mirror, and I'm reminded of one of the other reasons that Belle Mère feels like home. "Oh, honey. I don't do it for the grades."

. . .

WHEN WE REACH MY HOUSE, I do a double take when I spot a white Mercedes, still sleek with factory wax, in the driveway. "Does he have company?"

"If he does, she has good taste," Josie says appreciatively. She pulls in next to it and eye fucks the car for a few seconds. I can't blame her. Her Civic isn't much to look at, but it is dependable. Two characteristics that mean nothing to a teenager.

Meanwhile, I stare at the house. The blinds are drawn, as usual. Pawnography, my dad's pawn shop off the Strip, doesn't open for a few more hours, which means he's probably home. I haven't had the heart to check in with Jerry, his manager at the store, to see if Dad's been coming in.

"So, he's here." Leave Josie to face my conundrum head on.

"Yep." Facing things isn't my strong suit.

We lapse into silence and she finally makes a suggestion. "We can come back later."

"There's a pretty good possibility he'll be here later, too." I unbuckle my seat belt and take a deep, steadying breath. There's also a good possibility that he's passed out from whatever he drank the night before. If so, I can probably get in and out before he knows I'm here.

"Wait, if he has company, do you really want to go in there? They could be...you know..."

She rolls her hips for emphasis.

I roll my eyes, "Gross."

"Just saying. I can go in if you want."

But I've made my decision. "No, I can do this."

When I reach the front door, I find it's unlocked. I'll be lucky if the whole place hasn't been robbed in my absence. But everything is in its place and there's no evidence of squatters.

The only difference is that Dad isn't on the couch. I consider peeking into his bedroom, but if Josie's right and he has someone over, that's the last thing I want to see. I already have step-daddy issues thanks to Hans, there's no need to further scar me.

My room is exactly how I left it, unmade bed and all. Most of my luggage is in Palm Springs, so I gather whatever bags I can and shove the contents of my closet inside.

"Emma?"

I jump, discovering my dad holding onto the doorframe. I can't tell if sleep or booze weighs down his eyelids.

"You're home," he says, but I shake my head vehemently. I don't want to give him false hope. I'm not back to save him.

"No, I'm just here to get some stuff."

"Your mom called," he continues ignoring my denial. "She said you took off but she didn't say why. That's the car she got you in the driveway."

That's a better explanation for the phantom luxury vehicle's presence than I could have hoped for. Then I remember she bought it with Hans' money. Maybe later, I'll take it to the desert and torch it. "Where are the keys?"

"On your dresser." He points to the fob. "It's been waiting for you. I was tempted to take it out for a spin, but I was hoping you'd come home."

"I didn't," I repeat. "I'm staying with Josie, I just need some clothes."

"Look, Emma I think it would be better if you stayed here."

I abandon the packing and glare at him. "Right now what you think doesn't matter. I feel safer at the Deckards."

My words are a verbal slap across his face. He recoils, shame flitting over his features before he looks at the floor. "I know you don't believe this but it was an accident."

"Yeah, I accidentally got in the way of the fist you intended for Jameson." I don't miss how he winces when I say his name. "Then you accidentally filed the police report against him for assault. I could have done the same to you, but I didn't."

I zip my old gym bag shut and throw it over my shoulder. The rest of my stuff is shoved into a couple of reusable grocery bags I found at the bottom of my closet. There's a lifetime of memories in this room that can't be packed away.

But maybe it's time to leave them behind.

"You're still a minor," he says finally.

"Is that the only card parents have?" I ask him, recalling how my mom said the same thing last night in Palm Springs. "Because I won't be a minor in a few days. So if you want to force me to stay here until I turn eighteen, go ahead. But when I do turn eighteen, I'll walk out that door and you'll never see me again."

"I don't want that," he begins.

"No, I didn't think so," I continue, not allowing him to interrupt my diatribe. "I need to come back on my own if I decide to come back at all."

"I want to make this right." There's a vulnerability in his voice that I've never heard from my father. I guess dads aren't supposed to show their weaknesses. He'd never been able to hide his. I'd just never been one of them before.

"Then give it time," I advise him.

Sliding past him, I head down the hallway.

"Are you still seeing him?" he calls after me.

I stop and turn to face him. "Yes."

"Just to upset me?"

I shake my head. It's not the first time in my life I feel sorry for my father. What can make a person stop believing in other people? "No. I'm still seeing him because I love him."

I drop that bombshell and then I walk away, leaving him to figure out how to cope with the damage.

Chapter 10

IT TAKES an embarrassing amount of time for me to realize that there is no key or ignition in this car. If I wanted to torch it before, now I'm planning on driving straight to get some gasoline for the bonfire. It's Josie who finally figures it out.

"Try that," she says, pointing to a button that reads on/off.

I press the brake pedal and then I hit the button. The engine purrs to life.

"This car is so sexy." Josie runs her fingers over the leather armrest. If I'm not careful she's going to orgasm on the spot.

"I hate it," I say through clenched teeth.

"Because it's from your mom or do you have problems with luxury cars in general?"

"You want it?" I dangle the key fob between us.

Josie flicks the bottom of it, then sighs. "This is yours, girl. I'll keep looking until I find a sugar daddy who'll buy me my own."

I know one who would. I nearly gag at the thought.

"Enjoy it, Emma," she advises me. "It's been a shit year and it's just a car. Who cares where it came from?"

Maybe she has a point. I decide to christen the car *Pain and Suffering*. It's a fitting name. If I'm going to cover the cost of years of therapy by myself, I guess I can accept the car.

"Care to go on a joyride?" I offer.

"I'd love to but I promised my mom that I would drive her to work this summer so she didn't have to figure out parking."

"Isn't it a bit early for her to be going in?" I glance at the digital clock on the dash. I realize it's already 8:30 in the morning, but Vegas doesn't exactly run on traditional work schedules.

"She has a fitting." Josie groans as she pets the sleek console between us. "I really wish I could stay and play. I have a feeling this is the beginning of a beautiful friendship," she murmurs lustfully.

"Get out of my car." I shove her playfully. "Before you leave a stain on the passenger's seat. I need to run a few errands, anyway. I'll catch up with you later."

"Okay," she agrees, then she leans over and air kisses my cheeks.

"What was that for?" Trust Josie to make me laugh when I'm trying to be pissed off about something.

"You're a sophisticated woman now," she says. "You drive a Mercedes."

"That doesn't make me European."

"Whatever you say, darling." She blows me a kiss before she climbs into her car.

Considering that I hadn't planned on coming back to Belle Mère so soon, there's more than a few things I need to tackle on my to-do list. I know I should triage the items—decide which is most important and start there— but there's one activity I can't put off any longer.

Belle Pointe is a smaller hospital, not the trauma center that I'd been brought to after the accident at Jameson's penthouse.

After a few days, I'd been released from that hospital into my mother's care. Leighton hadn't been so lucky. Sometime in the last month, they moved her from Las Vegas General to the cushy private institution.

Undoubtedly, it's closer to her parents but it has to cost twice as much. She still hasn't woken up, so I'm not sure she appreciates the upgrade. I don't know what to expect when I stop at the front desk. "I'd like to visit a patient."

"Fill out the chart." The nurse doesn't bother to look up from the paperwork she's sorting. I search for a pen for a few seconds before she reaches out and plucks one out of a ceramic planter. The top of the pen has a flower glued to it.

"Cute." I take it from her.

"You'd be surprised how many pens wander off." She shrugs and returns to her work. Not only is this place super swanky, judging from how hard it is to tell the waiting area apart from a lobby of a 4-star hotel, but it also conducts social experiments on important topics like pen stealing. As if they couldn't afford to buy more pens given how much a place like this costs.

I write down Leighton's name, then mine, and the time before I hand the clipboard back.

She checks it, then eyes me for a second. "Are you a family member?"

"Do I have to be?" I ask, unwilling to commit to an actual answer.

"You just look a little like her."

I almost tell her that I was the other girl in the accident—the one who walked away with a few bad cuts and some stitches—but it's not a fact I want to boast about.

"How is she doing?" I ask.

"Not my floor," the nurse admits. "You can ask the attending when you get up there. She's in room 321."

Despite the hefty price tag this place comes with, they

don't bother with much security. I head toward the bank of elevators. Stepping inside, I spot Jonas just as the sliding doors shut. I guess I'm not the only one back in town. I hadn't seen him since the accident, but Josie, who somehow knows the geographical location of half of the school, has kept me up to date on his family's travels for the summer. I consider hitting the button to open the doors, instead I hit the one for the 3rd floor.

It seems impossible to go from wanting to talk to someone every day to having nothing left to say to them. Somehow Jonas and I accomplished that. Although, I'm pretty certain he perfected it years ago. I hung on to a relationship that had been over for an embarrassingly long time. Chasing after him now seems like a step in the wrong direction.

The third floor is relatively quiet. The woman at the nurse's station doesn't look up as I pass or when I double back to head in the right direction.

I stop in the doorway, realizing far too late that Leighton's room isn't empty. Hugo leans into view before I can make a quiet exit.

"Pawn Star," he says affectionately. Hugo Roth has the amazing ability to sound like he's complimenting you and insulting you at the same time. A stranger might have found his greeting friendly, but I know that its intended effect is to keep me in my place, beneath him on the social, financial, and sexual scales. He's one of the original Housers, the group of students at Belle Mère Prep, who make it their mission to squash as many people beneath them as possible.

"What are you doing here?" I ask him as I move hesitantly into the room. I don't mean to come off so accusatory, but he's always brought out the bitch in me.

"Someone needs to visit her," he says in a flat voice.

I don't push him on it because I can hear how much he hates this question in his reply. "I just got back in town," I explain to him. "My mom didn't want me to come back until I was fully recovered."

Hugo looks me up and down then turns away, and stares at Leighton. Something about him looks lost until he finally speaks. "You look fine."

"I guess I was the lucky one," I murmur in a low voice. Seeing Leighton connected to a half-dozen machines that monitor her heart rate, breathing, pulse, and a number of other things I don't recognize is a pretty harsh reminder that I was fortunate to walk away that night. In the giant hospital bed, she looks small. Her skin is too pale, and they've chopped off some of her blonde hair on one side where stitches still pucker her scalp. On the other, her hair still brushes her shoulder.

"What do her doctors say?" I ask the question and then realize how stupid it is. Why would Hugo know that?

To my surprise, he answers, "There's brain function although it's not as strong as they'd like. Really, it's just a waiting game."

"What are we waiting on?" I ask him.

"Whether or not she wakes up." His fingers twitch and it takes a second for me to realize that he nearly reached out for her hand. I back up a few steps, feeling the need to give them space. I should ask him about The Dealer and try to get the scoop on the rumors floating about Belle Mère. He's always had a finger on the pulse of what's going on in our tiny enclave. Instead I say, "I'll leave you two alone."

"You don't have to," he says. "She's not much of a conversationalist."

I tug my purse strap higher up my shoulder. Right now, I don't feel very social either. I search for a topic knowing that half the things on my mind, I shouldn't even bring up. "I saw Jonas," I blurt out.

"That must have been exciting for you," he says in a snarky voice, which I ignore.

"Just as I was coming up. He was leaving."

"You thought you saw Jonas." Hugo corrects me. "He's in Indiana, or Illinois, or Omaha visiting his grandmother."

"You just named like half the country," I say. There's no doubt in my mind that I spotted Jonas. Considering that Hugo can't even remember where his best friend is supposed to be, it hardly matters.

"He's somewhere in the middle then."

If 'by the middle' he means downstairs, then he's right, but I don't push him on the subject.

"What are your plans for the rest of vacation?" I ask when I can't come up with anything else to say to him.

Hugo groans loudly, running a hand through his spiky blond hair. "I think I might learn how to do macramé. What are yours?"

"The same." I don't miss the resentment in his voice. I roll my eyes recalling that when it comes to Hugo Roth, you need full body condom, because he's such a dick. "I guess I should go."

I should be the one in that bed. Not her. I back toward the doorway and when my foot hits the outside hall, Hugo calls after me, "Emma, thanks for stopping by."

I blink a couple of times trying to process that he just showed appreciation for something I did. "You're welcome."

I make it a few steps towards the elevator before I turn around and creep back to Leighton's room. Hugo has his hand over hers as he whispers to her. I can't make out what he's saying, but it's enough to make me comprehend that miracles are possible because Hugo Roth has a heart.

I'm inside the elevator when a far less welcome realization hits me. I do look like Leighton. It isn't that it *could* be me in that bed, I conclude with sickening certainty.

It was supposed to be me.

Chapter 11

A BELL over the door tinkles as I walk inside the shop. Nostalgia surges through me, not just because the store is full of crap but because I spent most of my life calling it home. There were times when I slept on a cot in the back with Becca. I'd been working off the clock since I could count in order to fly under child labor law regulations. I used to consider myself an integral part of keeping this place functioning, now I know I was just a Band-Aid. I can't spend my whole life being the glue that holds my dad together, and this is the first place I need to let go of if I'm going to send him that message.

Jerry pauses from rearranging a display of Civil War era pistols and glances up to greet his customer. His joy is instantaneous when he realizes it's me. I'll bet he's been waiting a long time for his lunch break. He hurries out from behind the counter to greet me, pushing his floppy hair out of his eyes.

"I was wondering when you would be coming back." He goes for a hug and I let him, patting him awkwardly on the shoulder as he squeezes. "This place isn't the same without you."

I'm pretty certain that what he means is paychecks are irregular, deposits aren't making it to the bank on time and he's stuck here all hours of the day. But I'll take the compliment.

"I just popped by to grab something." There's no way to soften the blow, so I don't try.

The smile falls from his face. "Oh. I thought you were home to help for the summer."

"My Mom doesn't want me working at the shop, because of...the accident," I lie.

Jerry lets out a long whistle. "Do you think that's wise? I don't know how we're going to keep this place running."

We're not.

"I'm sure dad will make sure everything stays on track." I sidle past him towards the cash register. He watches me with interest, but he doesn't try to stop me. I'm not here for money. I doubt there's any to speak of, anyway.

"We both know that isn't true, Emma. He can't keep this place up without you."

Apparently Jerry managed to grow some balls while I was away in Palm Springs. I've always pegged him as more of a 'take it and like it' type. The kind of guy who spends his nights in one of those scuzzy little hole in the walls getting spanked by a woman in leather. I open a drawer and dig until I find the business card I threw in here a couple weeks ago, sliding it into the back pocket of my cut-offs, and slide the drawer closed. Jerry deserves better than to be lied to, especially after all the years he's put into this store. "You're probably right, but I can't spend the rest of my life holding him up."

"You shouldn't have to," he says in a soft voice. "You're too young...and pretty," he tacks on awkwardly.

I give him a small smile, hoping it doesn't encourage the crush he's been nursing on me for the last few months. Jerry's sweet, but I can't stay behind to help him out. I head toward the door, finally ready to leave this place behind for good. I pause and drink it in one last time.

The jerseys signed by long-retired athletes, guitars played by former rock stars, guns used in war, and knickknacks collected by children who grew into adults who no longer needed their treasures. The whole place is like a warning to let things go. Here, time doesn't seem to flow. It just stops, and if you're not careful, you can get trapped. I turn, and push up on my tiptoes to give Jerry a kiss on the cheek. "You shouldn't get stuck here, either," I advise him.

"Somebody has to keep it running." He scratches his head, following my gaze around the large, open store, and I can see that he's trapped here.

"Yeah, my dad has to keep it running," I remind him. "These aren't your burdens, and they're not your treasures."

I leave it at that, calling out over my shoulder, one, last time. "See you around, Jerry."

"See you, Emma."

Before I get in the Mercedes, I pull the business card from my back pocket and stare at it for a moment.

Dominic Chamber.

He came to me with a forged Babe Ruth baseball card. In the end, he left with the fake and gave me this. I hadn't known I'd need to use it. Now I know why I saved it, but, asking for help—drawing attention to a problem I'm not sure exists—makes me feel sick.

I shove the card in my glove box. Maybe I'll let it marinate there for a few days until I know what I want to do. As I pull out of the parking lot of Pawnography, I know it's the last time I'll visit.

It's bittersweet. I thought this place was my future—a ball and chain, that I'd have to drag with me my whole life. Maybe things never would be the same between my Dad and I, but I have to admit that his actions finally set me free.

"Ugh, Emma," I say to myself, gagging a bit. "Can you sound sappier?"

Reaching into my purse, I search for a pair of sunglasses to ward off the midday glare coming through my windshield.

There's only one person I want to see right now. I'm about to call him when I notice a maroon Monte Carlo behind me. It sticks out, because the same Monte Carlo was parked at the back of Pawnography. You tend to notice the other car in an empty parking lot. Against my better judgement, I slide on my phone and hit Instagram. It looks like The Dealer's been busy today. On the top of his feed, there's a photo of Josie, carrying a Weckman's drugstore bag full of toilet paper. I try to scroll down while keeping my eyes primarily on the road, but, there's nothing new of me...yet.

The Monte Carlo's windows are tinted, so I can't get a good look inside and the driver is staying far enough back that I can't see any other details. Flipping on my turn signal, I decide to test my theory by maneuvering across a couple lanes of traffic at a suicidal speed to take the closest exit. Sure enough, Mr. Monte Carlo follows me.

I've got The Dealer in my sights, or at least my rear-view. Now I just have to figure out what to do with him. So far, this asshole has been content to channel his inner-paparazzo, but what happens if he realizes I know he's following me? The thought chills my blood, and I hit auto dial.

Jameson answers after one ring. "Morning, Duchess."

"It's nearly afternoon," I inform him.

"So it is," he says with a yawn. For a second, I'm distracted by the thought of him stretching his magnificent arms over his head, wearing nothing but a sheet.

"I have a problem." I have to remember to get to the point.

"What's wrong?" The languid sexiness is gone from his tone, replaced by urgency.

"I'm pretty sure someone's following me. I think, maybe, it's The Dealer." I glance in the mirror to check if he's still there. He is.

"Well, stay on the phone and come to me."

"No. I'm trying to think of a way to trap him. Like, maybe I'll pull into a store and wait, and when he goes to follow me in—"

"Come straight to my house," Jameson cuts me off before I can rattle off the rest of my half-hatched plan.

"I'm not driving all the way up to Mount Charleston."

"You're driving? Whose car?"

My hands tighten on the steering wheel. "Jameson! Where can I go? I'm not going to Mount Charleston."

"Our place in Belle Mère," Jameson corrects me.

"How many freaking houses do you have in this city?" I snap, panic getting the better of me. So much for calm and calculating. Apparently I'm going straight to uber-bitch.

But he ignores my attitude and begins to rattle off directions.

"I'm not going to remember any of that."

"Then just stay on the phone and tell me where you are." It takes me seconds to find the cross streets, but when I do, he heaves a sigh of relief. "Okay, I want you to take your next left."

He navigates me to his house with saint-like patience. The Monte Carlo follows me the whole way.

"Your gate's closed," I tell him when I turn into his drive and see the wrought iron monolith blocking me from safety.

"I just opened it." As if on cue, the panels begin to slide to the side. I wait just long enough to be certain the Mercedes can fit through before I zoom forward. Any other time, I might waste precious seconds by admiring his house, but the Wests' real estate portfolio is the last thing on my mind.

Jameson is waiting on the front drive, wearing nothing but a pair of jeans. His feet are bare, his abs are on display, and judging from the tousled mess of coppery hair sticking in every direction, he really had been in bed. All I can think about is having those strong arms wrapped tightly around me. I put the car in park, not even bothering to turn off the engine, and run to him. Burying my face in his chest I breathe in his scent: soap and the remnants of yesterday's cologne mixed with a little sweat, like he'd been tossing and turning in his sleep.

He tips my chin up with his index finger. "Promise me you won't go around acting like live bait?"

"I just thought—" I start, but he cuts me off.

"It's not safe, Emma, and I need you to stay safe."

"Yeah, I'm your alibi," I mutter, trying to pull away.

Jameson holds me tighter. "You know that's not why I need you to stay safe, Duchess."

"I'm sorry ..." But the apology dies on my lips when the Monte Carlo barrels down the driveway.

"You didn't shut the gate," I yell at Jameson.

"I need you to stay calm," he says.

I wrench away from him, instantly realizing that there is more to this situation than he's letting on. "What did you do?"

"I need you to stay safe," he repeats himself.

"What did you do, Jameson?" I demand. The driver of the Monte Carlo climbs out of the car and walks towards us. Pausing at my car, he leans in and turns off the engine.

That's weird behavior for a psycho.

I expected The Dealer to be someone we know—someone who has a stake in our secrets—but I've never seen this man before, and I know I'd remember him. The guy makes The Rock look like a weakling. He could probably eat The Rock for breakfast. His neck is wider than his head, bulging with veins that pulsate down to his broad shoulders and inhumanly large arms. If someone told me he was smuggling pythons around those biceps, I'd believe it.

"This is Maddox," Jameson informs me. "He's a former Navy Seal."

"And my new stalker," I add.

"And your new bodyguard," Jameson corrects.

I whip around to face Maddox, not realizing how much closer he's come to me. I have to crane my neck so that I can see his face when I tell him, "Thanks, Maddox. Nice to meet you. We won't be needing your services."

Maddox glances at Jameson, who gives a condescending tilt of his head, as if to say *you're dismissed for now* before he grabs my hand and drags me inside.

"I do not need a bodyguard," I say through gritted teeth. "The thought of someone following me around night and day is enough to drive me crazy."

"I disagree with you," Jameson says.

"That doesn't matter. I didn't give you permission to hire someone to follow me around."

"No, you didn't. But I cleared it with your mother."

"You spoke to my mother?" I begin to pace, needing to put distance between us, even if it's only a few steps. I guess he's siding with her on the whole *Emma is a minor, we can do whatever we want to her* issue.

"I assumed that you'd fight me on this."

"And you didn't think I'd fight my mom on it?" I ask. If that's true, then Jameson West doesn't know me half as well as he thinks he does.

"This is about your safety. I don't want to control you, I just need to know that you're safe."

"You keep using that word. I don't think you know what it

means, because I am safe. The accident was just that: *an accident.*"

It's obvious that he's been preparing for this reaction, because he doesn't blink. "Hans and your mother had security on you the whole time that you were in Palm Springs."

"What?" This I didn't expect. "I barely left the house."

"They sat outside the house, and when you did leave, they followed you."

How on earth had I missed that? "You all should win awards for paranoia. I'm going to get the lot of you tinfoil hats for Christmas."

"It's not paranoia, Duchess. Someone pushed you through that window. I can't be with you all the time." His tone isn't pleading, it's firm. This has been decided for me. "When you decided to leave Palm Springs, I reached out to your mother because I wanted my man on you."

"I don't want any man on me," I tell him, shoving him in the chest. "Especially not you at the moment."

A growl of frustration vibrates through him and he moves forward, backing me toward a wall. "They would have sent Hans' men," he informs me, "and I don't want that creep to know that you so much as ate breakfast this morning."

"That doesn't give you the right to have me followed."

"It's a precaution. Nothing more." When I go to argue, he smashes his mouth against mine, kissing me until I'm senseless. My rage seeps away. It's an effective way to the end the conversation.

My fingers run along the stacked plane of his abs, vibrating on each one. Now I know where they got the term *washboard*. I break away, panting heavily, my lips still brushing over his. "This conversation isn't over."

"I'm not stupid, Duchess." He licks my lower lip in invitation.

"You're very stupid," I moan. "With your stupid mouth and your stupid body."

"That's it, baby. Try to stay mad." He rocks against me, encouraging me to focus on a very different, but equally intense, range of emotions. "You're so cute when you're angry."

"I'm about to be goddamn gorgeous!" But I can't keep my lips away from him. Jameson answers my kiss with a groan as he lifts me off my feet. My thighs make contact with the heat of his bare skin and I give in to the wild woman trying to claw her way out.

I am mad at him. A message which he probably isn't getting since I'm wrapped around him like a pretzel. I snake my arms around his torso and dig my fingernails into his back. He responds by pressing me against the wall.

"Let it out, Duchess," he urges me. "Show me how pretty you are when you hate me."

Oh god, I wish I hated him. It would make it so much easier to walk out that door and take control of my own life.

"I hate you," I murmur against his mouth and he sucks my words away with a kiss, plunging his tongue deeply into my mouth. Since he's not going to let me verbally get my point across, I rake my nails down his back.

He winces audibly before whispering, "I told you I like it."

Rough? I'll give him that. When he goes to kiss me again, I bite down on his lip until iron floods over my tongue. He pulls back and runs his tongue over his injured lip. "If you aren't careful, I'm not going to be able to stop."

"Stop what?" I demand breathlessly.

He answers with a thrust that I feel through two layers of denim.

"Did I ask you to stop?" I ask.

"Be very careful with what you say now, Duchess," he warns me, "unless you want to find yourself naked in my bed."

"Maybe that's exactly what I want."

"You hate me," he reminds me.

I love you. The words trip over my tongue but I swallow them away. Now isn't the time to reward his behavior with affection.

"Goddammit, Jameson, take me to bed."

"No way," he says with a grin. "Not angry. At least, not for the first time."

I can't help but like the idea that there'll be a second time or a third. I don't think I could ever get enough of him, and if he keeps acting like this, we'll have plenty of angry sex in our future.

But there's an ache building inside me that can't be ignored, so I decide to change my tactics. "Don't you want to take me to bed?"

"Fight fair," he advises me. "I can't handle it when you pout."

I stick out my lower lip, realizing I have all the ammunition I need to get my way. I circle my hips, rubbing against him. There's more than one way to get a rise out of him. "Please?"

"Christ." He grabs my hips and forces me to stop. "I want to stay in control."

"And I want you to lose control," I whisper.

"Is that what this is about? A power struggle?" He nuzzles my neck before nipping the curve of my shoulder. "Because you hold all the cards, Duchess."

I stop pouting and revel in his admission.

"You look pleased with yourself," he notes.

I press my heels into his back, forcing him to crush his body harder against mine. "I hold the cards?"

"Yes," he mutters.

"Then take me to bed," I order him.

Chapter 12

HE KISSES me as he swiftly maneuvers our tangled bodies across the foyer toward the stairs, but before he can carry me to my requested destination, a familiar voice shrieks.

Jameson stops and we break apart, our eyes still locked together. "We have company."

"So it seems," I mutter. "What's a girl have to do to get some?"

Jameson chuckles softly as he extricates his body from mine, placing me safely on my feet.

"Jameson, dear," his mother calls, "please put a shirt on. It's nice to see you again, Emma."

"You, too, Mrs. West." I don't bother to pretend that I'm happy to see Monroe with her. The two of them are laden with shopping bags.

"Would you like some help?" Jameson offers, stepping away from me. I already miss the feel of his skin on mine.

Trust love to turn me into a wide-eyed, helpless sad sack.

"Shirt," she repeats. I have to smother a giggle at the frustration that flits across his face, but Jameson nods and dashes up the stairs.

I stand there for a minute, trying to decide where to go. Following him seems like a bad idea, because unless I'm mistaken, his mom just put the kibosh on our afternoon sexscapades. Instead I wander past the foyer until I find myself in the kitchen.

"Oh, hell," Monroe mutters when she spots me. "Mom, the maid forgot to take the trash out."

"I forgot. I got you a present," I tell her. Then, I give her my middle finger.

"Classy."

"I learned it from you," I say with a fake sob.

She twirls around, her stick-straight, blonde hair whipping over her shoulders as she drops her bags on the kitchen island. Jameson reappears with his mother on his heels. This time he's wearing a shirt, and grabs my hand, bringing it to his lips for a quick kiss. Evelyn studies him for a second before giving him an approving smile. "That's better."

He winks at me and heads towards the fridge, kissing his mom on the cheek as he goes. He pulls out a box of pizza but before he can open it, his mother bats his hand away.

"I can't believe you're going to eat that."

"I'm hungry," he protests, but he tosses the box in the trash.

She ruffles his hair in affection. "Did you just get up?"

Monroe glances at me and smirks. "Something's kept him in bed, obviously."

Jameson doesn't miss a beat, immediately picking up on what his sister is implying. He comes over and throws an arm around my shoulders. "Emma just got here. Unlike some, she's a lady."

"I don't know what you're insinuating." Monroe shrugs as

she studies her manicure. I know exactly what he's saying, but I keep that to myself. "I just call it like I see it."

As much as I despise Monroe, I like Jameson's mother. There's no need to make things any more awkward. I'm pretty certain her walking in on our make-out session covers that. Evelyn West has not only perfected the ability to look polished at any given time, but also the ability to ignore it when her children squabble.

"Emma, would you like something to eat?" she asks me as she pulls a vegetable tray out of the Sub-Zero and places it on the counter.

I shake my head. My nerves are still raw from trying to evade my own bodyguard this morning and I'm on edge after the fight that I've left unfinished with Jameson.

"Probably for the best," Monroe says. "It looks like you were eating well in Palm Springs."

This catches her mother's attention. She turns on Monroe and glares. "No daughter of mine will speak to another woman that way."

"Mom, I was just—"

Evelyn silences her with a single look. "No excuses."

"They're not ladylike," Jameson jumps in.

"I don't care if either of you are ladies. In my opinion, being a lady in this day and age is highly overrated, but girls have enough problems without being catty to one another." She speaks the truth and we both know it, which is why we all remain quiet.

"Show Jameson what we picked up today," Evelyn suggests after we've all been on our best behavior for a few minutes.

"He doesn't want to see it, mom." For the first time since I've known her, there's an embarrassed edge to Monroe's words. There's no way I'm going to miss this. I take a step back and watch as she pulls out some candles and a framed picture.

"I thought it was best if Monroe redid her room here," Evelyn tells Jameson, her voice tight with emotion. "I don't want either of you going back to the penthouse."

I expect them to put up a fight about this but instead they nod. I'd always assumed that Monroe's lack of respect for authority figures stemmed from her father's money. After all, who cares what people think of you when you can just buy their respect, or at least their silence. She's different around her mother. If I hadn't been subjected to such large doses of her bitchiness, I might even like her now.

"I left a few things in the car," Evelyn says to Jameson. "Can you help me with them?"

He glances at me, as if to check that this is okay, but she loops her arm through his.

"Do you mind if I borrow the man of the house?" Sadness coats her words and I can see what a struggle it is for her to keep a smile on her face.

"Of course not." It's not like I can answer any other way.

Plus I've just spent the better part of an hour trying to convince Jameson that I don't need a babysitter. If I want him to believe me and to tell Maddox to step down, then that means I'm going to have to learn to take care of myself in any situation, even those that involve Monroe, a.k.a. The Witched Bitch of the West.

Monroe and I stare at one another. Neither of us speak. She picks up a carrot stick from the tray of crudités her mother has set out for all of us and munches on it. The crunch of her teeth is the only sound in the kitchen, and I join her, absent-mindedly eating as a means to pass the time. We might not be capable of being nice to one another, but surely we can shut the hell up and tolerate each other for a few minutes.

"Hugo said you went by the hospital," Monroe says. Apparently, our relationship now includes casual conversation.

"I did," I mumble.

"How did she look? I can't stand to go in there," she admits. "Hospitals aren't my thing."

"You haven't gone to see her?"

Her eyes narrow at the judgment in my tone and I immediately regret my words. "I went," she says defensively. "But only once."

"Yeah. I don't like hospitals, either." I decide to take a different tact. The fact is that Jameson isn't going anywhere. Not if I have anything to say about it. So like it or not, his family is a package deal. Monroe included. As long as I don't have to move into some type of creepy, multi-generational compound with all of them, I need to at least try.

"She looked pale," I say at last. "I didn't stay long. I had no idea Hugo would be there."

"He's always there." Monroe confirms what I had suspected when I saw them. She doesn't have to say any more than that.

"I had no idea they were so close."

"I don't think he did, either," she confesses. "It's funny how you don't realize how you feel about somebody until you don't have a chance to tell them."

Is it opposite day? Because now I find myself wanting to hug her. I refrain, knowing that that would be too much, too soon. It probably always will be.

Jameson and Evelyn reappear, saving us from our uncomfortable attempt at discussion.

"I thought I'd cook dinner this evening." There's a brief glimmer of light in Evelyn West's eyes as she says this, but it immediately extinguishes. She's trying so hard to be strong; anyone can see that. Maybe that's why her kids are treating her with such care.

"Would you like to stay?"

"I'd love to, but I promised my best friend ..."

She waves off my excuse. "No need to explain. Another time."

Jameson's eyes dart to mine and he stops unpacking the grocery bags. "Mom, I'm going to walk Emma to her car."

She nods and begins to discuss what color Monroe would like to paint her bedroom. Jameson doesn't take my hand as he leads me back to my car. "I'm sorry about earlier," he offers.

"But you're still going to have Maddox follow me," I guess.

"You can be mad at me all you want."

"That's good," I jump in, "because I'm going to be."

Reaching out, he cups the side of my face with his palm. "You're a firecracker, Emma Southerly."

I smile sweetly. Just wait until he sees me go off.

Chapter 13

"I'M famous for buying toilet paper now," Josie announces as she slings her purse onto a chair in the corner. "Did you see?"

I glance up from my laptop and grimace. She's holding the bag from Weckman's that The Dealer snapped her with earlier. "I saw."

The real question is whether or not she's thought about what that means. Josie crosses to her dresser and pulls out an oversized t-shirt.

"My boobs are killing me." She strips off her top and bra and pulls the comfy shirt on. "I'm just glad all he caught was the Charmin and not my tampons. Paying Eve's penance is bad enough without photographic evidence."

I close the lid of my computer and search for the right way to bring this up. "So the picture was taken this afternoon?"

"There's the proof." She points to the t.p. sticking out of the plastic bag.

"Did you see anyone? Taking your picture, I mean?" I force myself to ask the hard question.

"No." She lies next to me on the bed and stares up at her

bedroom ceiling. I scoot down and join her. Dozens of plastic, glow-in-the-dark stars are still stuck overhead. "Remember when we put those up?"

"Your mom was convinced the landlord was going to kick you out," I remember with a laugh. "What were we, ten?"

"Eleven," Josie corrects me with a giggle. "I abided by the no posters on the wall for a whole year."

"And then you went on a rampage, starting with those." I grab her hand and we look up. When we were younger, we'd lie on the floor during sleepovers, and I would stare at those stars and make wishes. Right now I wish I still believed in their magic. "Josie, if that photo is from today, someone followed you."

Her grip on my hand tightens as I point this out.

"I know," she whispers. "How didn't I notice him?"

"It's a busy city. Whoever it is knows how to stay unseen." I sigh. It was a long shot that she might remember catching someone with a camera, but we need a break. "Why are you so certain it's a guy?"

"What do you mean?" Josie flips on her side and I do the same. We stare at each other, each clutching a pillow.

"You always say *him* or *he*."

"I guess I just assume this perv is a dude," she says.

The whole game does have a creepy, up-skirt camera vibe. But even narrowing it down to a *him*, doesn't get us any closer to discovering The Dealer's identity.

"You know my pic wasn't the most interesting one he posted. Did you see the other one?"

I frown. The other shot had been nonsensical at best. A cup o' joe labeled May. "The cup of coffee? May? Maybe The Dealer is behind on posting since it's June."

"No!" Josie sits up and tosses the pillow to the top of the bed. "What was under the cup of coffee."

I roll over and grab my phone from her bedside table. Opening Instagram, I scroll to the photo. "I stared at this thing forever."

"And you didn't notice the business card?" she asks dryly. Leaning over, she taps the screen and I immediately spot the black card poking out from beneath the mug.

"I was looking for lipstick or a logo on the cup." I leave out that I also studied the woodgrain of the table, hoping I might recognize the coffee shop where the photo was taken. I'd been so focused on minute details the whole time, I'd missed the most important element.

"What does it say?" she asks.

I raise an eyebrow. "You noticed but you didn't even try to read it?"

"Not all of us spent our afternoon working on our amateur sleuth badge," she teases. "I figured we'd tackle it later."

I pinch the screen and zoom in. It's hard to make out the card's gold foil lettering, especially since the cup cuts some of the info off. "It looks like a-c-h-è, but I know there's more."

"There's part of a phone number, too."

I sit up on the bed and reach for my laptop. "So we know The Dealer is in Vegas."

"He didn't take any pics of you in California," she says with a nod, "and he was obviously here today."

"That's about the only thing I miss about Palm Springs," I mutter as I open Google. Typing in what I can see on the business card, which is nothing more than the letters and a few digits of a phone number, I hold my breath and hit *search*.

"Anything?" Josies asks as the search results load.

Frowning, I scroll down and stop when I hit the third entry. Cachè. Half the phone number listed matches what I could read on the card. "That can't be a coincidence."

"What?" She worms her way next to me so that she can see the screen. "I don't get it."

"I forgot you failed French."

She jabs me in the stomach. "I didn't take French."

"Cachè means hidden." I give her a second to process this. "Like—"

"The Dealer," she finishes for me. "Holy shit."

"Did I earn my badge?" I ask her.

"With honors."

We both fidget as Cachè's homepage loads. The website is sleek and modern, carefully presented with very little information. "Let's see. They're located in Las Vegas. Big surprise. No clue what they're selling...or hiding."

"Click on that," Josie says, pointing to the company policy page.

The company policy consists of a single line:

Cachè provides singular companionship with uncompromising discretion.

"Wait," Josie fumbles for words as it hits both of us. "Cachè is a brothel."

"I think they use the term escort agency."

"Is there really a difference?"

We both know there is. You don't grow up in Nevada without knowing a bit more about issues of vice than most people your age. "Hand me my phone."

Josie sucks in a breath before she relinquishes it. "Are you sure this is a good idea?"

"You're right. This is why he posted this photo." I check the number on my computer screen as I begin to dial.

"So maybe it's a trap," she says nervously.

"I don't think The Dealer wants to hurt us." I hesitate before I hit the call button. Talking to the agency isn't dangerous. It's just about information, so why is my heart lodged in my throat?

"How do you know that?"

"Because whoever it is followed you around long enough today to get a photo of the most embarrassing part of your day." I tilt my head toward the Weckman's bag.

"Everybody poops, Emma." She jumps on the bed and begins to pace nervously. "What are you going to say?"

"I'm going to wing it," I admit before I press the green circle. It only rings twice before a breathy voice answers.

"Cachè."

"Yes, I'm calling to..." I look at Josie and say the first thing that comes to mind, "Find out about a job."

"YOU'VE OFFICIALLY LOST YOUR MIND," Josie informs me the next morning as we stand in the entry and go over today's plan. "Who is going to notice something like this?"

"Jameson West needs to be taught a lesson." I finish throwing my license in her purse, then pass her mine. I'd borrowed a black, lace romper from her that left little to the imagination. Between the fuck me pumps she'd insisted I wear for today's undercover operation, and handing off my purse, I feel more than a bit out of my element. "Little details are going to be important. Believe me, this Maddox is ex-military."

"What branch?"

"Why do you care, GI Jane?"

She grabs her bag from me and fishes out her plum lipgloss. "Don't wear that!" I grab it back. "I'd never wear that color."

"You're also not black, Emma," she points out dryly.

"I'm tan and wearing a hat," I shoot back.

She plants her hands on her hips and stares at me. "Hat and tan aside. No one has ever mistaken us for each other."

"As long as you stay far enough from him, he'll never know." I hand her my keys. "Plus, you get to drive the Mercedes."

Offering her the keys to my shiny, new ride was the only part of my insane plan that had interested her.

"You shouldn't go alone."

"It's my only choice unless I want to take Maddox along," I remind her.

"Why do you care if Jameson knows you're playing detective?" she asks, dropping the key chain into my bag.

"I don't. This is about teaching him a lesson."

"Isn't love grand?" she quips, but she doesn't press further. Neither of us are the type to appreciate a guy overstepping his boundaries. "Just promise me you'll be careful."

"I'm not doing anything dangerous." *Not really.* I've only told her about half of my plans for the day. If Maddox catches up with her, the less she knows, the better.

"Look, he's worried about you, and he has a right to be. I don't see why having a little hired muscle with you is so wrong." She squares her shoulders before she adds, "But I'm your best friend, so lecture over."

I kiss her cheek. "It's cute when you worry. I'll go out the garage. Wait a few minutes and then run out to my car."

With any luck, my newly hired shadow would be too distracted by both of us leaving to realize we'd switched cars.

Climbing into the driver's seat of the Civic, memories flood me. I'd learned to drive in this car courtesy of Josie and Becca. Dad was usually too drunk to give proper instruction. While I'm still not a fan of being behind the wheel, at least I'm comfortable here. I know what every button does. The stereo has a radio and a tape deck. I've never once needed to check a 300 page instruction manual to figure out how to open the fuel tank.

I don't bother to look at Maddox's car as I pull out, but

when I finally give in and peek in the rearview mirror, I see he's starting to pull away from the curb. Dammit, he must assume we're together. He's a few car lengths behind me when he comes to a stop. Josie's in the Mercedes, heading the opposite direction at breakneck speed.

"I hope I have full insurance on that," I say to myself. But her dramatic exit works. Maddox backs his car into a driveway and peels out to catch up with her. I blow a kiss.

It might be nice to think the hard part of the day is behind me, but I left a few errands off the list I shared with Josie when I convinced her to help me with my shenanigans.

Pulling over a few blocks away, I glance around to make certain that Maddox didn't wise up. When I know I'm alone, I dig Dominic Chamber's card from my wallet and input his address in my phone's GPS app. He's only fifteen minutes away, which gives me plenty of time to pay him a visit and still make my interview at Cachè.

With a full day of being in the wrong place at the right time ahead of me, I can't help hoping that I'll catch the attention of The Dealer. I failed to mention to Josie that today I'll be playing the role of live bait. If this amateur creep is interested in photos of Josie with toilet paper, I can only imagine how eager he'll be to catch me walking into an escort agency. This time, though, I'll be the one waiting to snap a picture of him.

Reaching into Josie's purse, I rifle through a handful of receipts from Weckman's until I find a few lipsticks stashed at the bottom. Pulling the caps off each, I search for the perfect color. The last one labeled Troublemaker is exactly what I'm searching for. Swiping the bright red over my lips, I smack them together in the mirror. The Dealer has no idea who he's messed with.

"Say cheese, asshole."

Chapter 14

THE CHAMBER DETECTIVE Agency looks like the set for an old film noir. Right down to the gold foil letters on the office door. A bell tinkles as I open it and look around to discover a cluttered desk and a half-dead fern. A familiar head pokes around the corner.

"Just a sec. You want coffee?" he calls out.

"No thanks." I don't trust my stomach to keep anything, even something as innocuous as coffee, down today. Butterflies are already churning up what's left of last night's late night snack with Josie.

I remember Dominic Chamber more for his woolly eyebrows than his detection skills. It's a long shot coming to him for help, especially given that he hadn't been keen enough to spot a fake Babe Ruth card. But since I don't know any other private investigators, he's what I have to work with.

Today he's in a velour jogging suit the color of overly cooked green beans. How he manages to wear it and keep the office at a balmy 85 degrees is beyond me. I fan myself with my hand as he pushes aside a stack of papers to make room for his coffee mug.

"Let me guess...cheating boyfriend?" he asks, sizing me up.

"Close," I grant him. "Cheating wife." Amongst so many other things, but I have to start somewhere.

"Well, the times, they're a-changing." He leans back in his chair and crosses his arms behind his nearly bald head. "Do I know you?"

"We had some business before." I hesitate to mention the baseball card. A shrewd business man doesn't accept payment in the form of collectibles.

"Hold on," he says before I can continue. "I'm good with faces." A few seconds later, he snaps his fingers. "The waitress from the Golden Nugget."

If we were playing hot and cold, he'd be in the arctic. I shake my head.

"The lady with the lost Shih Tzu."

Arguably, I'm about to lose my Shih Tzu just being here, but I can see that he's not going to stop guessing. "The girl from the pawn shop."

"The heartbreaker." He clutches his chest. Then he points to a frame on the far wall. I look over to find the forged card on display. "I decided who cares if it's real. It impresses clients."

"You know what? I think I need to be somewhere." I grab my purse from the floor, but before I can stand up, he starts to talk.

"That's not your purse," he tells me, "or your outfit. I'd wager you're as comfortable in that lipstick as you are in those heels. You're pretending to be someone else today, which means you're hiding from someone. Maybe your mother? She's the cheating wife, right? But you work in your father's shop, so why would you care?"

My mouth falls open and I have to force it closed. "How did you do that?"

"I might be bad with faces, but I'm good with details."

"No, really," I press. I don't think private investigators cling to their secrets as tightly as magicians, and I want to know his tricks.

"You looked at the floor for a second before you picked up the purse, like you were looking for a different one. You've been tugging up your top since you walked in. Whoever that belongs to has a smaller bust-line. No offense."

"None taken," I assure him. "Go on."

"I didn't recognize you at first because you don't look like the kid who threw that fake card in my face."

"Sorry," I interject, but he waves me off.

Taking a sip of coffee, he studies me for a moment. "Hiding from your mom is a guess. Girls your age like to dress up behind their mother's backs. I'm guessing she wouldn't want you walking around this city looking like that. No offense again."

At least, I'll look the part at the escort agency.

"You said cheating wife and I remembered that the other guy who works at that shop, who is less concerned about authenticity, by the way, mentioned the owner was out. He'd been coming in less since he got divorced. I gathered since you're here about a cheating wife and your parents are divorced that we're talking about your mom."

"Holy shit." I applaud politely and he bows his head.

"So what can I help you with, Miss?"

"Emma," I correct him. "Can I still call you Dominic?"

He nods, steepling his fingers as he waits for me to spill.

"It's about my sister," I begin. "She's...she died."

"I'm sorry to hear that."

"Anyway, I came across her death certificate recently and noticed that there's no father listed on it." I really hope his gift extends to reading between the lines, so I don't have to spell out anymore of this than I have to.

"And you want to know who her dad is? You thought you shared the same father," he guessed.

"Yes," I say in a quiet voice.

"I have to warn you, Emma. Paternity cases can dredge up some nasty secrets."

I think of how much my father drinks to deal with her death. Then to Hans and his unnerving relationship with Becca. "There are a lot of things I don't know about my sister. I have to start somewhere."

"I'll look into it." He picks up a card from a stack on his desk but I shake my head.

"I already have one."

"Then I'll just need you to fill this out. Basic information. Your name. Her name. Everything is kept confidential." He passes me a sheet of paper and a pen. "My standard rate is $100 an hour."

I flinch and force a smile. "Do you take credit cards?"

"And fake baseball cards," he says, grinning back.

I finish filling out the information form and check the time on my phone. "I have to go!"

"I look forward to working together," he calls after me. "I'll let you know as soon as I have anything."

I pause at the door and consider my next request. "There's one more thing," I say slowly. "My father had a grudge against Nathaniel West. I want to know how it started."

"It might raise some eyebrows if I go digging around looking for info on Nathaniel West," he warns me.

I think about my next appointment. "Be discreet."

. . .

CACHÈ IS NOT what I expect. The agency's office is as minimal as their website, the only sign of personality is the black paint coating the walls. But I guess you hide things in the dark. There's only one woman inside and she greets me at the door. Her dress suit matches the wall, the neckline dipping to display an impressive amount of cleavage. Other than a single silver streak at each temple her hair is fiery red.

"You must be Caroline." She extends a hand and I take it uncertainly. "I'm Suzanne."

"Um, yes, I am." I'd nearly forgotten the fake name I'd fed her when I made the appointment.

"If you don't mind my asking..." She pauses and I suspect whatever comes out of her mouth next is going to be a bit rude. "...how old are you?"

"I'll be eighteen next week." That isn't a lie. "Is that a problem?"

It's been a while since I brushed up on the Vegas prostitution guidelines. It's a joke at Belle Mère Prep that they hand out a pamphlet on the subject during career day in the local public schools.

"Oh, lovely!" She claps her hands together in delight, which I suppose means I'm good to *ho*. "You won't be able to start until then, of course, but we can begin all the necessary paperwork and tests."

"Tests?" I repeat back.

"The usual. We need to check for STDs and pregnancy as well as overall health." She gestures to the chair at her desk. I sit down and let this soak in. I don't know how far I'll have to go to find out why The Dealer led us here. Getting blood drawn might be my hard limit, never mind having someone poke around inside my vagina. Ironically. "Will that be a problem?"

"I guess I didn't realize that..." My blush finishes the sentence for me.

"Sexual relations are not a requirement. This is an escort agency." She gives me a practiced smile that feels as rehearsed as those lines. "You choose if you want to engage in sex with your clients."

"Then why the tests?"

Her smile grows forced. "Many of our girls enjoy sexual relations with our clients who are very wealthy men and *very appreciative.*"

Translation: they're willing to pay because they're old, fat, or desperate.

"As I mentioned, we don't encourage our girls to have sex, but..."

"I don't have a problem with it," I interject before she can end the interview. It's not like I'm actually taking the job, so what do I care about the semantics of it. "I just wanted to understand. I don't want to get into trouble."

"There will be no trouble." The warmth in her tone returns as she begins to click around with her mouse. "Our clients are very discreet. They know to expect a certain caliber of women and they follow the rules."

"If they don't?"

"I handle all appointments personally. Once you're on my blacklist, you can't beg or buy yourself off it."

I don't want to know what lands you on that list, judging by the cold undercurrent in her words.

"You'll want to choose a name," she advises. "We don't recommend that girls give their real names. It encourages stalking or romance, both activities we strictly prohibit."

So I'm not allowed to fall in love with the desperate old men. I think I can handle that. "So I can work here?"

I'm surprised by how little she needs to know to hire me. Then again, I think living, breathing, with a vagina might be the only non-negotiables.

"We'll have to wait for the tests and your birthday, but I think you're just what a few of my clients are looking for." She pushes her chair away from the desk. "Excuse me, while I get some forms off the printer."

She walks into the other room and I'm left with a choice. Since I don't have any time to waste, I gamble. Jumping up, I lean over her desk and grab her mouse. I click around until I find the appointments calendar on her desktop. Opening it, I scroll until I find what I'm looking for.

May.

Whoever she is, she's popular, because she's booked out through the end of the next week. Before I can talk myself out of it, I schedule a fake name in the next available time slot. I use my real number. Hopefully, they don't call to confirm bookings like the hair salon. The only thing left to decide is where, and I happen to have an in at the West Resort. It's going to be fun to explain this one to Jameson. I'm clicking finish when the screen freezes. Shooting daggers at the wheel of death that's replaced the mouse's curser, I count the seconds until it stops and I can close the schedule. I've just sat back down when Suzanne reappears.

"This has all your forms as well as the clinic information. Call and tell them Suzanne sent you when you make your appointment."

I nod as she continues, but my mind is elsewhere.

"Do you have any questions, Caroline? *Caroline?*"

It takes me a hot minute to remember she's talking to me. "Sorry. I started thinking about having my blood drawn," I lie. "I hate it."

"A necessary precaution." She passes the folder to me as she shows me to the door, then she winks. "I think you'll find it's worth it."

Chapter 15

MADDOX IS WAITING for me in the driveway, and it doesn't take me long to figure out how he knows we switched. Josie leans against the side of his car, wrapping a lock of hair around her finger and giggling. The girl could give lessons on how to flirt. I can't help but admire the scene. If my bodyguard is upset about the bait and switch, she's thoroughly distracted him. Then again, when I press the garage door button, he whips around and glares at me.

Busted.

I pull the car inside and brace myself as I get out. I knew there'd be a price to pay for my little stunt.

"Do you understand that when you pull shit like that I get in trouble?" Maddox yells at me as soon as I'm out of the garage. Veins pulse in his meaty neck as he continues, "I like my job. I like to eat."

For a second I imagine what it takes to feed him in a day: a couple dozen eggs, maybe a few whole chickens. He's that big. In past centuries, his ancestors were probably mistaken for gods. I swallow hard before I respond. "I'm sorry, but I tried to tell Jameson that I didn't want to be followed."

"So instead you made me look like a fool." Maddox crosses his arms and glares at me. "I'm going to have to tell him what happened."

That I expected. Part of me is surprised that he hasn't already been in contact with Jameson. "When you talk to him remind him that I'm his girlfriend not his child."

"I don't care if you're his prize canary, he hired me to protect you," Maddox grumbles.

"You don't have to tell him," Josie suggests. She moves to Maddox's side and strokes his shoulder. She practically has to stand on her tiptoes to reach it. I shoot her a warning look that she ignores with a shrug. "If he doesn't know, you can't get in trouble."

"That's very sweet of you, Miss Deckard." Maddox softens in her presence, shifting from a hardened military man to a cuddly teddy bear. It's simply further proof of Josie's magic touch in the man department. He smiles down at her but then he puffs out his chest as if to remind both of them what a big badass he is. "I have a duty, though."

"To protect and serve the highest bidder," I mutter under my breath. Thankfully, he's too mesmerized by my best friend to notice.

"I'm going in," I announce loudly in the hopes that I can convince Josie to stop playing with her new toy and come with me. There's so much to tell her.

"You have my phone number," Josie reminds him. She scampers into the house behind me, laughing. "You didn't tell me he was such a pushover."

"I'm not certain his training included warding off horny, teenage girls," I say dryly.

Josie wags her finger at me, but her lips twitch with a grin. "Hey, I resemble that remark."

We're still teasing each other when we walk in on Josie's mom in the living room. Well, not just her mom, but rather her mom kissing some guy. Josie halts on the spot and gasps. I do my best to shush her but the couple pulls apart.

"Oh girls, I didn't expect you home so soon!" She swipes at her smeared lipstick, doing her best to straighten her bunched skirt.

"School's out for the summer," Josie informs her. "You're lucky I was out."

"I saw Emma's notes," she says, obviously flustered.

I shoot Josie an apologetic look. After showing up at the ass-crack of dawn the other day, I thought it would be more courteous to give Marion a heads up on when I would and wouldn't be here.

"Hi." I step in to try to smooth over the situation. "I'm Emma."

Marion's date takes my outstretched hand tentatively. I can't decide if he's shy or if he's never seen a girl shake hands before. Either way, his palms are sweaty and when no one's looking I wipe my own hand on my romper.

"Emma, this is Anton." Marion smiles affectionately as she introduces the new man in her life. Anton for his part is as nondescript as they come except for two defining characteristics: thinning brown hair and round glasses that lean more toward spectacles than most modern eye wear.

When no one speaks again and Josie doesn't step forward to introduce herself, I take the initiative. "What do you do?"

"I'm an accountant." He sighs as he tells me. "Not very exciting, I guess."

Considering that my life could use a whole lot less excitement at the moment, I think dating an accountant sounds pretty sexy.

"Can I make you guys a snack?" Marion offers, tapping her finger nails together like a broken clock.

"We already ate," Josie says coldly.

I don't bother to correct her, even though I could go for a bite. If she isn't careful, we'll be making a pilgrimage to In-N-Out later to rectify the situation. Josie stomps down the hall and slams her bedroom door shut behind her.

When I duck into her room, Josie shuts the door softly behind me, then leans against it.

"What's wrong?" I ask.

"That guy," she whispers, and I lean in so that she can keep her conspiracy on the DL. "I dated him a few weeks ago."

I suck in a breath and try to think of something reassuring to say. It's pretty hard given that I want to yell at her. I have been waiting for this to happen; a single mom, who even I have to admit is a MILF, and her teenage daughter with a taste for older men, adds up to either a really bad sitcom or a really good V.C. Andrews novel.

"Let me have it," she says when I stay quiet.

"Sheesh, Josie! You have to have seen this coming. I don't know where to begin!"

"Maybe with the fact that this is all my fault," Josie suggests. "That you knew this was going to happen and it was only a matter of time until trouble?"

"Sounds like you have it covered. Let me know when you need me to jump in."

Her lower lip begins to tremble and I immediately regret what I just said. "What am I going to do?"

"Look, he can't have known, and now that he's seen you he's going to break up with her."

"Mom really likes him and I fucked it up."

"Um, he really likes seventeen-year-old girls. I'm not entirely certain that you're not doing her a favor."

"He didn't know how old I was. I lied about my age," she admits.

"Do you do that with all of them?"

"The nice ones," she says. "Some of them like knowing that I'm younger."

I shudder, thinking about that. I pat the bed next to me and she comes over to sit down. "So, he was a nice one?"

"Yeah." It's not like her to be so quiet, but, then again, she's not usually sorry about who she dates.

"Then he's going to break up with her, and if he doesn't, then we'll figure it out," I promise.

She rests her head on my shoulder, her curly locks tickling my neck.

"Besides, I have lots of things to tell you that I promise will prove a distraction."

"Oh," she claps her hands and jumps to her feet. Scientists should study how rapidly her moods swing. "I want to hear all about it but first I'm going to go to the bathroom, okay?"

I nod. Now that Maddox has figured out our little ploy, there's no need to keep up our Parent Trap pretense. By now, he'll have delivered news of my shenanigans to Jameson, who'll hopefully take the hint that I'm not putting up with a bodyguard.

I grab my purse and start taking out Josie's stuff from our earlier switcheroo. Before I can throw her phone on the bed, a notification pops up for Instagram. It takes me a second to remember what her lock screen code is, but before I can see what photographic delights our friendly, anonymous stalker has in store for us, Josie reappears and snatches it from my hands.

"What the hell are you doing?"

"Um, looking at your phone." It seems obvious to me, but

given the shock registered on her face I guess maybe it's not to her.

"I didn't tell you you could look at my phone."

"What crawled up your snatch?" I ask her.

"You!" she shrieks. "First you sit there and judge me after I've given you a place to sleep, even though you're keeping things from me."

Okay, she's totally lost it. Hadn't she been fine minutes ago? "I'm not keeping anything from you!"

"Oh, like where were you going today that I couldn't tag along?"

"Somewhere where I needed my bodyguard not to go," I remind her. "I was about to tell you everything I did."

"Save it, Emma. Ever since you met Jameson West you've been a different person."

Standing up, I dump the contents of her purse on the bed and grab my phone and wallet. She's being totally unreasonable. "You think I'm judging you?"

"I know you're judging me, but you're too nice to even say it to my face."

"Fine!" I explode. "You treat these little romances of yours like games and you always knew someone was going to get hurt. This time it's your mom. What happens when you ruin someone's marriage or get some poor schmuck arrested?"

"I'm going to be eighteen soon." She dismisses my argument with a roll of her eyes.

"But you weren't always eighteen. How old do these guys even think you are? Wait, don't answer that because I really don't want to know anything more about this."

"Of course you don't because you just want to pretend you're my best friend."

I have absolutely no clue how things escalated this quickly. A few minutes ago she was leaning on me for support and I was preparing to spill my guts about everything that happened in Palm Springs. Now I'm glad I hadn't. This betrayal cuts deeper than the others I experienced this summer, which is saying something. She's being irrational, but I'm not going to waste my time telling her that. "I thought I could count on you."

"You can. Here's a little judgement for you," she offers when I reach her bedroom door. "You have a boyfriend accused of murder who's hired a bodyguard to stalk you. Your step daddy is a movie producer and you're driving a brand new Mercedes. Stop acting like we should all feel sorry for you."

"Because my life is so perfect," I hiss. "You have no idea how hard things have been."

"Save it, Emma. If I want a dose of reality I'll take a look at my own life."

"Then I suggest you do that soon," I throw open the door. I rush out of the house past a startled Marion and her new boyfriend slash Josie's ex. As soon as I'm out the front door, I run directly into Jameson's chest, but I don't feel like being comforted by him right now.

"Get off me," I shove him and hurry down the sidewalk.

"Where are you going?" he demands.

"None of your goddamn business," I call over my shoulder.

"Emma, wait!"

But I don't listen. I jump in the car and back out, nearly running him over in the process. From now on no one is going to stop me, no one is going to make choices for me, and no one is going to tell me what to do.

Chapter 16

THE NICE THING about Las Vegas is that if you drive fast enough for long enough, you'll hit the desert. Then you can drive as angrily as you need to.

I don't bother to look at my odometer when I reach open road, all I know is that the Mercedes has sports mode and I'm going to put it through all its paces. I don't have to check behind me to know that Jameson is following. Maybe he gave Maddox the day off and decided he'd do the job himself. But either my car isn't as fast as his BMW or he just knows how to work his better because after a few minutes he pulls alongside me driving the wrong direction. He casts a furious glance my way and then cuts ahead of me.

I resist the urge to speed up when his brake lights flicker on. He's slowing us down, no doubt forcing me to come to a stop, but I'm not going to make this easy on him. Too many things have been handed to Jameson in his life. If he wants me he's going to have to fight for me.

Glancing down, I discover that he's slowed us down to

about thirty miles per hour. I've just decided to stop fighting him, when he races forward and screeches to a halt allowing the back of his car to slide so that he's blocking the road entirely. I slam on my own brakes and jump out of the car.

"What the hell do you think you're doing? Do you know how dangerous that is?"

"Please give me a lecture," he retorts, "when you're racing through Las Vegas going a hundred miles per hour!"

At another time that might have embarrassed me. I don't want to explain to him how I'm feeling. That I needed to get away from Josie's house and Belle Mère and this whole mess as quickly as possible. Two days with the car and I've already started treating it like a toy.

"We all have to die sometime," I say with a shrug.

"You don't mean that." I open my mouth to protest this, but he keeps going. "And if you do, then we have bigger problems. What you did was reckless."

"I know." I cross my arms over my chest, unable to ignore the wave of guilt that overcomes me. Speed had been a factor in Becca's death. It's one of the reasons I didn't want to drive. I didn't want the power of a car in my hands. The second I'd gotten one, I abused it. "I'll get rid of the car."

"I'm not talking about the car, Duchess." His gaze drops to the ground and he shakes his head, his frustration with me only making me feel worse. "I'm talking about tricking Maddox."

"That was for your own good," I informed him.

"Exactly how is putting yourself in danger for my own good?" His blue eyes flash like the tip of a flame and he lunges forward grabbing me by the arm. "Do you have any idea how much danger you're in?"

"Do you?" I ask him.

"I guess I do since I'm smart enough to realize that if

someone pushed you through a window, then you know something."

"I don't!" I scream. "This whole thing is a giant mix-up and I'm tired of trying to keep everything straight. We're all tangled together like a big bowl of noodles. I can't tell which lies are mine and which belong to other people anymore."

"Slow down and start from the beginning. Is there anything you haven't told me?"

I glower at him, but he may as well know. "I overheard something at your house that night. When I confronted Leighton about it—"

"Wait, what did you overhear?"

I wave off his question. "It's not important."

"Like hell it isn't!" he growls.

"Get your caveman in check," I warn him, "or I'm not telling you anything."

Jameson steps back and runs both his hands through his copper waves. He pauses like that, as if he's considering pulling out his own hair, but he waits for me to continue.

"I overheard something. I asked Leighton about it, someone pushed us."

"But you aren't in danger," he mutters. "What did she tell you?"

"Nothing. She never got a chance to."

He looks to the sky as if pleading with the Gods for patience. Then he turns the full force of his smoldering gaze on me. I can't say no to that look, not when it's coupled with his strong jawline and insane good looks.

"What did you want to find out from her?" He rephrases the question.

If I tell him what I overheard, he'll know I doubted him. I make a choice knowing that I can't quite anticipate what the consequences will be. "She was talking to Monroe, something about that she had seen what had happened and she was protecting *him*."

"Who is *him*?" Jameson asks in confusion.

"To be honest, I assumed it was you, at first."

"Go on," he says after a moment of silence that seems to extend farther than the desert surrounding us.

"I thought she was talking about you. She was telling Monroe that she had seen what had happened, but that she wasn't going to tell anyone what he had done."

"And you thought she was talking about me killing my father?"

"I didn't know what to think. Everything was chaos. You'd just been arrested and—"

"You don't have to explain yourself," he stops me in a soft voice, but the disappointment in his tone says otherwise.

"I only wanted to know what she was talking about. When I confronted her, she told me they'd been talking about Jonas."

"You told me that night you believed I was innocent, but you still jumped to that conclusion." He's not interested in what Leighton might know about Jonas, only in what conclusions I'd drawn about him.

"I did. I still do," I whisper.

"Why?" It's less of a question and more of a plea. "I don't understand how you can believe me. Sometimes I don't even believe myself."

"Don't say that." I move toward him but he looks away.

"I'm no good for you."

The sincerity in his words makes my heart sink. I grab his chin and force him to face me. "You're the best thing that's ever happened to me."

"How can you say that? Your dad hates me. I spend most of my time worrying so much about your safety that I hired someone to follow you, and you've been dragged into a murder investigation. I've done nothing to deserve you."

"You set me free," I whisper. "I didn't have a life before you. I refused to have one. I'd just accepted that nothing was ever going to change and had half-buried myself in other people's trinkets at the store. Then you changed everything."

"Out here"—he glances around before returning his gaze to mine—"I can see for miles in any direction, but right now, all I see is you. I think you're the only thing I've ever seen clearly."

I don't need him to explain, because it's exactly how I feel.

He takes a single step forward, closing the short space between us. "I love you, Emma Southerly."

It takes a moment for his words to soak into me. I've known I loved him for a while now, but hearing him say it, I can't find the words to respond.

Jameson doesn't wait for me to respond, he continues, "I think I fell in love with you when you walked into my kitchen and made me that macaroni and cheese."

"And you've made me work for it all this time?" I tease, sniffing as the first tears break loose and stream down my cheeks.

He brushes them away. "I can't be held accountable for acting crazy; you've driven me to it."

"Okay," I croak. For now, I'll concede on that point. It's not as if I've been the picture of mental health since we met. I guess that's why they say crazy in love. "I love you, too."

He heaves a sigh. "I don't know if I deserve that."

"Shut up and accept it," I order him. Grabbing a fistful of his t-shirt, I pop onto my toes and offer him my lips. His face slants over mine and he captures them like he's captured my heart.

We stumble toward the car. Jameson feels around behind me, refusing to break off the kiss until he finds the door handle.

He lays me across the back seat of the Mercedes before he creeps over me. My hand snakes around his neck, drawing our lips together again, as our bodies mold to one another.

Reaching down, I fumble as I try to unfasten his jeans. He groans and the sound of it vibrates through me. "Not in the car, Duchess."

"Jameson," I pull back and address him seriously, "I don't think I can wait any longer."

He laughs at my earnestness. "Which one of us is the guy again?"

"Let's take off our pants and find out." I wiggle my hips, hoping that he won't be able to resist my suggestion.

"I swear to god that the minute you turn eighteen, I'm going to find the nearest bed and take my sweet time claiming you."

"Claiming me?" I repeat.

He rocks his hips against me, sending a thrill pulsating between my legs. "Do you have a problem with that?"

"Claiming sounds good," I murmur, "but I don't want to wait."

"It will be worth it," he promises me.

Of that, I have no doubt. It's more of a patience thing. The trouble is that I don't have any left.

"I need you, Jamie." The nickname appears on my tongue and it's like it's been there my whole life—like he's been here my whole life.

"We don't have to wait for everything," he reassures me, pushing a renegade strand of hair from my face.

I arch my body against his, wondering if he can really hold out. His arm circles my waist and he holds me like that. Blood rushes to my head as he leans forward and catches the top of my strapless romper in his teeth. I'm beginning to see spots in my vision when he tugs it down, freeing my breasts. I strain to change position, so I can see what's happening, but when the heat of his mouth closes over my nipple, I go limp. He sucks it past his teeth, swirling the tip of his tongue around the swiftly hardening peak.

"I've waited my whole life for you, Duchess," he tells me as he releases it. "When this is over, I'm going to take you away from here."

"Where?" I murmur dreamily, ready to imagine what our life together will be like then.

"It doesn't matter," he teases, "because you won't see anything other than the bed."

I moan loudly as he follows that promise by taking my other nipple in his mouth. He lingers there, not trying to stop me as I begin to buck my hips against his to seek relief.

"That's it," he coaxes and I feel his free hand press between my legs. He pushes aside the scrap of lace that passes for shorts and runs his fingers down me. I feel one gently push inside and a throaty cry escapes me as he moves it in and out. "God, you are so tight. I'm going to have to do this as often as possible before your birthday."

"Promise?" I breathe. It's the only word that I can force out as he continues.

"Of course, Duchess. Now let go."

I feel another finger stretching me and that's all it takes. Jameson holds me as I release, his forehead pressed in the valley between my breasts as I ride out the gift he's just given me.

When I've regained control of my body, I smile shyly at him. "Your turn."

This time he doesn't argue. Instead, he licks his lips and unbuttons his pants. I scramble onto my knees but before I can return the favor the chime of an incoming text message interrupts.

"Ignore it," I command him just as his phone chimes again.

When the third message chimes before I have his pants down, I sit back and wait for him to check his texts.

"Levi and his goddam timing," Jameson grumbles when he sees his phone. "Apparently, I have a house guest."

Now seems like a good time to mention that he's going to have another one. It's probably also the right time to tell him that he needs to kick Levi Rowe to the curb. Even through my oxygen-drenched brain, I know I have to do something before Levi finds out something he shouldn't.

Jameson pockets his phone and lounges back. "He can wait."

"I don't think that's a good idea," I say hurriedly. "Plus, there are beds at your house."

He raises an eyebrow. "I thought I was clear about that."

He was crystal clear about it. I'm beginning to think his checklist is even more rigid than mine. "I was thinking we could practice. Clothes on or maybe clothes off and *everything but.*"

"It's going to be really hard to drive across town with blue balls."

I bite my lip and pout, remembering what he told me the other day. "Why are we in two separate cars?"

"Because someone wanted to race," he reminds me.

"We can leave mine here," I suggest, tracing the bulging outline in his pants, "and come back for it later."

"Seems like a lot of trouble." His breathing speeds up as I shake my head.

"I promise it will be worth it."

He doesn't argue with me any further. Jameson pulls my car off the road. "If anything happens to it, I'll buy you a new one."

I'm not in the least bit worried about what happens to that car, even though I have to admit that I like having my own set of wheels. I get into the passenger seat of the BMW.

"Buckle up," he demands as he shifts the car into drive and heads toward the city.

"I can't," I inform him. "Drive carefully. Oh, and Jameson, see if you can hold out."

Then I wiggle under the arm controlling the gear shift and give him no choice but to lose that challenge.

Chapter 17

THIS TIME when we arrive at Jameson's Belle Mère estate, I take a longer look. This home is modeled after a Mediterranean villa complete with tiled roof and a large fountain out front. I'd noticed that the last time I was here, but I hadn't been able to appreciate the details like I do now. If he told me that it had been dug up from an ancient village in Tuscany, I would believe it.

I let out a low whistle. "Impressive. So let's see, you have the penthouse at the top of the casino, a chalet up on Mt. Charleston, and a villa in town. Any other properties you want to tell me about?"

"There's the flat in London," he teases me. "Amongst others."

"Do you have a book I can peruse or..."

"I'd rather surprise you by taking you to each one."

I have to admit that I like the sound of that. He parks his BMW in the drive. I've learned to stay put until he opens my door. Everyone's always bitching that chivalry is dead. If he's its last dying breath, I'm not going to be the one to extinguish it.

He takes my hand as soon as I'm out and we head inside the house.

We've just stepped into the foyer when my phone rings. "That's my mom," I tell him, recognizing the ring tone. "I can only avoid her for so long before she sicks the police department on me. I've spent enough quality time with the Belle Mère PD to last me a couple of years."

"Take the call, I'll find Levi." He gives me a swift kiss before he heads off in the direction of the kitchen. One simple gesture and he's left me breathless. I'm in so much trouble with him.

"Hi mom," I greet her.

"Where are you?"

"Nice to talk to you, too." I turn toward an empty room that serves as some type of parlor, hoping no one else will hear my conversation with her. "I'm in Belle Mère."

"I've been trying to reach your father but—"

"I'm not staying with him," I stop her. There's no point in trying to keep the facts from her. I hear a sharp inhale on the other line.

"Where are you staying?"

"With Josie." It's not exactly a lie. I haven't brought up my fight with her to Jameson yet, so I don't know for sure that he'll let me stay here. If he doesn't, I guess I'll be begging her forgiveness after dark.

"Emma," she says in a warning tone.

"Call Marion if you don't believe me," I snap.

"Fine. Did you get your car at least?" Trust my mother to segue into a topic that makes her look good. She's doing damage control without knowing what caused the destruction in the first place.

"I did. It's nice."

"Maybe you could drive back down here and pick up your stuff," she suggests.

"Mom," I say it slowly, wanting to catch her attention. "I won't be coming back to Palm Springs unless Hans is out of town." I add the qualifier because as angry as I am with her, I know it's not her fault.

"Emma, what happened between you and Hans?" she asks in a soft voice.

And here it is. My chance to tell her the truth. But before I can, I remember Josie's face this afternoon after she saw Anton with her mother. She'd stepped over a line and she couldn't turn back. If I tell my mother, I know she'll side with me. I also know there's a prenup, that there will be a nasty divorce and that she'll have her heart broken all over again. She has to suspect what kind of man she's married to. She can't possibly know the depths of his depravity, though, and I'm not ready to be the one to tell her. Not yet. "I saw the script for Hans's movie." It's as good of a reason as any. "There's a sex scene in there between me and Jameson."

There's a long pause on the other end of the line.

"Did you have sex with him that night?" she asks.

I had no idea she was capable of such directness. "No, I didn't. I told Hans that, but he refuses to take it out."

"Honey, you can't make business decisions—"

Here come the apologetics. I've given her enough slack for the evening. "Mom, sorry, I need to go. Something's come up."

I hang up before she can stop me and turn the ringer off on my phone. Tonight I only want to be with Jameson. But as I round the corridor that leads to the kitchen, I realize that might be harder than I thought.

The gang's all here.

"I guess I shouldn't be surprised that I didn't get an invitation," I say to Monroe. She doesn't even bother to answer me. I suppose the brief moment we had the other day was a fluke.

Unlike the others, Jonas has the decency to come over to me.

"Good to see you," he says, hugging me awkwardly. It's hard to admit there was a time when I would have bottled up that momentary contact and clung to it for months. Finally being over Jonas, I'm having a hard time not judging how pitifully I'd acted.

I break away as soon as it's polite. "I saw you at the hospital."

"I'm sorry?"

"A few days ago." I attempt to jog his memory, but he still stares at me blankly. Then again, he's always been a bit of a beautiful nothing. Seeing him now, I can't help but wonder what Leighton felt the need to protect him from. "Did you go to visit Leighton?"

"No." He grabs a beer out of a six pack on the counter. "I just got back in town."

"You know what? Hugo mentioned that." He's not going to budge, so either he forgot or he's protecting himself as well. What does Jonas have to hide? "I guess I thought it was you."

I'm absolutely positive that I'd spotted Jonas at Belle Pointe, but why is he covering it up? Sure, his story is that he was out of town, but I know better. I might not always be great with names or facts, but faces I'm pretty good at—especially one I've nearly sucked the lips off.

"Trying to steal my girl?" Levi swaggers over and drops an arm around my shoulder with the confidence of a man who knows what's going to greet him when he looks in the mirror. Any other time, I might be flattered by his attention, but I saw that headshot in my stepfather's office, and I suspect Levi isn't at Casa de West to catch up with the family.

I shrug away from him and force a small smile. "Good to see you."

Judging from the scathing glare that Sabine, Monroe's less nice best friend gives me, he won't have a hard time finding another girl to feed his ego. She saunters over and wedges herself in the space between us. If she knew I was grateful that she's acting as a buffer, she'd probably lock me in a room with him. Sabine's bizarre need to look out for her own interests is only trumped by her uncompromising policy that the rest of humanity remain below her.

I take my chances anyway, knowing how much it will irk her, and lean to whisper in her ear. "Thanks. I couldn't get away from him to find my boyfriend."

The only thing that might annoy Sabine more than knowing that she's helped me is a reminder that I've landed Jameson West. Now that I've put that pot on to boil, I hurry away.

Jameson is nowhere to be seen, which sucks considering I'm stuck in the high school reunion from hell: ex-boyfriend, guy I slept with to get back at ex-boyfriend, ex-boyfriend's girlfriend, the first female anti-christ, and the hot guy planning to screw over one of his best friends for fame. I guess Friday nights are alright for fighting.

I duck out onto the back patio. Leave it to the Wests to eschew the traditional barbecue grill and picnic table and replace it with a full grotto, a gourmet outdoor kitchen, and not one, not two, but *three* guest houses on the far side of the pool's stone waterfall.

"Subtle," I mutter to myself.

A door opens behind me, but when I glance over my shoulder, my heart sinks. It isn't Jameson.

"Care to go for a swim?" Levi flashes me his signature smile.

"I don't have a suit."

He leans against a stone column and chuckles. "I've never found that to be a problem."

"I'm guessing you don't find many things to be a problem," I say to him. *Like your conscience, for instance.*

He blinks, looking a bit confused, then shrugs. "Do you mind if I swim?"

"Go right ahead, but I'm not jumping in if you start to drown."

Levi clutches his chest. "You wound me. What did I do to offend you so terribly, Emma...?" He pauses, trying to remember my last name.

"Southerly," I offer it to him, for reasons I can't even fathom. It's that goddamn charismatic grin of his.

He strips his t-shirt over his head, but before he can take off his pants, I think better of the situation. "Actually, I do care if you swim."

His fingers freeze on the button of his shorts. "I didn't take you for being a shy one."

"I'm not," I reassure him. "But I do have a shred of decency."

"I can keep my shorts on," he says, but I shake my head.

"That's not what this is about, Levi. When are you going to tell Jameson the truth?"

"I don't know what you mean." So that's how he's going to play it.

"You're going to have to lie better than that if you're going to land an award for playing him in 'Wild West.'" I make sure to put the title in air quotes.

"How do you know about that?" he demands.

"I'm guessing Jameson didn't fill you in on who my stepfather is."

When he continues his impression of total vacancy, I sigh and continue. "Hans Von Essen. Ring a bell?"

"Holy shit. I had no clue."

"Yeah." I put a hand up to stop him. "I guessed that from the fact you were stupid enough to come here."

"Why would it be stupid to visit an old friend?" There's definitely no Academy Award in his future. Maybe he finds it easier to act on screen than he does to lie to someone's face. Either way, he's charismatic, but he's not convincing.

"I find being lied to pretty insulting," I inform him.

"I'm not lying to you. I just came to catch up, and study his mannerisms, and find out how his family is doing," he continues and I see now that he's lying to himself. I suppose you'd have to, to betray a friend so deeply. "So what if I want to get him just right? Whoever plays Jameson should be emotionally true."

"Save it," I cut him off. "Have you told Jameson that you plan on playing him in this movie?"

"I'm going to," he hedges, but it's a safe bet that he's not. "You haven't told him, have you?"

"No. I've been trying to think of a way to break his heart even further. You know, his father was recently murdered, and the police are investigating him for the crime," I rattle off the facts in a flat voice.

"Wait," Levi says, taking a few steps closer to me. "If you're Hans's daughter…"

"Stepdaughter," I correct him. At the moment, that qualification feels pretty important. So does the fact that Levi isn't listening to a word that I say.

He whistles. "I'm a little surprised. I mean, I knew Hans was a kinky fucker, but…"

"Stop right there. I know about the sex scene."

"Don't you mean *scenes*? Personally, I'm all for them.

They're bringing Blake Lively in to test to play you." His mouth curls as if he's imagining her naked.

I groan, wondering how hard I have to hit my head against the stonework out here before I lose consciousness.

"Then again, Blake can't hold a candle to you." Levi takes another step toward me. This time, there's no hesitance in it.

I stare him down. "Keep your hands, and everything else, to yourself."

"I'd just like to know more about your side of the story." He brushes a finger down my bare shoulder, and I jump back.

"Here's a fun fact," I snap. "There's legitimately no part of that movie that's based in reality."

"That's because audiences don't want reality," Levi begins to explain.

Now I wish I'd let him go swimming after all. It would be a lot easier to drown him.

"Save the spin," I advise, "and get the hell out of here, before I tell the Wests why you really stopped in for a visit."

"It's a job. It's not personal."

"Do you really think they're going to feel that way?" I ask.

"I do."

"Then you're either stupid or you're lying to yourself. If you honestly believe they won't care, you should walk inside and tell them right now why you're here," I call his bluff.

"They've got a lot going on right now, and I wouldn't…"

"Yeah. That's what I thought," I mutter, ignoring his sorry excuse.

"Emma, you have to understand—"

"What's going on?" Jameson interrupts us. I don't have to look at my boyfriend to know that he's angry. Taking a mental step back, I evaluate the situation. Super-hot movie star friend standing way too close to current girlfriend, while he pleads with her. Yeah, this looks bad from any angle.

Levi comes to the same conclusion, because he backs away from me and holds up his hands in surrender. "It's not what it looks like, man."

"Really? Because it looks like you're hitting on my girlfriend."

"Is this the part where you two bump chests, and wrestle around on the ground?" I ask them. Jameson holds up a warning finger, but I slap it away.

"Have you still not figured out that I don't like to be told what to do?"

"And I don't like friends who overstep their bounds." As he moves in closer, I'm just starting to realize that this is about to come to blows.

"Look, man. I don't want to fight you. I have to be on set next week and..."

Jameson's fist finishes that sentence for him.

Levi grabs his nose, as blood begins to gush from it. "Did you just break my nose? Do you have any idea what this nose is worth?"

Jameson takes out his wallet and tosses a few hundred dollar bills at his feet. "That ought to cover it."

Turning toward me, he gestures towards the house. "Come inside."

I put my hands on my hips and shake my head. "I'm not taking your orders."

"Can we do this somewhere else?" Jameson suggests.

"No," I refuse, "because Levi has something to tell you."

"I do?" Levi adds in confusion.

Before he can work out that I'm forcing my hand to get him to confess, Jameson shoves him against the column. "Did you touch her? Did you lay a fucking hand on her?"

Levi shoves him away. "I don't want to hurt you."

"There's a difference between stage fighting and real fighting," Jameson warns him.

My stomach clenches in anticipation at his words. Maybe it's a little primeval of me to get off on watching two beautiful men make each other bleed, but if it's wrong, I don't want to be right.

"Tell him why you're here, Levi." I call out to them, hoping they can hear it past the roar of adrenaline that's taken over their reasoning.

"What's going on out here?" Monroe steps onto the patio, her eyes flashing from her brother to Levi. "You didn't start a fist fight, did you?"

"*I* didn't," Jameson says with emphasis.

I can't keep it in any longer.

"Levi came here because he's going to play you in the biopic that Hans Von Essen is directing." The truth explodes from me. Not telling them would be as bad is lying. Something Levi might feel comfortable with, but I can't anymore.

"Is this true?" Jameson asks in a hollow voice.

Levi hesitates, which is answer enough.

"Get the fuck out," Jameson orders him. "And stay away. Don't call. Don't come by. Our lawyers will handle this."

"Lawyers?" Levi repeats. "I don't have a lawyer."

"Then I suggest you get one." Jameson turns his back towards his former friend.

"You can't sue me because I'm taking a role."

"Maybe not, but I can find something to sue you for, and I will."

Levi balks at Jameson's threat. "You wouldn't actually do that."

"A day ago, I might have said, 'You wouldn't actually take a role where you say I murdered my father.' I guess we're both full of surprises. Do you know how easy it would be for me to pull the plug on you playing this role?"

"I'd like to see you try," Levi sneers. It's the most unattractive he's ever looked, and for the first time I notice that his teeth are slightly crooked. One ear is larger than the other, and there's slight acne scars on his face. I guess a good smile can really disguise an asshole.

"Monroe, back me up." Levi addresses her and turns on the charm, but she simply raises an eyebrow.

"You heard what he said. Get out."

"I thought we were friends."

"We were," she informs him. "But this is about family."

"Your family's fucked up. You both know it. You both know how much your father hid. How he treated your mom. You told me so yourself."

"Yeah, it's a fucked up family," Jameson takes a step closer, and Levi flinches. "But it's our family, and you're not a part of it."

"What did I miss?" Hugo asks, rubbing his hands together as he steps outside.

Levi wipes his bloody nose with the back of his hand, and then straightens up. "Nothing. You didn't miss anything. I was just leaving."

"That's too bad," Hugo says, clapping him on the back as he passes, oblivious to the tension between the four of us. "Next time, I want to hear all about you getting up on Blake Lively."

Levi casts a glance toward Jameson. "Sure. I'll tell you all about it."

Then he walks into the house and out of our lives.

"How long have you known about this?" Jameson asks me when the others go into the house.

"Since the night we left Palm Springs. I'm sorry. I should have told you."

"No. Don't apologize to me, Duchess. You didn't do anything wrong."

"I didn't know how to tell you that your best friend betrayed you," I admit.

"I think it's hard for someone like you to understand."

"Understand what?" I whisper, as he moves in closer, his lips slanting towards mine.

"Disloyalty."

"I know a thing or two about it," I think of Becca and the lies she kept from me.

"Maybe you do, but there's not an ounce of it in your body. It's one of the reasons…"

Before he can finish the sentence, I kiss him, because I trust him, and he trusts me. Right now with our worlds as fucked up as they are, that has to count for something.

When we break apart, I'm panting. Jameson presses his forehead against mine, lingering there despite the sweat from the heat of the evening.

"Can I stay with you for a while?"

"You can stay with me forever," he promises. Then, he seals that vow with a kiss.

Chapter 18

HIS MOM SHOWS me to a spare room. Obviously, things are a bit different when she's home. She smiles knowingly as she opens the closet and takes a guest robe out, laying it across the bed. She continues to point out where I can find towels, or shampoo, or a spare tooth brush.

"You didn't have to go to all this trouble," I say to her, when she asks if there's anything else I need.

"Nonsense, this is why we have guest rooms. Jameson mentioned that you're only seventeen. I don't feel comfortable allowing a seventeen-year-old to share a bed with her boyfriend."

I bite my lip, wondering why on earth I can't will the ground to open up and swallow me whole when I need it to.

"I knew your mother," she continues, "and I think she'd agree with me on this."

"You have no idea," I say under my breath. Of course, if it was up to her, I wouldn't be staying with the Wests; she'd be taking a restraining order out against them. I keep that to myself, though.

After she's left, I look around the large bedroom, feeling out of place. I creep quietly to the door when I hear voices in the hallway.

"You don't have to put us in separate rooms," Jameson says to her.

I hear her muffled laugh through the door. "I've seen how you look at her. It's for the best. There's enough police scrutiny on you at the moment. Keeping some distance between you and her is a good idea while she's still underage."

"I know, we've already talked about it."

"You have?" she says in surprise.

"We talk about a lot of things, Mom. She's not like other girls."

Those are the words we all long to hear because isn't every new boyfriend or girlfriend the same until one is different?

I'm different for Jameson.

The thought settles over me, sinking deep in my bones, and when I climb into the guest room bed, I drift away peacefully.

Sometime in the middle of the night, I'm awakened when he slips in beside me.

"You're not supposed to be in here," I murmur sleepily.

He spoons against me and presses a kiss to the back of my neck. "Try to keep me away, Duchess."

I wiggle closer to him, shamelessly pushing my ass against his groin.

"Duchess, what are you wearing?" he asks in a strangled voice.

"What I always wear to bed." It's harder to feign innocence when you're half asleep, but I do my best. "My panties and a tank top."

I already know what's gotten his attention. Ninety-nine percent of the time, I'm a boy shorts kind of girl, but since I'd had to wear that teeny tiny romper today, I'd opted for a thong. His hand skims over my bare ass cheek, and he groans.

"You're the one who wants to wait," I remind him.

"Shh," he hushes me. "I'm trying really hard to remember why." I giggle, enjoying the feel of his hands roaming all over me. "My mom is down the hall, remember?"

I flip over to face him, tucking my head against his shoulder. "I don't think she'll hear us."

"Duchess, if I have anything to say about it, they'll hear you in China," he promises. Then he kisses me on the forehead. "You're just going to have to wait."

"It would be easier if you didn't keep getting into bed with me," I tell him.

"It would be easier if you weren't half naked." He sighs deeply and moves his palms upward until they're resting on the small of my back. "Stop pouting."

"It's dark, how do you know I'm pouting?"

"You're pouting so loudly that I can hear it. Get some sleep," he advises me.

"Won't we get in trouble if she catches you in here?"

"Yeah," he says wearily. "She'll slap me on the wrist and then ask if I want breakfast."

"I wish my mom was like yours."

"Be careful what you wish for," he says mysteriously. I'm not certain what to make of that statement, so I let it slide. Every moment I've experienced with Evelyn West leads me to believe that she has a wonderful relationship with her children. Then again, it took her days to return home after her husband was murdered. She claimed her father was sick but if my own life proves anything, it's that appearances can be deceiving.

"I don't want to sleep," I admit to Jameson. "I have too many nightmares."

"I won't let you have any tonight." His arms tighten around

my waist. "Tonight you're only going to have good dreams. What do you want to dream about, Duchess?"

"My birthday," I say shyly.

"Why? Is there something you're looking forward to?" I can hear the smile in his voice.

"I have a feeling it's going to be the best birthday ever."

"If I have anything to say about it, it will be." He keeps his lips pressed to my forehead, whispering the words across my bare skin. They tingle across my scalp and race down my neck, settling low in my belly. "Have you thought any more about where you want to go?"

"Nowhere too far," I tell him.

"Paris and London are out?"

"Too far. I want to get there as quickly as possible," I admit.

"What about Mexico? There's this little resort in Playa del Carmen. We can sleep near the water."

"Sleep?" I repeat.

"Miss Southerly, what are you suggesting?" He says, in mock horror.

"It'd be easier for me to give you a preview," I murmur. Then I move my lips to his.

"I SHOULD HAVE KNOWN you'd be in here." Waking up to Monroe's smug voice is not my idea of a good morning. I burrow down into the covers, leaving Jameson to deal with his sister.

"What do you want, Monroe?" he mutters, rolling away from me and then instantly falling back to sleep. For a second, I'm reminded of how things used to be with Becca.

"You two have company."

"What time is it?" I whisper over his snores.

"Eight."

Monroe strikes me as the type to get up at the break of dawn to do two hours of cardio. When I sit up, my suspicions are confirmed when I see she's in a sports bra and shorts.

"Who is it?" I ask, praying it's not my dad.

There's no smugness in her tone when she says, "Detective Mackey."

She might as well have shot me up with espresso. I jump out of bed and shrug on the robe her mom left me.

"Don't wake him up," I order her.

She grabs my arm, digging her nails into my skin. "What are you hiding?"

"Nothing." I yank free of her grip. "In case you missed it, your brother doesn't always act rationally when he thinks I'm in trouble."

I take the stairs slowly. I'm not exactly excited for my reunion with my favorite federal investigator. The fact that she's here as early as is socially acceptable is a pretty good indicator that she's bringing bad news with her. It occurs to me too late that I should have asked Monroe for more details. Had Mackey come to see both Jameson and me? Or just him?

Or me?

When I reach the sitting room, I can't help but notice that the slick bob she'd sported when she came to town is a bit too long. She's been working overtime. I might feel sorry for her except for the fact that she's trying to put my boyfriend away for murder.

"Can I get you some coffee?" I ask.

Channel your inner hostess much, Emma. I don't even know where the coffeemaker is.

Mackey raises one eyebrow that's in serious need of intervention. "Making yourself at home, aren't you?"

I stopped fidgeting and sit up straighter.

"I'm attempting to be polite, you should try it."

There's a hint of a smile at her lips, but she doesn't give me the satisfaction. She leans back and crosses her legs, regarding me for a long moment before she comes to the point. "There's going to be a press conference today. I felt you should know."

"I had no idea that interest in the case has waned so much that you have to solicit attention door-to-door," I say with a shrug. If she's going to pretend that she doesn't find me amusing then I'll pretend that I don't find her or her games interesting.

She folds her hands in her lap. "Would you like to know what it's going to be about?"

"I'm assuming the murderer. Are you trying to tell me you've done some genuine police work and have a real suspect finally?"

"Yes, we do." Mackey tilts her head and meets my eyes. "You."

I don't blink. Partially because I don't want her to see that she's spooked me, but mostly because I'm frozen. I force myself to respond. "You really are desperate."

"Says the girl playing house at a billionaire's."

"Fine, I'll bite." I lean forward, placing my elbows on my knees to close some of the distance between us. "What do you have on me?"

"First, can I ask you a couple of questions?"

"Should I have a lawyer present?" I counter. If I'm smart I'll kick her out, but curiosity has gotten the better of me.

"You should," Jameson says from the doorway. There's no sign that he's been sleeping. He's dressed and alert while I can claim neither thing. Not bothering to look my way, he prowls into the room with his eyes trained on her.

"Mr. West, how lovely to see you." Mackey sounds anything but pleased that he's joined us. "I'm having a private conversation with your girlfriend."

"Anything you can say to her, you can say in front of me."

It's a line right out of a CSI episode.

"Is that true?" she asks me.

"Yeah," I say without hesitation. "I don't keep anything from him."

"So young to have so little secrets. How long have you two known each other?"

"Long enough," Jameson answers for me while I do the math. Has it really been less than two months? "Do you have actual questions? And can they wait for my lawyers to arrive?"

"You don't need a lawyer," Mackey corrects him. "She does."

"I misspoke. I meant *our* lawyers."

"You two have gotten close. It's surprising given that you've known each other such a short time—or did you know each other before?" she asks.

I groan and slouch back in my chair. Apparently, Mackey will be playing the role of good cop *and* bad cop today. It's hard to believe anyone actually falls for this crap, but pitting couples against one another must work if she's trying it.

"I waive my right to an attorney."

"Emma, I wouldn't advise that," Jameson begins, but I hold up a hand.

"Look, I don't feel like waiting around all day to get to the point. Let her ask her questions. We know the truth, so let's see what she believes is so rock solid that she's here accusing me of murder."

"Right now it's only gut," Mackey admits.

"You want me to be the one who killed him. Should I be flattered or offended?"

She doesn't answer my question. "You make the most sense."

"Enough theorizing," Jameson intercedes. "Ask your questions and get out."

"According to your statement, you were present at the West Casino on the night Nathaniel West was murdered." She takes a notepad from her purse and flips it open.

"Yes, and that's still true," I promise her. "The darn time machine I've been constructing isn't finished yet, so I haven't been able to change history."

She continues, ignoring my sarcasm. I guess my mom is right that my dark sense of humor isn't my friend.

"Furthermore, you claimed that that the two of you were together the entire evening."

"None of these are questions," Jameson points out.

"No," I respond, eager to get this over with so that I can separate the two of them. "I told you that we went skinning dipping, we spent some time together, and we fell asleep."

Her eyes narrow. So much for trying to call my bluff. What would be the point of trying to change my story now?

"Are you certain that's what happened?"

What do they say? The truth will set you free. Or you'll just get asked the same question over and over until you lie simply to break the cycle. "Yes, that's exactly what happened."

Jameson asked me not to lie on his behalf, which is why I don't bother to claim he was actually next to me the entire evening.

"So, either of you could have gotten up in your sleep, and the other one wouldn't have known." She's having a hard time asking actual questions. I guess it's a good thing that she's sticking to the law and not the order side. Leading the witness, anyone?

"I suppose." I grant her this one tiny admission, mostly because it's pretty fucking obvious.

"Who exactly do you think did it now, Detective Mackey?"

Jameson cuts straight to the point. "Because without evidence, this is becoming harassment."

"Isn't it wonderful that the Federal Bureau of Investigation is above such petty concerns?" She smiles serenely at him before turning her attention back to me. "Emma, are you a virgin?"

I snort in surprise. Of all the things Detective Mackey could be here to ask me, that's pretty far down on the list of possibilities.

"You don't have to answer that," Jameson says, but she holds up a hand to silence him once more.

"Miss Southerly wants to be cooperative."

Challenge accepted. "No, I am not."

"How long have you been sexually active?" she continues.

"I'm sorry, but what does this have to do with the murder?" I bypass her question because my answer is pretty embarrassing, especially when you consider I've been practically begging my boyfriend to screw me all week.

"I'd prefer if you would just answer the question."

"Fine." I cross my arms over my chest as if that can shield me from the oncoming humiliation. "I lost my virginity a couple of years ago in a rash moment of stupidity, and I haven't done it since then."

"So you aren't sexually active?"

It's strange to see Mackey unnerved. It isn't the response she expected, but I'm still not certain what this has to do with Nathaniel West or what happened that night.

"No, I'm not having sex if that answers your question."

"You'll pardon me if I find that surprising." She scribbles a note on her pad of paper.

"You mean: how did I land a billionaire without the aid of my vagina?" I retort. If I have to be uncomfortable, so does everybody. "Look, have me go to a doctor or something. It's probably been so long that it's closed back up."

"Vaginas don't close back up."

"Gee, thanks for the biology lesson," I tell her, "but these are the facts. I haven't had sex in over three years."

"So now that she's answered your question, would you care to elaborate on exactly what you were hoping to find out today?" Jameson asks.

She closes the notepad and shoves it inside her bag. "She's given me an answer, whether or not it proves to be true is another matter entirely."

Oh my god. Where is a wall to hit when you need one?

"If I had information to share with you, I would." I'm tired of the games and double speak, so I opt for being direct. "But I don't lie, and I don't appreciate people who show up and accuse me of doing so."

"Noted." Mackey stands up and smooths down her pants. "We'll be in touch if we have further questions."

"I'll be holding my breath," I promise her.

"Exactly what did any of this have to do with my father's murder?" Jameson asks as he shows her to the front door

"Well, since you two are so innocent, you can find out when everyone else does. Press conference is at noon."

I hate to admit it, but we both know we'll be watching.

Chapter 19

JAMESON TAKES me by the hand and leads me towards the stairs as soon as she's gone. We should talk or come up with a plan, but I can't find the energy to do either.

"I can't go back to sleep," I warn him.

"Can I have a moment with Emma?" Evelyn asks, stepping out of the shadows before we reach the stairwell. Jameson considers for a moment, but his mom must be on the pre-approved list because he excuses himself.

"I'll be waiting in your room," he says, before he leaves me with her.

Dark circles rim Evelyn's eyes. Is anyone in this house getting sleep?

"What did they want?" she asks when we're alone.

"To accuse me of murdering your husband," I blurt out. "I might as well tell you now because there's going to be a press conference."

I don't know how I expect her to react, but she surprises me by wrapping me in a tight hug.

"How can you know that I…" I let the thought trail away.

She steps back, her hands gripping my shoulders. "The same way I know Jamie is innocent."

"He's your son." It seems like an obvious fact to point out.

"He is, and he's in love with you. As far as I'm concerned that makes you my daughter and I know what my children are capable of."

I swallow hard, wishing I deserved her faith in me. If she knew the secrets I'm hiding, she wouldn't think so highly of me.

"Get some rest."

When I step into my room, Jameson closes the door behind us then he takes me in his arms.

"Mackey won't touch you," he vows.

"I don't understand why she was asking all those questions," I admit. "Jameson, you have to know that I had nothing to do—"

"I already know that, Duchess. I'm going to draw you a bath and then I'm going to go downstairs and get on the phone with my lawyer."

"You don't have to do that." He stops me with a kiss.

"Yes I do."

I blink against the prickly heat of tears. "She's going to try to turn us against one another."

"She's going to fail," he promises me.

"There's going to be interrogations, maybe even a trial." I'm too panicked to let him reassure me, but he grabs my chin in his hands and directs my gaze to his.

"I'm not going to let that happen, Emma"

"I don't have the resources you have unless I ask Hans for help," I rattle on.

"You have every resource at my disposal," he corrects me.

"They're going to make you go in there and talk about our sex life." *Or lack thereof*, I add silently.

He pauses and I see the wheels turning behind his blue eyes. "There's a way around that."

"How?" I plead. I need to know how he can fix this. I want to believe he can because for the first time since this started, I'm truly scared.

"You'll be eighteen soon." He doesn't have to remind me, it's all I've been thinking about. "Emma, they can't force you to testify against your spouse."

I jerk away as if he'd suddenly announced he has a contagious disease. "What?"

"Spousal privilege. If it comes to it, we can get married." His words are detached. He's suggesting a preemptive strike.

Call me old-fashioned, I'm not walking down the aisle as a strategic move. "We are not getting married." Disbelief mixes with fear. "We haven't even had sex yet, how are we having this conversation? I still have a year of high school and I'm pretty sure I don't want to spend it labelled as the gold-digger murderess."

"You're neither of those things," he reprimands me.

"Tell that to the rest of my graduating class," I grumble.

"Who cares what they think?"

Apparently I do. I'm too shocked over this moment of self-discovery to share it.

"Look, I'm not going to make you marry me," Jameson begins.

"Good because I'm not."

"I have to admit that I'm offended that you don't want to."

"It's not that…" I search for the right words to explain the crazy jumble of thoughts in my head. How on earth did things get this screwed up? I spent the better part of the last week begging him to take me to bed. Now he's offering to put a ring on it. Everything about this scenario is backwards. "You don't have to do something this extreme."

In the end, I opt to spare his feelings.

"It's not a big deal."

"It is a big deal." I don't bother to hide my incredulousness. "Marriage is a very big deal. At least it is to me."

"You have to remember I was raised by a billionaire. Jesus, I can afford to have a few wives."

"A few wives, huh?" My eyes narrow at the thought of someone else catching Jameson's attention.

"You look jealous, Duchess." I can hear how pleased he sounds.

"Don't worry about me. Continue to visualize your trophy wife collection. Might I suggest mahogany for the cabinet you keep them in?"

"You are jealous." He grabs the sash of my robe and tugs me closer. "I like jealous on you."

"I don't." How he's managed to distract me from the drama at hand is beyond me.

Jameson goes into the ensuite bathroom and begins to run water in the bathtub.

"I'm only going to be downstairs," he says as I slip off my clothes and grab a towel, waiting for the tub to finish filling up.

When he reaches the bathroom door, I call after him, "By the way, that was the worst marriage proposal of all time."

He pokes his head back in the door. "I'll do better next time."

What have I gotten myself into?

When the tub is nearly full, I turn off the tap. I'm about to get in when there's a knock on the bathroom door. I wrap my towel around me. Jameson wouldn't bother to knock, especially if there was a possibility of catching a glimpse of the goods. I expect to see Evelyn on the other side of the door, but it's Monroe. "I brought you this."

She offers me a glass of water before she opens her palm to reveal a small blue pill.

"Umm." I hesitate. I'm not exactly in the habit of taking drugs from strangers, not that Monroe is a stranger exactly. She's something worse: an enemy. Although, in the last few days, she seems to be heading into neutral territory.

"Xanax," she assures me. "I overheard what Mackey had to say."

"You can't tell anyone..." I say in a rush.

There's a struggle in her crystal blue eyes, but after a moment she says, "I'm not going to, Emma. I know you didn't do it."

I want to ask her how she knows and where her sudden suspicious faith has come from. Instead, I take the pill from her and pop it in my mouth.

"Try to relax," she advises me. "Jameson is already on the phone with the lawyers."

I swallow a gulp of water and hand her the glass. "Thank you."

It's hard for me to get it out, and, judging by the way she flinches, it's hard for her to accept my gratitude. Which is why I can't let this go.

"Why are you being so nice to me?" I ask her.

She shrugs. "You're a guest, and well...I get the impression you're not going anywhere."

"I'm not," I warn her.

"Then I guess we have to get used to each other." It's a mediocre truce at best. One we've been forced into, rather than chosen on our own, but it's a start.

"Need anything else?" she asks. I shake my head no, still too dumbfounded by her sudden generous spirit.

The Wests certainly know how to surprise you, I think as I sink into the bathtub.

"It's a good thing," I say to myself even as I wonder what curve ball they'll throw at me next.

"I DON'T UNDERSTAND why her parents don't take care of this."

I freeze outside the kitchen, waiting for Monroe to say more. I expect Jameson to defend me, but it's his mother who comes to my rescue.

"Not every family has the resources to cope with a scandal of this magnitude."

Scandal. I'm a scandal. And they're sitting around trying to figure out how to handle me.

"Her stepfather has money," Monroe points out.

"I won't allow it," Jameson informs them. There's a finality in his tone that leaves no room for questioning.

This impromptu family meeting is none of my business—except that it's obvious they're talking about me.

Jameson continues, finally shifting the topic away from his ill-begotten girlfriend. "I spoke with Richard yesterday. A number of new suits have been filed against the corporation."

"Fucking vultures." Monroe doesn't mince words.

"Watch your language," her mother chastises her.

"It's true," Monroe defends herself. "A man is dead, so why not try to bleed his assets dry."

"What can we do about it?" Evelyn asks. "Or do we do anything?"

"It could destroy most of our holdings," Jameson advises her.

"But we'd be fine?"

"Yes." He clears his throat, and I wish I could see his face. "But the people we employ won't be."

"Sometimes I forget how different you are from your father," she says softly.

"That's why I've decided to step in as interim CEO," he announces.

I gasp loudly enough that everyone in the other room falls silent. Next time I'll wear bells so they can hear me coming. Steeling myself, I wander into the kitchen.

Jameson shakes his head, not buying my casual entrance for a second. "Care to join in our family meeting, Duchess?"

"I'm not family," I say dismissively. "I thought I'd see about some coffee."

"Nonsense," Evelyn pipes up. "Sit down. These topics concern you. I'll get you some coffee."

I head towards the bar stool at the far end, but Monroe moves to it, allowing me to sit next to Jameson. I try to hide my surprise at the thoughtful gesture, but it's like I'm in the *Twilight Zone*.

"Catch Emma up." Evelyn hands me a mug. I cup it with both hands, savoring the warm ceramic against my palms. Jameson gives me a rundown of what they discussed. I can't bring myself to tell him that I overheard most of it already.

"That brings us back to the fact that I'm stepping in as CEO." His gaze locks with mine, and he waits for me to speak.

"Okay," I say, wondering if he wants more input or if he's torturing me for acting like I haven't already overheard all of this. But I'm less concerned with the fact that I've been caught eavesdropping. "Is that what you want?"

"That's a really good question," his mother backs me up. "You left business school."

"I don't know," he admits after a long pause, "but it is my responsibility."

I want to tell him to screw responsibility. He owes his father, and the legacy he left behind him, nothing. But sitting in this small circle, I realize that he's not doing it for himself. Risking the company's assets undermines his family's financial stability.

Isn't that the reason I'd stuck around the pawn shop for so long? The burdens we carry for those we love are the heaviest and hardest to release.

"Emma?" He wants my opinion and for a split second it's as if we're the only two people in the room.

"I'm with you," I reassure him. "Do what you have to."

"Then for the time being I'll take over."

Evelyn's eyes flick to mine and I catch a flash of approval that she quickly masks. That's when it hits me that she wants Jameson to step in. So why did she remind him that he'd abandoned business school?

I clear my throat awkwardly. Despite my initial reservations—and a lifetime of being spoon-fed a hatred of the West family—I can't take advantage of their kindness, even Monroe's begrudging civility. When I have their attention, I begin, "I overheard. I don't need help with lawyers."

"Like hell you don't," Jameson growls and all three of our heads swivel in his direction.

"Down, boy," Monroe orders him.

Jameson glowers at her, his face a stony mask that conceals a raging storm of emotions I can only sense. "You don't know everything. The situation…"

"Sucks," Monroe finishes for him. "But don't let Jamie fool you. We won't know much until the press conference."

"Except that scoop from the DA's office," he reminds her.

"What scoop?" I do my best to ignore the fifties slang term.

"They're leaving some information out during the press release today," Monroe says.

"I bet it won't be anything important," I grumble.

That's why Mackey came by—to watch me squirm. If she only knew that she'd left too soon.

"We should know what it is in a few days," Jameson tells me.

Pressing my lips together, I allow this to sink in. "How are we going to find out?"

"Do you want the truth or plausible deniability?"

"On second thought, I don't need to know." The West's money could buy any information he wants, and there's no way to talk him into leaving this case alone.

AT NOON, we gather in the rec room and turn on the local news channel. We don't have to wait long before the district attorney appears at the podium. Mackey takes her place beside them and they wait for the crowd to quiet.

"New evidence has been found in the investigation of one of Belle Mère's most prominent citizens..."

I dare a glance around the room. Nathaniel West's family wasn't invited onto that stage for this announcement. Not only is the FBI keeping the Wests out of the spotlight, they've already drawn their conclusions.

Jameson grabs my hand and squeezes it tightly as the DA hands the mic over to Detective Mackey.

"After extensive examination of Mr. West's body, investigators discovered trace DNA. A follow-up search of the crime scene produced an object with both Mr. West's DNA and that of an unidentified source. Due to the nature of the evidence, our team has concluded that the victim had participated in sexual intercourse on the night of his death—"

Jameson turns off the television. "I'm sorry, Mom."

"Ignoring it won't make it untrue." The exhaustion in her

voice is at odds with the cheerful attitude she turns on for most customers.

"That's why she came here." I clap my hand over my mouth. Detective Mackey assumes I had sex with Mr. West.

"At least we know what we're dealing with," Jameson says grimly.

"Most of it," I grumble.

Evelyn pushes onto her feet and glances around the room, unable to make eye contact. "I'm going to lie down."

No one makes a move to stop her and as soon as she's out of earshot, I turn on Jameson and Monroe. "Did she know your dad was a…"

"Cheater?" Jameson fills in the blank. "Everyone knew."

I glance in the direction she fled. "She seemed so surprised."

"Humiliated," Monroe clarifies.

It's one thing to have an unfaithful spouse and another to have your family's dirty laundry hung out to dry for the whole town to see. When she doesn't emerge from her room for dinner, I begin to worry.

"Should we check on her?" I ask Jameson.

"This isn't her first rodeo," Monroe jumps in. "She needs time."

I decide that she also needs tea. One of the few comforting memories I have of my own mom involves hot tea. She'd brew it when we had stomach bugs or colds. Other times she made it for no reason at all. I dig through the cupboards looking for teabags. When Jameson asks what I'm doing, he stays out of my way. Monroe, on the other hand, helps me raid the pantry.

She holds a box of tea bags triumphantly.

"It's herbal." She scrunches up her nose like decaffeinated is below her.

"Do you know how she takes it?" I ask. In the end, I set off to her room with a cup of tea sans milk or sugar. Knocking lightly, I wait until I hear a faint *come in*.

"I brought you some tea." I place the cup on her nightstand.

"I'm sorry that you're mixed up in this."

"I mixed myself up." I could have said no to Josie that night and stayed home. I could have blended into the party. I could have never met Jameson. All the fear and heartbreak is worth it, knowing that he's in my life.

She lowers her voice to a whisper that I have to lean to hear, "There are very few people in Belle Mère that you can trust. Jameson is one of them."

I don't point out that he's the only West on her list. I read between the lines instead.

Chapter 20

LIFE FALLS into a rhythm that's steady but building in intensity. Hopeful reporters hover at the end of the family's private drive. A handful of friends finagle invitations to sit by the grotto's pool. Television networks negotiate private interviews.

When I answer the door early one morning, I'm stupid enough to accept a package.

"Don't!" Jameson calls out but it's already in my hands. He snatches it away. Inside, there's a subpoena for me to appear at a medical clinic by the end of the week.

"I don't understand." I study the letter like it's written in ancient greek, but he's on the phone to his lawyers. He talks to them so often that we should ask them to move in.

They want your blood, he mouths before his call connects.

My life has become a game of playing house with a billionaire's toys all while under a microscope. If I'm not careful, whoever holds that lens might use it to set me on fire.

By the end of the week this is my new normal, and I hate it. The only positive in this whole nightmare is when Jameson appears at the breakfast table in a three-piece suit and tie.

I whistle when he comes into the room.

"Doesn't he clean up nicely?" Evelyn reaches out to ruffle his hair but he sidesteps her.

"Duchess, a word?"

I hurry after him, but when I round the corner to the living room, he sweeps me off my feet. I grip his tie as he kisses me deeply.

"Mr. West," I say breathlessly when we break apart.

"Mr. West was my father," he says in a tight voice.

"And now it's you," I whisper, straightening the knot of his tie. I bite my lip, and he groans.

"If you keep it up, I'll never make it out of here," he warns in a dark voice.

That's exactly what I want. I didn't know Nathaniel West. I grew up conditioned to be prejudiced against him. The more I learn now, the less I want to know. Something about Jameson willingly taking up his place, even if only in the family business, makes me uneasy.

"I want you to keep Maddox with you today."

"That almost sounds like a request," I murmur with approval.

The muscles in his jaw clench before he admits, "It is."

"I don't need a babysitter," I remind him.

"The reporters will—"

"Let me worry about that. We had an arrangement," I cut him off before he can renege on our agreement that Maddox is at *my* disposal. Brushing a renegade copper strand from his forehead, I continue, "Go play with your billions."

"Yes," he says dryly. "I think my first order of business will be building a large vault filled with gold coins that I can dive into Scrooge McDuck style."

"I'm sure the board will approve."

He chuckles, but there's a nervous edge to his laughter.

When he finally lowers me to my feet, he pauses with his hands on my waist. "I love you."

"I love you, too." With the whole world burning around us, it's amazing that those three little words nearly knock me off my feet every time he says them.

"Give Maddox a chance, and stay safe." It's not a request, it's an order. I salute him before I push him towards the front door. He steals one final kiss before he climbs into the back of a chauffeured sedan.

Getting out of the house without being hounded by wannabe reporters looking to score their big break is the real trick. The driver will deliver him to the West Corporation headquarters. I have no clue how I'll get by them. I dress in a black wrap dress, pinning my hair low on my neck. No make-up or lipstick. As much as possible, I need to blend in. I head towards my Mercedes, which has been parked in the driveway since Jameson had someone retrieve it from the desert.

Maddox appears as soon as I touch the handle.

"Can I drive you somewhere?" he asks.

I whirl around and give him a wicked smile. "No, but here's what you're going to do."

THE ONE BENEFIT of staying locked up for a week is that it's pretty easy to trick the reporters waiting on the other side. I send Maddox ahead of me, along with one of the Wests's house maids who needed to run some errands. When I reach the gate at the end of the private drive, there's nary a leach insight.

No one's seen this car, so I put as much distance between me and the West residence as possible before I begin to slow down. I double-check my rearview mirrors and turn left a bunch of times until I'm satisfied that no one is following me.

Who knew you could learn how to lose a tail online? Thanks Google.

It's strange how different it feels when I pull up to the boxy, two bedroom house that's only a few blocks away. The stark difference in Jameson's reality and my past can't be denied. But even as my stomach begins to churn from nerves, taking the walkway to the front door feels like coming home.

I nearly give up when no one answers after I knock twice. I have a key, but I can't shake how angry Josie had been when I'd touched her phone last week. How would she feel if I walked into her house? I stand there for a moment, staring at the locked door between us until it opens.

"Emma!" Marion tugs her robe tightly around her.

"I'm sorry!' I stare at her in wide-eyed horror as I realize how early it is at the Deckard house. She probably just got off work a few hours ago.

But Marion waves off my apology. "It's my day off. I'd invite you in, but Josie has the flu."

"How is she?" I ask.

"She's fine. Probably something she ate."

I want to know about more than her stomach cramps, but I don't push the topic. Marion Deckard didn't invite me into her house, which means Josie's either really sick or she doesn't want to see me.

"Tell her I stopped by?"

"Of course," she promises, her eyes darting around the street before she steps back inside.

Maybe they both would prefer not to see me.

I don't have time to throw myself a pity party. If misery loves company, it hates productivity. My time is running out. According to the court, I have to appear at the clinic by Monday. That gives me the weekend to piece together the bizarre trail of clues The Dealer left behind for us. His posts have become less frequent. I don't know what that means, but I'm not going to miss my opportunity to figure out what he's trying to tell me.

As if to back up that decision, a new photo appears on his feed in the late morning. It's from last week. I'm in the black romper walking into a nondescript office building. I know what that place is and I know what he's trying to tell me.

I have an appointment that I need to keep this evening. But first, I have time to make a house call.

Dominic Chamber's office is a reporter-free zone, so he must have upheld his word that no one would know he's been working for me. It's early enough in the day that he's at his desk. The creeps come out at night in this city.

He glances up from his computer and exhales when he makes eye contact. Pushing away from the desk, he gestures for me to take an empty chair before he lounges in his own seat. "You're a hard woman to reach."

"I've been a little more cautious with blocked callers. Next time go through the Belle Mère police. They seem to know where I am at all hours."

He frowns. Maybe I'm not as funny as I think I am. "I called from several numbers."

"Sorry, but my lawyer"—it still feels ridiculous to say that—"made me block unknown callers."

"Understandable, given the circumstances. However, if we're going to continue to work together, I'll need a way to reach you. Get yourself a prepaid cell phone to use as a burner."

"A burner?" I repeat. I thought those were only for spy movies, but he nods seriously.

"Done," I promise him. "So if you've been trying to reach me, does that mean you have something?"

He shuffles a few folders around on his desk before he finds the one he wants. I could probably pay him in secretarial services.

"There's no record of who your sister's father is." Before I can thank him for his lackluster bit of news, he goes on, "In fact, most of her medical records and vital statistics have been sealed."

"What do you mean by sealed?"

"It's not so much that her father is unknown. It's more that he's hidden. Well, I might add."

"Why would they do that?" I ask. None of this makes sense. It had been hard enough to process that we had different fathers, but hearing the lengths my parents have gone to in order to bury that information is inconceivable.

"I asked myself the same question, so I started doing a little digging. I looked for your parents' names in conjunction with other legal proceedings. Adoption records, court records."

"Did you find anything?"

"Were you aware that your family accepted a large settlement from Nathaniel West about thirteen years ago?" he asks.

I nod. "My dad sued him in civil court for cutting him out of the business they started."

My parents used the funds as seed money to start Pawnography in an attempt to recapture the American dream he'd lost to his business partner.

Dominic rubs his temples. It's not the answer he's hoping for. "That's all I have so far. It's not much."

I can't help but think it's a lot more than he thinks. Someone has gone to an awful lot of trouble to keep this quiet.

"How much do I owe you?" I ask him, taking my wallet from my purse.

Dominic holds up a chubby hand. "Nothing today. I haven't gotten the information you asked for."

"But you've been working on it," I say slowly.

"I'll be happy to bill you when I've figured this out."

I had no idea private investigators came with a satisfaction guarantee. Then again, considering his hourly billing rate, I deserve more answers.

"I'll be in touch," he promises.

I leave his office with more questions than answers. My mind churns through an endless stream of theories, many so ridiculous that I actually laugh at myself. I'm so distracted that I don't bother to check my surroundings when I exit his building. When I remember, I glance around, checking every angle. There's no one in sight.

Apparently being investigated for murder makes one both reckless and cautious.

As if he can read my thoughts, Jameson calls.

"World's best girlfriend," I answer glibly.

"Where are you, Duchess?" he asks in a lowered voice that's so deep that I get goosebumps.

"Running errands." It's not a lie technically.

"Without your bodyguard?" he guesses.

"Are you asking or do you know?"

"I know. Maddox called to tell me you had him running the maid to the grocery store," he says.

"We're out of eggs."

He pauses and I brace myself for a lecture. "Just promise me that you're being careful."

"I am. Look there's no safer place to be than on a suspect list." Whoever is framing me wants me alive. I could run around Vegas naked with my hair on fire and no one would touch me.

"Will I see you tonight?" he asks.

"You'll see me every night," I reassure him before we hang up. He'll see me tonight, but I have a very important date to keep first.

Chapter 21

LIES ARE SO easy to tell, but sins are so hard to forgive. It's odd how even something as simple as a coat of paint can be deceptive until viewed in the right light. I never knew what I preferred—a pretty lie or a sorry sinner—until now.

They've redone the lobby of the West Casino. I suppose if I ran a hotel that had seen a murder and an accident in less than two months, I might try to freshen up the joint, too.

It's a bit early to check-in, but as I get closer to my appointment with May from Cachè—and her secret identity—I get more nervous. I'd planned to ask Josie to come with me tonight. I'd never even gotten the chance to tell her about the plan before our falling out.

Before I reach the check-in counter, Mackey steps into my path. I halt, looking around to see if she's alone. I don't spot any other officers, but they are trained to blend in. It's good to see my tax dollars at work.

So much for flying under the radar.

"Are you here to arrest me?" I ask her directly.

"I'm here to talk to you *alone*."

Translation: she wants to speak to me without Jameson or lawyers.

"I have lunch plans," I lie to her, "so this can't take too long."

She glances at the gold watch on her wrist. "Late lunch."

"Early interrogation," I counter. "I have until Monday to comply with the subpoena orders."

"You do," she confirms. "Let's grab a seat."

"Let's stand." I'm not about to let her get comfortable.

"Your boyfriend is calling in every favor in town to find out more about the DNA evidence we've uncovered."

I shrug. She wants me to bite, which is something I can do. "I keep telling him to watch less CSI. Next thing you'll know he'll be doing blood spatter analysis."

"We found a towel in the residence containing seminal residue..."

I do my best not to gag.

"And blood—as well as some tissue."

"Tissue?" I repeat, hoping she's talking about Kleenex.

"Preliminary reports suggest it's hymenal."

Some things you can't unhear. "Are you saying that Nathaniel West..."

"Had sexual intercourse with a woman we believe was a virgin at the time."

"Then there you go," I tell her. "That clears me because I'm not eligible for a white wedding."

"Given your intriguing sexual history, it's possible it could be you."

"I already told you that I'm not a virgin," I whisper furiously as a group of Japanese tourists roll past.

"According to your statement, you've only had sexual intercourse once. It's very likely that your hy—"

"Enough theories revolving around my vagina. None of this

explains why you think it's me." I'm not a lawyer but there has to be some evidence actually linking me to the crime before they can start stealing my blood.

"That's why I'm here," she says. "I'm about to tell you what your boyfriend so desperately wants to know."

"Out of the goodness of your heart?"

"Before it's too late." It's not the answer I'm expecting. "Our investigations have discovered some interesting connections between your family and the Wests."

That hardly counts as brilliant detective work. "Everyone knows that our fathers hated one another."

"But why?" she asks. "It took some time to convince the court to unseal the documents, but we have our answer. Nathaniel West settled a civil suit with your father a number of years ago."

"I know. They had a disagreement about a business arrangement."

Mackey casts a wan smile at me and my heart skips a beat. "The matter was tried in a civil court, and the records were sealed to protect a minor."

In the middle of one of the busiest hotel lobbies in Las Vegas, the world stops.

"Did you know Nathaniel West was your sister's father?"

No seems like a grossly inadequate word.

Mackey continues, granting me no time to come to grips with this. "Both sets of DNA found at the murder scene were a partial match."

"I don't understand," I say slowly.

"One set belonged to Nathaniel West. The other belonged to his progeny."

. . .

MACKEY DOESN'T FOLLOW me when I run for the lobby's bathroom. Progeny. Child. Daughter. The words assault me as I wretch over the toilet. If Becca was his daughter, of course, Mackey suspects I am, too.

I'm not, but someone else is. It can't be Monroe. She'd given the entire freshman class a front row seat to her debauchery. I know it isn't me.

At least, I know I'm not the one who…

I throw up again just considering what she told me. I might not be the one she's looking for, but I can't ignore the other bombshell she's dropped.

Becca was Nathaniel West's daughter, a fact both my parents knew—parents who've been desperate to break up my relationship with my boyfriend.

I vomit until I'm dry heaving stomach acid in the public restroom of a five-star resort. If Mackey wanted to be certain I'll submit to that DNA test, she knew exactly what button to push.

When I finally gather my strength, I rinse out my mouth in the sink. I can't bring myself to look in the mirror. I'm too afraid I'll find Nathaniel West staring back at me.

I check in to my room, ignoring the annoying cheerfulness of the front desk attendant. The hotel room has been redone to have a sleek, modern appeal. Everything is white and minimal with clean lines and the most abstract of abstract art, but the stale scent of cigarette smoke still hangs in the room. It's proof that Vegas is a city out of time, or maybe just one unhinged from reality. If it weren't for the acrid smell assaulting my nostrils, the space might actually seem luxurious. No doubt the renovation had been a ploy to try to convince visitors that the hotel is worth the hefty price tag.

Next month, I'll have some serious explaining to do when

my mom and Hans get my emergency credit card bill. But if this situation doesn't count as a crisis, nothing ever will.

I sit on the edge of the bed and wait with my hands folded in my lap. Being nervous is strange. Of course, I've never called a service before. Until a few days ago, my only contact with call girls had been on the flyers littering the streets. Somehow it still feels inevitable. I'm in too deep not to follow the clues.

But *this* room in *this* hotel in *this* city could never hope to be more than a mirage. Because the one thing tourists never see is the truth. The bones of Las Vegas are rotten, weakened by greed and excess. Even in a fancy hotel room I can't see past that fact.

Just like I can't see past the fact that my whole life is a lie. Is it possible this should be my birthright?

Because I don't want it. Any of it. If what Mackey told me is true, she's stolen the only good thing in my life.

Jameson calls a few times while I wait, but I send the calls to voice mail. No doubt I'm whipping him into a frenzy by not answering, but will he care as much when he finds out I'm his sister?

If I'm his sister.

If.

I cling to the tiny word like it's my life raft in a stormy sea.

My phone vibrates with a notification and I can't help but check it. The Dealer has posted another photo. I half expect it to be a snap of me vomiting all over the West casino bathroom. But it's simply a photo of the Belle Mère Medical Clinic.

Whoever is behind this account knows exactly how to salt the wound. I look at the picture wondering if that place will be my deliverance or my damnation. I stare for so long that it blurs in and out of focus, and in the process, draws my attention to something I might not have noticed before.

The photo was taken from a car window. The Dealer must

have been in a hurry to get this out, because a bit of the driver's side mirror is in the shot. I zoom in on the picture until the fragment comes into focus.

I nearly drop the phone, but somehow I keep it in my trembling hands long enough to send one text.

I know who you are.

A knock on the door startles me, and I stand, smoothing my shirt as if I'm going to impress May while smelling like vomit. When I open the door, I'm met by familiar, if surprised eyes. The shock mirrored in them quickly shifts to anger.

Stepping to the side, I hold out my arm. I might not have expected May to be someone I know, but the pieces start to click together. "Won't you come in, Monroe?"

———

Ready for another sinful installment?
1-click BEAUTIFUL FOREVER, book 3 in the Sinners Saga trilogy now! Turn the page for a sneak peek.

Want updates, exclusive bonus content, including a newsletter only story? Become a VIP:
http://www.genevalee.com/vip

If you loved Beautiful Sinner, you'll love the dark, sensual, and dangerous *New York Times* Bestselling Royals Saga, book one COMMAND ME is free for a limited time! *A glance, a kiss, and nothing would be the same...*

Join my Facebook reader group, Geneva Lee's Loves, for exclusive giveaways, sneak peeks, live videos and more.

Keep reading for a sneak peek of Beautiful Forever!

———

IT'S NOT TRUE. *I am not Nathaniel West's daughter.*

I repeat the thought in my head like a new-age manifestation. I have to believe it, because if I don't the pit widening in my stomach will swallow me whole.

The question plagues me as I reach the revolving door, but before I can step inside, a hand closes over my shoulder and spins me around. With my mind lost in thoughts of felonies, I shriek. The sound is smothered by Jameson West's lips.

Jerking away, I try to ignore the urge to melt into him.

In his suit, he looks older than he really is. There's even a faint trace of stubble peppering his jaw. I run my fingers over it without thinking and he sighs. Rubbing it with his hand, he shakes his head. "I shaved this morning, Duchess."

"It makes you look powerful."

His eyebrow curves up like a question mark. "It makes me look old."

After his father's unexpected death, Jameson stepped up to run the family business. Given that the last argument he'd had with his father was about him dropping out of college, he hadn't planned to be running a Fortune 500 company. The new responsibilities might be aging him, and sharing any info I've learned today won't help.

I look for the truth in his face, but all I find is the strong set of his jawline and unreadable expression in his silver eyes. His unruly, coppery hair is tamed into submission. Today he's playing the part of the businessman. Aloof. Untouchable. Calculating. And I'm the one he's analyzing. I shrink away from him.

"What's wrong?" The suspicion in his voice only sharpens my edginess.

"Nothing," I lie too quickly to be believable. "You surprised me."

"I was about to say the same thing," he says slowly. "Are you hear to see me?"

"Why would I be here to see you?" I really need some verbal Pepto-Bismol right now to stop all the paranoia from spewing out of me.

"Because I work here, Duchess. I was overseeing the security updates." He pauses to give me a chance to connect the dots but my brain has gone haywire. "I sent you a text."

"My phone's acting strangely." Apparently, the dishonesty is going to give the paranoia a run for its money.

"I have a few minutes. Why don't I give you the private tour of the business offices?"

I sidestep him when he reaches for me. Hurt flashes over his features, but he smiles tightly. "I'm sorry. Josie's sick and I have to run and if we get started…"

He allows me to bow out, gracelessly I might add, without further comment, but before the revolving door seals behind me, he calls out one final question, "Why were you here?"

I step out on the other side, and we stare at each other through the glass. I could go back inside and explain, but facing him is painful enough. Maybe this was always our destiny: to see each other but never touch.

Keep reading: **1-click BEAUTIFUL FOREVER**

Who killed Nathaniel West?

BEAUTIFUL FOREVER

Later

At Belle Mère Prep, some kids come back to school after a summer in Europe. Others return with a few new notches on their Restoration Hardware bedposts. So? I'm coming back with a security detail.

They can stare at me in the hallways. Who can blame them? The fact is that I spent most of my summer as a lead suspect in a murder case. My classmates gawk as I take a seat. No doubt they're trying to spot a baby bump. It's the only way this could get any better for them.

Thanks a lot, TMZ.

But while they stare, I can only think of those people that aren't here this morning to start their senior year. I feel their absences as ominously as an unexplained shadow in an empty room. Some are long gone. One didn't see the end of the summer.

Living or dead, they're just ghosts now.

Chapter 1

CHANCES ARE CHOICES. Or something like that. For instance, take opening a door to find someone completely unexpected on the other side. To shut the door or feign surprise. A kind person might give the guilty party across from them a gracious out. But no one has ever accused me of being nice. Not to Monroe West, anyway.

"Monroe." I greet her by the name I know as she flies into the room. Then I remember myself. "I mean, May. I see you've landed yourself your dream job."

May West. There's a certain poetry to it. I wonder if she was being clever or if she unintentionally chose such a famous alias. Her usually stick-straight hair waves into soft curls over her shoulders and she's wearing enough eyeshadow to make a porn star blush. She's gone from looking like an entitled seventeen year-old Houser to passing for a hard-used twenty-five-year-old showgirl. If we weren't standing so closely I might not have recognized her as my fellow classmate, boyfriend's sister, and, dare I add, psychotic bitch? We'd made some minor progress on that front of late but something tells me this less-than-chance encounter would put us right back at square one.

Monroe tugs up the silver, sequined tube masquerading as a dress and glares at me. I have to give her credit. The momentary flash of fear that I'd spotted when I opened the door is hidden behind a mask of annoyance. Despite the audacious dress, she doesn't look out of place in the five-star hotel room. Then again every aspect of the West Casino hotel room from the slight sheen in the wallpaper to the overstocked mini bar screams style over substance. Apparently, it's a trait Nathaniel West's hotels shared with his own family.

"How much?" she asks through gritted teeth.

"I thought I was the one who paid you." I lean against the hotel door, closing it behind us. As soon as the lock clicks her eyes narrow.

"I'm not interested in your little jokes," she hisses. "Tell me how much you need to keep quiet."

I blow a stream of air between my lips. "A pony. The lost city of Atlantis. Maybe a trip to see the Wizard."

I don't suffer from any misconceptions. If the situation were reversed, the Wicked Bitch of the West, aka my darling Monroe, wouldn't hesitate to blast the news of my fall from virtue to every student at Belle Mère Prep. But I'm not here for that. I've come to this hotel room for one reason: The Dealer.

A few days ago, a mysterious new photo had shown up on The Dealer's feed. I hadn't expected it to lead me to an escort agency. When I realized where I was I gambled and pretended to be interested in a job. The ploy worked, granting me enough time to schedule an appointment with May: the only clue The Dealer had attached to his post.

But why lead me here? What did Monroe's extracurricular activities have to do with the night that Nathaniel West died? I thought the purpose of the Instagram account was to expose the killer. I'm not so certain anymore. Unless The Dealer's plan is simply to disgrace each of us as thoroughly as possible.

Monroe steps closer to me, jabbing a finger in my chest. "How did you even find out?"

I sidle away toward the minibar. Grabbing two tiny bottles of West Tennessee Whiskey, I toss her one. She can play it cool but I know she needs liquid courage as much as I do.

She rolls her eyes when she reads the label and sashays over. "I prefer gin."

"Doesn't your family own West Tennessee Whiskey?" I ask as I screw off the cap and down mine in a single gulp. It blazes down my throat, lighting a fire in my stomach.

"Yes, but my family owns everything." There's a brittle edge in her words but she swallows it down along with her shot of whiskey. Then she digs out another mini bottle of Beefeater.

"What are you doing?" I ask her and suddenly this isn't an interrogation. I'm not trying to pry information out of her. Instead I find myself wanting to shake her. I may have no love for Monroe West, but I know what this would do to her family. I like her mother, but I was in love with her brother. With everything the two of them have been through this year, this might destroy the fragile threads holding their family together.

"Why would you care?"

That's a cry for help if I've ever heard one. "Because The Dealer sent me here, which means that anyone else who's following his posts could have opened that door."

It's only a matter of time before the police and FBI catch on to the account. That will be bad enough. Right now, only a handful of people are following the mysterious feed, and each of them has good reason to want to know the identity of our friendly neighborhood stalker. The Dealer hasn't been posting our proudest moments so no one has started sharing the pictures—yet.

"What does he have on you?" she asks, her eyes flash as if something important has finally occurred to her.

So much for hoping that Monroe is as smart as she looks. I'd had my suspicions that the blonde, air-head heiress act was for show, now I know it is. If I'm following The Dealer closely enough to wind up here it's not out of curiosity.

I shrug. Two blondes can play dumb.

"Maybe the proof that Mackey is looking for." She pours another glass, but she doesn't down it this time. Sipping thoughtfully, she watches me for a sign that she's right.

"Sorry to disappoint you, but he's got nothing." None of the photos on the feed seemed directed at me, but plenty of them focused on people around me. Of course, the company I keep has as good as convicted me in the eyes of the FBI. "I know what it will take for me to keep quiet."

"Yes?" she snaps. For a second I almost swear her eyes flash a demonic red, but that's probably just me.

"The truth." If Monroe expects me to keep quiet about this discovery, then I'm going to need to know why she's doing it in the first place.

"The truth is in short supply these days." She drops into a chair and stares out the window at the sparkling city lights. Even in the daylight, Vegas flashes its best smile, calling tourists to come hither with promises of good luck and good fortune. Monroe's gaze grows distant as if she's as lost to this city as anyone else.

"Why?" I continue. "You have everything. Why throw it away?"

"You think I'm throwing it away?" Her head whips around so she can glare directly at me. "Do you know what Vegas is? A place for dreamers. It's easy to lose your way here. Ask your daddy."

"Ask yours," I counter coldly.

She flinches but shrugs it off with a hollow laugh. Flipping her hair over her shoulder, she goes on. "You can either lose yourself or you can make yourself."

I'm pretty certain that Monroe West already has it made, but I keep the thought to myself. If I keep provoking her, I'll never get my answer.

"My father made himself into a mogul. Everyone expects me to spend the rest of my life in the spa or shopping. I don't have to work." Her eyes flicker over to check if I'm listening. I nod for her to continue. "But I don't want to be another parasitic heiress. God knows the world has enough of those."

"You want to be a hooker instead?" The question slips out, and I clamp my mouth shut. When you operate at my level of sarcasm, it's hard to contain it.

"I'm not a hooker," she says with a withering look.

"Escort," I correct myself, tacking on a "sorry."

"My father made his fortune on gamblers. He made money on money. Jameson gets to take over that empire. No work. No hardship. It's just his."

"I doubt he sees it that way." Defensiveness flares in my chest at the mention of my boyfriend.

"Of course not. He, like most men, has the luxury of being able to complain about his circumstances while still taking advantage of them." She wags her finger at the space between us. "We don't."

Now I'm in the same class as Monroe? Will wonders never cease? Although, I don't expect that our two-girl Breakfast Club is going to meet again after we leave this room.

"There's plenty of money in Vegas. It's almost an insult to make money on money."

"So you're going to make money off sex?" I guess.

"I'm going to build my empire on sex," she corrects me.

"The youngest madam in Vegas history. I've learned the trade from some of the best, and let's face it, I'm well-educated."

I thought back to English class. I suppose you don't need a spectacular grasp of the classics to run an escort agency.

"I won't have any competition." She leaves the last statement lingering in the air as bait.

I bite. "And why is that?"

"Because they'll all be terrified that I'll reveal that they employed me while I was underage. Instead I get to play the part of business savant," she concludes.

She already has the part of idiot down, I think.

Monroe studies me for a moment. No doubt wondering what I think of her now. "If things don't work out with Jameson, I might have a job for you."

"I don't think we should be in business together," I say dryly. Having Monroe as my high school enemy and my pimp is a bit much to swallow.

"You know where to find me," she says, unfazed. "If you'll excuse me, I have better things to do with my day and you must have…something to do with yours."

Like your brother.

When she leaves, I settle onto the bed and stare at the ceiling above. Various shapes emerge from the spackle like pieces of a mysterious puzzle. There was one question I didn't think to ask Monroe: why would The Dealer want to out her? I'm beginning to question if my eyes were playing tricks on me before. I check my phone for a response but there is none. When I open Instagram, the photo is gone.

It looks like The Dealer got my message and made a move after all. It should be a victory but instead it feels like I've painted a big target on my back.

. . .

MY SANDALS CLICK across the marble floor of the West Resort lobby. Slot machines ring out in the distance and even here I can taste the stale cigarette smoke from the casino floor. It's the same as every hotel and casino in this town. Arguably a little nicer than most. So why is it the current epicenter for crime in a city that's no stranger to vice?

This is where the mystery began for me. Is this where it started for a murderer as well? It's hard to believe that months have passed since the deadly party that dragged me into this world. I hadn't even wanted to go, but my best friend, Josie, who desperately wants to be in with the cool crowd, shanghaied me into attending Monroe West's end-of-the-year party. It was supposed to be a celebration of the last day of our junior year—one that I wasn't invited to attend.

We crashed, and I'd be lying if I said I didn't enjoy the look on Monroe's face when she caught me. The two of us had never gotten along, especially after Monroe screwed my boyfriend in front of half of our freshman class. It had been war between the two of us ever since, and trespassing on her party was a declaration of battle. I'd wanted to leave after the confrontation, but instead of tracking down Josie, I met someone. He was a stranger, but something about him put me at ease. We'd spent the night together. Not in the Biblical sense but pretty damn close. The next morning, he was gone.

As if waking up alone in my best enemy's house wasn't bad enough, I'd been forced to hitch a ride with my ex-boyfriend, Jonas, and his smarmy best friend, Hugo. I thought that was the end to a night I'd rather forget—until news broke out that Nathaniel West had been murdered.

The prime suspects? Everyone who'd been at his daughter's party. I might have gotten away with a simple questioning until I found out that the guy I'd shacked up with that night was Jameson West—the heir to the West fortune and the victim's son. Obviously, I have questionable taste in men. Not as strange as my best friend Josie's penchant for older men—a vice that sent her to some dude's hotel room and left me needing an alibi.

Jameson was everyone's number one suspect, even mine. Especially after he started showing up wherever I was. Despite his stalker tendencies, I decided to find out for myself. I never expected to fall in love with him.

I know he's innocent, but that hasn't removed either of us from suspicion in the eyes of the FBI. So, when a mysterious Instagram account ran by someone known only as The Dealer started posting incriminating photos of Belle Mère Prep's most-likely-to-be-a-murderer list, I took it upon myself to investigate. I need to clear our names, and I can only do that if I figure out who killed Nathaniel West.

But as of this afternoon something weighs more heavily on my mind. Thanks to the FBI's resident pain in the ass, Agent Mackey, I have to worry if I can be in love with Jameson. I already learned that my sister was another man's child, a fact my parents kept from me even after her death, but I never considered that I might be as well. If Mackey isn't lying, and I think it's entrapment or some other Law and Order no-go if she is, then I have more than one mystery to solve. Only time will tell if Nancy Drew and the Mystery of the Baby Daddy, starring yours truly, will have a happy ending.

It's not true. I am not Nathaniel West's daughter.

I repeat the thought in my head like a new-age manifestation. I have to believe it, because if I don't the pit widening in my stomach will swallow me whole.

The question plagues me as I reach the revolving door, but before I can step inside, a hand closes over my shoulder and spins me around. With my mind lost in thoughts of felonies, I shriek. The sound is smothered by Jameson West's lips.

Jerking away, I try to ignore the urge to melt into him.

In his suit, he looks older than he really is. There's even a faint trace of stubble peppering his jaw. I run my fingers over it without thinking and he sighs. Rubbing it with his hand, he shakes his head. "I shaved this morning, Duchess."

"It makes you look powerful."

His eyebrow curves up like a question mark. "It makes me look old."

After his father's unexpected death, Jameson stepped up to run the family business. Given that the last argument he'd had with his father was about him dropping out of college, he hadn't planned to be running a Fortune 500 company. The new responsibilities might be aging him, and sharing any info I've learned today won't help.

I look for the truth in his face, but all I find is the strong set of his jawline and unreadable expression in his silver eyes. His unruly, coppery hair is tamed into submission. Today he's playing the part of the businessman. Aloof. Untouchable. Calculating. And I'm the one he's analyzing. I shrink away from him.

"What's wrong?" The suspicion in his voice only sharpens my edginess.

"Nothing," I lie too quickly to be believable. "You surprised me."

"I was about to say the same thing," he says slowly. "Are you hear to see me?"

"Why would I be here to see you?" I really need some verbal Pepto-Bismol right now to stop all the paranoia from spewing out of me.

"Because I work here, Duchess. I was overseeing the security updates." He pauses to give me a chance to connect the dots but my brain has gone haywire. "I sent you a text."

"My phone's acting strangely." Apparently, the dishonesty is going to give the paranoia a run for its money.

"I have a few minutes. Why don't I give you the private tour of the business offices?"

I sidestep him when he reaches for me. Hurt flashes over his features, but he smiles tightly. "I'm sorry. Josie's sick and I have to run and if we get started…"

He allows me to bow out, gracelessly I might add, without further comment, but before the revolving door seals behind me, he calls out one final question, "Why were you here?"

I step out on the other side, and we stare at each other through the glass. I could go back inside and explain, but facing him is painful enough. Maybe this was always our destiny: to see each other but never touch.

Chapter 2

STANDING outside Josie's cracker box house, I can't help but see it for the tiny two-bedroom block that it is. I'd been by earlier today in an attempt to make amends, and it hadn't struck me then, but with my world topsy-turvy, I guess I'm seeing everything in a new light. I've spent the last few months bouncing between billionaires like a bad episode of MTV's Cribs, but being here, now, all that matters is that it feels like I'm finally home. If I'm an impostor in my own life, then it's time to take a step back and return to the people who know and love me.

Even with this new-found resolve, I knock tentatively at the door. Marion, Josie's mother, opens it with a surprised look on her face.

"Since when did you knock?" she asks. And there it is: I am home. This is where I belong, and who I belong with. She's fresh faced with her hair pulled back in a tight knot. It takes a minute for me to remember that it's Friday night. "Sorry honey, but I'm on my way out. I have to get to the dressing rooms in 30 minutes."

Such is the life of a Las Vegas showgirl on the weekend. She'll spend the next couple of days fending off the advances of overly confident businessmen, and the scummy men in town for bachelor parties. They'll pop in and out of Vegas, leaving nothing but a forgettable trail of debt following their two-night stint.

"I actually came to see Josie," I tell her.

Her eyebrows quirk together. "She's sick, and you know how she is when she's sick."

"I do know how my best friend acts when she's sick."

Hospitals were invented for people like Josie Deckard who could turn every cough into consumption. Since I've known her, she's had a habit of quarantining herself at the first sign of a sniffle. Back then, I was allowed to leave offerings of Disney Channel movies at her door, but never permitted to enter. Even Marion had to talk her way inside. But today is a different story, and her hypochondria will have to take a backseat to me pulling the best friend card.

I hesitate. If I tell Marion my sad story, she'll offer me the couch, which is already mine. But this isn't a decision I can leave up to her. Not with things so weird between Josie and I.

"I'll risk it," I decide out loud. No matter how good it feels to be here, I'll need Josie's blessing if I'm going to reclaim my second home.

Marion kisses me on the cheek and the familiar token of affection eases some of my anxiety. Her skin brushes mine. It's soft and warm, like a mother's cheek is supposed to be. I've based that belief entirely on the maternal surrogacy she's shown me over the years. My own mother favors more of a European air kiss with both strangers and her progeny. The stark contrast between Josie's mom and mine has never felt more evident than at this moment. "Lock the door behind me."

I nod as a lump forms in my throat. This is where I should

have been this summer, watching Netflix between shifts at Pawnography, my Dad's shop, planning out every second of my upcoming senior year at Bell-Mère Prep, and keeping Josie and her love life in check. Instead, I'd found myself cast without warning into the role of bad girl socialite. It's time to shed that costume and come back to reality.

Turning the bolt on the front door, I take a deep breath and march down the short hallway to Josie's room. I don't bother to be timid with my knock. Dead silence greets me and after an eternity, a muffled, "Go away."

This is going about as well as I expected.

Trying the knob, I'm not surprised that it's locked, but since this house was built in the 70s, like so much of Vegas, all that stands between me and my reckoning with my best friend is a bobby pin. Slipping one out of my hair, I poke at the tiny hole next to the knob until I hit pay dirt. Home builders must have thought they were doing parents a favor. Give kids the illusion of autonomy by providing a lock on the door that a one cent piece of metal can open.

"Ready or not," I mutter to myself and throw open the door. Josie's buried under her covers, a pillow over her head. Instantly, she sits bolt upright, her cotton fortress crumbling around her as she stares at me.

"I'm not feeling good," she snaps.

I shrug.

"The world is in a state of economic crisis, a reality star is running for president, and we're stuck in a town that still believes second hand smoke is harmless. Nobody's feeling good," I retort. My hands find my hips and I plant them there, ready for whatever she throws at me first, but my defensive posture does nothing to help me when she throws herself backward on the bed.

It takes a second for me to gauge the actual situation in the room. Not much has changed. Neat piles of discarded clothes litter the perimeter. Stacks of notebooks and magazines wait on the desk. She hasn't redecorated or remodeled or turned it into a craft room. Everything is as it should be, but by the time I take my second look around I see a few things that are off. The clothing piles are bigger than they should be. The magazines on her desk are untouched, having been left unread for an entire summer meant to be spent poolside. And most disconcerting, the television isn't on. Everyone from infancy to the infirm knows that the only modern perk of illness is Netflix.

"You aren't sick," I accuse her. "You're hiding. We might as well get straight to the point. Did you run off when I showed up today?"

It's not like Josie to turn tail and hide from a situation.

"Someone has a pretty high opinion of herself. I guess that's naturally what happens when you're dating a West." She makes the name sound like a curse word, and I'd be lying if I said my hackles didn't rise at the provocation. I circle her bed looking for clues.

"Yep, they initiated me into the secret society of the Housers," I say, imbuing my words with the proper amount of disgust. Neither of us have ever been Housers. That accolade is reserved for Belle Mère's elite, the children of Las Vegas's upper, upper crust. They run the show while the rest of us hope for a spot in the audience. "My shit no longer stinks and I know their special handshake."

She only glares so I continue my analysis.

"Oh my God, would you stop," she finally says. "You're right. I'm not dying, vulture, so if you're waiting to consume my dead body, you can fly off somewhere else."

"Cute, but that's not why I'm here. I have a favor to ask you."

"This is how you ask for a favor?"

Okay, so she might have a point. One of the few pieces of good advice my mother ever gave me was that you catch more flies with honey. I've never been very good at utilizing that strategy, probably since my mother never bothered to model the behavior herself. Plus, Josie and I are past the candy-coated platitudes of false friendship. She's right though. We need to fix this before I can come home again. So naturally, I start by attacking her. "What's going on with you Josie? You've been acting strangely for weeks. Now you're hiding in bed pretending to be sick? Not just from me, but from your mom as well."

There's a silence that stretches the length of the bible, and then she slowly sits up. Now that she's not glaring at me, I can see that her eyes are red-rimmed and bloodshot. Her lip trembles a little. Josie Deckard has been crying. The idea of teenage girl sobbing into her pillow might not seem like an anomaly, but my best friend doesn't fit that description. She never has.

"Where have you been?" she asks me quietly.

It's not as simple a question as it appears to be, and it doesn't deserve a curt response or a cutesy answer. Instead, I lay it all on the line for her. "Under investigation for murder, falling in love, wrecking my entire family, doing incredibly stupid shit and realizing it's been for nothing."

But that's only the beginning, and we both know it. Sitting down on the edge of her bed, I fill her in on all of the details. I know I'm leaving things out, probably important things, but the gist is there. When I'm finished, a huge burden lifts off my shoulders. I've forgotten how hard it is to keep secrets. Even having one person to trust them with lifts the load off my back.

"What about you," I ask her. "I'm not the only one who's been unavailable this summer."

Josie and I were often separated over the last few years during school break. I'd be shipped off to Palm Springs to visit with my mother or be stuck working at my dad's pawn shop. Josie would be stuck at home or taking whatever job she could find to supplement her non-existent allowance. But we called. And later we texted and Facetimed. We made time for sleepovers and lunch dates and the occasional petty shoplifting. This summer, we have barely sent an emoji to each other.

Josie doesn't respond to my question. Instead, she gets out of bed. It takes a long time, as if she's ordering her limbs to move and willing her body to take each step. Opening her desk drawer, she rifles around for a few minutes until she pulls the false bottom up. We'd concocted that little secret spot to stash contraband over the years. Contraband being a pack of cigarettes when we were going through our we're older than we look phase. A bit of booze. Maybe some condoms. The kind of stuff every parent knows their kid is hiding, but we still bother to hide anyway.

Nothing prepares me for what she pulls out of that drawer though. Having little to no experience with the topic, I stare at the black and white photo for far too long. The paper is flimsy. The image is warped, but I can read.

I can read her name in the corner. I can decipher that the numbers mean weeks and days. Try as I might, the white noise photo in the center doesn't make sense.

"Is this..." I trail away, swallowing the words. If I don't say them, they won't be true.

"An ultrasound," she says. Her voice detaches from her body as she continues on in an all business tone. "The clinic I went to makes you have one before you can make any decisions, even if you already made your decision. Probably some politician's idea of punishment."

She continues on, as if she can replace the tension in the air with her tirades.

"Oh my God," I breath, basically ignoring her. "Did you ... Are you ..."

"I am," she admits.

"Why?" The question bursts out of me. Everything is starting to make sense: her distance and irritability. But there's no relief in this revelation. Rather it feels like I'm waking from a nightmare to discover I wasn't asleep.

She snatches the picture away and shoves it back in the drawer, as if hiding it is in any way dealing with the situation. "All that debate about it and no one tells you how expensive it is to get it done. I've been saving all summer. It's still not enough and ..." she doesn't finish the sentence, but she doesn't have to. The thought of actually going through with it is scary and I'm not even the one who has to do it.

"I can help." It's not an offer because she's taking my help, whether she wants it or not. "I would've helped. Why didn't you tell me?"

"It's complicated."

"Does the father know?"

"He's not in the picture," she says, her nostrils flaring in defiance.

I decide not to press the issue. When she's ready to share more, she will.

"All those years of her being so paranoid," she says absently, "and I've gone and done the one thing that will break my mom's heart."

"You don't have to tell her," I whisper.

She blinks as if remembering that I'm there and then stares at me. "Em, I can't do this alone."

"You won't have to," I promise.

Chapter 3

WE SPEND the next few days ignoring our situations in favor of binge-watching as much bad TV as we can stomach. Now that we've spilled our guts it's easier to just sit and digest in each other's presence than to continue strategizing our next moves. I need a break. A break from the investigating, from the suspicion, from watching over my shoulder. I can't even imagine how badly Josie needs a break. I do my best not to stare at her when reality invades my conscious mind over the on-screen action trying to drown it out.

She looks the same. That may be because she hasn't changed her pajama pants in like three days, but really, looking at her you wouldn't even know. Shouldn't there be some type of clue? Is this how getting knocked up works? If so, couldn't we all be knocked up all the time and not know it?

"Stop staring at me," she finally mutters one afternoon. "It's not going to burst out of my abdomen and do a song and dance."

"Sorry," I say sheepishly. "It's just so weird."

She groans, shaking her head as she flips through the Recently Addeds.

"You know what's weird? The fact that you have a security detail parked across the street from my house."

Okay, I can grant her that.

"Let's go back to being 12," I suggest, "when our biggest problem was hoping we could finally get our periods."

As soon as it's out of my mouth, I wish I could take it back, but she just gives a hollow laugh.

"Yeah. I actually kind of feel like I'm hoping to get my period all the time at the moment."

"And the award for shitty friend of the year goes to"— I clutch my chest dramatically—"me. I'd like to thank my mother, who taught me everything I know, my father, who also contributed, and generally just being surrounded by the worst possible role models a girl can have."

Josie's false laughter turns into bemused giggles. "What award do I win? Most likely to become her mother?"

I wince, then nearly jump out of my skin when Josie's mother actually opens the door. If there was an award for appearing innocent, neither of us would be winning it at the moment.

"Em, your mom called me." She stares me down.

I kind of expected that. "I might have blocked her phone number."

Marion pinches the bridge of her nose, sighing heavily and forming the perfect image of the maternal archetype at the same time. "You can't block your mother."

"Funny, my iPhone says I can." I tack on a smile as if to indicate I'm joking, even though we both know I'm not.

"She says that she really needs to talk to you." Marion bypasses the passive-aggressiveness and goes straight for the kill. "I can't have you staying here if your mother doesn't think it's okay."

"My mother wouldn't care if I was living under a bridge," I grumble, but I take out my phone and pull up her number. "I'll call her."

Marion disappears with a look of triumph and Josie bumps her shoulder against mine.

"You want a minute?"

"Nah." I'd already told her everything that had happened. What I'd discovered about Becca, how Hans had tried to corner me. She'd gotten the blow by blow. Whatever mitigating factors my mother wants to add to the drama I won't be keeping from her either.

Mom answers on the first ring.

"Emma," she says breathlessly, as if she's been pacing while waiting for my call.

"Vivian," I respond coolly. She doesn't bother to correct me, even though she hates that I call her by her first name. More than ever, I need that detachment and whatever small sense of self-confidence it grants me.

"We need to talk."

We've needed to talk for the last eight years, but I'm glad she's finally getting the memo.

"I'm not coming to Palm Springs," I say.

Mom isn't the type to have serious conversations over the phone. She believes in tearing someone down to their face, the good old-fashioned way.

"You don't have to," she assures me. "I'm here in Las Vegas."

"What restaurant?" I ask.

"I think it's better if I come to you."

It's taken a lot of years for me to build up enough scar tissue where my mom is concerned that her barbs and dismissals don't hurt me anymore, but apparently, she can still catch me off guard.

"I'm staying at Josie's," I tell her in broken fragments while I try to piece together what could be so terrible that she would deign to leave her five-star life and slum it in the burbs.

"I'll come over this evening," my mom says. "Should I bring McDonald's?"

"Yeah mom, get me a Happy Meal," I say flatly. We hang up and I wonder if she's experiencing some type of medical incident that's caused a temporary bought of amnesia. Maybe she hit her head and thinks I'm nine years-old and that I've been at Josie's for an extended sleepover.

"What was that about?" Josie asks as soon as I'm off the phone.

I give her a look that says way more than what comes out of my mouth next. "Guess who's coming to dinner?"

Chapter 4

THAT NIGHT my mother actually brings me a Happy Meal.

"I can't remember if you still hate ketchup," she says as she hands the box to me at the door.

"I've made peace with tomatoes," I reassure her as I try to concentrate on the carefully proportioned glut of calories that she's brought me. Who decided apple slices were fast food? But I can't distract myself from the fact that for the first time, in a very long time, it's my mother standing at the door. Not Vivian von Essen.

Her perfectly manicured nails are chewed down to the quick, and she twists her fingers nervously. She's wearing a simple wrap dress instead of a tailored suit and although her hair is done, it hangs flatly over her shoulders. Somehow she's become the before shot in a shampoo commercial.

This is the woman I grew up with—harried, nervous. My dad's gambling problems made it impossible for his business ventures to succeed. I'd watched her dreams slip away for years, until this was what she looked like. She'd turned herself around then and left behind anyone who might have dragged her back to this state. I'm not sure what it means that she's here now.

Josie tip-toes down the hall to greet her. "Hi Mrs. Von--"

My mother holds up a hand to stop her. "Mrs...um, I mean Vivian is perfectly acceptable, Josie."

Perfectly acceptable. Well, it's good to know that the rod that maintains her stiff formality is still in place.

Josie glances at me worriedly. I'm not imagining that she looks like hell.

"I'll leave you two to talk." With that she disappears.

Mom and I stare at each other. Usually we meet on neutral ground. When she's in Vegas, mom doesn't come to dad's house. We meet for brunches or afternoon tea. Occasionally, she convinces me to go shopping, and while the Deckard's house isn't home to either of us, it's far from neutral.

That means that in my mother's eyes, it's up to me to play the hostess.

"Uh, why don't we sit down and eat," I finally manage. That's about the time I realize she's holding another Happy Meal. Apparently, mom also wants to pretend she's a kid again. I guess adulting doesn't get any easier. She catches me staring at the bag.

"I brought one for Josie," she explains.

"I'll give it to her," I say, seizing the opportunity to run away for a minute.

Josie holds up the sign of the cross when I enter her bedroom.

"I brought you food." I toss the happy meal on her bed like a sacrificial offering.

"I'm still not bailing you out of this."

"Please do not make me talk to her alone," I beg.

"Un-uh."

"I'm revoking your friendship card," I tell her.

"I think I can find someone else to French braid my hair," she teases.

I shut the door a little too hard behind me.

"Josie's been battling the flu," I say as a means to explain why she's hiding out.

"Oh, that's too bad," mom says absently. "It's probably best that we talk alone anyway."

"Aren't you going to eat?" I ask her.

"I wasn't hungry."

That makes two of us. Later, I'm going to regret not eating these French fries, but right now I know I couldn't force them down. Not when my mouth is so dry, it feels like someone shoved half a package of cotton balls in it.

"You look well," she says at the same time I blurt out, "You look like hell."

"Don't say hell," she admonishes me.

"There's no such thing as hell, mom." I've been making the argument since I first dropped the h-bomb to her.

"There is. It's where sinners and unbaptized babies go."

"When did you go Roman Catholic on me?" I ask. She's not *Mèrely* acting strangely. I think she may have actually lost it, full-blown *One Flew Over the Cuckoo's Nest* style.

"I've been thinking a lot…" she begins.

In my experience thinking rarely leads to being born again. Something bigger is happening here.

"And?" I prompt her.

"I've had a lot on my mind," she says.

"I guess it's a good thing since you've been thinking," I say slowly.

"Do you always have to be so sarcastic? It's really unbecoming."

"You have your ways of landing your billionaires. I have mine."

She winces at my joke, and I feel a twinge of panic in my stomach. Is this where she lowers the boom? Is she about to admit to me that Becca is Nathaniel West's daughter? Is she about to admit to me that I am, too?

"There's something I need to tell you," she says in a strangled voice. "You need to know. I shouldn't have kept it from you for this long. I thought it was for the best, but..."

Oh, shit.

Shit.

Shit.

Shit.

Shit.

"It's about your father."

Shit.

This is not happening. Some part of me reverts back to being five years old and I have to resist the temptation to plug my ears so I can't hear what she's saying.

"We've split up," she says finally. I could swear I hear a record screech to a halt.

"Yeah, years ago." It's official. My mom has had a psychotic break. She's clearly forgotten the last eight years of her life, seeing as she can't remember she's remarried to a pedophiliac scumbag, but remarried none the less, and that I'm too old for Happy Meals.

"Not *your* father," she says with emphasis. "Your stepfather."

That's a clarification that should have been part of the original thrust of the argument. "Good. He's slime."

"Emma!" She says reproachfully, but her expression softens and my heart sinks. "I know what he did to you. I know what he did to Becca."

And just like that, a dam bursts inside of me. I haven't cried to my mom since I ... I don't think I ever cried to my mom. The idea that she found out and took action is baffling and reassuring at the same time. It's a gesture I didn't know I needed her to make. Now that she has, that only leaves one more thing. "He belongs in jail."

"Yes, but…"

There's always a *but*.

"Out with it mom. What did he buy you with?" I shouldn't expect more, but I suppose it's not too far-fetched that a woman who would leave her husband for what he did to her daughter would also want his ass in prison. But how could he pay alimony from a cell? Plus, there's the issue of how it will look to those on the outside. A divorce is hardly unprecedented in the land of filth and money, but scandal should be avoided when possible.

"That's unfair Emma. I had to think about both of us. About our financial well-being."

"And our reputations?" I add.

"He's forgoing the prenuptial agreement. I get half of everything."

"Do you get half of his guilt?" I spit back.

Nothing could ever make me feel more disgusting than when Hans von Essen admitted to me that he'd molested my sister for years. He could claim it was mutual all he wanted but in the eyes of the law, and in mine, it was rape. Although the fact that my mother can overlook this comes pretty close to that sickening.

"Emma, you have to think about the consequences, how it will affect all of our lives if this comes out."

"Yes, I wouldn't want to destroy his career making crappy movies."

"This isn't about his career," she shoots back.

"Then what is it about, Mom? Explain it to me."

No one has held Vivian von Essen accountable for far too

long. It's a little tragic that it has to be her daughter that finally does it.

"I don't want your sister to remembered that way."

"As a victim?" I ask her. "Because newsflash, she's already a victim. She's already remembered that way. Don't try to make this about anything more than the fact that you want to save face."

"And so what if I do?" she admits haughtily. Fire sparks in her eyes, bringing some life back to her weary appearance.

"What about the other girls, Mom?"

"What other girls," she asks in horror. She could always play the naïve ingénue on command.

"The other girls he's done this to," I explain to her. "Do you think Becca was the only one? Do you think I was a fluke? How many girls have found themselves on his casting couch?"

Tales of movie producer's ethics have always been the stuff of legends. There's no doubt in my mind that Hans had all too eagerly embraced that perk of his power.

"He told me there were no others," she says too quickly. She's not lying, but she knows that he is.

"Whatever helps you sleep at night."

"Look," she says, shifting tactics, "A trust fund has been set up in your name."

"I don't care."

"There's $10 million in it."

"I don't care," I repeat. "He can't buy my silence."

"You'll never have to worry about money."

One way or another I'm not going to have to worry about money without taking Hans' dirty money. "I don't need his money. After all, think of the other trust funds I might be privy to."

"I don't know what you mean," she says.

"I know about Becca. I know why Dad settled with

Nathaniel West all those years ago." I take a deep breath and ask the one question I'm not sure I want an answer to. "What I don't know is whether or not Nathaniel West is my father?"

It takes a second for my query to process through the shock frozen over her classic features.

"No, he's not," she tells me, but the pit in my stomach doesn't close.

How am I supposed to trust her when her idea of nurture has been telling me lies? Even now, she prefers the trussed-up lie to the ugly truth. Could she even admit it to me if Nathaniel was my father? "I think you should go."

"Emma, I need to know that you aren't going to tell anyone."

"I'm not," I interrupt her. I'm fighting too many battles right now to take on one more, especially one that should be hers.

"Thank you," she begins, but I stop her.

"You should be the one talking to the authorities. To the media. To everyone." I cross the room and dig a business card out of my purse, then I wait by the door until she gets the memo. She pauses at the threshold and I hand her the card.

"Agent Mackey, "she reads, shaking her head. "Oh, Emma."

"You'll just love her," I promise. "Isn't it convenient I know an FBI agent?"

Chapter 5

"I THINK you should talk to him," Josie announces the next day.

"Who?" I ask in confusion. "Maddox?"

Even Marion had begun to question having a safety detail parked outside her house at all hours. Personally, I'd taken to grabbing him Starbucks when I went out on errands. Considering Maddox doesn't get involved unless he's needed—and he hasn't been—he's a bit more like having a faithful guard dog. Plus, I've discovered, his bark is worse than his bite. He might look like a pit-bull but secretly he has the heart of an English bulldog. A little dumb and very lovable.

"Not Maddox. Jameson."

"Oh, him." Josie is probably right. I should talk to him. It's the rational thing to do, which is why I'm not doing it. Not a single aspect of my life falls into rational or logical at the moment. Why should he?

"Your mom told you that Nathaniel isn't your father."

"And you believe her?" I ask. "Because everything she says is so credible.

"I don't really have a reason not to believe her. She admitted that Becca was Nathaniel's."

"Here's a better question: does she even know who my dad is?" It seems my mom had spent the late 90's bed hopping. "My dad could be anyone."

"Your dad is your dad," Josie corrects me. "*My* dad could be anyone."

"Sorry, Jos. I didn't mean to make you feel bad." According to Marion, Josie's dad was a visiting businessman who gave her a bogus name and a bogus occupation. When she tried to track him down she discovered that the company he worked for didn't exist. "You know, I've been thinking your mom probably could've paid someone at the hotel to give her the registration information on the sly."

Josie shakes her head quickly. "Don't ever suggest that to her," she advises me. "Mom's feelings on it are pretty strong. She says that if he wanted her he wouldn't have lied to her in the first place, and…"

Neither of us have to finish that thought out loud. If he hadn't wanted Marion, he definitely didn't want Josie. Given the generally disappointing men I'd encountered in my life I'd say the Deckard women were both better off.

"Don't let your mom ruin what you have with Jameson," Josie interrupts my thoughts, bringing me back to the topic--one that I'd been trying to avoid.

"The fact that he might be my brother is what might ruin things with Jameson." I practically spell it out for her.

"Well, then he deserves to know too."

"Josie, we didn't do it, but we did other stuff," I say, striving to maintain some delicacy, "and you know, I just … I don't want him to be thinking about …"

"You don't want to wreck it?" she guesses.

"What if he starts thinking about the fact that I might be his sister and then if I'm not, he can't look at me."

"Psychologists don't analyze things this much, Em."

"You're probably right." I'd grant her that but it doesn't mean I'm going to call him.

"Um, are we expecting company?" Josie asks, pausing the TV so that we can both hear the car pulling into her driveway. We wait for a minute, half expecting it to turn around but it doesn't.

"Maybe it's Maddox. Probably wants to go on a caffeine run." I hop up and go to the window, but it's not Maddox's familiar black sedan parked out front. It's a tiny, gold convertible. The kind of ostentatious car that only one person I know could pull off driving.

"If I were you I'd hide," I tell Josie. "The Wicked Bitch of the West has come to call."

"Life was so much simpler six months ago," Josie says with a sigh, scrambling off the couch to seek sanctuary in her room.

"And yet you're the one who wants me to call Jameson."

"If you call him maybe my house won't be Grand Central Station," she yells before she shuts the door.

"Hormones much?" I say to the now empty living room.

I save Monroe the humiliation of having to come inside a 2-bedroom house and meet her outside. Judging from the fact that she hasn't gotten out of the car she already views this as a self-service errand. Her worst half, Sabine, glowers at me from the passenger seat.

"I see you're back from LA," I say, conversationally. Sabine doesn't reply.

She doesn't talk. She just exists.

Monroe pushes her Louis Vuitton sunglasses to the tip of her nose and looks me up and down. "You're alive."

"Thanks for the info." Whatever tenuous truce that Monroe and I had managed earlier this summer is fraying at both ends. She's never liked me, and I have the kind of dirt that could destroy her. She's not ready to let the cat out of the bag on her escort empire. What she doesn't know, though, is what I found out about who killed Nathaniel West. The information Mackey gave me points suspicion for the murder at Nathaniel's own daughter.

Since I know it wasn't me, she's the next possible suspect. The trouble is that the evidence doesn't match up. If Monroe really has been passing her free time working as an escort for an exclusive Las Vegas agency, then it doesn't seem likely that she had any remnants of virginity to shed on a towel after the murder. But this is a city based on illusion. One where you can win big, play with magic, and live without consequence. Have I ever seen the real Monroe West?

"Paging Emma Southerly," Monroe says. "My brother requests that you turn your cell phone on."

"My cell phone is on," I tell her dryly.

"Then unblock him." She smacks her steering wheel so hard that the horn honks.

"I don't see why it matters to you. I'd think you'd be glad to be rid of me."

"I like to keep my frenemies close," she informs me. "Plus he's impossible to live with. He's either moping or throwing shit. There is literally no in-between. He broke mom's Baccarat vase yesterday. She's going to have him arrested. Call him."

She flicks a platinum blonde strand of hair over her shoulder.

"I'll think about it," I tell her.

"He doesn't like you staying here," she continues, "and I can see why."

"Not enough room for the servants?"

Monroe's eyes narrow into slits. "He requests that you stay at one of our other residences."

"Our?" I repeat. When did I get inducted into the West hall of infamy? "I'll think about it, *sis*."

"Whatever. I'm just the messenger." Apparently, this is the new form of passing notes in class. Send your bitchy sister to handle the situation.

"It must've taken a lot for you to lower yourself to that position." I lean down on the door and drop my voice to a whisper. "Then again, you know all about lowering yourself into positions, don't you?"

"Come home," she says, with a wicked smile that displays two rows of sparkling white teeth, "so I can teach you to fight like a West. You need practice."

She throws the car into reverse, barely giving me enough time to jump back before she peels out of the driveway, leaving nothing but the glimmer of a Mercedes logo in her wake.

I GO to the only place where I know I'll never be judged. The graveyard is silent. The grounds-keeper must have been through recently, because the stones are swept free of dead grass clippings, artificial flowers are tucked neatly into their urns, and the whole place feels more like a museum of the dead than a cemetery. I sit at the end of Becca's grave and stare at her stone. Even now, those dates don't make sense to me.

"It doesn't feel real," I say to the wind. "How can I be 18? How can I be older than you?"

The brutality of that fact is one reason why I'm glad my birthday has been overshadowed by other events this year. Josie is busy weighing her options. Mom is focused on the divorce proceedings. On the off chance that Jameson remembers, his call can't get through to me anyway.

Even though I don't want to celebrate with other people, I pluck a Hostess cupcake out of my bag. This had been a tradition of mine and Becca's since we were kids. The other would stash the individually wrapped treat when dad remembered to get groceries, then present it like the holy grail. It was our job to remember each other's birthdays. Too many times to count, that one tiny snack cake had been our official birthday cake. As we got older, Marion took charge, picking up a small sheet cake from the grocery store and having our names put on it. But we'd kept this tradition alive quietly. It was a signal that we had each other, and that no matter how bad our family might get, we'd never lose that.

Now it's my job to remember for the both of us. I unwrap it, but I can't bring myself to eat a bite. Behind me footsteps crunch along the dry, sun-burnt grass, and I turn. The appearance of my dad at my sister's grave shouldn't be a shock, but as far as I know, he's never actually been here before.

"Hey, Pumpkin. I thought I might find you here." He nods to the cupcake. "Do you want me to sing you Happy Birthday?"

Tears prick at the corners of my eyes, but I do my best to blink them back. When I had said our birthdays were often forgotten, I should have clarified that it was mom who remembered when someone bothered. Dad? He was always a few days late. His apologies generally came with something gift wrapped from behind the counter at Pawnography.

"Do you mind if I sit down?" he asks.

I shrug, afraid to betray any more emotions.

"I'll take that as a yes." He groans as he settles onto the ground beside me.

"You can have it." I offer the cupcake to him.

"It's your birthday, kiddo. I can't believe you're 18."

He remembered my birthday, and he even got the year right. Color me plum surprised. I force myself to turn and look at him. By all accounts, he's been a lackluster father. His greatest accomplishment has been keeping a roof over our heads, which given the nature of Las Vegas and Belle Mère was actually something to brag about with his gambling addictions.

"You know, you could come home with me," he offers. "Your mom says you've been staying with Josie."

"You've been talking to mom, huh?" I wonder what else she's told him.

"I know about the divorce," he says, reading my mind.

"You can have the money," I say flatly. "Use it to expand the store or something."

"I don't want the money. I want you to be happy. Is there anything else you need to tell me?" Our eyes meet. I know what he's asking me now. It isn't like my mother to walk away from a cushy situation, especially given that Hans spent most of his time in Los Angeles, giving her free run of her own private Palm Springs resort. He suspects there's more to the story.

We stare each other down, but he doesn't push me for the information. I'm more surprised because, although he's the one seeking answers, I'm the one who finds them.

"We have the same eyes," I say softly.

"Yep. You got that from me, kiddo." He looks away then, as if the reality of what we're saying is too painful to face.

"Why didn't you tell me about Becca?" I ask him in a low voice as if she might be able to hear us talking about her.

"You two were young." His voice grows distant as he remembers. "I told myself that I would tell you when you were older, when you could understand."

"What did mom tell herself?"

"She didn't want to say anything. She said it wasn't important."

"It was important enough to sue Nathaniel West over," I choke out.

"People do stupid things when they're hurt, Em. You know that better than anyone."

"That doesn't mean I understand it," I say softly.

"You want the real answer? I guess I never told you because admitting it to you two meant admitting it to myself. When the lawyers finished fighting over the details, they sealed the records. We signed affidavits. At first it was easy to convince myself not to tell because I couldn't legally, and then it was easier to ignore it. But, you know, I realized something? Maybe a bit too late, but I realized it nonetheless. It never really mattered. Becca was my daughter, your sister. She carried my name, even if she didn't have my eyes."

"Sometimes I feel like I didn't know her at all," I admit to him.

"You knew her better than anyone." I want to tell him this isn't true, that it couldn't be. I want to spill the secrets she kept.

"There are things that I'm finding out about her now," I begin.

"You know the funny thing about lies?" Dad interrupts. "Sometimes we don't mean to lie to other people. Sometimes we're too busy lying to ourselves. Then, when we realize it, we feel guilty like we've pulled one over on them. Truth is, the people close to you, the people you love, they always see through it. They see you better than you see yourself. You saw Becca, just by loving her. I know what it's like to find something out, and to think it means a person's been taken away from you, but she wasn't taken away from you. She's right here." He doesn't point to her gravestone. Instead, he points directly at my chest. "She's here with both of us right now. Can't you feel her?"

I pause and wait, and ever so gradually, peace settles over me. "Yeah, I do."

We sit there for what could be minutes, or what could be

hours. It doesn't really matter. When the spell is broken, he speaks. "You aren't coming home, are you?"

It's hard to get words past the lump in my throat. "No, I'm not, but I'm staying at Josie's."

"You're 18 now. It doesn't matter." Sadness softens the edges of his words. "Jameson seems like a good kid. He was right to get you out of there that night. He isn't his father. I know that."

I can only nod. If only it were that simple.

"Can I drive you to Josie's? Maybe take you to dinner?"

"That would be …" I search for my answer, and I'm surprised when I find it. "Nice. That would be nice, Dad."

The night is starless when he drops me off at Josie's house a few hours later. The summer is already growing shorter. Autumn will be here in the blink of an eye, along with my senior year, but while everyone else is thinking about prom and college applications, I'm going to spend time worrying over paternity tests and murder investigations.

The house is quiet. I wasn't the only one to opt out of my self-imposed isolation. I find my cell phone on the kitchen island with a note. "You left this. It's been blowing up all day. Turn it on and call Mackey back."

I know what she's after. I ignored the subpoena delivered last week to Jameson's door. The one requesting a sample of my DNA. I can't keep hiding from the firing squad, and whatever magic Jameson's lawyers have worked to keep the court order from taking effect won't last forever. With or without her answers, she's not going to give up.

I turn on my phone and check my text messages. There's a couple from Josie, ending with a, "Oh, shit. Your phone is here. No wonder you aren't answering me," and an offer for a free sandwich, but that's all.

Still no response from The Dealer, who, judging from his

Instagram feed, is taking a texting and posting holiday. Maybe I had played my card too early, or maybe I had started seeing things I wanted to see. Mackey's dogged pursuit of me might just be proof that sometimes we're so desperate for clues, we fabricate them for ourselves. I send one more text—to my suspect, anyway. If Mackey can badger me into a response, then it's worth employing a similar tactic.

The next call I make is purely practical.

Dominic Chambers answers on the first ring.

"Southerly," he says gruffly. He isn't expecting my call. No doubt he put more work into trying to find out about my sister, but not enough to justify the stamp on another bill. He's moved on from my tragic backstory and on to someone else's current drama.

"I don't need you to keep looking into who my sister's father is," I inform him.

"Oh." I can tell from the way he responds that he'd already stopped. "I guess I can put a bill …"

"No. I have something else for you to do. You can bill as much as you want," I say, thinking of my unwanted trust fund. If I was going to be paid off, at least I could donate the money to a good cause.

I lay out what I want him to do, and he gives a low whistle. "That's not going to be easy."

"I know," I say, simply.

"Or cheap," he adds.

"I know."

This time I speak more forcefully. "I recently came into some money," I explain to him. "Price isn't an object."

"That's a real claim to make in a town like this, little lady."

"I'm not worried about it."

Judging from Dominic Chambers' velour jogging suits and penchant for accepting bogus baseball cards, he's the kind of guy who thinks in the hundreds instead of the millions. He'll be surprised when I suggest we meet in the thousands. "Mr. Chambers, you just won the lottery."

When I hang up with him, I make the last call. Mackey doesn't bother to answer her cell phone. No doubt it's some type of psychological maneuver on her end to make me question myself. Still, there's no turning back now. I'll know the truth even if I have to swallow it whole. When her voicemail beeps, I leave a one-line message.

"Where do I go to get my blood drawn?"

Chapter 6

NOTHING HAS CHANGED inside Pawnography since I stopped coming to work. It's still a haven of other people's crap: old autographs, unwanted instruments, antique pistols. Jerry blinks as if he's seen a ghost.

"Emma?" he says uncertainly.

"Hey, Jerry. How's the store?" The place looks intact, but I know appearances can be deceiving. We both know what I'm really asking: how's my dad? I'd purposefully decided on my impromptu visit tonight since I knew Dad was heading home after he dropped me off at Josie's. I didn't want to get his hopes up that I'd be returning to my job. He hadn't always been the best boss, often leaving me to handle the financial affairs. I'd also been the on-call owner when Dad didn't show for a shift. While no one could argue that I hadn't learned a lot of trivial information about collectibles and forgeries, I'd been so caught up in not letting the shop go under that I'd forgotten to have a life of my own.

"We're doing pretty well." I don't miss the strain in his words.

"And Dad?" I might as well get to the point.

"He's been on it," Jerry says to my surprise. "But we've been busier than normal. I guess a lot of people read about you on the Internet and..."

"People came here to see me?" Seriously, I'm only accused of murder. I'm not that famous.

"Yeah. Jake's really stepped up," he says in a lowered voice as a few tourists step through the front door. "But we could use a little help."

Gee, can I sign autographs at the same time?

"That's why I came by," I say.

"Thank god. We're really missing having you here and I know your dad will be so happy. He misses you."

I suspect Jerry misses me, too. He's been in love with me since my dad hired him out of community college a few years ago. Although he's never said it, it's written across his face even now. I feel like I'm letting them both down now, because I'm not here to offer my services. I square my shoulders and deliver the bad news.

"I'm not looking for a job." I'm too busy dodging indictments. "But my friend Josie could use a part-time gig. I came by to see if you could afford to hire her."

Jerry's face falls but he recovers his pride quickly. "That would be great."

"Excellent!" My phone begins to ring in my pocket and I back up a few steps. "I'll bring her in this week and show her the ropes."

Outside the shop I check my missed calls. I don't recognize the number but there's a voicemail.

"Call me back," Monroe orders me in the message. She really needs a life coach because her people skills are lacking. Despite that, I return the call.

"You rang?" I snap.

"Don't get your panties in a twist," she advises coolly. "I just got some news that I thought you'd be interested to hear."

"Okay," I say slowly. Monroe and I don't necessarily share the same concept of news.

"You know I don't have to go out of my way to include you."

"I'm sorry. Will you please share your news with me?" I pretend to plead, but neither of us are buying it.

However, it must have sounded moderately sincere because she continues. "Leighton woke up from her coma yesterday."

"Oh my god," I breathe. "Is she alright?"

The doctors hadn't been certain she would recover fully the last I had heard. After the trauma she'd experienced, they couldn't judge the extent of the brain damage.

"I guess," Monroe says.

I refrain from reminding her that Leighton is supposed to be one of her best friends. Mostly because my own interest is far from selfless. "Has she said anything about that night?"

"I don't know, but I think we need to find out."

"Wouldn't want anyone to find out you lied," I accuse.

"Play nicely if you want answers," Monroe warns me.

"Can she have visitors?" I ignore her rebuke. I didn't lie about that night but I didn't correct the story Monroe fed the authorities. If Leighton is awake, there's no telling what she remembers or who she has told.

"I'll meet you at the hospital in half an hour," Monroe says and hangs up. Apparently, I'm not the only one who wants to know if Leighton is talking.

I don't spot Monroe's gold convertible in visitor parking, but knowing her she has a private parking space reserved in her name. Heading inside, I pause at the information desk.

"My friend just woke up from a coma, and I was told I could visit her."

The attendant gives me a doubtful look but turns toward her computer screen and asks for the name. If Monroe was with me, we'd already be in Leighton's room. I glance around the waiting area but she's nowhere to be found.

"Visiting hours are nearly over," she informs me.

I force a tight smile. My questions can't wait for tomorrow morning.

"She can have visitors but only if you're on the approved list." The attendant studies me over the top of her wire-rim glasses. "Are you on the approved list?"

"She is," a voice answers behind me. A male voice. A familiar male voice. A voice that makes my heart leap into my throat and my stomach bottom out at the same time.

You've been played.

I should have known better than to fall for Monroe's sudden concern for a friend. Pivoting slowly around, I face the last person I want to see and the person I want to see the most.

Like my feelings, he's a study in contrast. His strong, chiseled jawline looks as if it's been expertly carved from marble even as his coppery, brown hair falls over his eyes. The loosened tie and suit jacket are at odds with the hopeful smirk creeping over his lips, and the placid depths of his gray eyes flash with lightning as our gaze meets.

I want to kiss and I want to smack him at the same time. Instead I stand there, dumbfounded.

"Come with me," he commands, taking me by the arm and hauling me toward the elevator.

Normally I would push back at the bossy gesture, but I can't think with his skin touching mine, even in such an innocent touch. We step inside and stare at the doors as they shut. I should step away and put some distance between us but I can't seem to will my body to move. When the doors slide open, he presses his hand to the small of my back and guides me into the corridor.

I refrain from melting into a puddle over the gesture. Barely.

It's easier to get to Leighton's room now that she's out of the ICU. Although judging from the harried look on the nurse's face, we aren't the only ones who've come to visit. I wonder just how many people are on the approved list of visitors. Leave it to hospital staff not to share the joy when someone wakes up from a coma.

"Sign here," the nurse says pertly, "and I'll need to see some identification."

"I thought she was getting out of the ICU," I grumble as I dig my driver's license out of my purse. They hadn't asked for ID the first time I visited her.

"New policy," she tells us. "The police suspect that her accident might have been purposeful."

It seems that Leighton has been talking. I want to tell her that the accident was actually a lie, and that I know because I was the other girl who went through the window that night, but Jameson steps in before I confess. Flashing her a crooked grin, he passes her his ID.

She glances at it, and then her eyes widen. He might be everyone's favorite suspect in the murder of the century, but his family's contributions to Belle Mère Hospital are the stuff of legend. The Wests had built more than one wing of the institution, judging by the names and plaques displayed everywhere I look. They were the reason the hospital could afford to have nurses in the first place.

"I'm sorry, Mr. West," she stammers, blushing furiously. "Go right in."

"If that's how they treat you when they think you're a murderer," I say under my breath as we turn.

"The adjective billionaire somehow mitigates whatever noun follows it." He steers me down the hall until we're in front of room forty-seven. The door opens and a middle-aged woman steps out, her red-rimmed eyes completely undermining all the plastic surgery she's undergone. She swipes at tears and smiles widely.

"Jameson!" she says fondly. Apparently, my would-be boyfriend gets around in the middle-age social circles.

"Mrs.—" he begins.

"Cheryl," she stops him with a hug. "Isn't it wonderful?"

"Yes. We've been praying for this moment." He's indulging her. The small display of charm he'd put on for the nurse turns into an entire charismatic show. I've never seen him like this, except when we first met. It hits me like a semi-truck: he's flirting with her. It might piss some girls off, but I just stand back and let him work his magic. "Can I introduce my girlfriend, Emma Southerly?"

I swallow at the term of endearment. So, Jameson West still thinks of me as his girlfriend? Does it matter? Judging from the butterflies whirling around my stomach, it matters a lot.

A shadow passes over Cheryl's face but she recovers admirably. "Of course. I know your mother."

And not my father, I add silently. I've always loved my name but right now I'm reminded that it carries a history with it that's not entirely my own. I can't help but wonder which tragedy she's recalling in her head: my alcoholic father, my parents' divorce, or my sister's death. All of them seem like the kind of low-hanging fruit, someone like her would take a bite from.

We continue our pleasantries until Cheryl pops her head in the door. "Frank, Leighton has some visitors. Let's give them a moment with her." She turns back to us. "It will give me a chance to get some food in him. He hasn't left her side since she woke up. He's almost as bad as her boyfriend. I should warn you that she doesn't remember everything. The doctor says it will come back with time."

"Her boyfriend," Jameson repeats, zeroing in on that small aside, and I can't help but notice how his smile tightens.

Cheryl winks at him. "She couldn't moon after you forever."

I shoot Jameson a meaningful look. Apparently, he'd left out some bits about his relationship to his younger sister's bestie.

"Don't be jealous Duchess. She was just some kid who always hung around when I was home," he whispers as Leighton's mother ducks into the room for her purse.

"I was just some kid hanging around," I remind him tartly.

"Jealousy suits you," he teases.

Before I can give him more grief about how many of my peers he's strung along with his impish smile, we're welcomed in to her room. There are less machines tracking her every heartbeat and breath. A dozen fresh flower arrangements take up every flat surface. No doubt well wishes from her numerous pals who sent flowers rather than interrupt their Mediterranean summer holidays. Before when I'd visited the room felt cold and sterile, but now it's as alive as the girl sitting up in her hospital bed with a wide smile on her face. But she's not looking at us. Instead her gaze is fixed on her boyfriend.

Hugo Roth can barely tear his eyes away from her as if she might vanish, but he nods a hello.

"We'll leave you kids alone," Cheryl calls, tugging her husband out the door.

Kids. The repeated use of the term annoys me. We aren't kids anymore. Our childhood was stolen by this city and its sins. Pretending that we're going to have some Leave It to

Beaver catch-up session is as naïve as believing you could raise us kids here in the first place.

"Hey," I say awkwardly by way of greeting as the door shuts behind them.

Leighton blinks owlishly as if her vision needs adjustment. Then she realizes she's not seeing things. "Hi...Emma."

"I hope you don't mind us stopping by." Jameson interjects himself before things can get any weirder.

Maybe I should have brought her flowers. I could have played the part of concerned friend better and she might have thought she'd forgotten our relationship. As it is, whatever Leighton can't remember, she knows I don't belong here.

"Of course not." She waves him off with a tired hand. "I'm surprised. I expected to see a West today, just not..."

She trails off and I know what she's hinting at. She didn't expect to see Jameson. Not when she's spent the last three years being Monroe West's pet sidekick.

"I'm not certain my sister has heard yet," Jameson lies smoothly.

"Ugh." Leighton smacks the plastic, hospital mattress with an audible thwack. "My parents are being tyrants about letting me have my phone. I've had to use Hugo's."

At the mention of his name, Hugo startles out of his reverie and runs his hand over his spiky hair. "Sorry, guys. What?"

"Your girlfriend was just telling us about your chivalry," I say dryly. As of a few months ago, Hugo's reputation as a party boy had been intact. I'd witnessed his devotion to her firsthand the night that Nathaniel West died when he'd been surrounded by a gaggle of freshmen girls. "I didn't know you two were dating."

"We weren't." Leighton flushes. "Not really."

"And now?" I ask pointedly. Hooking up while one party was unconscious seems like a strange way to start a relationship. But what do I know? My romance is the result of needing an alibi.

"Things are different," Hugo says as if that settles it. I open my mouth to press the point but he shuts me up by adding, "I'm sure you both understand how quickly things change."

That I did.

"Tell me," Hugo continues, shirking some of the facade of respectability. "Are the rumors true?"

"Which ones?" Jameson asks with the practiced air of a tycoon's son.

"All of them. Murder of the century is quite the accomplishment," he says with a smirk.

So much for no one reading the tabloids. Leighton leans forward, some color returning to her usually tan face. Apparently gossip can serve to heal as much as damage. One person's nightmare is another person's Lifetime movie of the week.

"You know better than to believe rumors." Jameson takes the interrogation in stride, but I can't help looking at the floor. Maybe someday I'll get used to being analyzed by everyone we meet, even people we already know, but today's not that day.

As it is my patience with social pleasantries is up. "Look, we came for a reason. I didn't see who pushed us through that window, but I know you did."

Jameson sighs next to me, but I ignore him. His social caste might get off on their games of cat and mouse, but I live in the real world where bluntness will suffice.

"I don't remember," Leighton says in a small voice.

It's probably best that there are still a few monitors hooked up to her, because I really want to shake an answer out of her. Instead I'll have to stick to gentle encouragement. Two traits I'm not known for.

"I remember your face right before the...accident." I decide to go with the lie. If Leighton doesn't believe she's ratting someone out maybe we'll get more out of her. "You looked happy."

"Happy?" Her voice is hollow as she repeats me. I realize then that she's as lost as to who did it as I am. But maybe I can draw her a map.

"We were talking about someone," I remind her, taking a step forward. Out of the corner of my eye, I see Hugo stiffen and I stop. No need to upset her guard dog. "Do you remember?"

Her blue eyes are misty as she shakes her head.

Okay, I have to give her a little more to work with. "I thought I overheard you talking to Monroe about Jameson, but you told me you were talking to her about Jonas."

"Jonas?" Hugo says. "What does he have to do with anything?"

"That's what I'm trying to figure out." My words grate off my tongue as I try to hold on to gentle or encouraging—and fail.

"I don't remember," she says miserably.

"She just woke up," Hugo reminds us.

If I'd just woken up from a coma after some psycho pushed me out a window, I'd be screaming his or her name until they were under arrest. But comme ci, comme ça.

"I don't think Jonas was the one who pushed us." There's an apology written in her voice.

"Was he even in town?" Jameson asks and I realize I'd left my boyfriend out of my manic, conspiracy theories.

"Yeah, he wasn't on my list either until…"

"Until what?" Hugo's face darkens. Apparently in the war between the girl he loves and his best friend, Hugo's already taken sides.

"Until I saw this." I pull up the screen shot of The Dealer's Instagram account on my phone. "He erased this but I took a picture."

"That's Josie," Jameson points out in a quiet voice.

"Yeah, but she's not the only one in the picture," I inform them, not bothering to smother my annoyance. No one had been safe from The Dealer's unwanted attention this summer and he'd used that to his advantage. We'd all been too distracted by analyzing the people in the photos to notice something like a reflection.

"I never saw this photo," Hugo says slowly.

"The Dealer deleted this photo, and there's a reason." They pass my phone around, studying the picture. No one speaks, which is how I know that they all see exactly what I saw.

"Why is Jonas posting pictures as The Dealer?" Hugo asks.

"Who's The Dealer?" Leighton's confusion is excusable since she's been in a coma.

"Someone's been posting pictures." I explain the whole thing to her, but it doesn't seem like she processes it. I've known her long enough that I'm not certain if her slowness is the result of her injuries or her IQ. But before I can explain anymore, Hugo is on his feet.

"Where are you going?" I ask as he leans down and kisses Leighton's head in a gesture of farewell.

"I need to talk to my best friend." He pushes past me, and I shoot a pleading look to Jameson. He takes the hint and follows him.

"What's happening?" Leighton cries out.

I'm torn between running after them and comforting her. "I think I just started a fight."

"Emma, he isn't the one who pushed us," she says firmly. "You can't let Hugo attack him. He'll never forgive himself."

"How can you be so certain?" If there's one thing I've learned this summer, it's that people aren't always what they seem.

"Because I remember why I was talking to Monroe about Jonas."

"And?" I demand.

"I can't tell you, but he's not the one. He couldn't be."

There's enough certainty in her words to make me doubt my own cynicism, but if I give that up, what will I have left?

Chapter 7

JAMESON WEAVES in and out of traffic, trying to keep up with the taillights of Hugo's Porsche. I'm torn between my desire to batter him with questions and my need to clutch the armrest for dear life.

"Why didn't you tell me about Jonas? About the picture?" His eyes flicker over to mine before returning to the pursuit.

"We haven't really been talking," I remind him through clenched teeth.

"And why is that, Duchess? Why are you avoiding me?"

I gasp as he narrowly misses a car pulling into traffic. "That's kind of complicated."

"I'm listening."

"I'd rather you drive, West," I hiss as he swerves into another lane. "Does he even know where he's going?"

We're not on the way to Jonas's house, but Hugo hadn't hesitated when he went flying out of the hospital parking lot. I'd barely slammed my door shut before we had to take off after him.

"Don't change the subject," Jameson warns me. "I've been patient, but if you wanted out, you could have told me."

"Out?" I repeat. As if whatever this was between us could ever be that easy. "Why would you think that?"

I'm in love with you. My heart pounds against my chest as if trying to break free of the cage I'm keeping it in. It hurts like hell to hold the words back, but I know I have to until I know the truth.

Jameson slams on the brakes and I'm surprised to see we're parked in front of the Belle Mère gymnasium. He shuts off the engine and dares one look at me. "Because why else would you want to hurt me?"

He's out of the car and heading inside after Hugo before I can process what he's said. Tears sting my eyes. I want him to understand. I want to explain why I've stayed away, but how can I? Either way, I'm destined to hurt him.

"Now is not the time," I coach myself. It takes a good deal of effort to climb out of the car, but once my feet hit the pavement I'm running toward the double doors. I have no idea what anyone is doing here so late, but the school must not be locked up. Or Jonas has a key.

The scene that greets me looks as if it's been staged. Jonas is frozen, basketball in hand, in the middle of the court with Hugo stopped a few feet away, screaming so loudly that I can't understand him. Jameson glances at me from the door frame.

"Should we jump in?" I ask, my nerves rattled by Hugo's fury.

"Give it a sec," he advises, but we move closer. Jonas glances to us as if we might be able to explain what's happening. But when my eyes meet his, Jonas turns away. It's enough to confirm my suspicions. I'd given him a chance to come forward to me privately, offering him an out via text message, but he hadn't taken it. Now he has to face the consequences.

"I don't know what you're asking me, man." Jonas manages to punctuate Hugo's screams with a response.

"Did you push her?" Hugo repeats, enunciating each word carefully.

"Who?" Jonas looks genuinely confused, but its neither a denial or a confession and Hugo is here for one or the other.

Hugo lunges at his best friend, knocking the ball out of his hands and sending them both flying into a heap.

"Who?" Jonas screams, but the repeated question is met with a right hook to his face.

"Did you push Leighton?" Hugo demands as we rush over to break up the fight, but before we reach them he's started punching Jonas again.

"I wasn't the one who pushed her." Jonas's answer is nearly lost as Hugo pummels him.

He doesn't fight back, so by the time Jameson hauls Hugo off of him, Jonas's face is already swelling from the repeated impact. Scrambling away from the court, Jonas slumps against the wall and wipes the back of his hand over his bloody lip. He inspects it for a second as if he's surprised. "Let him go."

"I don't think that's a good idea." Jameson's grip on Hugo doesn't loosen.

"He's my best friend," Jonas says, "and I trust him to let me tell my side of the story. I wasn't the one who pushed Leighton."

"It's your funeral," Jameson mutters before he drops his hold on Hugo. Despite the rage radiating from Hugo, he stays still. I expected Hugo to pounce again. Even after his change of heart this summer, I didn't think Hugo could help but allow himself to be more than a mass of impulses, especially given how angry he is at the moment. Apparently, Jonas does know him better than the rest of us.

"Start explaining," Hugo orders. His hands are still clenched into fists, a reminder that he could strike at any time.

"I wasn't the one who pushed Leighton," he repeats himself.

"You said that already." Hugo practically growls the words.

Letting the two of them work this out on their own is going to get us nowhere. I step forward until I'm nearly between the two of them, and Jameson frowns. I ignore his concern. We might not have been the ones throwing punches but we've been a part of the fray for a while. "Then why would someone push us? She had something on you."

"On him?" Hugo asks, his confusion growing. He moves forward and I wedge myself further between them.

"Duchess!" Jameson calls in a low voice, but I ignore his warning.

"I overheard Leighton and Monroe talking. I thought they were discussing Jameson, but Leighton told me it was Jonas. It was the last thing she said before…" There's no need to bring up the accident again. Hugo is revved enough already. I can't bring myself to look at Jameson. He'd thought that I trusted him that night and then I'd questioned that at the first opportunity. Whatever Jonas had to tell us now better make up for all the damage he'd been doing this summer.

Hugo relaxes a bit as if he's interested in this explanation, but the color drains from Jonas's face. I can see the struggle in his eyes. There's no doubt in my mind that he knows what Leighton and Monroe were talking about that night.

"Okay, you didn't push us," I say when the silence drags on. "Did you kill Nathaniel?"

Jonas shakes his head. I believe him despite the guilt written in white across his face. Apparently, Hugo does as well, because he unballs his fists. I have the sinking suspicion that whatever he's hiding has nothing to do with us. It feels dirty and wrong to force his secrets into the open, but as long as secrets stand between us, we can't trust each other.

The trouble is that I know what it's like to hide out in the open. Jonas looks like a cornered animal, and I can't bring myself to be the one who destroys him. "Then we're done here. Whatever secret he's keeping doesn't affect us."

Jameson's head tilts in surprise as he studies me.

"You never stop surprising me, Duchess," he whispers so only I can hear him.

But my gift of amnesty doesn't mean that he can keep it trapped inside him any longer. Jonas slides to the ground, hanging his head to hide his face. The rest of us freeze, uncertain what to say. When he looks up to us, his face is tear-stained. No one speaks. It's an unspoken agreement to give him the time he needs to open up to us. After a few minutes of silence, he begins.

"Monroe knows something about me. Something no one else knows. At least no one at Belle Mère Prep. She's been keeping it a secret for a long time."

"Yeah, she's your girlfriend, man." Hugo drops to the ground beside him. Could I transition from angry to supportive that quickly, even with Josie? I hope I never have to find out. Half an hour ago, I honestly thought Hugo might kill him. Now he's practically holding his hand. Maybe he's a better friend than I am, or maybe Hugo Roth is a better person than we've—okay, I've—given him credit for.

"I'm not sure where the story begins," he admits.

I almost suggest he start with why he screwed Monroe at the freshman desert party but I keep the suggestion to myself. Will wonders never cease?

"We'll listen," Hugo says encouragingly.

Dammit, Hugo Roth really is a nice guy parading around in a pariah suit.

"Don't worry," he says to me as if he can read my mind, "I'm still a dick."

"No, you're not." Jonas's voice is almost wistful and the dreamy undertone deepens as he begins his story. "Most of you don't know my older sister. My parents sent her off to school in London not long after I turned ten. Hugo's met her." He pauses waiting for Hugo to nod, then continues, "There's always been rumors around it. She was fourteen at the time, and well, you know my parents. They make Donald Trump look like a liberal. Most people believed she'd gotten herself in trouble."

Did people still think like that? Especially in Vegas? And what did that even mean in trouble? It seems to me that half the adults I know didn't want their own kids. Why blame a girl for getting pregnant when you did it yourself?

"She didn't do anything. She was the perfect daughter. I was the reason she got sent away. I suppose they thought that they'd better keep their real problem child close to home."

"But why send your sister away?" I blurt out before I can stop myself.

"I think that the main reason was because Jessica was my only ally in the house. She understood me and more than that, she sympathized. Our parents weren't just hard on us. They expected perfection. I was their dirty little secret. Their son that liked to play with his sister's dolls. It was easier to send the only other person that knew away. Jessica made a lot of friends there—powerful, rich friends. She's marrying some duke or baron or something next year. I haven't even met him," Jonas confesses. "I guess it was better for her to go there. Sending me away would have been a reward for what my parents saw as acting out. So, I stayed here and with Jessica and her dolls gone, they shaped me into a man, by their standards. Lacrosse, soccer. Any sport imaginable. When I hit high school, they didn't encourage me to date. They demanded it. If there was a party, I had to be there. Drinking, sex—they could forgive all my sins as long as they were red-blooded, male sins."

As he spoke pieces of Jonas that had always been a puzzle to me began to click into place. When we'd dated, he hadn't breached the second base barrier. Being with him had been warm and comfortable. Of course, I'd been smitten as a kitten. What girl wouldn't have fallen for the second coming of Justin Bieber at that age? When he'd gotten together with Monroe, I assumed he'd wanted sex and she'd been a more willing participant. That's how I'd wound up in his best friend's bed trying to prove something to myself. But maybe Jonas hadn't wanted to have sex with me...or her. But if that was the case, why had he?

"It was fine for a while. I had a girlfriend that didn't mind making out, and she was nice. She never pushed me for more, and I don't think she suspected who I really was." His eyes stray over to mine, and I can see the silent apologies in them. "And then I screwed up, and Monroe West was there to catch me as I fell."

"Monroe has never caught anyone," Jameson says coolly.

"I don't mean that she helped me," Jonas clarifies. "She saw my indiscretion as an opportunity. She had a secret of her own, which she revealed to me along with some pretty damning cell phone photos. It was my worst nightmare but she gave me an out. She wanted the whole school to know that she was taken. All I had to do was get drunk and screw her at a party with enough witnesses."

"Why?" The question I've wanted him to answer for years slips out, but I'm not the one asking. Hugo is.

"It was the perfect alibi. I knew it would get back to my parents, and that in their own messed up rationale, they would think they fixed me. Do you know how fucked it is when your dad pours you a whiskey and slaps you on the back for something like that? I mean, they bought me a car. As far as they were concerned, I was normal again. All I had to do was sell my soul to Monroe."

"What did she have on you?" Hugo demands. Jonas is skirting the issue, and even though all the clues are there, we all need to hear him say it.

"I was drunk. I spent a lot of my time my freshman year drunk. It was easier to cope most of the time. Emma usually came to the parties with me, but she stayed home for some reason." He looks at me to see if I remember. I do. I'd gone out with Becca that night. Jonas had acted strangely after that night. Every day it felt as if he was going through the motions. I'd expected him to dump me, but he'd chosen a far more humiliating and hurtful way to end our relationship.

"I remember," I say softly, and try as I might, I can't place any forgiveness in my words.

"I didn't know what I was doing when I kissed him." Jonas barely pauses to let the truth sink in before he goes on. "He was drunk, too. More drunk than I was, but even as I did it, I knew I was lying to myself. He was straight and he probably would have kicked my ass if he knew what I did. I barely remembered it myself. I thought maybe I'd dreamed it until Monroe showed up with photographic evidence. She left it up to me. I could help her cover up her own secret and ensure that no one found out the truth or she could blast the proof all over Facebook. I didn't know what my parents would do if they found out, but, honestly, I was more ashamed. I didn't want to lose my friends. So, I went along with it. I am truly sorry, Emma."

His words work like alchemy, melting the cold, stoniness in my heart and creating acceptance. I'd held onto my grudge against him long enough, tricking myself into believing it was merely unrequited love. "I forgive you."

"Are you saying you're gay?" Hugo asks in a strangled voice.

Jonas takes a deep breath as if to steady himself. "Yes, I am. I'm s—"

"Why are you sorry?" Hugo cuts him off. "It's not a big deal, man."

Another moment of acceptance and maybe Jonas can finally shake free of the fear that's crippled him for so long, but the terror lingers in his eyes.

"I need to tell you something." His voice is shaky and my breath catches as realization dawns on me. Jameson grips my arm as if he senses my urge to interrupt this confession before Jonas gets hurt.

"It was you," Jonas admits. "Monroe caught me kissing you."

Hugo's eyes widen and then he does the last thing I expect: he laughs. "I'm flattered. If I played for that team...well, you know."

"You're not pissed?" The tension in Jonas's body relaxes and he practically slumps to the floor. He'd been bracing himself for a fight.

"Look, you've seen me drunk. I doubt you're the only guy I've kissed." Hugo continues to roll with it. "I get why you didn't tell me, but I don't understand why you had to be The Dealer."

I suck in a breath and wait for his response. Jonas might have less to atone for than I previously thought, but this was thing I wanted to understand.

"It's simple, really. The whole world was going crazy. I saw all of you there that night, and I was so tired of hiding who I was. Those pictures all tell more of a story than you think. That one of you"—he looks to Hugo— "carrying that girl? You just made sure she laid down on a bed."

That wasn't the conclusion I'd drawn when I saw it. That photo might have been innocent but what about the others. What story was he trying to tell? "And the others?"

"It's felt like karma has been on vacation for too long in Belle Mère."

"So you took over her job?" I guess.

"Someone had to. I know that whoever killed Nathaniel West was there that night. It was the perfect opportunity to hold people accountable."

"While still hiding," I bite out.

"I guess it's what I'm good at," he says in a flat voice.

"So you don't know who did it?" I ask. "Who killed Nathaniel?"

"Not any more than you do." He shakes his head and I feel myself deflate. So, Jonas thinks I'm innocent, but he has no way to prove it. He also has no idea who is responsible. We're back to square one.

Hugo stands up, brushing off his jeans, before he hauls Jonas to his feet. We stand awkwardly around each other, none of us certain what to say. After a minute, Jameson tugs at my hand. I step closer and he whispers in my ear, "Let's give them some space."

That's exactly what we should do. The answers aren't here, and the healing that needs to be done has nothing to do with us. But leaving them here will give Jameson exactly what he wants: me—alone.

A devilish grin curves across his mouth, and I know he has me right where he wants me.

Chapter 8

I WAIT until we're out of the school before I lower the boom. "Jameson, I have to go."

He steps in front of me blocking my exit. There are about twelve ways out of Belle Mère Prep and I know all of them, but somehow I don't doubt that Jameson will beat me to each exit.

"We need to talk, Duchess, you can't keep hiding from me." This time he doesn't cover the pain in his voice. He allows it to pierce his words and I feel it as acutely as I feel my own pain. "We can work through this."

I doubt it, but admitting that to him, as well as myself, means facing the truth. I want to talk. I want to explain, but I hesitate, only daring to lift my eyes to his. It's a mistake. Because what might have been an innocent gesture feels too intimate.

If Mackey's hunch is correct and Nathaniel West is my father, how can I feel this way about Jameson? More than ever, I want to believe what my mother told me. That whatever moment of insanity led to her conceiving Nathaniel's daughter, and my sister, didn't happen twice. But seeing as I've been a regular lightening rod this summer, I'm not sure I'll be that lucky. I want to be Jake Southerly's daughter. Because that obstacle—a Southerly falling for a West—feels a lot more surmountable than this.

"I know what's going on," he says, interrupting my thoughts.

"No, you don't." I shake my head, trying to clear it and things only grow hazier. Or is that the Jameson effect? I'm not really certain anymore.

"I do know." This time his tone is firm. There's no doubt that he is Nathaniel West's son. Unyielding, commanding, powerful—he got all those traits from his father.

"Jameson, I—"

But he cuts me off. "I'm not your brother."

You know that old cliché: time stands still? Well, it really fucking *can* happen. Everything around me grinds to a halt.

Jameson takes my hand, apparently unaffected by this time warp, and snaps me out of my daze.

"How? What? Why?" I stumble, looking for exactly the right question to ask.

Of course, Jameson already knows the answers. "I'm not stupid, Duchess. There are a lot of people willing to be bought in law enforcement. A little information for a lot of money isn't hard to understand when you've seen the pension plan."

"You bought someone off?" I ask in confusion. He nods, and tightens his grip on my fingers. That's both disturbing and reassuring. There's only one problem. "But I haven't taken the DNA test yet."

Did he think it would be this easy to trip me up? My anxiety and I have been friends far too long to be so easily soothed.

"I know that. I also know that you arranged to have your

blood drawn at the Las Vegas Medical Clinic next Wednesday. That won't be necessary, by the way."

Confusion shifts to annoyance. "Jameson West, I am not one of your family's puppets that can be ordered about. There are no strings attached to me. If you think you're going to make me dance around, you are completely mistaken."

"You're wrong about that." He takes a step closer, until our bodies are Mère inches apart. Spicy notes of citron and sandalwood tug at latent memories that I've been trying hard to forget. "There is a string attached to you. Only one."

"And you think you can pull it?" I surmise, jutting my chin to show how wrong he is. But who are we kidding? We both know he can pull it anytime he wants. That's why I've been hiding out in my best friend's bedroom for the better part of a week.

"I'm not trying to pull your strings, Duchess. That string that I'm talking about, can't you feel it? Running between the two of us?" His thumb traces the back of my wrist, and my pulse speeds up as if he's willing it to race. "We're connected. Nothing can change that. Stop being so afraid of it."

"I'm not afraid of it!" I explode. "I'm afraid that you're my brother, and that's really, really creepy."

"I'm not," he insists.

"We won't know until next Wednesday. Actually, probably longer. I'm guessing they don't have one-step paternity tests on hand." Given the frequency the topic shows up on daytime talk shows, you'd think you could get a one-prick test at the supermarket that could tell you who your baby-daddy is in less than three minutes.

"If you'd let me finish talking to you, I could explain how I know."

I need to break the connection sizzling between us before the lightening crackling around us becomes a full-blown storm.

I pull my hand away gently, allowing the regret to show on my face. I have a tendency to hide behind my bitchiness like it's my own feminist fortress, but Jameson hasn't done anything to hurt me intentionally. The sins that stand between us are those of our parents, and if he can, I'll allow him to tear them down. But while they're still up, I need the physical and emotional barriers to remain intact.

"I imagine I found out like you did. My lawyers and researchers were able to uncover the nature of the lawsuit that was settled between our parents when we were both much younger. When I read the details of your sister's paternity report, I knew what was troubling you. About the same time, a leak came through in Mackey's team, revealing that my suspicions were correct. The FBI also knew my father was your sister's father. The source also confirmed that Mackey had been in contact with you, using this information to pressure you into getting the DNA test my lawyers had worked so hard to prevent. It was easy to see why. If my father and your mother had had an affair, who's to say you also weren't his daughter?" He clears his throat. It's a small sign of discomfort, but it's there. Good to know that the thought bothered him as much as it bothered me. "But I knew you couldn't't be."

"That makes one of us," I mutter.

"I knew you'd think you were," he continues. "That's your biggest weakness. You need to have a little faith."

"In whom?" I retort. I hadn't been given a lot of opportunities to have faith in my life. My mom blowing up her marriage to my father hadn't instilled faith and love. My father's inability to keep the electricity on for more than six months at a time didn't instill a lot of faith in authority. But really, watching my sister die because of one stupid decision in a car, that's when I lost faith in the universe.

"I know you have a lot of reasons not to believe. And I

know it might take you a lifetime to heal from all the terrible things that happened to you. But I'm going to be there for that lifetime. I'm going to spend every day reminding you that good things can happen. That it's okay to believe and to hope and to have faith in other people."

"What if I can't?" I ask in a breathless voice. I don't have a successful track record when it came to blind trust.

"Baby steps, Duchess." He reaches out and brushes his knuckle under my chin. "Start with me. Have some faith in me. We'll go from there."

I had faith in Jameson, and it had been taken away from me. Why can't he see that my cynicism isn't rooted in some warped fixation on the past, but in the continued barrage of unfortunate events that had both brought us together and torn us apart?

"I can't just have faith," I admit to him in a small voice. I want to, and I want to tell him that. But he'll take my foolish desires as a sign that I'm capable of this tremendous feat he's asking of me.

"How about we start with something concrete?" he says softly.

I raise one eyebrow. He's going to need a miracle if he's asking me to make this leap. Then again, I'm going to need a miracle if I plan to walk out of here alone tonight. I want him, and I want the picture he's painting. But is it a future I can ever have?

"Oh Duchess, I'm sorry they broke you." The light finger on my jaw shifts and his whole palm cups the side of my face. His touch feels warm and comforting and right, so how could it ever be wrong? "But I'm going to fix you."

"You can't." The sooner he figures that out, the better off we'll both be.

"Look at me," he demands, and when I open my eyes, his

burn into mine. "I'm Jameson West, and I can do anything I want. So, when I say I'll spend my life teaching you how to have faith—when I say I'm going to fix you—I will."

I want so badly to trust him, but in my experience, dreams don't come true.

"I told you that I had proof. We'll start with one concrete reason why you should believe in us."

"And what is that?" I snap, as I feel the wounds in my heart begin to crack open.

"Your DNA," he says. "It doesn't match my father's. For good measure, it doesn't match mine, either. You aren't related to me, Emma Southerly."

I can't process what he's saying, how he knows this. He takes my silence for exactly what it is, disbelief. Sighing, he reveals the source of his findings. "You were sleeping at my house, remember? I borrowed your hairbrush, your toothbrush. Hell, there was a whole team in the guest bedroom. You could probably be cloned."

"What does that mean? How can they know so soon? Mackey said..."

"Mackey's using the resources of a government-funded laboratory. I had labs in New York, Switzerland and London test and send results. Their findings were all quite clear. We're not related. So, as to your question, what does that mean? It means that you're going to lock your car, and then you're going to get into the passenger seat of mine. My jet is waiting on standby. It's your birthday, Duchess, and I'm taking you wherever you want to go. The registered flight plan has us going to New York, but from there we can go wherever, so long as that place has a bed."

"A bed?" I choke out the word. My cheeks flush with heat as the memories I've done my best to erase flash through my mind. There's no stopping them now that Jameson has drained the fight from me.

"It's your birthday." His voice is low and suggestive. Apparently, he hasn't forgotten the date or why it is important. He had been the one to set the rule and force me to agree: we wouldn't sleep together until then. He smirks as if reading my mind. "You're 18, Duchess, and that means you're mine."

Chapter 9

MY HAND STAYS TIGHTLY CLUTCHED in Jameson's until we reach the airfield. The only time I let it go is to send Josie a text that I won't be back tonight. I spot Maddox's bulky form waiting by the plane. I guess there's no way that I'm going anywhere without protection. Jameson gives me an apologetic smile as he releases my hand, but he's out of the car and around to my door before the heat of his touch has fully dissipated. This time, when his fingers knit through mine, I suspect he won't be letting go.

We climb the stairs into the main cabin of the jet together. Jameson pauses to whisper instruction to Maddox and the rest of the crew.

I've been in the West family private jet before, but that fact does nothing to lessen the excitement I feel now. Luxurious private travel had usually been available to me when it came to one route only: Las Vegas to Palm Springs and back again. Knowing this plane could take me anywhere is the best birthday present I could ever ask for.

"We're going to take off soon, Duchess." Jameson guides me

to a cushy leather chair, and I laugh when he begins to buckle my seat restraint.

"I can do that myself," I assure him.

He does it anyway, kissing me on the forehead in the process. "I have to protect what's mine."

He isn't saying it, but I know the last few days of separation nearly drove him crazy. If it hadn't been for Josie, I'd probably be stark raving mad as well. It's going to take more than a few serious conversations to heal the damage that's been done to our relationship, but right now I think we're simply relieved to be together. We can piece together the events of the last week later.

Jameson takes the seat next to mine, and I raise an eyebrow when he doesn't buckle up.

"Do I need to buckle you in?" I ask.

He heaves a sigh and fastens the safety belt.

"Just protecting what's mine," I tease him. The butterflies in my stomach take flight as the jet begins to wheel down the runway.

"Are you okay?" he asks next to me, and I realize I'm clutching the arms of my seat.

"This isn't how I saw my day going," I admit. Heading on a romantic adventure hadn't been on my radar.

"Monroe packed a bag of your things that you left at my house."

I think that information is supposed to reassure me, but I've met his sister. I can't imagine what she thinks is necessary for a weekend holiday. Beggars can't be choosers, so I cross my fingers there are clean panties. Anything else is cake.

He holds my hand until we're in the air. As soon as I feel the landing gear lock into place, I'm out of my seat, and scrambling onto his lap. Strong arms wrap around my waist as I straddle him, and I feel even safer than I did before.

"I missed you," I murmur. I can't seem to bring myself to meet his eyes because Jameson's right. I didn't have faith. I'd been the one to nearly give up on us. I can blame my crappy childhood all I want, but I chose to believe the worst.

"Look at me, Duchess," he commands in a low voice, and I dare to lift my face to his. "It's behind us now."

Such simple words, but they carry so much meaning. We'd already faced what felt like an insurmountable obstacle. Whatever comes next, I know we will have each other.

"I don't deserve you," I whisper.

"No, you deserve more."

I take a deep breath, a leap of faith, and choose to believe him.

"What have you been doing while you hid from me this week?" Jameson asks, tucking a strand of hair behind my ear.

I nuzzle against his hand. This week has been full of terrible and right now, I want to be with him.

"Talk to me," he urges. "When we were apart, I nearly went crazy wondering what you were doing."

"I was hiding from my life," I confess. My life had managed to intrude anyway, and it will keep doing so. "Let's see, my mom is getting a divorce."

Jameson's eyes darken, and I know he's thinking about the night he saved me from my stepfather. He clears his throat. "Because of what he did to you and your sister?"

I nod as I begin to feel tears pricking my eyes. "She refuses to take the information to the police."

"I can handle that," he practically growls.

"No," I say resolutely. "I could, but this isn't my battle anymore. I don't want any more to do with it. Even though..."

I hesitate, because I don't like bringing up money, especially not with a West.

"Out with it, Duchess," he commands.

"She's arranged for a trust fund in my name. Hans was more than happy to settle the separation quietly," I say. I know Jameson can read between the lines. My stepfather paid my mother off. "It's blood money."

"You don't have to take it."

I don't tell him that I've already used some for a good cause: looking into our case with a private investigator. After his miraculous feat, hiring a P.I. hardly seems like a groundbreaking contribution.

"I won't." I leave it at that. "I'll donate it. With global warming, there's always some new disaster relief fund that needs money."

"Be serious for just a second," he advises, kissing the tip of my nose.

"I am. I can't think of a better way to spend his bribe than to erase some of the bad from the world with some good."

"Whatever you think is best. Besides we don't need money."

"We?" I repeat. "When did we sign up for a joint checking account?"

It's meant as a joke but Jameson shows no signs of laughing.

"You get serious," I say, smacking his shoulder. Although all signs point to the fact that he is serious—very serious.

"Wests don't joke about money." He doesn't clarify further. Before I can push the topic, because it seems pretty important that he know I don't want his money, Maddox joins us. He's carrying a small birthday cake blazing with so many candles I half expect that he'll start a cabin fire. Without a flight attendant, I'm not certain if oxygen masks will drop down in that event.

"You don't look like a stewardess," I say when he places the cake on the table in front of Jameson and I.

"I left my pantyhose at home," he says dryly.

I don't complain when they insist on singing happy birthday to me. I turn to face the cake but remain on Jameson's lap. He sings the words softly into my left ear, and when he finishes he whispers, "Make a wish."

I don't have to, because it's already come true.

When the candles are all blown out, Maddox ducks back into the crew quarters to give us some privacy. I twist in Jameson's arms until I'm staring into his stormy eyes.

"What did you wish for, Duchess?"

"You." Then I seal my mouth to his.

Chapter 10

IT'S a few hours before dawn when we arrive at the West Hotel in New York City. Perched at the top of Wall Street, it's a haven for business travelers and the elite who value privacy and luxury over nightlife. It may be the city that never sleeps but I doze in and out to the sound of trash trucks and delivery vans preparing for the busy day ahead. Despite my best attempts I couldn't keep my eyes open long enough to take in much of the city. Sight-seeing will have to come later. Right now the only sight I want to see is a pillow.

Our car pulls up to the valet station and a weary looking bellhop rushes out to meet us. I wonder if he's starting his shift or nearing the end of it. Either way I feel his pain.

"You look dead on your feet," Jameson notes as he helps me out of the Lincoln Continental that's delivered us to his family's local hotel-away-from-home.

"I'm fine." But the veracity of my claim is undermined when I immediately punctuate it with a yawn. The trouble is that I don't want to be tired. Not here. Not since Jameson and I are finally together again. "I just need some coffee."

Jameson casts a doubtful look at me. As we step inside, he pulls me close. The lobby is nearly empty save for a few staff members milling about dusting and polishing the floors. It's unlike the West Resort and Casino in Las Vegas. This hotel is that hotel's big brother: grown up, sophisticated, and aiming for partner at his law firm. Its elegance is understated, relying on subtle, but expensive décor choices. I drink in the leather club chair dotting the periphery and the black veined marble I can only assume has been imported from somewhere so far away that it cost twice as much to ship as it did buy. The West New York whispers wealth while its casino brother screams debauchery.

Whatever travel arrangements Jameson has made seem to be in order. Maddox and our driver bypass waiting with us at the front desk and go straight to the elevators.

"It will only be a minute," Jameson promises me, "and then I can get you into bed."

Bed.

The word jolts me awake faster than a triple espresso. We're going to bed. Together. And I'm eighteen.

A middle-aged man in an expensive three-piece scuttles out from the door marked private access and zeros in on us. His hands steeple together and he bobs his head as if bowing to a patriarch.

I'll never get used to these reactions. Jameson has my respect, because he's earned it. Everywhere else we go the deference he receives is born of his family name. He takes the man proffered hands smoothly, accepting the introduction while I zone out. The two can feign business talk, I have other things on my mind.

I can't help but be preoccupied what with words like bed being casually tossed about. This time when Jameson and I go to bed together there will be no push and pull. I won't peer pressure, and he won't say no. I've been planning to sleep with Jameson for months. Why am I getting so nervous now?

Probably because it's such a big deal that he's flown me across the country to one of the most romantic cities in the world just so he can have me all to himself.

"Ready?" Jameson asks.

I blink. Am I ready?

"To go upstairs, Duchess?"

I wonder how long he's been trying to get my attention.

"Yes," I squeak, my nerves showing through the thin layer of calm I'm clinging to.

"If you need anything at all, please don't hesitate to let me know," the hotel manager interjects before we can exit.

"We will, Mr. White," Jameson reassures him. His hand settles over the small of my back, directing me toward the elevators. As soon as we're a few feet away his voice lowers, "I didn't think we were going to get rid of him. I thought our early arrival might allow us to delay that formality. Hotel managers always think they need to greet the boss."

"It's fine," I say while absently chewing on my lip.

Jameson studies me as we step through the gold, sliding doors into the mirrored elevator. "Don't worry, Duchess. I'll get you into bed."

Bed. There's that word again. My stomach drops out as the elevator begins to ascend. Each button lights up, taking us from the one marked L past the single digits then the double toward the very last button emblazoned with a PH. When we reach it, Jameson extends his arm. "After you."

We step into something that looks more like a foyer than a hotel corridor. Other than the emergency exit and a service lift there's only one marked door on this level.

Penthouse.

Jameson opens the door, but I look around in confusion.

"What did you do with Maddox?" I ask when I spot our bags waiting for us in the entry.

"I told him I could handle you from here." I don't miss the double entendre in his words.

"Would you like to freshen up?" Jameson asks after he locks the door behind us. "Or maybe I could draw you a bath?"

"No!" I practically shout but recover quickly. "Maybe just a quick shower."

Jameson's lips twitch, but he nods. "Follow me."

He doesn't bother to give me the grand tour. It's pretty easy to make out the dining room table from the living room couch. That said, the space is huge and framed by large glass doors that overlook the city. Past them a small patio leads to a balcony. I can't help but shiver. I've had enough rooftop patios and plate glass for the summer. Thank you very much.

We pass through a corridor with several closed doors.

"What's behind those?" I point to them like a game show host.

"Other bedrooms," he says nonchalantly.

More than one bedroom? It's my understanding that most New Yorkers live in something roughly the size of a shoe box. We have a whole house at our disposal. This much extra space feels a bit like an insult.

"This is the master bedroom," he says, drawing me away from my thoughts.

I dare a peek at the king-sized bed that commands the center of the room.

"Maybe you should rest," he suggests, mistaking my interest in it.

I shake my head. I'm tired, but there's no way I'm about to fall asleep. He doesn't argue with me. Maybe he feels the tension, too. Instead he opens the door to the ensuite bathroom.

"You should have everything you need in here," he assures me before stepping away. "I'll give you some privacy."

Privacy isn't something I usually want from Jameson, but right now I'm glad to have it.

The bathroom is nearly as big as the bedroom and decorated in warm shades of white. I'm pretty certain we could fit a cocktail party's worth of people in the Jacuzzi. Actually, I could probably open my own spa here.

I opt for the walk-in shower, turning the water on to the sear setting. I can barely get my clothes off because I'm shaking so hard. Rummaging through the drawers of the vanity I find toothpaste, a razor, and a few other necessities like lip gloss and a hair tie. I also discover the handful of cosmetic items I occasionally use. Jameson didn't miss any details.

The steam from the shower rolls through the space, misting over the mirror. Shower's ready. I step under the cascade and hope the heat will clear my thoughts. But this isn't a sinus infection. This is sex, and my head is a muddled mess. I decide to go through the motions. I wash my hair and shave my legs. Then I just stand there and allow the water to flow over me as if I'm cleansing myself for some type of ceremonial offering.

"This is not your first time, Emma," I remind myself. But really it may as well be. I don't remember being nervous when I lost my virginity. Then again I didn't remember all that much about that night.

This is different. I want Jameson. I've wanted him since the first night we met. I'd stuck to my guns then, not allowing him entrance into my treasure chest. I'd promised myself I'd be in love before I had sex again, and I've been in love with Jameson for months. Now as summer days drifted away, I should be jumping into bed while I had the chance.

We'd had other opportunities this summer and there'd been

no nerves in the heat of the moment. Jameson had been the one to stick to his rule about waiting until I was eighteen. Most of the time I'd been embarrassingly ready to go. The spontaneous horniness that accompanied a good make-out session had served as some sort of readiness lubricant. There'd been no room for over-analysis in my hormone-riddled brain.

"There's only one thing for it," I decide. "Close your eyes and think of England."

I shut off the water and realize my fingers look like raisins. "Super hot."

I vacillate between pumping myself up and tearing myself down as I towel off. Now comes the hard part: do I wrap myself in this or opt for my birthday suit? My eyes land on the solution to my problem: a silky robe hanging from a hook on the back of the door. I have no doubt it's been placed here especially for me. How long had Jameson been planning this little impromptu getaway?

Slipping it on, I knot the sash tightly as if girding my loins. Steam escapes into the empty bedroom. I half expected to find Jameson waiting for me here. Tiptoeing through the suite, I spot him on the patio outside. The first ribbons of dawn are creeping along the horizon, casting citrus hues over the buildings surrounding the hotel. With each passing second, the noises from the street below grow louder as the city begins its day.

So much for avoiding the roof top, I think to myself as I head toward him. Jameson doesn't turn as I step onto the patio behind him. When I reach him, I place my hand over his on the balcony.

"Did you find everything you needed?" His voice is thick with emotion. When he finally faces me, his gray eyes blaze with a ferocity I've never seen before.

I nod. I have now. I'm not the only who's worked up over finally going to bed together. Maybe he's not nervous, but it's as important to him as it is to me. It's all I really need to know.

"Jameson, I'm ready," I say in a soft voice.

He doesn't ask me to explain. Instead he sweeps me into his arms and carries me inside. The bed welcomes me as Jameson lays me across it. He takes a seat on the edge of the bed and reaches for his top button.

"Let me," I stop him. My fingers tremble as I undo each one until I'm shaking so hard that I fumble. His hands close over mine and he takes over the job until the button-down falls open. He shrugs it off and I reach for the flat panel of his chest, running my palm along the carved ridges of his pecs. I pause there feeling his heart beating under my hand.

Jameson's eyes find mine and I see the unspoken question in them. Can I feel the connection? The thread binding me to him? With my free hand, I untie the sash of my robe and allow it to fall. It's as good an answer as I can manage.

There aren't words to describe the feeling that's overcome me. He seems to understand this, and he moves beside me, drawing my body close to his. Brushing the wet hair from my face, he kisses each cheek, then my forehead, then along my jawline. He worships me slowly and my body softens under his touch.

Still after all this time, I'd expected a little more urgency. Jameson seems to understand the need to take it slow. We've been through a lot recently.

But my paranoia gets the best of me. Am I just laying here like some cold, dead fish? I reach up and tangle my fingers through his hair, tugging his face closer so that I can capture his lips. He surrenders, but only long enough to steal my breath away.

"There's no need to rush," he murmurs the reassurance.

I let him take charge then. There will be plenty of time for the more female-empowering positions of the Kama Sutra later. Right now, I give him my faith, my body, my everything.

He accepts it with each sweep of his mouth over mine and each caress of his hands on my body. I give myself to him, and he offers himself to me. We take and we give, allowing the heat of our bodies to conquer any apprehension we might feel. When my fingers find the buckle of his pants, his hands close over my wrist.

"Are you sure?" he asks.

I can't find the words, not with all the emotions swelling inside of me, so I nod. This simple act of consent speeds us along a bit, and my heels shove his pants down. He settles against me and I can feel the heat of him. Even with our bodies still separate, in so many ways, we're closer that we've ever been before. We pause on the cusp of something that might change our relationship forever.

"I love you." His words are a vow. He traces them along the soft, bare contours of my body.

I find my voice, so I can repeat the precious statement. Three simple words that carry more weight than any others in the world.

Our lips crash together, his tongue flicking my mouth open so that he can deepen the kiss. I arch against him, but he doesn't accept the invitation. Instead, he breaks away, panting. Brushing his thumb over my lower lip, he smiles. "Hold on a sec, Duchess."

When he breaks contact, I bite my lip where he touched it, trying to resist the impulse to squirm. He tears open a foil packet. For a split second, I realize there's a lot of things we haven't discussed, and I make a mental note that it's time for me to get on the pill. Before I can berate myself for not being more cautious, he lowers his body over mine and the worries melt away.

I wiggle my hips, and he grabs them, holding me steady. His patience can be infuriating, but when I finally feel the first, hard edge of pressure, I gasp. My hands seek the sheets, and I grip them tightly.

A look of concern settles over his face. "Do you want me to stop?"

I shake my head. I guess my one and done experience a few years ago didn't qualify me as broken in. "I'm okay."

He moves slowly, gradually closing the last bit of distance between us and pausing occasionally to allow me to adjust. Once we've managed it, we stay like that for a few moments. Finally, I release my grip on the sheets, and hook my arms around him to signal that I'm ready. Jameson brushes his lips over mine, allowing the kiss to become something more organic. Our bodies take the hint, moving in rhythm with one another, until the slight discomfort I feel morphs into a small ripple of pleasure. Jameson responds to my pleased gasp with gentle urgency, rocking against me, and coaxing me towards my shattering moment of bliss. He meets me there with a low growl that tears through him.

Neither of us move for a moment. It took us so long to get here that the idea of breaking up the party now is unthinkable. Instead, our limbs twine together and we shift until we're on our sides, never breaking contact.

I've never really been one for long walks on the beach or love letters. But staring into the eyes of the guy you love after making love is pretty all right.

"What are you thinking?" he asks softly.

"That it was worth the wait," I confess, not bothering to hide a sheepish grin.

"And?" he presses.

"That I hope you're not going to make me wait that long for the next time," I tease.

He presses his forehead against mine. Our skin is damp with sweat, but he laughs. "How about we do it again right now?"

Chapter 11

WE FALL ASLEEP, tangled together, as dawn bursts into view outside our windows. When I blink dreamily a few hours later, the orange glow of sunrise has been replaced by late morning sunlight. I'm alone in the bed, so I roll over and stare at the ceiling.

Everything has changed and nothing has changed.

Except that I'm in a better mood then I can remember having been in for weeks. I giggle as I draw the sheet over my body. Then I yank it off the bed.

Tucking it around myself, I go exploring. When I reach the living room, Jameson grins at me over a cup of coffee.

"I thought you might be hungry." He gestures to the dining room table. It's been laden with silver platters and pitchers. I take the lid off a plate and then another.

"Did you order everything on the menu?" I ask.

"I thought the Duchess might have an appetite this morning," he teases.

I shove a piece of bacon in my mouth "The Duchess does."

I could stay like this forever, but I am in New York City.

"What are our plans today?" I ask as I pluck a promising looking croissant from a platter of pastries.

"I thought we could go out and see the city."

"Or we could stay in?" I suggest mischievously, my carnal side getting the better of me. "Neither of us are dressed after all."

Jameson abandons his coffee and prowls toward me, "What are you suggesting Miss Southerly?"

There's no resistance from me when he throws me over his shoulder and carries me back to bed.

IT'S NEARLY noon by the time either of us manage to get dressed. Jameson suggests another round of room service but I shake my head. "We'll never leave this suite if we do that."

"Tired of me already?" he asks.

"Never," I promise. I don't have to say more, he understands.

I've never been to New York and while I know the laundry list of tourist spots that I'm supposed to see, I defer to his wisdom.

We barely make it into the lobby before Mr. White accosts us.

"Mr. West, I was wondering if I might have a word with you?" he begins, but Jameson cuts him off.

"It's Saturday, Mr. White," he reminds him, "and I need to show my girl the town."

My girl, I think to myself. Everything sounds a little sexier coming out of his mouth this morning. Then again he'd given me a few demonstrations last night that showed just how sexy that mouth could be.

"Of course, of course!" Mr. White steps away and waves cheerfully, "Have a lovely day!"

"Unbelievable," Jameson mutters through clenched teeth.

"Give him a break." I can't help feeling benevolent today.

"If it was up to that man, I'd spend the entire weekend with his lips attached to my ass."

"No you wouldn't, I'd fight him for you," I promise.

"Oh yes?" he asks with a raised eyebrow.

"Definitely, that ass is mine."

I'm surprised when the car heads north. "Are we going away from the city?"

"Greenwich," he confirms. "I need to feed you. It's my responsibility after draining you of all your strength."

He takes me to a falafel place that's so small there's only room for a few bar stools at the counter. A charming mish-mash of colors compliments the simple menu of three items. Having never ordered falafel nor eaten it, I allow him to order for me. When he presents me with my food in a paper basket, I study it first.

"Trust me," he urges. I narrow my eyes but pick it the pita.

"What's in it?" I ask.

"Heaven," he says with a full mouth.

I take a bite and a variety of exotic, unrecognizable spices explode on my tongue. Next to me Jameson watches, clearly on edge, as I finish chewing and swallow.

"You know how you have all that money?" I ask. His face falls, no doubt he expects me to admonish him for not taking me to a fancy restaurant instead of this hole in the wall. "Can you buy one of these and put it in Belle Mère?"

"Your wish is my command, Duchess."

When we're finished, I'm stuffed. I can spy our car and driver, idling around the corner, but I stop Jameson before he can beckon it to us.

"Let's walk for a second," I suggest. I need to move if I'm going to digest this food baby I'm packing.

Greenwich, as it turns out, is charming. We find a row of brownstones lined by a canopy of trees. The emerald shade of their leaves makes it a few degrees cooler as we wander along. I sigh, my arm looped through Jameson's.

"Like it here?" he asks.

"So far I've only seen a king-sized bed and a falafel joint, and it's already my favorite place in the world. I might be biased though." Resting my head on his shoulder, I wonder how many times he's been here before. Maybe New York isn't as charming the hundredth time you visit, but it will always hold a special place in my heart. Jameson has been to cities all over the world. Do they hold a candle to this? "What is your favorite city?"

He flashes me a crooked grin that makes my knees weaken. "The one you're in."

"Charm will get you everywhere with me." I push onto my toes and kiss his cheek.

"Noted." He points to a brownstone with red lacquered steps leading to the front door. "That one."

"What about it?" I ask.

"It's for sale."

"What are we going to do with a place in New York? Especially when you own an entire hotel?" I ask. I'm guessing there might be a few other real estate holdings in the West family's New York portfolio. "Are you planning on leaving me any time soon?"

"Not if I can help it."

"Because I still have a year of prep left." I don't want the fairytale to end, but summer is fading around us. Soon we'll have to face the reality of our responsibilities in Belle Mère.

"And then what?" he asks.

"And then..." My mother had mentioned college before, but I'd always planned on sticking around and bailing Dad out of whatever new mess he found himself in at Pawnography. I never thought I'd get out of town. Las Vegas is a fly strip that's hard to break free from, but now it seems possible. So, where does that leave me? "I don't know."

"We'll figure it out," he promises me. "Maybe we can go on some college visits this fall. NYU. You'd probably love Boston."

"I'm not certain I have Harvard grades."

"You have Harvard money," he reminds me.

"What about you?" I interject, not wanting to consider if Hans's blood money could be used for that expense. "Don't you want to finish your degree?"

Jameson had left school—and the prescribed life his father had planned for him. Now that there is no one around to hold him to a vision of the future he didn't share, he has decisions to make as well.

"Most people go to undergrad and business school in the hopes that they'll land themselves at a fortune five hundred company," he says. "I'm already acting CEO of one."

No shit, Sherlock.

"But do you want it?" I ask in a small voice.

"I don't think it's forever," he admits. "In a few years, Monroe will be able to take over. I know she's always wanted to. My Dad was too stupid to realize she was the better choice for heir to the throne."

I gulp and look away before he can catch the suspicion I suspect is written across my face. Monroe has plans of her own but it's not my place to tell him about them. "What if it all crashed and burned?"

"Crashed and burned?" he repeats. "Are you plotting arson?"

"No need to call the lawyers." Or the nice men with the strait jackets. "What if you just gave it up? You let it all fall apart? Without a West at the helm, what would happen?"

"Someone else would take over. There would be no crashing or burning. My family is invested enough within the company that we wouldn't even notice."

"Then why did you take over?" After the murder, Jameson had stepped up to take his father's place. I'd assumed the move was made out of necessity, since he hadn't wanted to inherit his father's position. But if what he's saying is true, then he did it for another reason.

"People needed reassurances," he explains. "My family, my mother, my sister. The people who work for our company. It's easier to accept the next person in line than to survive a power struggle within. If I play my cards right, I'll be able to step away when I'm ready and hand it over to someone else. It's figuring out how everything works and who everyone is first."

I don't have the smallest comprehension of what he's talking about. My family business employs one person and relies on the slave labor of its owner and daughter to survive. But I am relieved that he isn't stuck with West Enterprises forever. How long could he play the role of Nathaniel West before he became his father?

Jameson not too subtly shifts the topic of conversation from the serious turn it's taken to what I want to do this afternoon. That far ahead I can commit to. He suggests everything from a visit to the iconic Tiffany to a Broadway show, but I already know my answer. "Central Park."

"Central Park?" he repeats in disbelief.

"Horse-drawn carriage rides, mimes, there's a zoo."

"I thought you hadn't been here before," he says in an amused voice.

"I haven't, which is why I need to see Central Park." No amount of persuasion can sway me from this plan of action.

By the time we circle the block and find ourselves in front of the falafel shop once again, he's given up.

"This time of day it is going to be murder to get there," he grumbles as we climb into the back of the Lincoln.

I trail my finger down his thigh and blow him a kiss. "I have a few ideas on how we can pass the time."

AT ONE OF the many entrances to the park, there is a man who has painted himself entirely in white—his clothing to his face and his hands. I can't tear my eyes away from him. Apparently, this living statue gig is par for the course in Central Park, because Jameson is unimpressed.

"Take my picture!" I plant myself next to the man, who still doesn't move. Jameson groans and digs a few dollars out of his pocket. It's only then that I realize that this living art show is less about art and more about making money.

Regardless, I have mad respect for anyone who will brave body paint in this humidity.

After we get our shot, Jameson reluctantly agrees to allow me to eat a hot dog from a cart.

"How can you be hungry?" he asks.

"I'm battling an increased appetite. I feel like I ran a marathon this morning." Sex has to be good for the metabolism.

"Hopefully, that appetite doesn't lead to food poisoning." He ignores the dirty look the vendor shoots him from behind the cart.

As we meander through the twisting lanes of New York's most famous green space, I can't help becoming enchanted.

"I think I could be a New Yorker," I announce.

"That's a tall order," Jameson warns me.

"You don't think I could hack it? I grew up on the strip," I remind him as I toss the hot dog wrapper in a nearby trash can.

"You grew up in Belle Mère," he corrects me.

"And survived," I point out.

"Then you could probably make it anywhere," he agrees. Somehow we manage to miss the zoo. Instead, we happen upon a small pond surrounded by a low brick wall and a restaurant on one side. Little kids watch toy boats drift along its surface as their moms visit nearby.

"Most of New York is not this idyllic," Jameson tells me, but it doesn't matter.

Today of all days he can't scar my perfect vision of the world.

We find a spot under a nearby tree. Before I can claim the empty bench, I realize Jameson isn't beside me any longer. Whipping around to look for him, I find him the last place I'd expect.

"What are you doing down there?" I ask in a strangled voice. I can't help hoping that he's had a sudden onset of early arthritis to explain why he hasn't dropped to the ground like a normal person. Because he's not sitting on the grass. Instead, he is perched on one knee.

It takes a few seconds for me to process what's happening. When I finally do, I'm left with a choice but not the one he's given me. I opt to join him on the ground. Screw tradition. I need for us to be on an equal footing.

Dropping to my knees, I come face-to-face with the velvet box waiting in his palm.

"You don't have to do this," I whisper. "We're going to make it through this."

"That's exactly why I'm asking." Sincerity shines in his eyes. "Because we're going to get through this, and we'll get through whatever life throws at us next."

"Jameson, I can't—"

"Because you're too young?" he guesses. "You don't have to earn love. It's not a rite of passage. My love is yours. My everything is yours. That's not going to change."

"How can you be certain?"

"Are you certain?" he asks, turning the tide against me.

I don't hesitate. There's nothing to consider, because I know my answer to that question. "Yes."

"And I'm certain about this." Jameson flips open the box, forcing me to face the crossroads we've come to. "Will you marry me?"

I don't even have to think. My answer is already on my tongue. "Have you lost your mind?"

Jameson blinks. He wasn't expecting that answer. To be fair, I'm not entirely certain I meant to say it. I clap a hand over my mouth before it can get me in more trouble.

"No, I haven't lost my mind," he says in a flat tone.

"Then why?" I ask. "Are you still worried about being forced to testify against me? Because I think we've cleared that problem up. The FBI isn't—"

"This has nothing to do with that. That's our past. I'm focused on our future, Duchess."

"Does our future have to include the words 'till death do us part'?"

"Not if you don't want it to," he says fiercely. He snaps the box shut.

Crap. What have I gotten myself into this time? I grab it from his hands before he can shove it back into his pocket or toss it into the pond. There's no telling what he'll do.

Thinking quickly, I come up with a much more reasonable response. "I need to think about it."

The scowl darkening his face lightens.

"That's not a yes," I remind him.

"It's not a no, either," he says, interpreting my non-answer in his favor.

He leans closer, nuzzling my neck until I'm practically

putty in his hands. "Is there anything I can do to persuade you?"

"Yes," I say, shoving him away. "Let me think about it. Also, maybe let me take a nap."

Between two lunches, a few broken hours of sleep, and the emotional whirlwind he's just unleashed on me, being unconscious sounds pretty good. In fact, that my reaction to his proposal is to retreat or fall asleep should say a lot to him about my overall readiness for something as important as marriage. By agreeing to consider, though, I've rescued our weekend holiday.

Despite that, conversation is at an all-time low in the car. When we step back into the West New York's lobby, I'm relieved to see Mr. White waiting for us. I'm not certain he's ever moved.

Jameson lifts my hand to his lips and kisses it.

"Why don't you get some rest," he suggests. Before I can escape, he takes out the ring box that I'd given back to him in the car. He thrusts it into my hands. Apparently, we're going to play hot potato with it. "To help you think."

He winks before he turns to the over-eager White.

How can something so tiny feel so heavy? I wonder as I head up to the penthouse.

Maddox is waiting in the corridor. He unlocks the door for me, and I flush when his eyes linger on the ring in my hands.

So naturally I act like an adult and hide it behind my back.

"Did you have a good afternoon?" he asks. I don't miss the insinuation in his voice.

"It was interesting." I leave it at that, resisting the urge to treat him like a therapist and seek sanctuary in the suite instead. Heading straight for the bedroom, I deposit the box onto the dresser. But when I climb into the bed, it looks as if it's hovering above me. Scrambling up, I grab the box and put it on the nightstand. Then I turn over and squeeze my eyes closed. It's no use. I know it's there.

I had been too caught up in the insanity of the moment to even check it out before.

"You promised to think about it," I remind myself out loud. Rolling over, I pick the box up and open the lid. It's a whole lot of flawless. I'd seen enough diamond rings pass through the Pawnography showcase to know this one is worth a small fortune. I try not to think about that fact. If I had been the type of girl who dressed up as a princess or cried during romantic comedies, I might have pictured what my own engagement ring would look like. The truth is that the thought has never crossed my mind.

Now I know it could only ever be this ring. The square diamond in the center sparkles with a fiery brilliance that even I can't ignore. Smaller diamonds circle its edge and adorn the band.

I pluck it out of the box, and I'm surprised that something so sparkling and delicate could be so solid. I study it more closely and that's when I notice the inscription: To my leap of faith.

"I'm not crying. You're crying," I announce to the empty room. Hesitantly, I hold it over the tip of my ring finger as I blink back the moisture pooling in my eyes. It's too much change, too soon. But would it hurt to try it on?

Before I can decide, I hear Jameson enter the suite. Shoving the ring back in the box, I abandon it on the nightstand and nearly jump out of my skin when Jameson appears in the doorway.

"I didn't mean to scare you, Duchess."

Too late, I think, glancing at the box on the table next to me.

"I thought you were going to take a nap." His eyes stray to where his engagement ring sits unworn.

"I'm having a hard time turning my mind off."

"I can help you with that." He saunters, forward tugging his t-shirt over his head. The site of his perfectly stacked abs does a lot to relieve my anxiety. "Of course, maybe I don't want to take your mind off things."

He plays with the button on his jean, and I can't help licking my lips. "Maybe you could work on persuading me."

I don't bother to tell him that right now a few blissful moments of oblivion are exactly what I need.

"I can do that." He lets his jeans fall to the floor before he pounces onto the bed. "Allow me to show you one of the many benefits of marrying me, Duchess."

Chapter 12

THE NEXT MORNING, the siren song of New York lures me out of bed. I leave Jameson sleeping peacefully, eager to venture out on my own. It's liberating to be in a city hundreds of miles from where you live especially given my newfound infamy in my hometown. Tugging my hair into a messy knot at the top of my head, I slip into a sun dress and sandals. I barely remember to grab my sunglasses before I head out the door. The hotel is quiet. In a few hours, the halls will be filled with people checking in and out, businessmen meeting for lunch, and the cleaning staff coming to make beds. I prefer it this way. I enjoy the relative anonymity of the crowds bustling along the street and the sense of being lost in the chaos.

It's nearly impossible to go unnoticed here, not when you're walking down the halls with Jameson West. It's a bit like being caught with the commanding general. The staff doesn't salute him, but everyone stops what they're doing and grovel. He's accustomed to it having spent his whole life bouncing around between his father's properties, shaking hands, and glad-handing; it's second nature to him. I prefer to blend into the wallpaper. The elevator delivers me to the first floor. I'm a few steps toward the staircase that will deposit me into the main lobby when I spot Mr. White; so much for going unnoticed. While the manager's effusive hospitality is understandable, I'm not up for it at seven in the morning.

I freeze at the top landing and begin to pivot slowly. If I take the elevator another flight down, I could exit through the bellhops' entrance; but before I can flee, Mr. White calls my name. "Miss Southerly. Miss Southerly." I do what any confident, well-adjusted woman would do in this situation. I pretend I don't hear him. Scurrying back toward the elevator, I jabbed the button and pray the cars haven't been called to higher floors. A light ding over my head, and I'm relieved when one opens just as Mr. White's insistent call grows closer. Inside, I press the button to close the doors and head to the lower lobby. It's empty, save for a bellhop who's too busy tagging stored luggage to notice me.

I push the sunglasses onto the bridge of my nose and head out the side door. Despite the early hour, it's already muggy. My forehead instantly dampens in the presence of the unfamiliar humidity. Growing up in Las Vegas I'm no stranger to heat, but desert heat isn't like this. By the time I happen upon a little pastry shop a few blocks away, I'm swiping at the sweat collecting under the rim of my sunglasses. I can't help but wonder as I stare into the pastry case if New Yorkers know how good they have it. Sure, back home I could choose between a gourmet champagne brunch courtesy of whatever celebrity chef has plastered his name on the local hotel or a massive buffet at all hours. There's no such thing as quaint in Las Vegas which means there's nothing like this there.

I order a bagful of French pastries that I can't pronounce and cappuccino. At least growing up in the desert has taught me how to drink hot coffee regardless of the temperature. I take my time heading back and watch as New York City comes to life, store fronts open, cars begin to clog the streets, and swarms of people descend on to the financial district to start the day. I try to maintain a leisurely pace but soon find myself swept along, forced to keep up with the current rushing about me. By the time I spot the familiar W emblazoned on the West New York Tower, I've finished my cappuccino and I'm ready for a cold shower. Zigzagging through the crowds toward the front entrance, I don't notice anything unusual until my feet hit the small courtyard outside the door.

Instantly, the air fills with shouted questions and camera clicks.

Click, click.

"Ms. Southerly, why are you in New York?"

Click, click, click.

"Can you confirm that you eloped with Jameson West?"

Click, click, click.

"What do you think about the allegations against your stepfather?"

Click, click, click.

"Is it true that you're pregnant with Jameson West's baby?"

I stumble forward, trying to worm my way past them. Somewhere along the line, I lose the bag of pastry. If the paparazzi think they're getting a photo op when I just lost my éclairs, they've got another thing coming. They crush forward hiding behind the cameras that they push into my face. I'm seriously considering going all Baldwin on them when a firm hand closes over my elbow.

I'm relieved to see Maddox standing in front of me. He pulls me through the crowd and whether it's due to the sheer size of him, or the unmistakable fury rolling off his body, the crowd of reporters parts like the Red Sea before us. Security guards are stationed at each door, providing a flesh and blood barrier to any journalists intrepid enough to try to get inside the West New York.

Jameson is at the front desk barking orders in a low voice to a trembling Mr. White, who looks even paler than his name suggests. Thankfully, the other hotel guests accustomed to five star establishments, and their celebrity clientele, discreetly look past us as Maddox delivers me to his boss.

"What were you doing?" Jameson turns his wrath on me.

I give him a blank stare.

"What were you doing out there?" he repeats.

Apparently, he's not getting the message. "I'm not on your payroll, Jameson West, so don't talk to me like I'm one of your ass-kissing employees."

Mr. White shrinks back behind the desk either afraid that this argument is about to go nuclear or seizing the opportunity to detach himself before Jameson can continue berating him.

"Mr. White says he tried to stop you." Jameson jerks his head at the manager, but he's no longer standing there. My boyfriend looks around for a moment before he gives up. "He says you ran off."

"That might have happened." I admit feeling a trifle sheepish for fleeing the premises earlier.

"Why would you do that?"

"Hold on." I cut him off. "I thought he was going to ask me how the room was and if we needed anything and give me those overeager puppy-dog eyes."

"No one stopped you on your way out?" Jameson asks. "There were no reporters?"

"I went out through the bellhops' entrance. It seemed like a good idea."

Jameson rubs his temples and his shoulders slowly slump into a normal position. "It was a good idea, Duchess. I'm sorry I yelled. When Mr. White called up to the room he was frantic, and to make matters worse, you weren't answering your phone."

I fish it out of my pocket and see several missed calls on its blank screen. "I didn't hear it ring."

He drops an arm around my shoulders and kisses my forehead. "It's okay, but we should probably go and pack."

"New York's been breached," I note with disdain.

"Two days of quiet are apparently the most we can hope for. Next time I'll take you to the Mediterranean. We have a private island in the south of France."

"Of course you do." I slip my arm around his waist as we wait for the elevator. But any semblance of normality is dashed by the hovering presence of Maddox. Although he stays a few feet away, he is impossible to ignore. "Is he going to follow us upstairs?"

"Yes, I think it's best that Maddox stays close by."

"Kinky," I whisper before sighing. "I had no idea the paparazzi was so virulent here."

"About that." Jameson tenses again, and I can feel the muscles in his back go rigid beneath my palm. "There have been some developments at home."

I move away from him. "What kind of developments?"

He doesn't answer. Instead he seizes my hand as we reach the top floor. Maddox arrives and takes up watch outside the door as Jameson leads us into the penthouse.

"What's going on?" I demand as soon as the door closes behind us.

"I already have my people on it," he says, but in no way reassures me.

Away from the crush of reporters screaming nonsensical questions at me, I start to recall what they were asking me. "Oh my God! They think … and…"

"Maybe you should sit down," Jameson suggests. "I'll fill you in in a moment."

"Fill me in now."

"I will, but first I'm going to order you breakfast, Duchess."

"Oh, my pastries." I say, remembering how the bag fell underfoot, only to be trampled by the dozen people surrounding me. In the background, Jameson orders coffee and juice, eggs and bacon. I began to lose track. "Are we in this for the long haul?"

I wonder how long it will take to arrange for us to return home.

"The plane is on standby but there's no need to rush." Somehow I doubt that, but I keep this opinion to myself.

Whatever new scandal we've found ourselves embroiled in can wait.

"Can I see your phone?" he asks me. I hand it to him, not bothering to hide my suspicion. "What do you need it for?"

"You can have it back after your breakfast." He slides it into his pocket.

"What's going on, West?"

"Food first." He's not going to budge.

Room service arrives with lightning speed, one of the perks of being here with the owner. Jameson sits across from me sipping coffee and not speaking as I pile food onto my plate.

"Aren't you hungry?" I ask, between bites of eggs.

He shakes his head.

"I could have sworn you worked up an appetite last night."

He laughs, but his eyes remain distant. Swallowing my last bite, I slam the fork down on the table. "Out with it."

"It's on the cover of every major daily newspaper," he says in a steady voice.

"If you're trying to keep me calm, it's not working." My imagination has already kicked into overdrive. Do they have pictures of the proposal? Or, I gulp at the thought, something more personal. Maybe our late-night rendezvous on the patio last night was a bad idea.

"The FBI has arrested Hans on multiple counts of abuse, molestation, and child pornography."

The list of allegations especially the last one make my stomach flip over. *Child pornography*. If that's true, then he has pictures of Becca, and maybe even …

I don't finish the thought before I'm running for the bathroom. Jameson follows and kneels besides me as I wretch up breakfast.

"Maybe food was a bad idea," he says apologetically. "I thought it would be better if you ate before."

I shake my head to try to tell him this isn't his fault but the next round of vomiting sends another message. When everything is up, I sit on my heels and wipe my mouth. My knees shake as Jameson helps me to my feet. He oversees the appearance of a toothbrush and a glass of water.

"What else? I rasp out, my throat scratchy from vomiting.

"I'm having my people look into it, but otherwise it's the usual stuff."

"Usual stuff?" I raise an eyebrow. What's usual to Jameson West is prime tabloid fodder for the rest of us.

"It doesn't matter."

"I think it does." I plant my hands on my hips, refusing to follow him into the bedroom.

"The press got wind of us being here together and they might have jumped to conclusions."

"What kind of conclusions?" I ask slowly as I sort through the questions the paparazzi yelled at me.

"You've seen the cover of *Us Weekly*."

I have actually seen the cover of *Us Weekly*. My whole life I've been staring at it in the line at the grocery store or gas station. It's always plastered with news of celebrity divorces, marriages, births, and various scandals.

"Let me guess," I say, "not only did I murder your father, I'm also pregnant with your baby."

It takes me a second to realize that he isn't laughing because I'm actually right.

"Oh my God, are they saying I'm pregnant? We just had sex."

"I'll be sure to tell them that," he promises me dryly. "I don't think they're interested in the facts."

"Give me my phone." I hold out my hand.

"Duchess, I don't think that's a good idea."

"Give me my phone, West." He relinquishes it reluctantly.

"It's only rumors. We know that." I ignore him and google my name along with his, only to discover a whole fresh crop of ridiculousness has been fed to the gossip rags in the last few days.

"They think we got married?" I shout as I scroll through. "Oh my God, does it look like I have a baby bump?" I run a hand over the plane of my abdomen as I stare at a photo that's headline news on TMZ.

"You do not have a baby bump. It's called Photoshop." Jameson gently pries the phone from my fingers before I can find the next horror story. "They've been running stories about us for months."

"Not like this." Conjecture has turned into rampant, imaginative bullshit. "I should call my mom, my dad, and I don't know, the *New York Times*? Somebody needs to set this record straight."

"I already have people working on it," he reassures me.

"Then why do we need to go home?" I ask after a long pause, "Let's go to the Mediterranean. Let's run away."

The truth is that the baby and wedding rumors are easy to

face compared to what's going on with my stepfather. I can't bring myself to ask more about Hans. If I call my mother, will she want to talk about it?

"Wait," I say as realization dawns on me. "What do you know about the charges against Hans?"

If he already has people working on the fallout, it must be bad.

"We don't need to think about that right now."

"Now is a pretty good time. There's no food in my stomach. I'm less likely to throw up all over you."

"That's not it," he hedges. "I need confirmation before …"

"Before what?" My eyes narrow and I advance on him. If Jameson West thinks he's going to keep a secret from me right now, he's very much mistaken.

"I can't say this with absolute certainty," he says as I continue to corner him, "but the information we've gotten so far suggests your mother turned him into the FBI."

If Jameson thought this was going to upset me, he's wrong.

"She did?" I ask, awestruck.

"It's not confirmed, but it seems like it."

It hardly seems possible that I could ask so much. First, my dad showed up at the cemetery, remembering my birthday. Now, my mother has put aside her selfish fear of embarrassment and done the right thing.

"My parents are finally growing up," I whisper. I just had to show them how. Jameson doesn't respond. He simply wraps two strong arms around my shoulders and draws me close.

We stay like that for a long moment, gathering strength from one other. Then we walk out of this hotel. There will be more scandals to face, more questions, more scrutiny, but at least we'll face them together this time. It's a comforting thought.

Jameson's cell phone begins to buzz in his pocket. "Sorry, Duchess."

He kisses me quickly before he answers it. He remains silent so long that I begin to question if there's anyone on the other line. But I know from the way his face goes blank that he's listening.

"I understand. I can assure you that's not the case," he says in a clipped tone. "Of course, we'll see you soon."

"What was that about?" I ask as he pockets his phone.

"Time to pack. We've been called to a family meeting."

Chapter 13

MY DREAMS of joining the Mile-High Club are dashed by the perpetual influx of calls Jameson takes on the way back to Las Vegas. Considering the shock numbing my body, it's probably for the best.

The entire cabin of the West private jet has been turned into a miniature war room. The stack of newspapers waiting on the table when we boarded has been strewn across its entire surface. Each of the headlines is a glimpse into the situation awaiting us at home, and the picture it paints is bleak. Not only are the allegations against Hans as sickening as expected, but the reporters are doing an admirable job of tying all of the summer scandals into one big story.

Nathaniel West's murder has nothing to do with Hans van Essen but the fact that my former step-father had been planning to make a movie based on his death has encouraged journalists to jump to bizarre conclusions. The coincidence might have been left at that if it weren't for one common denominator between the two stories: me.

The milder features and editorials are in reputable newspapers. But the stack of gossip magazines delivered fresh from the presses take a bad situation and turn it into a nightmare. I'd been kidding when I joked earlier that the tabloids were reporting that I murdered Nathaniel West and was pregnant with Jameson's baby. Apparently, I have a knack for creative journalism, but the tales the tabloids spun of treachery and twisted family loyalties were beyond my scope of imagination.

Jameson takes another call and I sneak one of the gossip rags off the table and begin to read the cover story.

Summer arrived with murder in Belle Mère, Nevada, Las Vegas's most exclusive enclave. In a crime that shocked the nation, real estate mogul Nathaniel West was found murdered in his home atop the West Casino and Resort on the Las Vegas Strip. The discovery was made after his daughter, former reality star Monroe West, threw an end of the year party for her classmates at Belle Mère Prep.

The bizarre story doesn't end there. Initial investigation seemed to be directed at Nathaniel's son, heir to the West real estate empire. But what young billionaire is going to get his own hands dirty? Sources close to the investigation say that Emma Southerly, a friend of West's sister and a party-goer that fateful night, was so lovesick over Jameson that she agreed to carry out his plans for Nathaniel's murder.

What's in it for her? Newly released pictures have us speculating that she's providing Jameson West with more than an alibi. Is that a baby bump we spot? The two were seen canoodling in a New York eatery this weekend. According to a friend of Southerly, the couple was in New York to quietly elope. Has Emma Southerly seduced Jameson West or is this simply an attempt to secure their love child's future claim to the West fortune?

Regardless, Jameson West better watch his back where Ms. Southerly is concerned. According to a friend of the couple, the eighteen-year-old prep-school senior has major daddy issues and might have been one of her step-father, Hans van Essen's many victims.

If the two are looking for honeymoon suggestions, might we suggest a brief trip to couple's therapy?

I reach the end of the page and a strange emotion begins to bubble inside me. A few seconds later, I'm laughing. Jameson steps back into the main cabin, eying me with concern as he finishes his latest phone call.

"No one will believe that," he informs me, taking the magazine from my hands and dumping it ceremoniously into a nearby trashcan.

"People will believe it," I tell him. "They're always going to believe these things about me. I'm just a gold-digger desperate to get my claws into you, after all."

Jameson's jaw twitches. "If that's the case, I take it I finally have my answer."

It takes me a minute to realize he's referring to his proposal. The gossip rags might take away my dignity, but they won't take my freedom. I shake my head. "I'm not going to make life decisions based on tabloids. But you're right. I have made my decision."

"And?" he asks through gritted teeth.

"No," I tell him softly. He begins to turn away before I add, "And yes."

"That's not an answer, Duchess," he warns me in a cold voice.

"Let me clarify." I stand up just as we hit a pocket of turbulence, and I'm thrown forward. Jameson catches me. I half expect him not to, given the chilling distance he's demonstrating.

"Not right now. In five years, when I'm done with college, or my first parole has been granted"—at the rate we're going, either seems equally possible—"then yes, I will marry you…if you still want me."

"I will always want you." His promise takes my breath away. There's an absolute certainty to it that not even I can doubt.

"But I'm not marrying you to solidify an alibi or to legally prevent you from having to testify against me." I need to be clear in this, especially as we jump into the fray at home.

"I don't want you to marry me for those reasons. I want you to marry me because you love me," he says sharply. "I didn't ask you as a means of strategy. I asked you because you ran away and I thought I'd lost you. I never want to lose you again."

"You won't. But you don't have to put a ring on it to keep me from running away again."

"But you ran the first time," he reminds me. A note of accusation in his tone.

"I had a reason to then."

"There is never a reason to run from me, Duchess," he growls. I want to point out that he's completely wrong about that, or at least I thought he was. "Promise me you won't run again."

"I won't run again," I vow, starring up into his eyes. His arms tighten around my waist possessively.

"What does it matter if we get married young?"

"You aren't going to let this go, are you, West?" I push onto my tiptoes and give him a soft kiss.

"That wasn't an answer." Before we can continue to debate our relationship in philosophical terms, his phone rings again.

"Go on and take it," I urge him. "I'll still be here when you get back."

He hesitates long enough that the phone goes to voicemail.

"Just one thing." His arms fall away from me, and, a moment later, he retrieves something from his pocket.

"Technically you said yes, Duchess," he says as he pops open the ring box.

"Listen," I say, pulling away. "Your mom demanded we come home, probably because she wants to make sure we didn't go to New York to elope. I don't want to give her a heart attack."

"Believe me. My mother has endured far worse shocks than this." He ignores my protest and slips the platinum band onto my ring finger.

"The tabloids are going to have a field day with this," I warn him.

"Let them." And for the first time today, a genuine grin brightens his handsome face. "I want the world to know you belong to me."

"Belong, huh? They think I'm a blood-thirsty, psychopathic gold-digger. I think the world assumes you belong to me."

His laughter dissipates the tension in the air. "Then they'll know you're my psychopathic gold-digger."

Chapter 14

MONROE'S NAILS click on the polished mahogany top of the dining room table. If being under the scrutiny on tabloid surveillance teams is awkward, this is unbearable.

"He'll be out in just a minute," I say apologetically for the tenth time. Later tonight I'm going to have to talk to Jameson about abandoning me to the mercy of his mother and sister in the middle of a crisis. Maybe it's unfair given that he's probably on the phone trying to handle the situation, but his absence only gives them more time to sharpen their claws.

Monroe runs her tongue along her teeth across the table from me.

She's going to eat you alive, a tiny voice warns me. Tell me something I don't know.

Evelyn, Jameson's mother, has been eerily silent since our arrival. Usually she's the warmest member of the family, having gone out of her way to make me feel welcome, despite the circumstances under which Jameson and I met. Tonight, she seems to have taken a page out of her son's book, keeping her thoughts and emotions under wraps.

She sits at the head of the table; her black silk blouse a stark contract against the creamy white of her throat. A string of pearls nestles against her collarbone. From all outward appearances, this woman is in mourning. Knowing what I know about the nature of the West family, her show of grief is less about actual sadness and more about propriety—a topic I have a feeling I'm about to get a lecture in.

"Mother. Monroe." Jameson greets his family as he strides into the dining room. It feels like ages since we've both been in his Mount Charleston home. Can it really only have been a few days? The boy who brought me here a few months ago has been replaced by a man in a white oxford and suit pants with his sleeves rolled up to the elbows and his tie unknotted at his neck. I miss the t-shirt and jeans. I miss the picnic basket with crunchy peanut butter sandwiches, but most of all I regret that he's given it all up to protect me.

Monroe clears her throat. "Can we get going with this? I have plans this evening."

I shoot her a look that suggests I suspect what those plans might be, but she maintains her studied indifference as she inspects her manicure.

"Of course we can—now that we're all here," Evelyn West says in a benevolent tone. Jameson takes the seat at the opposite end of the table, and the tension between them is palpable. On one end, his mother still reeling from the murder of his father, has been left to parent two children who took the Autobahn into adulthood. On the other end sits her son, who has risen to power in the absence of his father. I'm glad I'm not battling for which end is up, but being stuck in the middle sucks.

"Well, you called this meeting," Jameson prompts.

"We're sorry to interrupt your little holiday in New York," Monroe sneers, "but you left a mess behind yourselves."

I grip the edge of the table, trying to maintain some sense of decorum. Considering that my relationship with Monroe has primarily consisted of flipping the bird to each other behind the backs of teachers for the last three years, this is harder than it sounds.

"Monroe." Her mother's voice is rich with admonishment. "I asked us all to be here because this concerns all of us."

"I don't see how what her stepfather did…"

I'm halfway out of my seat when Jameson cuts her off.

"Shut up, Monroe."

"You can't speak to me like that."

"I don't know why you think I can't," he growls.

"You will both be quiet." Evelyn's fist pounds the table. "Neither of your names have been dragged through the mud half so much as poor Emma's, and you don't see her starting fights."

I shrink further into my chair, thankful that she doesn't realize how close I'd been to lunging across the table for Monroe's throat. Jameson takes the heat for me, squaring his shoulders and meeting his mother's gaze with defiance.

"Is this a family meeting or a lecture?"

"It seems you are in need of both, my son." Their eyes stay locked on each other, providing Monroe and I with some common ground as we glance at them nervously.

I hadn't expected a play for power between the two of them, but then again, I never expected to find myself in this situation at all.

"I called this meeting to clarify some points of interest," his mother explains.

"Then why is she here?" Monroe asks.

"Because she is a part of this family," Jameson informs her tersely. Meanwhile, I twist the engagement ring he insists I wear around to hide the diamond, stealing a glance at my hands and my lap. I wonder if it would be better to change it to the other hand. There's something blatant about wearing it on this one.

"Is it true?" Monroe demands. "Is that why she's hiding that rock she showed up wearing? You can take it out from under the table. You aren't fooling anyone."

So much for that plan. Evelyn keeps her eyes trained on her son.

"Of course Emma is welcome as a member of this family. You've made your feelings about her quite clear, and while I can respect that, I would like to know if congratulations are in order."

I open my mouth, my cheeks turning a lovely shade of candy apple red, but Jameson beats me to the punch.

"Do you believe everything you read on the Internet, Mother?" he asks dismissively.

"No, I don't." She folds her hands in front of her. "But, as your sister pointed out, and as my accountants informed me, your girlfriend is wearing a stunning, million-dollar engagement ring."

"Holy shit," I blurt out. I'd expected the ring cost bank, but not the actually contents of a small bank.

"Don't get practical now, gold-digger," Monroe says.

"You will not call her that," her mother informs her as Jameson gets to his feet.

"None of this is any of your concern."

"On the contrary"—Evelyn gestures for him to sit back down—"given the concerns Agent Mackey and the FBI have presented to me, and the speculations of the media, it's very much my concern."

"I've already addressed those concerns," he says through gritted teeth.

"I'm not here to be part of a cover-up," Monroe interjects.

"Maybe I should go," I say nervously. The West family has

enough to deal with without being overly concerned with my problems.

"Nonsense, this concerns you. I simply want to know if you two are married."

"No," I cry out, overwhelming Jameson's more calm denial. He might not care about what his mother thinks of me, but I do. "And we're not getting married."

"Is that a placeholder, then?" Monroe asks.

"I told him he has to wait. I'm not marrying him to get the FBI to back off, and I'm not not marrying him to avoid the scandal. I just told him that I would marry him in a couple of years if we still want to get married."

"That sounds very practical." Evelyn's lips twitch, but she keeps smile to herself. "I'm glad one of you is thinking clearly."

"I'm old enough to get married," Jameson reminds his mother.

"Yes," she admits, "but your girlfriend it not. I'm glad you finally found someone to ground you in reality. Lord knows, I've never been able to."

"Well, now that that's out of the way." Jameson's voice is cold, showing neither the embarrassment I feel or the amusement his mother is hiding. "We should be going."

"Don't be ridiculous. There are other matters to consider."

"I'm not pregnant," I jump in, wondering if she's concerned over that particular headline as well.

"I didn't think you were, given that Jameson and I had an understanding." She gives him a pointed look. "It would be quite miraculous if you were. Of course, now that you're eighteen, I would ask that you wait a few years before you make me a grandmother."

I flush. She knows exactly why he took me to New York.

"I think we need to discuss other situations, particularly the allegations your father is facing."

"Stepfather," I corrected her. Monroe rolls her eyes across the table. I don't care if it seems like a petty difference to her, it's a huge difference to me.

"Stepfather," Evelyn grants me. "I have a few questions."

I gulp, feeling a hard knot forming in my throat. "Of course."

"You don't have to talk about anything unless you want to, Duchess," Jameson calls from the other end of the table, but I hold up my hand.

"I want to. This is a family meeting after all, and apparently, I'm officially a West, married or not."

"Some of my questions are a trifle delicate," she warns me, and I nod. "First of all, our lawyers would like to talk with you when you have a moment about the film project your stepfather was involved with regarding my late husband."

"I'll tell them what I know about it," I promise, adding silently, *which isn't much.*

"Secondly, Monroe would like to say something." Evelyn turns her attention to her daughter.

"It's come to my attention that I allowed a snake to get too close to the family, and she's struck."

"Stop talking in riddles," Jameson demands.

"Sabine," Monroe clarifies. "Apparently, she was quite smitten with Levi. The two of them have been seeing each other behind my back for a couple of weeks."

"Christ, Monroe," Jameson mutters, running his hands through his hair. I don't need her to continue. I know exactly what this means. Sabine has always been Monroe's right-hand bitch, which means she knows more about the sordid affairs that go on behind the West family's closed doors than nearly anyone not sitting at this table.

"I apologize," Monroe continues, "and I'll be more judicious in my choice of friends in the future."

Judicious? It's more like she's taking the SAT's than apologizing, but I keep my mouth shut. Sabine might have seemed like a loyal lapdog; however, their friendship had always been based on fear and control. None of us should be surprised that she took the opportunity to stab Monroe in the back at the first opportunity. Judging from Monroe's detachment, she even seems a little proud.

"Now that that's settled." Evelyn swivels to face me. "I would like to know if the allegation that your stepfather molested you is true."

"Mother, that is none of your business," Jameson interrupts her.

"You've made your intentions towards Emma clear."

"So you want to embarrass her?" he asks.

She levels a stare that could probably melt iron at him. "Embarrass? Is that what you think of me? My support, financially and emotionally is entirely behind your girlfriend."

"Fiancée," he corrects her, and I wince.

"Let's let her get used to the idea," his mother suggests. "I'm asking her, because if it's true, I'd like to arrange for her to see a therapist."

"I don't think," I begin.

"That's not your place," Jameson interjects.

"You'd like this woman to be my daughter," she points out to him, "so I'm treating her as I would my own daughter. If Monroe were in this situation, I would urge her to do the same."

I can't help but stare at Monroe. If Evelyn West had any idea what type of situation she's in, we'd be having a different conversation right now. Monroe's facade of disinterest slips, and I see the fear in her eyes. She knows I can burn her, and I have every reason to do so. Particularly, after learning how she's used Jonas for the last couple of years, but this is a family meeting, and if Evelyn West wants to treat me like a daughter, then I need to treat Monroe like a sister.

"I don't think it's necessary," I explain to Jameson's mother, "because he didn't molest me."

She releases a deep breath. Someday she'll learn the particulars—that Hans von Essen raped my sister—but, for now, she needn't know it was his actions towards me that brought him to his knees. No, Evelyn West doesn't have to worry about me. Hans von Essen didn't get the better of me.

I destroyed him.

Now that the emotional part is out of the way, she shifts into business mode. "Naturally our lawyers and publicity team have been following the events. They will be at your disposal should you need them when dealing with the authorities or with the press."

"Of course." I swallow hard at the thought. Is this what the rest of my life will be if I join this inimitable family? Family meetings and strategy sessions, all designed to dictate how the world sees us. It's overwhelming to consider.

"Jameson, might I have a minute with you alone?" his mother asks. The two of them step into the study across the hall, leaving Monroe and I to face one another.

"You didn't rat me out," she says.

"I thought it in poor taste, given …" I trail away. I can't bring myself to say it.

"That you're a West now?" she finishes for me.

"I guess," I say with a shrug, hoping that I appear nonchalant, even as my heart speeds up.

"Why do you think I advised you to stay here this summer?" Monroe asks. "There's a lot you have to learn about this family."

I glance toward the study doors, which have been shut behind mother and son. "You're telling me."

"Just to clarify, we're not best friends or anything," Monroe says.

"Agreed. So long as you tell me you're not planning to sabotage me at the first opportunity."

"Do you think I wouldn't sabotage my friends?" She laughs, as though the suggestion of her loyalty is preposterous.

"Remember how you told me you needed to teach me how to be a West?" I ask her. "I think maybe it's time for me to teach you how to be a decent human being."

"Too late for that, I'm not interested." If my barb stings, she doesn't show it. "But rest assured, you're better off being my family than my friend."

My eyebrow arches. "And why is that?"

"Because this family protects each other. *No matter what.*"

"So I'm one of you then?"

"You could have delivered me to my mother. You could have told her the truth about what you know. She'll find out eventually, of course. It's an inevitability in my plan, but it wouldn't have done you any good with her or with me. You've proved yourself to be a West with your loyalty."

"I'm not even sure what that means," I admit.

"It means you know how to keep a secret, and it means you'll protect us, *no matter what you know.*"

Chapter 15

THAT I'M DATING a real estate mogul's heir has never seemed more important than when Jameson unlocks the door to a penthouse suite in an off-the-strip property. The idea of going anywhere that people might recognize us makes me want to vomit and after tonight's awkward family meeting, I need a little distance from the rest of the Wests. If I'd thought that being labeled as a prime suspect in a murder trial was going to be my worst memory of summer vacation, I know now that I was wrong.

As if facing the impending storm of questions from my parents and friends isn't bad enough, Jameson hadn't said one word to me since we left Mount Charleston. Whatever his mother had spoken to him about in private hangs between us, dampening the mood.

"This is nice," I say conversationally, but he only shrugs. The resort he's brought us to is one of those luxury joints masquerading as a haven from the bright lights and business of Las Vegas. Judging from the info I'd skimmed while Jameson did his bit to shake hands and make nice with the management, it's a timeshare for gambling addicts that have the good sense to keep some mileage between their wallet and the craps table.

The suite is decorated in subdued hues of beige, perfect for whoever might call it home for a week at a time. It's more nondescript and a lot less stylish than the other West resorts I've seen, but the leather couch still shines with furniture polish and the pillows on the gigantic bed remain fluffed.

I eye it and realize that I have one weapon in this cold war we're silently battling. As I slip my sundress over my head, catching Jameson's attention, I realize how fortunate I am to be a female. The low back of my dress and its tiny straps made wearing a bra impossible. Yes, it's completely unfair to flaunt my body to get my boyfriend to talk to me, and some might argue I'm setting women back like a hundred years, but personally, I've never been so happy to have boobs.

"Not going to work, Duchess," he calls from the living room as I drop onto the bed.

Arranging myself artfully like the chick in Titanic, I respond. "I can't hear you. Come closer."

"I said you are infuriating," he growls as he steps into the bedroom. But the annoyance in his words can't mask the ways his eyes linger on me.

"What big eyes you have, Mr. West."

"I'm not playing around here." He grabs a robe from the back of the door and tosses it to me.

I shrug it on angrily. So much for my irresistible feminine wiles. "I'm not either, but I'll do what I have to if it means you'll talk to me."

"Why don't you try talking to me?" he suggests in a flat voice.

That hadn't occurred to me, but I'm not letting go of my bruised ego so easily. "I've been talking to you."

"Small talk about the decor isn't a hot conversation starter."

If he's trying to up the alert level of my fury, he's doing a damn good job.

"I don't want to fight with you," he says in a soft voice.

"Your mom is pissed, isn't she?" I guess. When he nods, I wish a sinkhole would form and swallow me alive.

"Not at you," he clarifies when he sees my expression.

"If she's mad at you, then it's because of me."

He doesn't bother to challenge that assumption. "I knew we would get flack for being engaged. This will pass."

"Maybe I shouldn't..." I twist the ring he's given me around until it reaches my knuckle but he strides over and pushes it back down my finger.

"That's your birthday present," he reminds me.

"It's a whole lot more than a birthday present." Staring at it, I wonder how such a little thing can mean so much. Then I remember the price tag and the disdainful look in Monroe's eyes when she called me a gold-digger. "I don't need a ring. I'm not really the jewelry type."

I fail to add that every girl I know is the diamond type even if they've never owned so much as a friendship bracelet before.

"Duchess, I want you to wear it." He leans over the bed and tilts my chin up with his finger. "It's important to me and since you won't marry me yet, let's call it a compromise."

I narrow my eyes at him. He's not fighting fair. How am I supposed to say no with those silvery-gray eyes gazing into mine? It's not even a discussion. "I thought we were calling it a present."

Jameson laughs, slipping his hands under the collar of my robe and gently shucking it free from my shoulders. I allow the sleeves to slide off my arms and the garment falls off, pooling behind me. His eyes stay glued to mine even as his jaw twitches. "I've been imagining that ring—and only that ring—on you since I bought it."

"And aren't you going to look?" I purr. I'm not entirely certain if I've won or lost this argument, but I can't seem to care.

His gaze sweeps over me, leaving goosebumps in its wake. I drape my arm over my bare hip and put his ring on display. He lingers on it and with each passing second, my pulse ratchets up in speed. Finally, I reach up and grip his shirt, urging him to join me on the bed. As I unbutton it, his face slants down, nuzzling into the curve of my neck.

"It's not just a present," he whispers.

My answer catches in my throat. "I know."

He pulls back and studies me for a moment. "You don't have to wear it."

I cup his face with my palm and smile shyly. "I think I want to. I just never expected to have something so…"

Extreme? Expensive? Unexpected? I can't find the right word.

"It's a ring fit for a duchess." But Jameson understands, taking my hand in his, he lays me across the bed. "For my Duchess."

Biting my lip, I marvel as his body moves against mine, slowly pushing all my doubts away.

THE NEXT MORNING I'm alone in bed, stretching my muscles. Is everyone this gloriously sore after sex? Or has Jameson West cornered the market on wearing a girl out? Either way, I'm not complaining. I find a note next to a fresh pot of coffee in the living quarters.

Dealing with fall-out. Call me when you're up.
    Love,
    Jamie

I take a risqué selfie instead. His response is immediate and I answer the phone as soon as it begins to vibrate.

"Thank god you're eighteen," he says gruffly.

"Why are you whispering?" I ask, unintentionally lowering my own voice.

"Because I'm in a boardroom with a bunch of middle-aged men who already drool over my fiancée. I don't need to give them any more material to fantasize about," he admits.

"Then you better delete that photo." I pour a cup of coffee and take a slow sip.

"That photo and I are going to have some alone time together later," he promises.

"How about you hold out for the real thing?"

"Just promise you'll stay like that the rest of the day and we have a deal." I can hear the wicked smile in his voice. "Duchess, I have to go. I love you."

"I love you, too." I hang up and look around the room. I'm not entirely sure how I'm not floating mid-air right now. Before I can come down from my high, my phone rings again and I answer it immediately.

"Yes, I am naked, but you're going to have to be patient."

"I'll keep that in mind," Agent Mackey says dryly. "I guess you didn't want to wait for your test results—or you didn't care."

My temper flares and I have to set my coffee mug down to avoid spilling it all over myself. I'm mad at myself more than her, but that doesn't mean she's getting a free pass. Not this time. "We had private testing done. Your lab didn't seem as concerned with the results as we were."

"Ah, the royal *we*. How is the pedestal he's placed you on?" she asks.

"Did you call for anything else?" I can barely get the words past my gritted teeth.

"Mostly to deliver the good news, but when you have a moment I'd like to get a statement from you regarding your stepfather."

I swallow against the bile rising in my throat. Mackey is never going to allow me to be happy. She'll always find a way to disrupt my life. "I have nothing to say about him."

"That's interesting. I'd still prefer we talked," she presses.

"You're never going to let this go, are you?"

"Let what go, Miss Southerly? Or are you Mrs. West now? It's hard to keep up with the gossip."

I bypass the jab and focus on the real issue. "You have your DNA results. You know it wasn't me. You know it's not Jameson. When are you going to stop this persecution?"

"Persecution is a strong word," she warns me. "As far as the FBI is concerned, you've been cleared. There's no evidence to substantiate your involvement."

"And as far as you're concerned?"

"I'll let it go when I know who's responsible for Nathaniel West's murder."

"It wasn't us!" I've completely lost my cool now.

"But it was. Maybe not you or Jameson, but it was one of you. Someone at that party killed Nathaniel West and whoever he or she is, they think they've gotten away with it. I'm here to make certain that you can't go on buying your way out of trouble. Don't fool yourself. A lot of people wanted him dead, and someone close to you saw that it happened. How well do you know your new family, Emma? How much will they pay to keep the truth locked away?"

"I've never bought my way out of trouble," I say flatly.

"No, but you sold your soul to a man who did."

. . .

WHAT JAMESON DOESN'T KNOW CAN'T hurt him, which is why I don't tell him I'm leaving the suite. I bribe Maddox to keep quiet with a venti white chocolate mocha, his guilty pleasure. I even allow him to drive me. Given the increased interest in my personal life, having a body guard the size of The Rock around seems like a good idea. Plus, it's pretty easy to feed Maddox bullshit.

"I need to run an errand for my dad," I say. "This guy brought a bogus baseball card into the shop the other day and I have to deliver the bad news that it's a fake."

Tucking a little kernel of truth into my lie makes it easier to sell. Don't say I never taught you anything.

Maddox pulls into a spot in front of Dominic Chamber's office and I jump out before he can unbuckle his seat belt.

"I'll only be a minute," I promise him. He looks unconvinced. Probably because I've pulled a few over on him. I take my phone out of my bag and drop the bag on the passenger seat. "Consider this collateral. I'll be right back."

Chambers puts out a cigarette as soon as I enter. "Sorry, about the smoke, Miss Southerly."

"Not going to ask if I've changed my name?" I ask dryly. He'll be the first person I've seen since my return to Las Vegas not to.

"Why would I ask that?" His bushy eyebrows knit into one woolly caterpillar over his eyes.

"Nothing. Rumors. Tabloids." I'm more than happy to not explain.

"Oh that." He waves a hand. "I never believe that crap."

I nod in agreement. Finally, a reasonable response.

"Plus, I checked wedding license applications in New York. I know you didn't get married," he adds.

"I think that's a breach of my privacy," I inform him.

"I am a private eye," he says as if that absolves him of his nosiness.

"Did you receive my advance?" I'd taken the liberty of PayPal-ing a significant sum through Chamber's website, hoping it would encourage him.

"I did. Much appreciated. I'm happy to report that I have something for you as well." He tosses a folder across his desk to me.

"Is this...?"

"Better than a few pictures, huh?" he says with pride.

I'd asked Dominic for a picture or a document that only the police would have. Instead he delivered the mother lode.

"Las Vegas PD is surprisingly easy to bribe," he continues. "Plus, I think they want to stick it to that FBI agent who thinks she's running the show."

"They aren't the only ones," I mutter. I skim through the contents of the Nathaniel West case file, glancing away when I reach the crime scene photos.

"He was a bastard, but he didn't deserve that," Chamber says thoughtfully.

"No, he didn't," I agree. Standing to leave, I assure him that the rest of the agreed upon fee will be arriving shortly. Before I reach the door, he stops me.

"If you don't mind my asking: what are you going to use it for?"

I flash the detective a coy smile. "Bait."

Chapter 16

THE WEST RESORT and Casino has a lovely afternoon brunch even during weekdays, which is why I choose it for a bite to eat. Plus, it gives me a chance to put my invited guest in her discomfort zone. I need Monroe West if I'm going to use the information I've gotten from Dominic Chamber to my advantage. I'm already seated by the time she arrives, and my earliness makes me feel as if I have the upper hand.

Perhaps that's why my mother always gets to a restaurant thirty minutes in advance.

Monroe's annoyance radiates from her. While her lacy, navy dress and nude flats make her look the part of the innocent, I know exactly how I got her to meet me today. That's probably why her sharp blue eyes cast daggers at me from across the dining room.

"Did you have to call my agency?" Monroe hisses as she takes the seat across from me.

I shrug, stirring a packet of sugar into my tea. I'm not certain this is what people mean when they say kill them with sweetness. "It seemed the easiest way to reach you."

"You have my phone number." She orders a mimosa from the waiter and then turns her fury back on me.

"I forgot."

She considers this for a moment, and I hold my ground. Bullies respond to strength, so if I want to bond with my future sister-in-law, I'm going to have to show her exactly what I'm made of.

"So did you miss me or is there a point to this little afternoon tea party?" she asks, lounging into her seat. She's getting comfortable, which means she's letting me win this round.

Score one for Emma.

"I received some good news today. I've officially been cleared in your father's murder case."

"We've known that for a while, though."

I can't quite hide my surprise. I had no clue that Jameson had shared the DNA issue with the rest of his family.

"Don't look so shocked," she says. "We keep each other's secrets, remember? Although no wonder he was so upset. It would have been pretty fucking twisted if you were his half-sister."

Score one for Monroe.

"Of course, maybe that gets you off," she continues, smothering a roll with butter before proceeding to pick at it.

"You're more of the expert on fetish," I assure her as I take a sip from my straw.

I don't miss the slight flinch she tries to hide.

Score two for Emma.

"I thought we could celebrate," I begin.

"That you aren't screwing your brother? Sure, why not?" She rolls her eyes and abandons the uneaten roll on her plate.

"That I'm free and clear. Unless there's a reason we should be concerned about familial involvement." I don't hide the implication of my words. I'm calling Monroe's bluff. I'm not Nathaniel West's daughter, but she is.

"Don't be a pervert," she says flatly. "So you want to have a party."

I nod, trying not to look too self-satisfied that I've gotten her on the same page. "Here."

"Here?" Monroe repeats. "You mean upstairs? Is that a little tasteless?"

"I had no idea you were so concerned with other people's opinions. Maybe we should burn the place down and rebuild." Monroe doesn't seem to care that her father was murdered in this building. She's stayed here, conducted business here. Hell, she even threw another party here.

"My mother is concerned with saving face," she reminds me.

"This is about showing our strength," I counter, hoping that this fledgling family connection is strong enough to get this done. "To whoever is watching. We own this town and they aren't going to scare us away."

"You aren't a West yet. We might protect you but let's wait for the prenup before you go claiming to own my family's empire," she suggests drolly.

I slide my hand around my glass and lift it so that my engagement ring sparkles in the afternoon sunlight. "Oh honey, I already own it."

WHEN I STEP off the escalators to the lobby, I'm met with half of the hotel's security team. So much for keeping a low profile. Maddox shrugs through the crowd of suits. We both know that when Jameson wants to make a scene he's going to.

"Miss Southerly, I've been asked to escort you upstairs." It's hard to take the man speaking to me seriously given that he's wearing sunglasses inside the building, but I do my best.

Following him toward the bank of elevators that lead to the business offices, I spot Jameson waiting for me. His tie is still knotted tightly at his throat and his suit is pressed. I'm used to seeing him later in the day when he's ditched the veneer of respectability. The man standing in front of me is far too respectable and it's having an undeniable effect on me.

He takes me by the hand, thanking the guard.

"I thought you were staying home," he whispers. "I have to admit that I was rather enjoying visualizing you naked in bed, waiting for me."

"Are you disappointed to see me?" I ask, brushing a chaste kiss over his lips.

"Never," he promises, rubbing the stubble peppering his jaw. Without thinking, I reach up and run a finger along it.

"You need to shave," I murmur.

"I shaved this morning." His mouth closes over mine before I can continue to critique his appearance. Despite the tension coiling through my limbs, I melt against him. When we finally break apart, I gasp for breath. "Just think of it as friction, Duchess."

"I like it," I simper.

He doesn't mistake the double meaning and without a word, he grabs my hand and strides toward the elevator.

"Are you on a break?" I call, trying to fish my phone out of my bag with my free hand.

"No." He continues forward and to my surprise, he bypasses the private elevator and steps into one crowded with people. Jameson shifts behind me to make room for another passenger, giving him the opportunity to grab my hips and pull me against him. His dick presses against my butt and my breath hitches. Just imagining what's about to happen, tightens my stomach and when we step off the elevator a few floors later. I glance around.

"Where are the hotel rooms?" I ask in confusion, staring at a corridor of meeting rooms and banquet halls.

"If I take you near a bed, I won't get back to work today, and"—he checks his phone— "I have a meeting in fifteen minutes."

"Don't let me keep you," I taunt him, letting my hips sway a bit as I walk.

"Not until you answer a question." He grabs me around the waist and holds me. Meanwhile I've stopped breathing. Jameson didn't spot me by chance in the hotel lobby. He'd sought me out.

Leading me into a meeting room, he picks me up and sets me on the edge of a table. "What are you doing here?"

"How did you know I was here?" I hate the idea of lying to him, so I counter with a question of my own.

"We were overseeing the implementation of a new security system." He smiles tightly. I don't need him to explain why it's necessary. Jameson has been gradually increasing security around his hotel, his family, and to my annoyance, his girlfriend, since his dad was killed. "Were you hoping to see me?"

He steps between my legs, angling his face to nuzzle my neck. I hook my arms around his neck, my fingers lingering in his mess of auburn hair. "I'm always hoping to see you, but I had lunch with Monroe."

I'm leaving a few important details out, but I'm not certain he's going to be thrilled about this party. I need to butter him up first.

"Monroe?" he repeats.

"She wants me to feel like part of the family." I prop my index finger over his lips when he tries to speak. "Don't worry. I'm keeping her close without letting her get too close."

"Smart girl," he breathes. Jameson is content with my answer or he's lost his patience. Either way, he's distracted from his interrogation. His hands creep under my shirt to massage my breasts while he kisses my collarbone. Within a few seconds, I'm practically vibrating under his touch.

"You were saying something about friction, Duchess?" he whispers against my skin before brushing his cheek across my neck. My body answers for me, erupting in goosebumps. Jameson chuckles under his breath. He rocks against me and I clutch his tie, lowering my back to the table. I don't bother to ask if he's locked the door, even after he's stripped me from the waist down. One of the perks of being with the owner of a resort is that no one is calling security if they stumble in. Plus, the idea of getting caught sends a throb traveling between my legs.

Jameson's jaw trails along the soft inner skin of my thigh, sending a ripple of pleasure that bubbles out of me in giggles.

"Are you ticklish?" He lingers in the spot until I'm laughing and panting, torn between giddiness and anticipation. Finally, his head pops into view, a smug grin plastered on his face. "You sound like a squeak toy."

I glare at him, too weak from his physical teasing to come up with a retort. My lack of response only encourages him to laugh, too. Hooking his arms around my legs, he drags me to the edge of the table. "Don't worry, Duchess. I'm not done playing with my toy yet."

ARRANGING my last visit of the day takes a little more finesse. Explaining to Maddox that I want to visit Monroe's now ex-boyfriend results in a blank stare.

"He got into a fight," I tell him. "He was beaten up pretty badly, and I wanted to check in on him."

"That's considerate of you." Either Maddox isn't buying what I'm selling or he's really more teddy bear than human. I'm happy regardless. As it turns out Maddox is the easy one to appease. Jonas's mother is far less happy to see me.

I smile broadly when she opens the door. "I came to check on Jonas."

"He told me company was coming." It's clear from the way her lips purse like she accidentally sucked on a lemon wedge that he forgot to mention I was the company.

I take her acknowledgment as an invitation and waltz into the house. Unless they've changed things around, I know exactly where his bedroom is. If what Jonas told us was true, then his mom will be thrilled to see a girl going inside.

Well, maybe if that girl was someone other than me. But given my current notoriety, I can't blame her.

Jonas is strung across his bed, absorbed in a PlayStation game.

"I didn't know they still made those," I say. It had been years since I'd played a video game, but, at the moment, I understood the appeal of delaying adolescence.

Jonas looks up and grins. He won't be smiling for much longer, not when I tell him why I'm here. I clutch my purse a little closer. It feels heavier with the police file inside.

"How are you feeling?" I ask, checking out the deep, purple bruises on his cheek bones. A few have begun to fade to green along the edges.

"Fine," he promises. "I think Hugo actually gave me some street cred. My Dad says I look like a real man." Jonas's smile slips and he forces it back on his face, but it no longer reaches his eyes. We both knew that if his father knew the truth, he wouldn't be so proud.

"One more year," I remind him, "and then we can get out of here."

"Not sticking around?" Of course, Jonas remembers my plan to stay in town and run my dad's shop. Because regardless of the mistakes he's made, he's a genuinely decent guy. I'm counting on that decency to help me out.

"I think I'd prefer to get the hell out of town," I say with a laugh.

"I'm glad you aren't staying here," he says conspiratorially, his chocolate brown eyes rich with concern. "This place will poison you—turn you into someone you aren't."

Like someone willing to use anyone and everyone she knows to get what she wants? I try to push my self-disgust down but it keeps rising to the top. If I don't find out who killed Nathaniel West, I'll have the crime hanging over my head for the rest of my life. I tell myself it's not self-service that compels me to use every resource I have to uncover the truth, but rather self-preservation.

"I need your help." I can't stomach sitting here and pretending to be a considerate friend regardless.

Jonas sighs and settles back against his bed. He points to his desk chair, and I take a seat. "I was worried you were going to say that."

"Am I that transparent?" I ask.

"Consider it a good thing. But after all these years, and what I did to you, I don't deserve a house call. That's what gave you away." He winks at me but I see the sorrow hiding in his eyes.

"Maybe you aren't as bad as you think." I pull the folder out of my bag and hold it up. "But you're right I came here for a reason."

"What is that?" he asks, not bothering to get up. In this town, I wouldn't take a nondescript folder either.

"The case file on Nathaniel West's murder." If this is going to work, I have to be completely honest with him. It's a leap of faith to spill my plans to another soul, but I was recently told I needed to be a bit more trusting. I believed Jonas when he said he had nothing to do with the murder, but that's not the reason I've come to him.

"And why do you have it?"

"I paid for it." I toss it on the bed. "You might want to skip the pictures. They're hard to get out of your head."

Jonas doesn't pick it up. "Why are you telling me this, Emma?"

"Because we both know that whoever did this is following your account."

"I'm not posting anymore," he says flatly.

"Look, you created The Dealer to restore some karmic balance to Belle Mère."

"All it did was hurt people," he stops me.

"Then this is your chance to make things right."

"How?" he asks.

"By catching the person who killed Nathaniel West once and for all." I shove a few papers that have fallen out back into the folder. "I'm having a party at the Wests. All I need you to do is post a photo of this in the office."

"Where he was killed?" Jonas's face is ashen.

"Whoever did it will know it's a message. They'll come looking for the file."

"And you'll catch them red-handed." Jonas pauses to considerate, then he shakes his head. "You can't be sure they're still following the account."

"They are," I say firmly.

"But how do you know?" He doesn't share my certainty, but that's not important.

"I know they'll come looking for one reason, because they haven't been caught yet."

"You aren't as clever as you think you are," Maddox says,

drawing my attention away from my cell phone after we leave Jonas's house.

"What?"

"Running around town, whipping everyone into a frenzy. I know you're up to something." He keeps his eyes on the road, occasionally checking his blind spots. Maddox is always watching. Of course, he saw through my errands.

I have a choice: keep trying to lie to him or get him on my side. Considering I'm not the one paying his salary, he has no real reason to keep quiet—unless I give him one.

"Fine," I level with him. "I am up to something, but it's the only way to clear all our names."

"And what happens when you catch who did it? What if it's one of you?" he asks bluntly.

That's the second time today I've been forced to face that possibility, but it doesn't lessen my resolve. "It wasn't me and it wasn't Jameson."

He chuckles. "So everyone else is on their own?"

The photos of the crime scene flash through my mind. Jameson found his father like that. No matter what had passed between them, he had faced that gruesome discovery. Someone left his father for him to find, and that person is going to pay.

Chapter 17

PAWNOGRAPHY'S newest sales associate waves to me from behind the counter. There's something comforting about knowing that she's here to keep the store in check. The shop is swarming with customers, which is its new normal following the media storm that is my life Suddenly, my impulse to retrieve the Venetian mask I bought ages ago feels foolish. Tugging the tie from my ponytail I let my hair fall like a curtain over my face. If this keeps up, I'm going to have to invest in a wardrobe of over-sized sunglasses and wide-brimmed hats. I ninja through the crowd, careful not to make eye contact with any of the patrons. Most of their attention is on the items under the glass and the girl behind the counter.

    I blend in, so no one notices me, but I stop in my tracks when a woman bustles up to Josie at the counter. She's dressed in a Las Vegas t-shirt that screams tourist. Judging from her mom jeans, she's a Midwesterner. In my experience Kansans love a good souvenir shirt and a pair of high-waters. I suspect that if she turns around, there will be a fanny pack buckled around her ample waistline.

"Where's the girl?" she demands.

Josie blinks innocently, but I can tell by how forcefully she stares the woman down that she knows exactly what she's asking. "I'm sorry?"

"The girl they keep talking about on television and the world-wide web." The customer twirls her hand impatiently as if a nondescript gesticulation will help clarify her point.

"She doesn't work here." Josie smiles as she delivers the bad news, and I want to hug her.

"The television said she works her." The woman pulls out her phone and I groan inwardly. "Look at this article. That's this shop."

"Yes, it is," Josie confirms.

"So, where is she?"

"I'm sorry, but if you would like to make a purchase—"

"I came all the way from Nebraska..."

Nebraska. Kansas. What's the difference? I lose interest as the woman continues her tirade. After a few minutes a weary looking man retrieves her with an apologetic look to Josie.

"The internet said she works here," the woman reminds him angrily.

"I know."

"She needs to repent for her sins. I came here..."

I'm saved from hearing exactly why she came here as the couple exit the shop without their prize.

"Didn't want to give them an autograph?" Josie whispers conspiratorially. She tugs at the hem of her green tank top self-consciously and I do my best not to look. "That was conspicuous."

"What?" I hold up my hands.

"The baby bump check you just did. I'm not showing. Mom just shrunk this shirt," Josie explains.

"I wasn't looking." But I guess I can't lie to her.

"I have an appointment." Josie keeps her voice low so that no one can overhear. "It can't get here fast enough."

On the outside with her stylish, dark curls, and fuchsia lipstick, Josie plays the part of a grown woman, but I can see the fear she'd trying to hide. I can't blame her. If it were me in her shoes, I'd be freaking out. I hesitate, uncertain how she'll feel about my next question. "Can I go with you?"

"If you want." She shrugs but I don't miss how her lower lip trembles. That's a definite yes.

"So, are you coming to my party?" I decide a change of topic is in order. I haven't had the chance to give her the lowdown on my plan to catch Nathaniel West's murderer at my birthday bash, so I distract her with the info now.

"Yes, but explain to me why we're having a party there? Isn't that the last place you would want to celebrate your birthday?"

"Can't a girl throw a rager for her eighteenth birthday? I can legally vote. It's time to celebrate." I slide along the glass case, looking for what I came in for. When I spot the mask, I tap the spot. "I'm going to need that."

Josie takes it from the case and raises an eyebrow. "What are you up to?"

It's a fair point, but not one I can explain without a lot more time and possibly some visual aids. "If you promise to come, I promise you'll find out."

"You're being very mysterious." She wraps it in some paper and hands me the bag.

"Aren't I?" I tease. "Oh, you're going to need one of these, too."

"Like a costume?"

Before I can tell her anymore, a customer butts in. I'm relieved when he asks to see an autographed baseball card in the case instead of wanting to take a photo with me. The longer

I stick around the shop, the more chance there is that I'll be recognized.

"I'll text you," I promise, waving goodbye.

Pushing open the glass security door, I escape from that life and return to the one I've chosen. To outsiders my decision to host a masquerade ball in honor of my eighteenth birthday signals that I've just becoming another showy Houser. I think it's one of my more brilliant ideas, though. What better safety net could you offer a murderer if you were hoping they'd come to call?

By the weekend, Monroe has acquired every bottle of good champagne in Las Vegas. I stare at the lines of bottles displayed on the bar. The previous shindig I'd crashed had utilized the West's private stock of liquor.

"Why do we need this much champagne again?" I ask.

"For the theme," she says as if this makes perfect sense. "I'm going for nouveau riche. Think *The Great Gatsby* meets trailer park." She sweeps her hand in the air as if to share her vision.

"Have I told you you're a bitch today?" I ask, crossing my arms.

"Not today." She bats her eyelashes like I've paid her a compliment. Knowing Monroe, I have.

"You're a bitch."

She ignores me and begins to point out various details I couldn't care less about. I nod when appropriate, but she isn't buying it. "This party was your idea."

I shrug. I could care less if she's taken it over. I had expected her to when I pitched the idea. I need Monroe to play hostess because she was the one who invited the guests earlier this summer. All of that is important to me. I just don't give a damn about the drinks or the decorations.

"Your outfit is in Jameson's room," she says, clearly washing her hands of me. "Go get dressed."

"I'm wearing this." I gesture to the flowing, yellow maxi I put on this morning. It's simple but comfortable, and tonight I'll have enough attention directed at me no matter what I wear.

"Don't argue with me," she snaps. "If you're going to be a West, you need to dress like one."

"But won't I look more nouveau riche in this?" I ask flatly.

"I'm making Jameson wear a tuxedo, you'll be underdressed," she informs me. The change in tactics works. It's hard enough to hold a candle next to him. If the right clothes can help ease the feeling of inferiority I'm apt to fall victim to I should take her up on the offer.

"How did your mom feel about the party?" I ask Monroe as she signs a delivery sheet.

"She's not thrilled," Monroe admits, "but she'll get over it."

"I want her to like me." Immediately, I wish I hadn't shared that snippet with Monroe. In her world, information is power.

"She does," Monroe says to my surprise. "I told her the party was my idea."

"Why would you do that?" I've watched how critical Evelyn West can be of her daughter's choices this summer. Letting her mom believe it's her idea to host a party in the same space where her dad was murdered didn't seem like the best plan.

"Strategy. Mom wants us to get along, so I told her I was dying to throw you a birthday party."

"In other words, you lied?" I ask.

"Yes. My mother is a sucker for lies if it paints the picture she wants to see. She's too eager to watch us bond to cause trouble."

"So she actually likes me?" Despite the kindness Jameson's mother has shown me, I had to wonder if her opinion of me had reversed in light of our "engagement."

"Yes, Pollyanna," Monroe confirms dryly. "She thinks you hung the moon."

Armed with this good news, I surrender to Monroe's request and dismiss myself to dress, which has the added benefit of getting me away from the party planning. The outfit, or lack of it, that she's picked out for me is laid out on Jameson's bed.

Band-aids have more surface area than this thing, and don't get me started on the lacy scraps of string that accompany it. The tiny dress is covered in gold sequins that sparkle luminously in the light. When I lift it from the bed, I discover a gorgeous mask hiding underneath. I had planned on wearing the one I picked up at Pawnography, but I can't help but admire the one Monroe has selected. The mask itself is made of a creamy porcelain with subtle facial features painted on in gold. The gilt effect around the eyes looks like long feathers. I hold it up to my face and peer through the openings.

The heat of my breath collects inside it, but there's something comforting about having the mask on. Behind this, I can be Emma Southerly again instead of Jameson's girlfriend or murder suspect or gold digger. With this on, none of those labels seem to stick. There's liberation in deception.

I place the mask gently onto the nightstand and begin to strip. I'll have to do something with my hair, but make-up won't be as important if I stay hidden all night. I hadn't considered that perk of a masquerade party. Squirming into the dress, I realize that it's not compatible with my current underwear. My gaze strays to the thong I've left on the bed.

"Seriously?" I say to myself.

A soft laugh startles me and I pivot to find Jameson standing the doorway.

"Do you knock?" I ask, trying to tug up the stuck zipper.

"It's my room," he reminds me. He pushes the door closed behind him.

"I'll knock next time." I give up on the zipper and cross my arms over my chest.

"You're in a mood," he notes as he comes closer. When he reaches me, he runs the back of his hand down my arm. The effect of his touch is both soothing and exciting.

"This party is a terrible idea," I admit. "Is it too late to cancel?"

"And disappoint all those people who want to be your friends now?"

Jameson has no idea the real reason that I've planned this gathering tonight. The more people who know, the worse are chances are of catching the murderer. But as the party gets closer, I'm beginning to wonder if it's a good idea at all. What if I'm wrong? I'll be exposing myself and Jonas to even more scrutiny from the police.

A pit opens in my stomach as I consider an even worse possibility: what if I don't want to know who killed Nathaniel West?

"None of the people coming tonight matter," he continues, mistaking my silence as hesitance. "If you want to cancel, then we will. Although might I request you wear this dress tonight regardless."

"I don't think I can wear this dress period," I say absently, picking up the collection of strings I'm pretty certain are supposed to be underwear. "I mean, look at this! Why bother?"

Jameson adjusts his collar with one hand. "You should give them a fair chance."

"Oh yeah?"

He takes them from me and dangles them off his index finger. "You should definitely give these a chance."

"Aren't you worried about me bending over?" I ask.

"I'll just have to stay behind you all night and keep the view to myself."

It's too late to call tonight off, and I can't freak myself out a second longer, so when Jameson backs me toward his bedroom wall, I don't resist. His breath is hot on my neck as he trails his lips down to the curve of my shoulder.

"When is this party?" he whispers.

"Who cares?" I breathe.

Jameson's hands bunch my flimsy skirt around my waist as he presses his body against mine. "That's the right answer, Duchess."

WHEN JOSIE ARRIVES AN HOUR LATER, I'm in a much better mood. The party doesn't start for another hour but she's already dressed in a slinky, red wrap dress. The mask she's chosen is the same brilliant crimson.

"Va va voom!" I exclaim when she parks herself in the kitchen. Monroe's made it clear that I'm not to touch anything. I've been cut out of the party planning entirely. Instead, I'm stealing nibbles from the food trays.

Josie holds up her mask so I can see the two tiny horns protruding from the top. "I'm going for she-devil."

"And winning," I assure her, offering her a tiny sandwich from a fancy, silver platter.

She takes one and pops the whole thing in her mouth. Then she gives a thumbs up. "You didn't tell me this party was going to be so…"

"Over-the-top?" I suggest.

"Actually I was thinking serious. Passed hors d'oeuvres and champagne. It's a little different from…" she trails away as horror slackens her face.

"We thought we'd try something a little different." I shrug

my shoulders to show she hasn't wrecked the evening by mentioning that the only other party she had been to here was on the night of the murder. I, on the other hand, had crashed another a few weeks later, but only by accident. Those parties had been the equivalent of a rich kid's kegger not the dressed-up event we'd concocted this evening. Maybe the subterfuge aspect had appealed to Monroe on some personal wavelength. Either way she'd gone out of her way to make this a memorable evening, and if I had my way, it would be even more so. "Or Monroe did at least."

At the mention of her name the blonde flies through the kitchen like a demonic fireball. "Have you seen the menu cards?"

Josie and I help her search until we've tracked them down. She hardly notices that Josie is here, even after my best friend discovers where the cards have been put.

"She's crankier than usual." Josie purses her lips thoughtfully, and I can't help but realize that she has a point. Monroe is acting strangely.

"In all fairness, I used blackmail to get her to throw this party," I admit.

Josie links her arm through mine. "Do tell."

It isn't my secret, but the gossip is too good not to share. I've kept Monroe's hidden life quiet from her family and friends. But Josie isn't her family or her friend. She's mine, and I trust her.

"Promise not to tell," I ask.

"Cross my heart and hope to die." Josie slashes her fingers over her chest for emphasis.

I dish the dirt in whispers. Josie's eyes widen until I think they're going to bulge out. When I finish, she shakes her head. "You must have been pretty scary?"

"Why would you say that?" I'm a bit offended by the idea.

"Because she's acting like her whole life is riding on this. She must be worried that you're going to rat her out."

There's no reason Monroe should believe that. I'd used the information I'd had as leverage, but if I'd wanted to tattle, I would have done so. I make up my mind to keep a closer eye on my adoptive sister this evening. After all, she's not the only one with a lot riding on tonight.

Chapter 18

NO ONE IS late to the party. When the doors ceremonially open at 8:30, every student at Belle Mere Prep is waiting. Security does a decent job weeding undercover reporters from the crowd, but my heartbeat speeds up as I survey the group of strangers before me. Behind their masks, I can't recognize any of them, and I realize without their masks, I wouldn't know most of them anyway. The uppermost floor of West Casino has been transformed into a golden playground. Ropes of sparking lights drip from the ceiling, casting a warm glow that feels out of place in the modern setting. Dozens of white roses dipped in gold-leaf are staged strategically throughout the space.

"It's gorgeous," Josie says as she comes up beside.

"It's gaudy," I correct her. "Actually, it's nouveau riche."

The whole scene screams wealth and debauchery. Monroe has made her point. In the future, if I'm going to fit in I might try to do so with a bit less theatricality.

"What?" Josie asks.

"Inside joke," I say dryly. I haven't had the heart to tell Josie how much money Hans put in my trust fund before he went upriver. Between my relationship with Jameson and everything going on in her private life, I don't want the gulf between us to widen any further.

"When did that happen?" she shrieks. I follow her finger to find Hugo and Leighton entering, hand in hand.

Leave it to him to be the only person late to the party of the century. Behind my mask I study the way Hugo hovers near Leighton. I can't imagine what it took to convince him to let her come back here. Not after she'd nearly died. Glancing over I realize I can't even tell which window we went through. It's been repaired—erased as if it never happened.

"I didn't tell you? They were together when I went to the hospital. He's been there since she woke up."

"I did not call that," Josie admits, waving her hand under her mask. "Screw this."

She pulls off her mask and smiles tightly.

"Too hot?" I ask.

"Yeah. Besides no one here knows who I am anyway. My face is as good as a mask," she says with a laugh.

I don't miss the pain that lingers in her eyes. Josie has never felt like she belongs here. I can't imagine how she feels at the moment.

"Let's find you some water," I suggest, but before I can abscond with her to the kitchen, a man steps into our path. "Excuse me."

He catches me around the waist when I try to push past him. Tipping his masked face lower, he whispers, "You don't recognize me, Duchess?"

"Of course, I do." My fingers trace the broad shoulders accentuated by the dark cashmere of his tuxedo jacket. "You're supposed to be watching my back."

Literally and figuratively.

"A West is always fashionably late," he advises me, pushing

his mask up. He points to the corridor that leads to the private family rooms. "Case in point."

Monroe is the last to arrive, despite the obsessive care she took planning it. She sweeps into the room in a long black gown that dips low, exposing the valley between her breasts. Unlike the mask she chose for me, hers is a simple lace strip tied around her eyes. Monroe West is on display for all of us to see, but how many people see past the image she projects?

Josie clears her throat to remind us that she's still here. "I'll give you two some space."

Before I can tear myself away from Jameson to join her, Monroe marches up to us.

"How did they get past security?" she hisses, pointing to Sabine, her former best friend, and Levi, Jameson's former roommate. She's not the only one late to the party.

"Were they on the list?" Jameson asks indifferently. He's much more calm than the last time he was in the same room as Levi. He's had time to cope with his fair-weather friend's betrayal.

"How can you just stand there?" Monroe demands, and I can't help but agree with her.

"That movie will never get made. Levi will continue to be a B-list star whose destiny depends on his looks. Karma has done its part as far as I'm concerned."

"You're a bigger person than I am." Monroe sweeps across the room after them.

I tug Jameson's arm, forcing him to follow.

"My sister can fight her own battles," he reassures me, but I ignore him.

"You broke it, you bought it."

I have no idea how Sabine and Levi got up here," he says gruffly. "Security has been notified that they can't so much as step foot on the sidewalk."

"And yet, they're here." Judging from Monroe's reaction, they wouldn't be for much longer. A chilling thought occurs to me as we approach them. If it was that easy for two people to crash this party after all the security upgrades that had been made since Nathaniel's death, how many other people can get past the surveillance and guards—tonight and the night of the murder?

As we approach the threesome, we're joined by Hugo and Leighton. My pulse speeds up and I clutch Jameson's hand. I'd once considered them the Belle Mere axis of evil. Circumstances had torn them apart this summer, which means there's no way to know how ugly this argument could get.

"You weren't invited." Monroe delivers her dismissal in a lowered voice, but Sabine only laughs at her.

"I know every staff member of this hotel. I'm always invited." Sabine has eschewed the traditional uniform of pink I usually see her in. Instead, she's rocking an electric blue number and a silver, Venetian carnival mask. Next to her Levi shifts on his heels.

Jameson doesn't bother to tell his former friend that he's unwelcome. He handed down that edict when he first learned that Levi planned to play him in a damning biopic. The role would have made Levi's career. Now the movie was dead in the water along with their friendship.

The tilt of Jameson's head is hardly perceptible but a few moments later, Maddox appears behind our small group.

"Mr. Stone, please follow me."

Levi shoots Jameson a pleading look, but it's too little too late. Sabine stays frozen in place even as her boyfriend follows our hulking private muscle toward the elevator.

"Monroe," Sabine begins, but Monroe holds up her palm.

"Leave," she commands.

"What's going on with you two?" Leighton interjects. She

doesn't bother to keep her voice quiet, and all around us, heads turn. Apparently, she's still a little hazy on what's happened in her absence. I glare at Hugo accusatorily. He brought her here knowing full well that their little friendship circle is broken forever.

"Tell her," Sabine says, stamping her heel on the tile. Now the whole party is watching. "Tell her what's going on with us, Monroe."

"It's best you go." Monroe turns but not before Sabine moves closer.

"Tell her who pushed her out the window."

A low buzz breaks out around us as people figure out what she's saying.

"Get her out of here," Monroe shouts to the security guards who are standing by hesitantly.

"No." Hugo steps in. "I want to hear what she has to say."

"Tell them," Sabine sneers. She might lose the war but she's going to win this battle and it seems there will be casualties.

"It was a misunderstanding," Monroe begins, her eyes flash to each of us. No doubt she's hoping one of us will save her. The trouble is that none of us have reason to.

"You pushed her through the window," Hugo screams, and I'm reminded of how swiftly he'd turned on someone he considers his best friend. It doesn't matter if Monroe did it so long as Hugo believes she did.

Before I can nudge Jameson to intervene, Jonas steps out from the crowd. More than anyone, he doesn't owe Monroe any favors. But when Hugo takes a purposeful step toward her, Jonas grabs him from behind.

"Let's cool off," he coaxes his best friend.

"Why? Because I can't hit a girl?" Hugo asks. "Because she's no lady. She's a cold-blooded bitch. You know that."

"Drop it," Jonas urges, struggling to keep his hold as Hugo

thrashes. After a few moments, Hugo goes limp. But before we can breathe a collective sigh of relief. He casts a scornful glare at Monroe. "Assault. Prostitution. What else are you capable of, Madam West?"

The accusation goes off like a bomb and the low murmurs of gossip die down as everyone strains to hear her response. Looking around, I realize more than a few people have been filming this encounter. Within hours, Monroe West's private life will be subject to an online smear campaign.

Monroe raises her chin in defiance and then she does the last thing any of us expects: she shrugs.

"Caught me," she says with a wicked smirk. Next to me Jameson doesn't move. I'd wondered before if he knew what she was up to, and now I know. He had no clue.

Security finally does their job and escorts Sabine to the elevator. Hugo begins to follow but Leighton just stands there staring. Monroe doesn't meet her minion's eyes until Leighton's soft voice calls for her attention.

"It was you. Emma told me I saw someone that night and that I smiled at them before we went through the window." She repeats the story I told her as if she's finally remembering. "You tried to kill me."

"I overreacted," Monroe admits, and more than a few people around us boo her. When this news leaks, she'll be the talk of the town. The question is whether or not her temper flared up so dramatically on the night her father was murdered. I can't be the only one wondering that now.

But despite the demonstration of what she's capable of, somehow I know it wasn't her. Monroe and Jameson didn't hate their father regardless of his faults. Rational or not, Monroe had a reason for why she'd pushed us out the window that night. What would make her hurt her father? All these people surrounding us now were there as well. The room is full of opportunity, but I still can't find the motive?

Monroe seems to realize that she's playing to a crowd that's turned on her, so she beats a hasty retreat.

"I need to talk to my sister," Jameson says, his voice so frigid that a chill runs down my spine. He follows her away from the crowd and I contemplate stepping in. Monroe certainly owes me an apology, although I don't want her explanations. The reasons behind her actions are quite clear to me. In the end, I stay put, watching as most of my top suspects take the elevator. They'd all been hiding something, but if they aren't the ones behind the murder, who is?

As the crowd begins to disperse, waiting for whatever unexpected entertainment comes next, Jonas steps beside me.

"We have a problem."

It's the last thing I want to hear. He gestures for me to follow him. As soon as we're in an empty corridor, he levels with me.

"It's gone," he says.

"What's gone?" I ask even as dread floods through me. I don't wait for him to say it before I rushing down the hall to Nathaniel West's office.

The FBI had unsealed the room weeks ago, but I hadn't bothered to come in here. Not even when I arrived to prepare for the party this morning. That had been Jonas's job. I considered it remuneration for the emotional distress he caused me when he posted photos of me online.

The office is as Spartan as ever, but I ransack the drawers anyway. "Maybe a maid came along and put it away."

"Emma, it's not there," he insists. "I checked."

"Then where could it possibly be?" Stress seizes my chest, making me feel as though I'm in a choke hold. Without that file, we have nothing.

"As soon as I got here, I checked to make sure you'd left it where you were supposed to," he explains. "But when I came back a few minutes ago, it was gone."

"Did you get the picture? Did you post it?"

He shakes his head and my heart sinks, drowning my hopes along with it. "Without the bait…"

"Emma," Jonas says slowly, his brown eyes nearly black in the dark, "could someone have known it was here?"

"No. I didn't tell anyone else." Panic gets the better of me and I kick the desk chair. Most of my suspects just walked out of the casino lobby, and, like it or not, none of them seemed capable of murder. They were all too caught up in their problems. "We're missing something."

I think for a moment before I hold out my hand. "Let me see your phone."

Jonas unlocks the screen and hands it to me. He already has The Dealer account pulled up. So much for the best laid plans. I scroll through, studying each picture.

"Why these people?" I ask him. There'd been dozens of party-goers there the night that Nathaniel was murdered, but Jonas had only focused his attention on a handful.

"Hunches. Weird behavior. Bias," he admits.

As I look at the stream, I notice something that hadn't occurred to me before. Naturally, I'd gravitated toward analyzing photos of myself and Jameson. People I didn't trust were already suspects in my book. That left one person whose presence in the stream I'd hardly questioned.

"You said you wanted to deal out some karma." It was a desire I understood. I'd been the victim of Monroe and her posse's bullying, and I'd fallen prey to Hugo Roth's playboy antics. That didn't explain everyone who'd caught The Dealer's attention. "What did Josie do to deserve such a prominent feature on your thread?"

"It's not only about karma," he says slowly. "I guess I wanted to expose what people try to keep hidden."

So, he knew Josie's secret, or one of them. He'd posted pictures of her with older men. Since he'd followed her to the family planning clinic, Jonas had probably guessed the other item Josie wanted to keep undercover.

"That wasn't your right," I say through gritted teeth. "Josie has issues..."

I feel like a turncoat for even speaking the words, but it's the truth. I don't understand how Jonas can't see that. His own parents had rejected who he was. Josie didn't even have a father to reject her.

"I wanted to figure out who killed Nathaniel West, so I couldn't ignore her."

"She was barely at the party." I'm really losing my cool now.

Why? the tiny voice in my head asks, but I ignore it.

"I saw her late that night," he corrects me. "Nearly everyone had gone home or passed out, but she was running. She looked totally wrecked. I tried to go after her but Monroe stopped me. I knew you two hadn't been invited, so I distracted Monroe so there wouldn't be a scene."

I can feel my heart slowing down as his words sink in. "Are you saying that Josie—"

"Knows who killed Nathaniel West?" he finishes my thought. "I'm sure she does."

Chapter 19

THERE'S no time to consider any of the questions flooding through me as I run out of the office. But despite telling myself there is rational explanation, I can't help but wonder how I've been so blind. Rushing into the party, I search for Josie's red mask in the crowd. Following Monroe's exit, the drinking has begun in earnest. More than a few champagne bottles lie empty on their sides, and as I stand there I jump when more corks are popped. The hired waiters have given up in the face of mob mentality.

They're celebrating Monroe's overthrow. I don't miss the irony that she provided the champagne they're using to toast her demise. It will take all the West's people to clean up this mess. I can only guess that Jameson is still addressing the debacle privately. But right now I need him at my side.

I've fucked this up royally, and he's the only person I trust to know what to do.

Jonas appears at my side, and I resist the urge to strangle him. Why hadn't he told me about seeing Josie at the party? Why hadn't he told anyone?

Because he'd been scared like she is now. He'd misunderstood that fear. We both had.

Without knowing where Jameson is, he'll do—but only in a pinch.

"I need to find Josie. She's wearing a red dress and a red mask." I leave him to search through the crowd while I go to find Jameson. I'm halfway to the family bedrooms when I hear raised voices. I pause. They're coming from the room across the hall from his.

I don't bother to knock.

Monroe looks up with tear-stained eyes and runny mascara when I enter. She opens her mouth to order me out, but I cut her off.

"I need you now," I tell Jameson.

"Can this wait?" he asks as we step into the hall. "I'm not done crucifying my sister."

"Nail her to the cross in the morning. I need you. I fucked up."

Jameson's face goes blank and he doesn't speak, which is probably a good thing since it's all pouring out now.

"I made a mistake. I thought I could smoke out the murderer, but I was wrong. And now, I can't take it back."

Jameson grabs me by the shoulders and looks me dead in the eye. "What's going on?"

"We were wrong," I continue, the first hysterical sob breaking loose. "It wasn't murder. It couldn't be."

"Emma, you aren't making sense."

I force my mouth closed then I inhale deeply. When I speak again, I keep it simple. "We have to find Josie."

He doesn't ask questions, although I'm certain he has as many as I do. Maybe he's responding to my panic or perhaps he has simply kicked into crisis mode. Grabbing my hand, we join the crush of people partying. He doesn't let go as we weave in and out.

When I see a red mask, I yank it off without looking. But none of the red masks are hers. When we make it to the other side of the crowd, we huddle together.

"Did you see her?" he asks.

I shake my head as my breathing speeds up.

"Calm down," he orders me. "What is going on?"

"I don't have time to explain!"

"Then give me the CliffsNotes," he recommends.

"I might have gotten ahold of the police file for your dad's murder." I don't stop to see how he reacts to this information. "I convinced Jonas to use The Dealer to bait the murderer."

"You did what?"

"It was reckless. I realize that now, but I thought it was the only way." I'm screwing up this whole explanation thing, but I'm too distracted by the possible consequences of what I've done to care.

"What does this have to do with Josie?"

"I think she has the file." I can't bring myself to admit why I think she took it.

Jameson seems to understand though. "We'll find her. She's going to be okay."

How can he say that? How can anything ever be okay again? But I'm reminded of the inscription on the ring I wear. If ever I need to take a leap of faith, it's now. He leads me around the bar and past a security guard stationed to prevent unauthorized guests from entering the private spaces of his home. The guard is busy flirting with a few drunk girls I recognize as a year younger than me.

"Has anyone been through here?" Jameson demands as the guard jumps to his feet.

"Only our people."

"Who?" I press. I no longer know who to count as our people. The distinctions between friends and strangers feels more acute than ever before.

"Steve and your guy, Maddox. But they took off." I can see the gears whirring in his head as he searches his memory. "And your friend."

My blood turns to ice and it takes all the strength I have to respond. "The one in the red dress?"

He nods.

She'd been here before the party. She had been in Jameson's bedroom. We'd snacked in the kitchen. Of course, the guards would see her as an authorized friend of the family.

"Where was she going?"

As soon as he points in the direction of the kitchen, I take off running with Jameson at my heels. A few members of the wait staff stare when we round the corner. She isn't here. Whipping around, I consider where she might have gone.

"If she came for the file, would she leave?" Jameson asks.

"I don't know." Taking it wouldn't destroy the evidence that it contains. After all, it's only a copy. But she'd come. I'd been wrong earlier when I told Jonas that no one else knew about our plan. Josie knew.

Because I had told her.

She knew it was a trap and she'd walked into it. The realization nearly knocks me off my feet. Jameson catches me as I stumble and that's when I spot the black and white photo caught in the track of the sliding door.

Forcing myself forward, I open it and step onto the patio. The night is unusually still. This high up I might expect a breeze, but nothing disturbs the scene I find. Photos and affidavits litter the concrete as if they've been strewn along like breadcrumbs.

She's leading me straight to her. I spot a dot of red in the pool and I run toward the water. I fall before I reach it, scraping my knees on the pavement.

Jameson makes it all the way, but he stops at the edge. "It's just a mask."

I cry out with relief and then force myself to stand. I have to find her. When my gaze falls on her, I freeze. She's perched on the rail of the balcony with her back to us as she looks out over the strip below.

"Josie," I call out tentatively.

She glances over her shoulder and gives me a sad smile. It's all the encouragement I need to step closer.

"You came," she says. "I knew you would."

"Whatever happened, everything is going to be okay."

Her laughter comes out as a harsh bark. "Tell me, Jameson"—she moves, twisting on the slippery metal railing and my heart stops until she's turned herself around to face us—"is it okay? I killed your father. Is that okay?"

I can't bring myself to look at him, so I stand there between the two people I love most in the world while the truth slowly tears us apart.

"I think I understand. He was your father, too, wasn't he?" Jameson's voice is steady and sympathetic, and for the first time since the horrible realization dawned on me, I believe it can be okay.

"You need to know…I didn't know that," she says as a tear streaks down her cheek. "I didn't plan this."

"We know that," I tell her. "Let's talk about this." I beckon for her to come down, but her hands tighten on the railing.

"No one knows the truth but us. It can stay that way," Jameson promises her.

"You really are the brother I never had." She sniffles, hesitating for a moment as if to consider his offer. "But you don't know the truth."

"I do," I say. I've pieced it together in fragments.

"I was looking for you." She turns her attention to me. "We got separated and…I didn't mean to wind up in his office. But when I did he was nothing like I expected. He wanted me there. I knew why. I've had enough older men try to take me home."

I nod encouragingly. She needs to confess so that we can all move on.

"You know I never slept with any of those guys," she admits. "I'd let them buy me dinner and feel me up."

I take a step closer. If I reach out I can grab her. "You were a virgin."

It's not a question. It's a fact.

"I'm all talk. After all these years, even people don't know the rumors about me." She tilts her head up as if looking into heaven. "I was tired of being all talk. And I was tired of being treated like dirt. We weren't invited to that party. Did she tell you that?"

"Yes," Jameson says. He hasn't moved. No doubt he doesn't want to frighten her. He, far more than me, holds the absolution she needs to receive.

"We both met the men that would change our lives." An unexpected gust of wind whips her skirt around her legs, and I leap forward afraid it will push her over. She holds up a hand to stop me.

"Josie, please come down," I beg her.

She ignores me. "I didn't put up a fight. I wanted it. I wanted to look Monroe West in the eyes and know I screwed her daddy. I told myself that she didn't deserve any of it, and that all I wanted was a taste."

"He was rough." Her eyes grow distant, rewinding back to that fateful night. "But I didn't cry. He told me he liked that—that I was a good girl."

"Why?" Jameson finally chokes out. "What did he do to you?"

"He asked for my name. He wanted to call me, and I just didn't care anymore. I thought maybe I'd get taken care of for once, so I told him my name. Josie Deckard. I'll never forget the look on his face when he asked me if Marion Deckard was my mother. When I said yes, he lost it. He grabbed me and he asked me why I was there. He wanted to know if I'd come on purpose. How I'd found out. I don't think he knew he was hurting me," she says softly. "I don't think I realized I'd grabbed the letter opener. When he accused me of coming there to fuck him for more of his money, I didn't understand. Not until he asked me what kind of sick girl screws her father."

I clamp my hand over my mouth to hold back the sobs threatening to escape. Now I understood her erratic behavior over the last few months. Josie had wanted to meet her father her whole life. No one could have expected the truth.

"I can't remember much, except for the way his skin popped when the blade struck him. I hear it all the time. I still feel the way it vibrated across my skin each time I stabbed him. And then I ran and waited for them to come for me."

"No one's coming for you," I say, hoping it will reassure her.

"They should. I've stood by and watched while they accused you. I've been too scared to make a move. Even when I found out I was pregnant, and I couldn't lie to myself about what happened, I was stuck."

Her admission startles Jameson, who lurches back a few steps. I'd kept her pregnancy from him because it wasn't his business. Now he's facing it at the worst possible moment.

"What do you think of me now?" she asks him. "Am I so easy to forgive?"

I hold my breath as I wait for his answer.

"Yes," he says. "I forgive you."

"We're going to make it through this." I hold out my hand and she lifts her slowly, her eyes brimming with tears. "We'll take care of things."

"No, you won't." She shakes her head, her hand still hovering within reach. "My mom used to tell me that we make our own beds. Mine's a mess, Em."

"All of ours are," I reassure her.

"I've got to clean it up. You understand, don't you?"

I nod, inching toward her. "I'll help you."

She laughs and the emptiness of it fills the quiet night. "Deckard girls don't ask for help, remember?"

"Josie!"

She smiles one last time, and then she lets go.

Chapter 20

A THICK BLANKET wraps around my shoulders. I blink as Jameson swims into focus, the night sky a black canvas overhead. No stars twinkle above as if they've gone silent, too.

"You're trembling," Jameson explains.

"I am?" I hadn't noticed.

He rubs my shoulders, allowing me to sit quietly in the midst of chaos. I'm aware of the officers and agents sweeping the scene for evidence. I wince as a camera flashes, but I don't move.

I'd collapsed there moments after it happened and I still can't bring myself to get up. Not while strangers piece together the last few moments of my best friend's life.

A medic comes over and explains that I might be in shock. I nod, not bothering to tell him that I don't care. When he suggests that I lie on a stretcher, Jameson intervenes.

"She's fine," he says firmly.

"It would be best if—"

Jameson cuts the man off before he can get any farther. "I know what's best for her."

I stare at him and then slowly I lift my hand to his. I need him to anchor me while my world spins out of control. Later, we'll discuss what happened. Later, we'll deal with it.

Later, I'll feel something other than numbness.

The silence is interrupted by the click of heels across concrete. I can hear each purposeful step coming closer. Jameson straightens, but I don't bother to look up.

"Emma." Agent Mackey's voice is unusually gentle. I find myself wishing she would scream. "We have a few questions."

"I'll be happy to talk with you later," Jameson interrupts.

"We really need statements from both of you." She's straining to keep her voice soft. She wants to scream.

I don't blame her.

"We can arrange for her to make a statement in a few days."

"Given the situation, I would think you'd be eager to get this behind you," Mackey finally snaps, unleashing her inner dragon.

"It is behind us," Jameson says, his tone remaining even, "which is why my lawyers will be in touch in a few days."

"Mr. West," she starts.

"You can speak with my lawyers." He leans down so that only I can hear. "I want to take you home."

"I don't have a home," I mumble. At most, I've always had pillars, and now that one of them has fallen, I can't stand on my own.

"I'm your home," he reminds me. "Do you want me to carry you?"

When I don't answer, he lifts me into his arms and carries me away from this nightmare. He drives us into the mountains to the closest thing either of us has to a home.

That night he holds me against him. No words pass between us, even though neither of us sleep. The clock on the nightstand slowly counts the minutes and I watch each one drain away. One moment snuffed out for eternity. When the first light of dawn slashes across the horizon, it seems impossible that the sun will ever rise again.

    It does anyway.

After

Dr. O'Donnell never asks me how I feel, which is the only reason I continue to see her.

Her office is decorated with framed Rorschach tests. I still can't decide if the one hanging over her desk is a dog or an elephant. She won't tell me what that means.

She takes her seat across from the couch and crosses her legs. There's no notepad and I don't lie down. Mostly, we talk.

"Have you cried?" she asks gently.

I shake my head. I'd cried at the funeral. Seeing Marion bury her daughter had broken me into pieces so small that there's no room for tears any longer.

"How are you feeling about tomorrow?"

"I'm not really," I admit. Part of the reason I agreed to go to therapy the numbness that hadn't abated since the night Josie jumped.

"Part of what you're coping with is a sense of futility," she explains. "Everything feels inevitable."

"Isn't it?" I ask. Life. Death. Taxes. I couldn't escape any of it.

"Have you spoken to your mom?"

"She's coming to grips with my pseudo-engagement." After everything went down, Mom went through a sudden bout of maternal paranoia. She refused to accept the seriousness of my relationship with Jameson, but she stopped demanding I move in with her. "And she's finally packed up all of Hans's things."

Mentioning my stepfather doesn't move me either. I'm just as numb to what he did.

"How is Jameson?" she broaches the one topic that never fails to elicit an emotional reaction.

I smile begrudgingly. "Perfect."

She knew this, of course. He'd been seeing her for the past few weeks as well. While my therapy consisted of open-ended questions and encouragement, he'd chosen a more proactive path.

"I have to ask, Emma, are you certain you want to return to Belle Mère tomorrow?"

O'Donnell isn't the type to worry, but there's concern in her voice. Given that I'm a walking time bomb, I can't blame her.

"Yes." I have other options, but I don't want to cut and run. "It's not the first time I'll go back without…"

"Have you spoken with Monroe? She'll be returning as well."

My lips twitch as the suggestion that Jameson's sister could be a source of companionship. I keep the thought to myself. Despite the fallout from that night's revelations, Monroe had been there. It's true that the Wests stick together.

"Well, you have my number. If you need to chat, I'll be on standby."

For the hourly rate she charges, I almost expect her to come with me and hold my hand tomorrow.

Outside the office, a comforting sight waits for me: Jameson paging through a magazine. When the door opens, he glances up and a blinding smile spreads across his face. His therapy has been going better, judging from how often he gives me that look. "Ready?"

"If you are." I hold out my hand and he takes it.

It's been a little harder for him to let me out of his sight of late. It's one of the issues he's working on with Dr. O'Donnell. Considering that I'm returning for my last year in the morning, I hope they're making progress.

The truth is: being together is the only medicine that seems to work. When he's beside me, I can think about the future without pain. He makes me laugh. At night, we escape in each other's arms for heated, fleeting moments, and when he falls asleep beside me, there are no nightmares.

Despite my objections, our new house has a gate. When I refused to skip out on my last year at Belle Mere, I had to compromise. When we pass, the reporters camped in front of it, it reminds me why he insisted.

"The sale went through," he says, eying me for my reaction.

"Good." I don't think any other response is necessary. When he first told me that he wanted to sell the West Casino, I told him not to bother. Even if a new company slapped another name on it, it would still be there, lingering like a bad memory in the Las Vegas skyline. When he added that the terms of the sale required it to be torn down, I got on board. He's been selling off most of the West real estate holdings ever since.

His phone rings as I grab the milk carton out of the fridge. He checks the screen and sighs.

"Mom or Monroe?" I ask.

"Mom." He accepts the call, wandering into his office.

Getting rid of the casino has freed him up to mediate between his mother and sister. Monroe had surprised all of us when she turned the scandalous leak about her secret identity into a reality show. Jameson took me house shopping the next day.

My own mother had opted to keep her place in Palm Springs, even after I turned down her offer to move in with her. She, along with my dad, had given their blessing for my new living arrangements after some coercion. I'd been forced to flash my diamond ring and ask if they wanted grandbabies now or later. We quickly came to an understanding.

"It's just crass enough to work," Jameson says with disgust as he reappears. "A high school madam. What will reality TV think of next?"

I shudder thinking about it. "She's not going to stop until we're the Kardashians."

"I will never let you be a Kardashian," Jameson promises, earning him a genuine smile.

"That's true love."

"Speaking of love." Jameson swoops down, lifting me off my chair and waiting for my orders.

"Take me to bed," I command.

We linger between the sheets, soaking up our final solitary afternoon before life interrupts our private healing process. This is how we communicate best. Each touch provides a reassurance that we can find nowhere else. We speak to one another in sighs and murmurs with trembling mouths and hungry hands.

When we finally collapse into a heap together, words are still there to fill the space between lovemaking.

"What happens when it's all gone?" I ask in a soft voice.

"What's gone?" he murmurs, nuzzling against my ear.

"The hotels and properties and businesses. What will there be then?"

"You and me," he says simply.

It's not the answer I expect. "That's not much."

"No, it's everything."

The next morning inevitability comes to call. I reluctantly agree to let Jameson drive me to the first day but balk when he offers to pack me a lunch. When we arrive in the parking lot, a few people give us the thumbs up and my throat swells.

"They think I'm a fucking saint." I roll my eyes behind my sunglasses. I'd finally given in and purchased several over-sized pairs.

"Then give them hell, Duchess."

I don't need any encouragement on that end. The board of directors had, in their infinite wisdom, declared that school would start late this year. Extending summer vacation would give students time to mourn and reflect on the tragic events.

You can't make this stuff up.

For most of my peers it just meant impromptu, last-minute vacations.

A car zooms into the spot beside us and honks. Monroe traded in her gold convertible for a Porsche in a shade she deemed "hooker red." I have to hand it to the girl. She has no problem branding herself.

She waits for me to get out, and I sigh. Glancing out the back window, I ask Jameson one more time. "Are you certain Maddox is necessary?"

"Ask me if you want him around when Monroe's film crews show up," he says dryly.

He has a point.

"It's not too late to run."

Jameson's offer is tempting, but I shake my head. "I'm not supposed to run, remember?"

"From me. Running from high school is both understandable and acceptable."

He kisses me long and hard so that my lips are swollen

when we break apart. It's a reminder that I'll carry with me throughout the day.

"Finally!" Monroe exclaims, slamming her car door shut. "It's a little creepy that he drops you off."

"You're a call girl," I remind her.

"Touché." She shoulders her bag and prattles on about non-compete clauses and waivers. If nothing else she's taken it as her responsibility to bore me the details of her new show. I interpret it as a sign that she cares.

We both stop short of the entrance.

"This is the last time we'll walk through those doors on a first day." It's uncharacteristically sentimental moment until she adds, "thank God."

But I know she feels the same unwelcoming atmosphere as we enter the building. A sea of unfamiliar faces greets us. Monroe doesn't say it, but I know I'm the closest thing she has to a friend here this year. Even if she had made up with Sabine and Leighton, they'd both transferred to new schools. Jonas had opted to trade places with his sister, going off to school while she came home. And the last I heard, Hugo Roth told the headmaster he was taking a 'leave of absence.'

Monroe bids farewell until later at the door to Advanced Economics. I'm willing to bet she'll teach them a thing or two. Meanwhile, I do my best to ignore the attention I receive as I head toward AP Literature.

Mr. Hunter glances up from the blackboard and I enter.

"Miss Southerly," he says warmly. "I trust you finished your summer reading list."

The normality with which he states this makes my jaw drop open.

"I'm a little behind," I admit.

"Better catch up," he advises, passing out the class syllabus. It's a comfortingly mundane gesture.

After

At Belle Mère Prep, some kids come back to school after a summer in Europe. Others return with a few new notches on their Restoration Hardware bedposts. So? I'm coming back with a security detail.

They can stare at me in the hallways. Who can blame them? The fact is that I spent most of my summer as a lead suspect in a murder case. My classmates gawk as I take a seat. No doubt they're trying to spot a baby bump. It's the only way this could get any better for them.

Thanks a lot, TMZ.

But while they stare, I can only think of those people that aren't here this morning to start their senior year. I feel their absences as ominously as an unexplained shadow in an empty room. Some are long gone. One didn't see the end of the summer.

Living or dead, they're just ghosts now, and even though they haunt me, I owe it to them to live fully.

Beautiful Memories: A Sinners Epilogue

"MISS SOUTHERLY, there is some concern that your notoriety may have an unwanted consequence for the campus." Dean Reynolds taps her pen on a stack of papers that I hope are my application and not printed internet articles about last summer.

I shimmy in my seat until I glimpse the TMZ web header at the top of the paper. No such luck. It shouldn't surprise me that my part in the murder case of the previous year is as important as my SAT scores—and given that my fiancé was once kicked out of this prestigious institution Stanford was always a long shot. It's not the best start to my round of college interviews in the golden state.

If I'm doomed, I might as well go straight to hell. No handbasket necessary.

"I think the campus has seen its fair share of infamous students. Wasn't Lila Moore going here when she led the police and paparazzi on a high speed chase? But I guess the rules are different for coked-out movie stars." My purse is already on my shoulder as I stand to leave. This isn't my first time dealing with the misplaced disapproval of authority figures. I'd endured a bounty of that during the last school year at Belle Mère Prep. Going off to college has been the light at the end of a very long tunnel, but maybe the past isn't going to let me go so easily.

"Miss Moore is no longer a student." She doesn't ask me to sit back down. Instead she shifts the stack of papers as if already mentally filing my admission decision. "I'll leave you to decide if Stanford is right for you. It seems you might have other plans for your future."

I don't have to read through the articles she's gathered to know that she's making a none-too-subtle dig at my much publicized engagement to Jameson West. "I think I already have. I thought Stanford was a little more serious about academics and less interested in salacious gossip. Maybe you need to take a refresher course of sourcing your research materials."

I don't look back as I leave the Admissions office. Instead, I head straight toward the one decision I've already made about my life. Jameson grins at me from the steps of the building, sliding his sunglasses down to take in my frown.

"I take it that went well." He's at my side, taking my hand before I reach the second step.

"Why did I think applying to the school that kicked you out was a good idea?" I glance over and can't stop myself from appreciating the way he's trying to keep a smirk off his handsome face.

"Point of clarification: I left Stanford." He squeezes my hand even as he teases me—a small gesture of reassurance I desperately need.

"Only because they were going to kick you out," I say.

"I think the real reason was that my destiny was calling me elsewhere. You needed me, Duchess." He pauses and pulls me into his chest. It's warm and solid and safe—just like him.

"I think you needed me." I keep my voice light even as dark memories churn inside me. The truth is I did need him. Before we'd met, my life was a mess. It got even worse after that between finding out the truth about my sister and her death, being accused of a murder my best friend committed, and then losing her, it was amazing today had come at all. I know it's because of Jameson that I'm standing here now. I take a step back and glance over my shoulder. "You know I don't think Northern California suits a girl from Vegas."

Jameson's answering smile splits his whole face. "I'd say it's time to head south."

LOS ANGELES IS MORE my speed. The sun, the palm trees, the even distribution of Priuses to Porsches—it all reminds me of home. But there's one important distinction, it isn't Las Vegas. This is where dreams go to come true instead of where they go to die. At least, it could be for me, especially given that I have no interest in becoming an actress. I might have a different opinion if I'd come here to try my hand at Hollywood. I'd had a front-row seat for that sideshow for years. It was riskier than a roulette. I'd seen enough gambling for a lifetime.

A car meets us at the private airport as soon as we land. I breathe a sigh of relief when Jameson takes the keys and gets behind the wheel. The last thing I need is to show up at another interview with a private driver.

The Wests have a house in the hills, but like most of the legacy his father left him, Jameson can't stomach it. Instead we stay at a hotel in Santa Monica, close enough to the pier that I can see the rides.

"Where are we headed first?" Jameson asks as he tosses his overnight bed on a chair in the hotel suite.

I stare out the window and remember the last time I was here when my mom had flown Josie, Becca and me here for a week to watch my new stepdad filming a movie. We'd gone to the pier and eaten hot dogs and cotton candy. Josie had nearly vomited during one ride. My own stomach turns over as the memories of that week flash through my head. So much has changed since, I've lost so much.

"Duchess?" Jameson slips his arms around my waist and calls me back to the present.

I blink and tear my gaze from the window as I remember where I am and who I'm with. "UCLA."

"They already accepted you," he says, beginning to kiss the back of my neck.

"I want to check it out anyway. Just in case..." After yesterday, I know that's not going to be enough. Maybe I'll never get a fresh start. Maybe I'll never escape my past. Maybe I shouldn't care, but I do. I can't explain that to him, but somehow I know he understands. Probably, because he's gone through it with me.

"Do you want to talk?" He pauses his worship of my shoulder and props his chin there instead, abandoning his attempt to lure me to bed.

"Do you ever want to be someone else?" I force the question past the lump in my throat. I need him to understand that this isn't about him or us. It's about me and who I've become.

"All the time before I met you," he says quietly. "I am someone else when I'm with you. Someone better. Someone happier."

"And what about when we're not together?" That's the real question. The one I've been too scared to ask. He's gone along on this college tour despite both of us knowing that he's needed in Las Vegas to run the heart of his family's empire. Being in different states for four years could put a serious strain on our relationship. He hasn't brought it up either, which means he's not worried or he's as concerned about it as I am.

"Nah, you don't understand." He spins me to face him and

cups my chin in his hand. "It doesn't matter where you are. You could be across the world and you'd still be right here with me. You've changed me. I don't ever want to the man I was."

"Even if you could shuck the West family name?" I ask.

"Emma Southerly fell for Jameson West."

"I didn't know your name then."

"That was before you fell for me," he corrects me.

He has a point, but I don't dare concede it. It's too early in our relationship to set a dangerous precedent like admitting I was wrong. Not when I have the rest of my life to share with him.

"You knew who I was, and you fell for me." It's a miracle that never ceases to surprise me.

"The moment I saw you, I knew who you were and I knew I loved you."

My mouth finds his because I can't think of anything to say, and when he carries me to bed, there's no need to say anything at all.

TO AVOID any more unnecessary *notoriety*, Jameson drops me off at campus the next day. I'm jealous of his board shorts and loose t-shirt. He's at home everywhere we go, but he seems lighter in Southern California. I, on the other hand, feel like someone's wrapped an anchor around my waist as I head to the admissions office. Since I've been admitted, the university has gone the extra mile and arranged a campus tour, classroom observation and an interview. For most of the day, it feels like I'm being taken on a date instead of interrogated. I only catch people snapping photos of me a handful of times and my tour guide pretends like she's never heard of me. She's a terrible actress, but I go along with it.

The unwanted attention is minimal, which is just one of

the perks of the school. The truth is I'd known I wanted Los Angeles since the plane had landed. Maybe it was all those years living in the dessert, but now I need the ocean. It's time for a fresh start and the Pacific Ocean could wash away all my sins. Plus it scores bonus points for having a noncraptastic admissions officer who waves off my past like I'd been accused of not paying a parking ticket. When Jameson pulls up in the Porsche in the late afternoon, I already feel at home.

"You're glowing," he says as I climb into the passenger seat. "I'm a little jealous. I thought I was the only one who had that affect on you, Duchess."

I don't bother to massage his ego. His billions do that well enough without my help. Instead I finally say aloud the one thought that keeps running through my head. "It's perfect."

He doesn't say anything, and I realize that I've made the decision without asking him what he thought. "You know it doesn't matter where we are, right? I'm with you, remember?" I remind him of his own words the night before, but he pulls onto the highway without a word. The sun begins to set and we ride in silence, leaving me to wonder what we have left to say. He's navigating the treacherous switchbacks of the Hollywood hills by the time I figure out that I do have something to say. "Jameson, if you don't want me to go here. Well, that's too bad. I want to be with you. I am with you, but I can't stay in Vegas. I understand if you have to, but we'll find a way to make it work."

I'd make good on that promise. So being apart would suck, but we'd been through a lot worse. I'm just about to tell him that when he pulls off the windy road into a private drive. I raise an eyebrow at the mid-century masterpiece that he parks in front of.

"Where are we?" I ask suspiciously when he turns the car off.

"Home." He's out of the car before I can ask for a more

detailed explanation. It takes an eternity for him to round the front of the car while I try to unbuckle my seatbelt, my brain still processing the info bomb he's just dropped. When I finally free myself, he opens the door and helps me out.

"Whose home? Or are we speaking in code now?" I ask.

In response, he takes my hand and leads me to the front door. I can't speak when he turns the knob and lets us inside. The entrance opens into a great room with floor to ceiling windows that look over the sparkling valley below. It's no stretch to imagine that I can see all of Los Angeles from here. From above, in the haze of twilight, the lights look like a blanket of stars.

"Whose house is this?" I whisper.

"Ours. If that's okay."

I whirl around and shake my head. "Your dad's?"

As amazing as this is, I know that being under his father's roof won't help either of us move forward. Given the view that's a pretty tough pill to swallow.

"Ours," he repeats. "I sold the West property months ago. I put it on the market the day you got your acceptance letter to UCLA."

"I'm not sure how to take that," I admit slowly.

He crosses to me, a determined glint in his blue eyes. "It felt stupid to have two houses here. Monroe is going to kill me for selling it, because I believe we had a Kardashian neighbor."

"That's real estate gold. You made a big mistake there, West."

"Nope. All my money's on you. It always will be."

"So you bought a house in LA?" I can't wrap my head around it. "A few hours ago I wasn't even certain where I wanted to go to school."

"You can take the man out of Vegas, but he'll always know when to gamble." A sly smile creeps over his lips. He's so damn sure of himself that I almost want to call his bluff. The trouble is that he's right and I love him for it.

"Can I take the man out of Vegas?" I'm breathless with the possibility.

"I'm not stopping that rescue mission. I know I said that it wouldn't matter where you went and it won't. Wherever you are, that's where I'll be."

"But what about—"

"It might be time to transplant the heart of the West company," he cuts me off.

"To the city of stars?" I ask.

"That's up to you," he says.

I hesitate, knowing that this decision isn't just about me, but then I remember that he's a part of me. We are in this together and we have a future ahead of us that no one gets to write but us. So I hold out my hand and with it my heart—my everything.

"I love you, Emma Southerly," he says as he takes it.

"I love you, Jameson West." It's strange how those words still thrill me. He is everything I never expected and everything I needed.

His fingers twine through mine and he tugs playfully. "Now let me show you our bedroom."

———

Acknowledgments

Very few people knew about this super secret project until it was finished, so I have to give them major props for being patient with me as I figured out all the twists and turns.

First off, I could not survive without my partner in crime, sister, and business manager, Elise Lee. Copper boom!

Rebecca Yarros, you are the best cheerleader and soul sister that I can imagine. S.L. Scott, your enthusiasm is limitless and I always walk away from my conversations feeling inspired. Shayla, I'm not going to butcher your last name, but thank you for all the late night talks and writing sprints. I'm so blessed to have you all in my life.

Louise Fury, your name suits you. I pinch myself whenever I tell someone I am your client. Thank you for your support and guidance. This is the beginning of a beautiful relationship.

Becca Mysoor, you walked into my world with fabulous lipstick and I knew we would be friends. You are the sweetest lipstick guru I know and one hell of an editor. Thank you for taking a chance on me.

To the authors who inspire me every single day to keep

writing and telling stories by being the genuine article. Thank you, Meredith Wild for raising the bar and limo rides. Audrey Carlan, your beautiful spirit encourages me every day. There are so many others I could name here but it would take another book. I am beyond privileged to be part of this industry with you.

Jackie, thank you for being the glue I need when I'm on deadline.

To the entire Ivy Estate team, you're making my dreams come true.

To the Loves, I don't know where to begin. You make me want to write every single day. Thank you for letting me tell you stories.

No book would have a life without its readers. Thank YOU for reading this book. You're the reason I do this.

And to Josh, I'm so glad that we can talk or not talk all day long. You make me believe in true love.

Printed in Great Britain
by Amazon